PHIL BOOTH was born in Southport in 1953. As w.. ..
Rigby novels, he is the author of several critically-acclaimed plays.
For more information please visit www.philboothwriter.com

Online reviews for Sam Rigby's first adventure, *Late Swim*:

'Really clever and funny.'

'Wonderful writing with a page-turning plot that kept me up at
night and made me laugh out loud.'

'A cracking good read. I was entranced by the murky world of
1970s Southaven.'

'Brilliant detective novel with a gripping storyline. Can't wait for
the sequel.'

'I couldn't put it down.'

'Full of humour, superb characterisations, and a plot that keeps
you guessing until the very end.'

'Excellent.'

Cover picture: Queen Victoria by Sir George Frampton, RA
(definitely not by Sir George Cattermole). Frampton also created
statues of Victoria to be found in Kolkata and Newcastle upon
Tyne, but this one in Southport has a magic all of its own.

Cover design and photograph: Jamie Davidson.

**Phil Booth**

# STILL LIFE WITH HAMMER

**the second Sam Rigby novel**

*set in Constantia*

*copyright © Phil Booth 2019*

*first published 2019*

ISBN 978-1-5272-3452-9

*www.philboothwriter.com*

### *a note on Southaven*

The events and characters of Sam Rigby's world are fiction. Southaven doesn't exist, but it shares a grid reference with a similar town which does. I've sometimes played fast and loose with the geography and history of Southaven's original. (For example, the Grand Hotel was inspired by the Victoria Hotel, which had actually been demolished by 1971, when the novel is set.) I hope no one will find cause to be offended.

### *acknowledgements*

Once again, thanks are due to the wonderful staff of Sefton public libraries, especially at the Atkinson in Southport. Thanks also to Francesca Baker for assistance in bringing the book to publication. Early readers of the text performed a sterling service in pointing out anachronisms (Surprise Peas were of course dried, not frozen – how could I have forgotten?). Any mistakes which have slipped through the net are entirely my own work.

*in memory of my mother*

# THE FIRST BOOK

## *one*

I was sitting up in bed one afternoon trying to read *Moby Dick*, when unknown knuckles rapped at the door of my flat. The only person in the building I can be said to get on with reasonably well is my downstairs neighbour Florrie, who's elderly and very deaf and normally too self-sufficient to seek out the company of others. The rent boy – that's to say, the boy who collects the rent – wasn't due to pay his weekly visit for another couple of days. Anyone else would surely have buzzed at the front door.

So naturally I felt curious, but was I curious enough actually to get out of bed and investigate? It was February, a thin sleet fell from a gunmetal sky, and this year's 'flu had for the past three days been making itself thoroughly at home in every region of my body, inflaming the tonsils, pounding away at the cerebrum, and giving rise to a dull, omnipresent ache which could only be the harbinger of my tragic early death. As the landlord was in the habit of fiddling our electricity meters, I could afford to resist the day's bitter cold with nothing more than a single-barred electric fire which I'd bought at a second-hand shop on Mission Street, and the rest of the flat remained unheated. But with a hot water bottle at my feet, and my Woolworth's continental quilt pulled up tight around my shoulders, I'd begun at moments to feel almost warm, warm enough to relish Herman Melville's description of the even colder bedroom at the Spouter Inn where Ishmael was about to spend the night. Why get up when I could luxuriate here in a fug of viral misery?

The knuckles tapped again. There was something apologetic in the sound, as if anxious not to cause inconvenience. Now I came to think about it, on the very rare occasions when Florrie had wanted to speak to me, rather than knock she'd merely slipped a note under the door, leaving me with the task of knocking on her

3

own door later, repeatedly and very loudly, until finally she heard me over the screeching of the Light Programme, or whatever they call it these days. So it couldn't be her.

I knew very well that if I didn't unmask the owner of the knuckles I would inevitably be lying there wondering about them at four o'clock in the morning, when I ought to have been enjoying recuperative sleep. The sad fact is, I'm an investigator by compulsion as well as occupation. Sighing dramatically despite the absence of an audience, I put the book down and swung my feet out of bed.

The smart blue quilted dressing gown which I was wearing had been given to me at Christmas by my ex-colleague Detective Constable Mark Howell. You may be thinking that this was kind of him, but was it? Since our brief affair had ended seven or eight years previously we'd not been in the habit of exchanging presents, and even someone lacking my suspicious nature might have found themselves harbouring doubts as they loosened the meticulously knotted string. He wanted something, no question about it, but what? Unless, of course, he was seeking to revive the corpse of our relationship, but it would take a lot more than a dressing gown to achieve that.

As I padded on stockinged feet down the narrow hallway, the knuckles once more brushed at the door, more faintly this time, perhaps asking themselves now why they should put themselves to all this trouble when there was clearly no one at home. I tried to call out, 'Just a moment!' but various diseased body parts interfered with my delivery. When I opened the door, the knuckles were already moving towards the stairs, together with their executive arm.

Hearing the sound behind him, my landlord, Sidney Flint, turned and said, 'Ah – Sam! You're here, then?' I toyed with the idea of denying it, but before I could speak he went on. 'Any chance of a quick word?'

On another occasion I might have ushered him immediately into the flat, but with a sharpness of mind remarkable in one so close to death I saw the possibility of making a point first. Continuing to obstruct the doorway, I glanced down to my left, where an enamelled bucket collected the water which dripped at a steady rate from the skylight above. I then looked back to the face of my landlord, with an expression in which I tried to blend accusation with impatience. I would have told him what I thought of him too, but I was afraid my tonsils might spoil the effect.

At least Flint had the decency not to pretend he hadn't understood. Shaking his head sadly, he steepled his hands in front of his chest as if invoking whatever deity it was that supervised the affairs of ruthless, tight-fisted landlords such as himself. 'Ah, Sam, Sam,' he said, and shook the head again. 'It breaks my heart to see the old place going down like this, truly it does! This was a fine building when I had it first, they're all the same in Leigh Terrace, built to last, not like the rubbish they're throwing up nowadays. Those new flats by the roundabout? I give them twenty years at the most, they're practically crumbling away as you look at them. This house is in a different league. It's the craftsmanship, you see. People took a pride in their work in those days, but not now. Did you say I could come in?'

I cleared my throat and said, 'That roof needs fixing.'

Sidney Flint nodded complacently. 'It does, doesn't it? I've been saying so for months. Someone needs to get up there and sort it out.'

After an interlude of silence, I realized that my landlord considered these brief remarks to have brought discussion of the leaking roof to a close. I tried again. 'It seems to have slipped your mind, Sidney, but you are in fact the landlord. You own this building, and others equally decrepit. It's you who needs to get up there and sort it out, or if not you then persons under your instruction. It's been leaking since last April.'

The hands steepled again as Flint's long face adopted a look of pious resignation. 'I'd love to fix it, Sam, you know I would. Leaving things to go from bad to worse like this – it's criminal neglect, that's what it is.' Sidney Flint had this much in common with God, that they both saw all but flatly refused to do anything about it. 'My hands are tied, though.'

'Tied? How? What's tying them?'

'Business, Sam, that's what – business! There's no money in

property these days, anyone will tell you. I'm doing you all a big favour just keeping the place on, yet here you are wanting me to tart it up like it was the Ritz! The way I see it, you should be grateful you've got a roof over your head at all.'

I reminded him that every week for the last ten years substantial sums had been passing from my pocket into his. Surely it was reasonable to expect that I could take a turn on my landing without water cascading down all over me?

He sniffed a little. 'Cascading? You call this cascading? You should have seen the state of some of the places I lived when I was starting out. But did I complain? Not for one minute. Moaning on about a few drips, you're worse than a girl.'

A long time had passed since Sidney Flint had 'started out'. He must be around sixty-five, almost twice my age, and the years showed in his face, where they'd dug deep ravines of care. Rumour had it – or at any rate, my mother had it, which is more or less the same thing – that in years gone by he'd been something of a ladies' man, but that he'd abandoned this hobby when he discovered that the ladies liked a little cash laying out on them from time to time. Since then he'd lived in abstemious solitude in a neglected inter-war semi near Crowburn Park, from which he also ran his business.

Given that my mother was old enough to remember Flint's glory days, it's unsurprising that I'd once woken in the night gripped by the dread conviction that he must be my father. Someone had to be, and my mother had never specifically ruled him out, nor anyone else for that matter. But after an hour or two of sweat-drenched horror I'd calmed down again, reasoning that for Sidney Flint to be my father there would need to be something drastically wrong with Mendelian genetics, since, apart from above average height, we possessed few if any traits in common. All the same, it was a nasty scare.

The chill of the unheated landing had begun to strike through now, and I shivered. Clearly my plan to ambush Flint with the leaking roof had failed, and it would be prudent to admit defeat, if only on health grounds. Without speaking, I stepped back and to one side, allowing my landlord to gain access to the property, then closed the door behind him. I followed him into the living room, where I risked igniting the gas fire with my cigarette lighter while he nosed around.

Flint said, 'Don't believe in tidying up, do you?' I blenched at this calumny. I'd made a noble effort to bring my belongings under control as recently as Christmas. 'Have you actually read all these books?'

Amongst the objects scattered liberally about the room, books featured disproportionately. 'Most of them, yeah.' The fire blazed into life. I wasn't sure how long it would run before I'd have to feed the meter.

Flint was shaking his head again. 'Complete waste of time if you ask me.' He crossed to admire the view of the fire station tower from my window. 'A grand little flat, isn't it? Worth every penny of the rent, and more besides.'

As far as my state of health would allow, I followed the gas fire's recent example and blazed up in my turn. 'You can't be thinking of increasing the rent? It went up two shillings only last year!'

'It's decimalisation though, isn't it? Business folk like me can't afford to absorb the costs, we've got to pass them on.'

'Costs, what costs?'

'I'll have to change all the meters.'

'No you won't. The new ten pence is exactly the same size as a florin, you know it is.'

'There'll be extra paperwork.'

'Bollocks. I warn you, if you try putting our rents up because of decimalisation you'll have a fight on your hands, believe me.' I'd have said more, but a fit of coughing intervened.

By way of conciliation, Flint held up two palms. 'Now steady on, no one's talking about putting up the rent.'

'But you just said – '

'Purely hypothetical. When you're in business, you have to consider every angle. Of course the rent's an issue, with inflation on the up and up, but that's not why I'm here.'

In my excitement over the leaking roof, and now this loose talk about the rent, I'd forgotten that there must be some purpose behind my landlord's unexpected visit. Because I'd survived Leigh Terrace longer than any other tenant, Sidney and I were on first name terms, but it was unlikely that I saw him more than two or three times a year. Normally all business was conducted through his proxy, Dennis the rent boy, a pale, asthmatic youth, who, with his air of a Victorian foundling and ability to imply that he'd die of disappointment if you didn't stump up the readies, was probably a far more effective collector than any regulation thug. (I say 'youth', but, remarkably, Dennis had somehow affected the appearance of spotty late adolescence for over ten years now.)

Nevertheless, Sidney Flint had just climbed four flights of stairs with the intention of speaking to me, and the fact needed explaining. He said, 'Would I be right in thinking you're unwell?'

I admitted it.

'I see. I expect you've got that thing that's going round. I hope you're not going to tell me you're unfit for work?'

'Work? Are you offering me work?' Unaccountably, I felt a sudden surge of robust good health.

'Yes, I am, if you'll take it. You did a good job for me back in '69 when that Doris Lively did a flit.'

I'd soon managed to trace the errant Doris, who was enjoying the good life with a piano salesman in Burnley, and well able to afford her outstanding rent. I said, 'Has another one gone AWOL?'

'No, it's nothing like that. It's – I've been sent a letter.' After a moment's indecision, Sidney Flint abandoned his position near the window, unbuttoned his raincoat, then reached into the inside pocket and withdrew a manila envelope. 'You'd best see for yourself.' He took out a single folded foolscap sheet, unfolded it, and handed it to me.

According to the information printed at the top of the page, the letter emanated from the offices of Messrs. Tipton, Buxton and Lamb, solicitors, of Shoreditch High Street. After preliminaries, it ran as follows:

> *It has come to our attention that you hold a portfolio of property in the Southaven area. In the present economic circumstances, property maintenance places a severe strain*

*on the profitability of small businesses such as your own. Our client therefore anticipates that you would welcome the opportunity to sell off a proportion of your holding, say, fifty per cent, at a sensible price which acknowledges today's poor market expectations. This would leave you free to invest some of the released capital in your remaining properties, thus increasing both their value and marketability.*

*This is clearly a very attractive offer, but in the event that you find yourself unwilling to sell, we would urge you to reconsider. Our client may be unable to offer such generous terms where a sale has been needlessly delayed.*

*We look forward to hearing from you at your earliest convenience.*

The letter was signed, not by Mr Tipton, nor yet by Messrs. Buxton or Lamb, all of them presumably too busy or too dead to complete the task, but instead by one C.T. Frazer, LL.B.

As I was reading this unusual document, the inscrutable sang-froid for which I'm locally feted must have deserted me, because Flint now said, 'I see you don't like the look of it any more than I do.'

'See? How do you see?'

'Your eyebrow twitched. And you shifted your weight a little, like you were squaring up for a spot of aggravation.' Clearly a lifetime of closely observing those who owed him money had brought keenness to the man's perceptions. 'A nasty thing, isn't it? And there's more.'

Sidney now passed me the envelope. It bore his name and address, neatly printed. There was no stamp – we were in the third week of a postal strike – and written in the top right-hand corner stood the chilling words BY HAND.

I said, 'They've been to your house.'

Sidney said, 'They've got someone here in Southaven acting for them. For all I know, they're watching my every move.'

Privately, I felt that Sidney had this the wrong way round: it looked rather as if the solicitors were acting for someone in Southaven, someone intent on taking a short cut to a bit of nice, steady income.

With hindsight, this was probably the moment when my intuition first proposed the most likely candidate, but for personal reasons I didn't want to hear what it was saying. Instead, I moved further away from the fire. I'd begun to smell the hairs singeing on the backs of my calves. 'Have you had any previous contact with these people?'

'What, Tipton, Lipton and Skipton? Never heard of them. And before you ask, I haven't the foggiest notion who this mysterious client of theirs might be.'

'Whoever it is, he seems to have set his sights on buying out half your portfolio for peanuts. Whether you agree to it or not.'

'That's the tone, isn't it? They're too smart to threaten me in so many words, but you can't mistake the meaning.'

I tried chewing my tongue, but I didn't much care for the taste. I said, 'I don't suppose there's any chance you might want to go along with this?'

'Sell half my property? I'd have to be mad. It's all doing very nicely at the moment.'

Perhaps it was childish of me, but I couldn't let this pass. 'Doing very nicely? Not five minutes ago you were complaining there's no money in property these days.'

Sidney Flint scowled, causing new and previously unsuspected channels to etch themselves into his face. 'No, well, of course, there isn't. I mean, if you look at it like that. But all the same, I wouldn't want to sell. I take my responsibilities as a landlord very seriously. It's easy enough to guess what sort of character's behind a piece of work like this. I can't have my properties falling into the hands of some unscrupulous, unprincipled miser who would fail to maintain the fabric of the buildings and squeeze the tenants until the pips squeaked.'

Though the description sounded all too familiar, as I stood there holding the unsavoury letter by one corner I realized that unless I took decisive action it was possible I could fall prey to a landlord even more grasping and hard-boiled than Sidney Flint. I would have to do something about this.

Flint said, 'What do you reckon? Do you think I could get away with ignoring it?'

I shook my head, and instantly regretted it. Huge lumps of granite had apparently worked themselves loose, and were now scraping against the walls of the cranium. 'Not a chance. These people mean business, you can tell.'

'Then what should I do? I've been racking my brains over this for the last three days.'

'Well you can stop worrying now. You're turning the whole affair over to a professional.'

'Am I? Who?' He must have caught my expression. 'Oh, you mean you. But what can you do about it?'

'First of all, you need to reply to this letter.'

'How? There's a strike on, if you hadn't noticed.'

'You can use a courier firm. There's private postal services cropping up all over the place at the moment.'

Sidney's face violently discomposed itself. 'The price!'

'Listen, Sidney, you've got thousands resting on this. It's no use fretting over a couple of quid.'

'I haven't got where I am today by throwing good money after bad.'

I sighed, recalling similar penny-pinching in the case of Doris Lively. 'We have to reply to this letter. It's the only way to regain some sort of control.'

Sidney shook his head. 'No courier. It's outrageous what these people charge.'

I thought for a moment. 'Actually, I might be able to get a letter to London for nothing.'

Sidney tried not to look too interested. 'Really? And how would you manage that?'

But I merely tapped the side of my nose. 'Commercially sensitive information. If you don't mind, I'd rather draft the reply myself. We need to strike the right tone, leave them a little uncertain just what they're dealing with. My guess is, they probably don't know much about you.'

'But how will that get them off my back?'

'It won't. We're just playing for time. Meanwhile, I've got to find out who's pulling the strings.'

'Some mobster in London, presumably.'

'Perhaps. But anyone can employ a dodgy London solicitor.'

Sidney Flint stood silent for a moment, chewing over this latest development in a long, undistinguished life. In the fading winter light he looked old and vulnerable. He said, 'Do you think you can pull it off? Do you think you can get their claws out of me, whoever they are? I'm no expert on your job, but it strikes me this is a far tougher proposition than winkling out Doris Lively.'

I didn't answer Flint's question. How could I? I didn't even have a plan. I said, 'Suppose they try to get heavy – suppose they send the boys round. Have you got people you can call on?'

'I used to have, in the old days. I had collectors who turned out for me when tenants dragged their feet.'

'Then I suggest you put them on alert.'

'No chance of that, I'm afraid. Jacob's got a hernia, can't even bend down to tie his laces. Besides, he's seventy-three. And Dick's dead.'

'I suppose you can't very well set Dennis on them, can you?'

He seemed to bridle at this remark. 'There's no need to be facetious. Dennis may not be Charles Atlas but he's a very reliable worker.'

'So what do you do these days when you need a bit of muscle? I can't believe all your tenants are as obliging as me and Florrie.'

'I employ bailiffs, a Liverpool firm. They do well enough, but I hardly think they'd branch out into personal protection.'

I paused for thought, as far as thought was possible in my enfeebled state. Though I'd prefer not to lose this job before I even started, the omens looked unfavourable. I said, 'Have you considered going to the police?'

'No!' The reply was instantaneous, and accompanied by much heat. 'We don't want the police sniffing around, do we? In my experience, they never know when to stop. I'm placing this matter exclusively in your hands.'

Apparently I was about to work for Sidney Flint again. With the end of the interview in sight, I turned down the gas now, hoping to save a few coppers. Then holding up the letter I said, 'All right if I keep this?'

'You'll need it to draft that reply. Shall I come back tomorrow to see where you've got to?'

'Make it late afternoon, if that's OK. I'll need some cash up front, by the way.'

'Up front?' It would be hard to overstate the degree of horror with which this was spoken. 'You mean – now?'

'Yes, now. I charge ten quid a day plus expenses, minimum charge thirty pounds per investigation. I'll not start without ten quid on the table.'

Flint tried to smile, but from long disuse the relevant muscles failed to respond. 'But we're old friends! I thought you'd be giving me a special rate.'

'I am doing. Normally I'd expect the full thirty quid down, but I'm making an exception.'

'Sam, Sam! Do I look like a man who can afford ten pounds a day?'

He didn't, as a matter of fact. With his soiled raincoat and egg-stained tie, he looked more like a man who'd just escaped from the workhouse, but I knew he could afford the money nevertheless. Cruel as it was to place demands of any kind on my brain in its present condition, I now subjected it to mental arithmetic. The opportunity was too good to pass up. 'All right, Sidney, I tell you what. Knock five bob a week off my rent – twenty-five pence, I should say – and I'll take ten per cent off your bill in return. How's that? Nine quid down, and I'm yours.'

The face furrowed again while rival mental arithmetic went on in the back room somewhere. 'I don't know, I could be selling myself short. It all depends how long you end up working for me.'

'A gamble, isn't it? Come on, Sidney! You need this problem sorting out, and I'm your best hope. Be a man, put your hand in your pocket.'

There was still a brief delay while Flint's practised business mind canvassed other possibilities. I replaced the letter in its envelope and lodged it behind an empty cigar box on the mantel piece. If you stuck your nose in this box, you could still just about detect the rich aroma of its former contents, though in fact years had passed since I'd nicked it from the home of a robbery suspect when I was still on the police force.

Meanwhile Flint must have run out of alternatives, because at last he took out his wallet, possibly the oldest, most decayed such object I'd ever seen in use, removed a worn fiver, handed it to me, then put the wallet away. Next he reached into a side pocket of his old grey suit jacket and produced a roll of one pound notes held by a rubber band. Releasing the band, he gave me three of the notes, then secured the roll and pocketed it again. He said, 'You don't mind a little loose change?'

'Why not give me another one of those pound notes? You've got loads.'

'I find they come in useful. And it's all worth the same, isn't it?' Now he delved into his trousers and scooped out a great handful of coins. I held open my palm, and he counted out five florins or ten pence pieces, another thirty pence in shillings and five pence pieces, and the rest in an assortment of copper. Other people might have done this for effect, but not Sidney Flint. He was in the compulsive grip of some inner rulebook governing cash transactions.

I thanked him and placed all the cash on the coffee table. I was wondering how to broach my next question. 'Sidney – ' There was no point in being too delicate, I needed to know where we stood. 'Are you hiding anything?'

He stepped backwards, astonished. 'Hiding anything? What kind of damn fool question is that?'

'It's just – well, if you decide not to play ball with whoever this is, what exactly are their options? Obviously they could send the boys round, like I said. But for all they know you might have bigger boys, and they'd have wasted their time. They don't sound like the sort of people who waste their time, though, do they?'

Flint acknowledged the truth of this point with a slight inclination of the head.

I went on. 'So naturally I'm wondering if they know something. Because then they wouldn't need to send the boys round at all, would they? They'd have you right where they wanted you. Is there anything you'd sooner keep out of the public domain, Sidney? Possibly some old business deal which wouldn't bear close examination – '

'I've always conducted my business affairs with the very strictest probity.'

'Well then, something in your private life. Some personal peccadillo – '

'What are you insinuating?'

'Now don't blow up at me, I'm not insinuating anything. But you might turn out to have had a secret love child with Nana Mouskouri. I'm just making sure you're not exposed to blackmail. Because if you are, you can wave bye-bye to half your property straight away. And I wouldn't be surprised if they came back later for the other half.'

Not a man of high colour at the best of times, Flint had turned a whiter shade. 'I assure you, Sam, that there is absolutely nothing of that sort. For many years now I've led an ascetic existence dedicated to business and the service of my tenants. If these thieves – because that's what they are, in my opinion – if they think they can intimidate me by digging around in my past, they've got another think coming.' He re-buttoned the coat now, ready to protect himself against the keen winter blast. 'If that's all, I'll be on my way.'

I followed Sidney Flint out into the hallway, and watched from the door as he slowly descended the stairs, his shoulders slanting wearily from the accumulated care of years, but his head still proud and upright. At every other step, the cash chinked in his trouser pocket.

Back in the hallway with the door closed behind me, I no longer had the illusion of returning health. In the living room I switched off the gas fire and closed the curtains. It wasn't dark yet, but then you couldn't say it had ever been light all day, and I'd grown sick of the pretence.

In the kitchen I took another aspirin and made tea. Neither would do much to help with the 'flu, but that wasn't my real problem any more. My problem now was Sidney Flint.

Sitting up in bed again, with Ishmael's adventures laid aside on the quilt and the warm mug pressed between my hands, I sacrificed an imaginary dove and picked around amongst the entrails. I didn't much like what I saw.

On the positive side, life in Southaven was about to get a lot less dull. But Sidney Flint wouldn't be the only one forced to pick up the bill.

If I was reading the signs correctly, organized crime had come to town.

**two**

As a side-effect of the fever which attended my illness, my dreams had for the past few days been nothing short of lurid, displaying in febrile colours a range of activities likely to turn the stomach and warp the mind. The night of my meeting with Sidney Flint, this image factory acquired fresh material in the form of an article I'd tried to read just before going to sleep. It appeared in New Scientist, had been written by one Professor Z. Nussbaum, and was called *Are Three Dimensions Really Necessary?*

Here, the good professor hypothesized that human consciousness could have evolved just as effectively in a two-dimensional universe. We already know, he said, that it's possible to create a representation of three dimensions in two, through the magic of perspective; though I felt obliged to point out that this only worked when the image was viewed along an intersecting plane, or, to put it another way, from Somewhere Else, a place the Prof was keen to abolish. Therefore, he went on, if consciousness arose through the workings of the brain in three dimensions, it should be possible to design a two-dimensional analogue of this process which might be of use in developing systems of Artificial Intelligence. This was a subject which had crossed my path before, when an AI buff had obstructed my efforts to solve a murder case the previous summer.

Though I couldn't claim to have understood much of this article – Nussbaum lost me soon after the title – the consequence for my dreams was, predictably, that they all took place in an M.C. Escher world of impossible surfaces, whose shifting logic left me nauseous. Dream turned to nightmare when the Great White Whale suddenly materialized through a worm-hole between dimensions and began buffeting my craft with its Great White Head (of course, all this took place at sea). So it came as a relief when a familiar voice said, 'Sam! Sam!' and a hand roughly shook me awake.

The return of consciousness, in however many dimensions, also brought a return of the headache, the sore throat, the aching limbs, and the sense that death would be a blessed release. This must have caused me to groan, because the voice now said, 'For heaven's sake! You're not still pretending you're ill? We've got work to do!'

I opened my eyes. Teaming up with the brain, their first task of the day was to interpret the two grey forms in front of them, which turned out to be the trousered legs of my assistant, Matt Standish. I was rather fond of those legs, as I was of the rest of him, but a nurse called Eileen had got there first.

I said, 'Tea,' and didn't move.

A steaming mug now came into view between my eyes and the trousers. Matt said, 'If you want it, you'll have to get up. I'll be in the other room.' After which the mug and the trousers quit the scene.

This kind of behaviour was all too typical of my young deputy. From the earliest days of his employment Matt had shown a marked tendency to harass, hector and harangue. Of course I understood that he was just compensating for a quite natural feeling of inferiority – he the rookie or cadet, his boss the highly-regarded investigator with years of experience and unparalleled deductive powers. But it was still very annoying. In the beginning this hadn't seemed to matter so much because, technically, I wasn't actually paying him. That arrangement soon came to an abrupt end when Matt was hospitalized after an unfortunate incident for which his family, and in particular his mother, held me responsible. Small wonder that she was less than overjoyed when he took up the post again in September. Luckily, she had a large family and a part-time job to take her mind off such things, not to mention the fact that Matt's behaviour hardly stood out in a family whose members showed a pronounced disregard for their personal safety. The first disadvantage of his return to work was that this time he'd held out obstinately for a wage of fourteen quid a week (he asked for fifteen but I talked him down), so there was now a constant need to attract clients who could keep us active and solvent. The second disadvantage was that, incredibly, I was now actually paying someone to lecture me on my laziness and poor organizational skills, and I don't mind admitting it sometimes stuck in the craw.

I heaved myself out of bed. The dressing gown Mark Howell had given me lay in its usual place of honour on the floor, so I slipped it on, pottered through to use the bathroom, then joined Matt in the living room, where my tea awaited me on the small table in front of the settee. The gas fire had had some effect by now, but still the room was cool. I pulled the dressing gown more closely around me, enjoyed a first sip of the tea, then took a moment to reflect and ask myself how I was. When the answer came, if it hadn't been for Matt I'd have gone straight back to bed.

Matt had adopted his favourite position in the room, the bench seat under the gable window. Back in the old days, when my life was still my own, this bench had always been the resting place of various books and magazines, but now Matt kept it clear for the express use of his behind. The room faced north-east and the light could be poor at this time of year, but nevertheless he was attempting to read a copy of the local paper, which he'd brought in with him. It was scarcely daylight yet in any case, since we were in the third year of a mad experiment in permanent British Summer Time. Farmers in the north of Scotland weren't the only ones who hated it.

I said, 'Any news?'

'What, in the *Gazelle*?' Matt had taken to calling the Southaven *Gazette* by this sobriquet in honour of its notorious typographical waywardness. In low moods I could sometimes cheer myself up by recalling an instance from as far back as the previous August, when a picture of some children in a muddy field bore the caption, *'Youngsters from St Mark's Sunday School enjoy their annual threat.'* The first time Matt favoured me with this Gazelle gag, I'd been amused. The second time, I'd tried to be. Now it just annoyed the heck out of me.

'Yes, in the Gazelle. Or from any other source. Is there anything new in the world which you think I should know?'

'You still sound terrible. Drink some more of that tea.'

'Thanks. I will.' I did.

'No, I don't see anything interesting here. Just more stuff about the local government reorganization.' The latest stupid proposal to come out of Whitehall involved lumping Southaven council in with some districts on the north side of Liverpool, supposedly to save money.

I said, 'That'll never happen. People here wouldn't stand for it, they'd be on the streets. Hand that over.' I reached across, and Matt gave me the newspaper, which he'd disordered to a high degree. I reassembled it as best I could, and then noticed that the editor, Morgan Williams, had in fact led with a different front page story, the surprise takeover of the Marine Lodge by its larger neighbour, the Grand Hotel. After standing empty for several years, the Grand had reopened at Christmas, and it seemed odd that they should already feel confident enough of success to think of expanding. 'Did you see this about the Grand?'

'Yeah. Hadn't you heard about it? You're never out of the Grand Vaults this last few weeks, I'd have thought your little friend Nicky would have let you in on the secret.'

'It's not Nicky, it's Mickey, as you very well know. And he's not my friend.'

'Shame, after all the money you've spent. The way you look at him it's a miracle you've not been arrested.'

'He happens to have a very nice nose.'

'He looks like that Bluebottle puppet from the Goons on TV.'

'And he's an admirable professional barman with a broad conversational range.'

'And very tight trousers.'

'I thought you didn't notice that kind of thing any more.'

There was a silence. I drank tea guiltily. References to Matt's sexual history always got the wrong side of him. He'd been with Eileen for nearly a year now, but before that it had been a very different story. A better friend might tactfully have drawn a veil over the dead past, but where would be the fun in that?

As evidence that my remark had hit home, I now saw that Matt had started fiddling with the risible arrangement of downy hairs on his upper lip, which he was pleased to call his moustache. This offence against nature had begun its young life on New Year's Day. If Matt had been hoping for a bold, dark, authoritative piece of lip furniture, he must have been disappointed, but I could have told him the experiment would end in tears. Apart from the auburn tangle which pleasingly framed his pleasing face, Matt was not an hairy man. As with the legs, I'd always been fond of his upper lip, no less than of his lower lip, and so found myself unremittingly hostile to this ill-advised attempt to thatch it.

You didn't need to be Sigmund Freud to fathom Matt's motivation, nor to understand why an implied reference to Eileen should have set him stroking his furry chum like this. Eileen was Matt's senior by nearly four years. Inevitably, people passed comment. And though Matt quite reasonably objected that if the sexes had been reversed no one would have batted an eyelid at so small an age gap, the fact remained that the sexes weren't reversed, and eyelids went on batting. What could he do but try to make himself look older than his twenty-one years? Hence the fluffy interloper currently marring his appearance.

But after a few seconds of moustache-buffing, Matt stopped and rounded on me instead. 'You know you can be horrible sometimes?'

'Me? What have I done now?'

'I'm with Eileen, and you won't accept it. You still think I should be running after blokes, the same as you.'

'No I don't.' As a matter of fact I did, but this was no time to start dabbling in the truth. 'I really like Eileen, you know I do.'

'That's not the point. You don't like her being my girlfriend.'

'Nonsense, you're perfectly suited. Eileen is patient, tolerant and long-suffering, and you give her ample scope to practise her virtues.'

'Very funny.'

'I have no quarrel with her. It's all in your head.'

In my present reduced state I could really have done without the conversation we were having. But Matt wouldn't let it go. 'You never talk about her. You never ask me how she is. And if we have a bit of a falling out it actually cheers you up. You try to hide it, but I can tell.'

Suspicion dawned. 'Have you two had another row?'

'No. Why should we?' I thought he answered too quickly. On top of that, he started fiddling with the moustache again.

'Come on, out with it. What is it this time?'

He hesitated, then said, 'It's nothing.'

'No it's not. You're definitely moping this morning. If I hadn't been dying of this disease I'd have noticed it before.'

The index finger continued fussing with the offending follicles. I imagined lathering Matt's upper lip and getting to work with a cut-throat razor. After a while he said, 'You know it's Valentine's Day on Sunday? I was going to take Eileen out for a meal in the evening, but now she says there's some kind of work thing she has to go to, out of town.'

'What, a course or something? On a Sunday?'

'I'm not sure. She was really vague, it made me uneasy. She said she couldn't get back in time.' He shook his head sadly, as if recalling happier days now lost for ever. 'I'd already booked a table at the Hen and Chickens.'

'I don't see the problem. Take her out another night instead.'

'Yeah. But – ' He fell silent.

'Let me guess. You couldn't resist saying something.'

He turned to me with evident feeling. 'I only said I didn't seem to be much of a priority with her.'

'I see.'

'And she said I shouldn't make such an issue of it, it's not as if we're engaged or anything like that. So I said, would she like us to be?'

'Strewth, Matt. You didn't propose?'

'I don't think so, not exactly. But in any case she said, "Of course not." Of course not!'

21

'And you didn't care for her tone.'

'I said what did she mean, "Of course not"? She said we hadn't been together long enough, and besides, I was too young.'

'Oops.'

'And I didn't have a proper job either.'

While privately agreeing with Eileen's previous objections, I felt that she'd now strayed wildly from the facts. 'What on earth is the woman talking about? You're Sam Rigby's right-hand man. There can't be a finer career opportunity in all of Southaven.'

A change had occurred in Matt's expression. 'You normally say assistant. Am I really your right-hand man?' I could see he was pleased.

'Naturally. And my mainstay. Also my prop, solace, and shelter from the storm. Which is why I can't have you distracted like this by affairs of the heart. Especially when we have a new client.'

I told Matt about Sidney Flint and the threatening letter. He asked to see it, so I pointed him in the direction of the cigar box and he got up to read it for himself. Reading was not his strong point, and nor was writing. Perplexed by this trait in one so sharp, I'd done some sleuthing. It seemed Matt's difficulties could be put down to a condition called dyslexia, marked by symptoms which varied depending on who you asked. There didn't seem to be any cure for it, but the practice common when I'd been at school of whacking poor readers over the knuckles and singling them out for humiliation was believed to be ineffective. Now I'd adopted the policy of never rushing Matt when he read, unless of course I was in a hurry, or he just happened to be getting up my nose at the time.

So it was with saintly forbearance that I waited while Matt slowly worked his way through the text of Messrs Tipton, Buxton and Lamb's toxic missive, chewing his lip in characteristic fashion as he did so. Then I said, 'Well?'

Matt said, 'I've never seen anything like this before.'

'I don't think Sidney had, either.'

'Sounds like someone trying to make a fast buck. How much property does he have, exactly?'

'I don't know. I didn't ask him.'

'Why not? We need to be clear what's at stake.'

'I'm ill. It was all I could do to stand there while he laid out the facts.'

'You're not ill, you're just malingering. I've been out on building sites in a far worse state than you.' This was a reference to Matt's pre-Rigby employment. 'You'll have to talk to this Flint character again.'

'At least give me credit for one thing: I did manage to extract nine actual pounds sterling from the man. Anyone who knows him would say that was a miracle.'

'Nine? Why not ten?'

'I gave him a discount in return for lowering my rent.'

'I hope you know what you're doing, he'll be asking for green stamps next. Are you sure you're fit to deal with this while I'm gone?'

Matt was engaged on a lucrative inquiry of his own. An affluent Welldale woman named Beryl Asprey, finding long blonde hairs on her husband Gordon's clothing, had concluded that his frequent business trips were nothing of the kind. Now Matt had discovered that, unknown to Beryl, Gordon also owned a flat in Manchester. With Gordon due to make another trip today, Matt was off to stake the place out.

Apart from concocting a reply to the letter, and making a phone call to see what I could learn about Tipton and Co., I doubted whether there would be much action in the case of S. Flint over the next few days. So I was confident that I could manage, but nevertheless I said, 'Don't stay away too long, will you? Something might come up.'

'I'd be back every night if I could, I don't much like the sound of this B&B you've booked me into.'

'You've got to be around late and early, that's when things are most likely to happen. And I'm sure it's a perfectly good hotel.'

'They said I should take my own soap.'

'What do you expect on a budget, the Hilton? Now, have you got the camera?'

'Of course.'

'When's your train?'

'Ten fifteen. I should be making a move.' Matt returned the letter to its home behind the cigar box. 'I suppose you'll go back to bed now, won't you?'

The phone rang. While I searched for it, Matt said, 'Why on earth you can't just keep it on the table I'll never know.' Then he went out into the hallway to fetch his coat.

I found the telephone hiding under the brown corduroy bean bag which I kept as a seating option for people who found the settee too conventional. I lifted the receiver. 'Sam Rigby.'

'Your office phone's ringing.' The unmistakable voice – severe, and rarely without some hint of accusation in its tone – belonged to my mother's older sister Winnie. She and Uncle Fred were the live-in caretakers at Crowburn House on the Boulevard, where my office was located.

'Good morning, Aunt Winnie.'

'Never mind "good morning", are you going to come down and answer it? It's never stopped since half past seven, when I was polishing the handrail on the stairs. If you kept proper hours, like normal people, you could have dealt with it by now.'

Pathetically, I tried mounting a defence. 'I'd have been down before, but I'm ill.'

'Again? You were ill last year. What is it this time, bubonic plague?' I thanked her for the sympathy. 'It's not sympathy you need, it's regular hours, three square meals a day, and no more booze or cigarettes. Do you want to end up like your mother?'

The answer to that was no, but I said, 'I'll be round there as soon as I can. And I appreciate you letting me know. Sounds like it could be something important.' Because although she exacted a heavy toll in sarcasm and was an even worse haranguer than Matt, it couldn't be doubted that Aunt Winnie had my best interests at heart.

'And do try to look presentable for a change. When you bumped into the Old Man in the hall last week, he thought we'd got squatters.' By the Old Man she meant William Leighton, chief agent to the Crowburn Estate, from whom I leased my office. Recently turned eighty-three, his notion of a presentable appearance probably involved spats and a monocle, and if he

24

found my casual chic challenging he only had himself to blame for not retiring at sixty-five when he had the chance.

At that moment the gas fire died. Not thinking, I said, 'Oh, bugger.'

'Sam!'

'Sorry, Aunt Winnie. The fire went out.'

And then Matt was behind me, kissing me on the top of the head. He said, 'I'm off now.'

Aunt Winnie said, 'You know I can't abide that sort of language.'

'It just slipped out. Matt – !' He was already half way to the door.

Aunt Winnie said, 'Who are you talking to?'

'My assistant's here, we're working.'

'Working? I suppose there's a first time for everything.'

This seemed harsh, even from my aunt. Piqued, I said, 'Would it hurt that much to say something nice occasionally?' and put down the receiver. She'd make me pay later, but it felt good at the time.

Matt gripped an ancient holdall which probably belonged to his parents. He was still living at home and showed little sign of escaping the family's sometimes stifling embrace. He said, 'What do you want? I'll be late for my train.'

The fact was, I didn't want anything in particular. Or rather, I wanted to say I'd miss him, but I knew that would be a mistake. I said, 'It's nothing. You'd better go. Ring me if you make any progress.' Matt nodded and walked out. I heard the flat door close behind him.

You may be wondering why, given the situation with Eileen, and Matt's sensitivity about his past, he'd allowed himself the pleasure of the chaste kiss on my skull mentioned above. In less guarded moments he would even risk the forehead, the cheek, or, God help us, the lips. The previous summer, during Matt's first significant rift from Eileen, there'd been a moment under the lime trees on the Boulevard when it had seemed that Eileen's loss was about to become my gain. A couple of hours later Matt was in hospital, fighting for his life, with nurse Eileen the ministering angel and myself barred from the presence by indignant Standishes. It's well known that the key to maintaining good relationships is never to talk things over, and since we'd resumed working together we'd both kept shtumm about the lime trees. But I knew he hadn't forgotten, and he knew I knew. These brief kisses, and sometimes an affectionate touch, were the only acknowledgement of what had almost been.

Whether it was the tea, or the business conference, or the phone call from my aunt, I can't say, but as I got up to turn off the gas fire it occurred to me that I was feeling marginally less ill. After days of abject suffering, the first sign of improvement is always cherishable, no matter how slight. It might not be long now before I felt fit to start smoking again. So it was with raised spirits that I found the assortment of loose change donated by Sidney Flint the previous day, fed the meter, and wallowed for twenty minutes in a hot bath. The phone at Crowburn House could ring off the hook for all I cared, I wasn't about to be cheated of this indulgence. I then shaved my several days' stubble, ate toast (Matt had brought in a loaf and other supplies), dressed in my usual dark trousers, coloured shirt and brown leather jacket, and with the threatening letter in my pocket clattered down the uncarpeted stairs to the street.

When you've not been out for three days, it's remarkable how the world can surprise you. I'd genuinely forgotten how dismal it was. A cold rain fell steadily, and a thin north-westerly off the Irish Sea gusted around me on Preston Street while I tried to remember where I'd parked the Minx. I recalled the hot bath. Did my mystery caller really matter so much? Might it not be better to wait another day before replying to the Shoreditch solicitors? Was it wise to be out and about when in all probability my glands were still swollen? Then I spotted the Hillman, a few doors down. With a sigh, I committed myself to life in the world, climbed into the driver's seat, and, after a couple of false starts, fired up the engine.

I quite liked the Minx. If you could once get it going, it responded very well to even a light touch on the gas pedal, unlike the skittish Cortina which it had replaced. True, I strongly suspected that it had been stitched together from the remnants of two damaged vehicles, but for ninety quid you could hardly grumble.

In a couple of minutes I was parking up round the back of Crowburn House. Some people would have made this short journey on foot, but I was ill and it was raining. I then walked round to the front of the building. Often I use the back entrance and have a word with Winnie and Fred on my way past their flat, but after my earlier exchange with Aunt Winnie it seemed best to let her cool off for a while.

Crowburn House always exuded a reassuring smell of polish and old leather, which greatly enhanced the client's approach to my office. The broad staircase too spoke of dignity and permanence. Clearly any private investigator with an office in this building must be a man of depth and integrity, even if these qualities were tempered just now by a headache and a nagging throat.

As I reached the top landing with its wide expanse of brown pre-war linoleum, a woman in a well-cut pea-green coat was just turning away from my office door. I said, 'Are you looking for me?'

In her left hand she held a large leather handbag, from which a copy of today's Gazette protruded. She said, 'Mr Rigby?' Her expression was business-like, but anxious too.

'That's me.'

The anxiety seemed only to increase. 'Do you never answer your phone? I've been calling you all morning.'

'I'm sorry, I've been detained. We've got a lot on at present.'

Now the anxiety completely got the better of her. 'Please don't tell me you're too busy!' She drew the Gazette from her handbag. 'Look at this.' Unfolding the newspaper, she presented the front page which I'd seen earlier. 'I'm Alice Haig from the Marine Lodge. It says here we're selling up to the Grand. That's a lie! They offered to buy us out for a pittance but I turned them down.' She smacked the page with the back of her hand as if it were a naughty child. 'This is outrageous! What do you propose to do about it?'

## *three*

I unlocked the office door and showed Alice Haig into the room.

My office at Crowburn House had always represented a refuge from the disorder which characterised other areas of my existence. For example, the floor showed a definite absence of books, magazines, newspapers, overflowing ashtrays, half-full mugs of abandoned tea, pencil stubs, biros, discarded socks, empty envelopes, cotton buds, paper clips, tubes of ointment (don't ask), and all the other paraphernalia essential to the preservation of life in the Leigh Terrace flat. Here, it was possible to cross the floor with ease from one corner of the room to another, and there was almost no risk that you would need to peel a wine gum off the sole of your shoe afterwards.

But under the influence of Matt, this minimalist approach had been softened by concessions to comfort and aesthetics. The rug was new, or at any rate new to me. An easy chair in the window now provided an alternative to the two upright chairs on either side of my desk. A counter against the wall hosted an electric kettle and other tea-making equipment, though we still hadn't invested in a fridge, which meant a trek to the downstairs scullery whenever someone of conservative tastes insisted on milk. On the wall hung a framed London Midland Railways advertising poster from Southaven's heyday, extolling its charms as a winter resort. The desk and filing cabinet still dominated, the overall effect remained businesslike, but the Standish touch offered a gentle reminder that business was not the whole of life.

All this was wasted on Alice Haig. She declined tea, and sat very upright in one of the upright chairs without waiting to be asked, laying the Gazette down emphatically on my side of the desk. I doubt whether she'd even seen the rug, nor indeed the picture. If Matt had been present, it would have broken his heart.

I hung my jacket up behind the door then took a seat opposite

Alice Haig. She said, 'Well?'

I nearly said, 'Well what?' but stopped myself in time. With this particular client, or prospective client, I suspected it would be more than usually vital to appear one step ahead. So I said, 'A pittance?'

Her face, still handsome at what I guessed might have been forty-five or so, briefly registered that she'd heard this word somewhere recently, then the recollection that it had been she herself who'd spoken it. 'Yes, Mr Rigby. A derisory sum. They were offering less than half the market value of the hotel. I had no hesitation in refusing.'

'When you say "they" – ?'

'The owners of the Grand.'

'The Goldings?'

If Alice Haig was surprised that I knew the name, she didn't show it. 'That's correct.'

I quickly skimmed the newspaper story, but there was no direct mention of the Goldings. 'Have you had dealings with them face to face?'

'No. When this first came up I did try to speak with them in person, but they seem remarkably elusive. As a matter of fact I'd like to give them a damn good piece of my mind.'

I stroked my chin contemplatively. The lack of stubble came as a surprise. I said, 'I'm not sure if you're aware of this, but there's a very good reason why Frank Golding is so elusive, as you put it. He's doing fifteen years in Wormwood Scrubs.'

Pleasingly, this went over big. 'Good heavens!' The exclamation was accompanied by a facial expression all too familiar in Southaven, which could be termed small-town affright. Clearly, objects such as Wormwood Scrubs rarely passed within Alice Haig's field of vision. 'Whatever for, do you know?'

'Sorry, can't remember. But I think violence came into it somewhere.' As it happens, an old colleague of mine from the Southaven force had had a hand in putting Frank Golding behind bars. 'It's Frank's wife Lou who's in charge at the Grand.'

'I hadn't realized I was dealing with such dubious characters. I'd assumed the Goldings were respectable business people.'

'And so they are, some of the time. But they do like to have things their own way.'

'So when I refused their offer – '

I indicated the newspaper in front of me. 'It would seem only natural to them to exert a little pressure.' There was an issue which I'd been tiptoeing around. I said, 'According to this, Marine Lodge is in financial difficulties. Is that true, or are they just trying to undermine you?'

Alice Haig was silent for a moment. Then she said, 'Have you ever run a business, Mr Rigby?'

I found this hurtful. 'Aren't I running one now? And call me Sam, won't you. Everyone does.'

'Everyone except me. I prefer to keep a clear boundary around my business affairs. Yes, of course you're running a business, after a fashion, but I was thinking of something more substantial, with a significant public profile. The point is, confidence is everything. Since my husband died two years ago I've done all in my power to maintain the illusion that Marine Lodge is flourishing. But we have significant debts.'

'I'm sorry to hear it.'

'Don't be. I have a sound business plan, bookings for the spring are well up on last year, and we're beginning to attract more and more event bookings from local organizations, all very profitable. What I don't have is money in the bank, and that's what makes me vulnerable. I've had to take out a loan. When the first letter came, offering to buy me out, not only did they know this, they knew the exact amount. How could they possibly have found that out?'

'Which is presumably where I come in. You want me to find the leak and plug it.'

'Yes. At least, that's part of it. The Gazette only speaks in general terms, I'm sure people won't have taken it too seriously. But if the exact figure were to be published, it could be disastrous for us. People would say, No point in booking into Marine Lodge, they're going bust, we'll lose our deposit.'

'I see what you mean.' I sat back in my chair, as far as that was possible, and took a couple of slow breaths. Alice's anxiety was ramping up my headache. On the one hand, I had several reasons for feeling unusually positive about this case. On the other hand, all I really wanted to do was take two aspirin and dive back under the quilt. Perhaps I'd get the chance for that later on. I said, 'Do you have any idea how they could have got hold of those figures?'

Again there was some hesitation before she said, 'No. None at all.'

'And you trust your staff?'

'They've all been with me for a while now. Except our bell-boy, he only started last summer. But he's too stupid for anything like this.'

'Would you mind if I talked to them?'

Anxiety became alarm. 'I can't have them thinking they're under suspicion! My housekeeper's already sulking because I complained she'd lost a laundry receipt, and the chef resigns every time his soufflés fail. You've no idea how difficult it is.'

I said, 'I can be very diplomatic,' and my nose grew about six inches.

'Well – all right, but make sure you are. Good staff don't grow on trees.'

This looked as if it would be a simple enough assignment. Unless there'd been a break-in, it seemed likely that one of Alice's trusted employees couldn't be trusted after all, and had engaged in a little spying on behalf of a competitor. 'But you said that's only part of what you want me to do?'

Another silence. I admired the way Alice Haig never spoke before she was ready. Perhaps she could give me a few tips some time. Finally she said, 'I don't quite know how to put this.'

Well, I couldn't just let her sit there looking shifty. 'You want me to dig some dirt on the Goldings.'

It was a safe guess that I'd voiced her thoughts to the letter. But she couldn't be sure whether industrial espionage chimed with the exacting Rigby Code, and her cool grey eyes searched my face for clues. 'Would that be so very wrong? I turned them down unequivocally, but now we have this charade in the Gazette. From what you've told me, I doubt whether they'll let go until they get what they want. But I'm not selling! Marine Lodge is my life now – and the children, of course.'

The situation required a clear head. Lacking this, I tried looking out of the window for inspiration, through the naked branches of the sycamore trees towards the shops across the Boulevard. The rain was still falling, the sky was still grey. It took some chutzpah to promote Southaven as a winter paradise.

As it happened, I already had an informant on the inside at the Grand Hotel, but today's events had made me suspect that he could be cavalier with the truth. Mickey the barman was none other than Frank Golding's youngest son. He'd already sold me the line that the Grand represented a quiet little retirement project for his mother Lou, who, unavoidably separated from her husband, had abandoned the cut and thrust of life in the capital for the gentler pace of Southaven, leaving Frank's other business interests in the hands of their two older boys. But Mickey had neglected to mention that Lou's idea of genteel withdrawal from the world included attempting to acquire the neighbouring property fraudulently at a knock-down price.

Matt hadn't been wrong to detect that I enjoyed Mickey's company. Any excuse to enjoy more of it was welcome, but I wasn't going to mention that to Alice Haig. I said, 'I hope you wouldn't expect me to do anything illegal.'

She eyed me squarely. 'Your methods are your own affair. Do you agree to do this work?' I told her my terms, and she reached into the handbag for her cheque book. 'This won't bounce, by the way. The loan came through last week. If we can just survive this unwanted attention from next door, I think we'll have an excellent year.' She wrote out the cheque and handed it to me. 'How do you intend to begin?'

I mulled. 'I take it you've been on to the Gazette?'

'Of course. The girl who answered the phone seemed to be retarded in some way, but she did eventually put me through to Morgan Williams. I doubt if he'll forget the conversation in a hurry.'

I smiled. 'Presumably he's printing an apology?'

'Yes. But he absolutely refused to reveal his sources. It was as though I'd committed blasphemy just by asking.'

With the Gazette taken care of, my agenda moved on to the

leak from Marine Lodge. 'Is there some way you can get me into the hotel informally, so I don't start putting people's backs up?'

Now it was Alice's turn to mull. 'Why don't you join us this afternoon? We're having a little birthday tea for one of our winter residents. In fact you may have heard of him – he's an actor, retired now of course. Giles Rawley.'

In my sickly state I'd rather been coasting through the interview so far. Mention of Giles Rawley sent a jolt right through me. 'Giles! I'd forgotten all about it.'

Alice Haig looked baffled. 'You'll have to explain.'

'Giles has already invited me. I've been a little off colour for the last few days and it slipped my mind.'

'How do you come to know someone like Giles?' Her tone suggested all too clearly that she thought Giles was a cut above me. I wondered whether she talked to her staff like that too.

'Oh, just socially.' I wasn't sure that it would be wise to reveal all. With clients I seldom do. In fact, I sometimes keep more affluent clients hanging for days after I've actually resolved their case, drip-feeding information on a selective basis. This inflates their bill somewhat, but they don't need the money and I do.

But the simple fact was, Mickey Golding had a twin sister, Lena, who shared bar duties with him at the Grand Vaults and had proved as big a hit with Giles Rawley as her brother had with me. In the process, Giles and I had become drinking buddies, albeit of the most superficial kind. The birthday in question would be his seventy-sixth.

I agreed to put in an appearance at Marine Lodge round about three thirty. There seemed no point in prolonging the interview, but as I was pushing back my chair to get up, the thought which for the past fifteen minutes had been hiding coyly behind the shrubbery of my nether brain suddenly stepped into view. It was an arresting thought, and worth the wait. I said, 'Just one more thing. If you haven't been in direct contact with the Goldings, who was it that sent you the original letter?'

Alice Haig's lips pursed as she recalled this unpleasant event. 'It was their solicitors.'

'That wouldn't be Tipton, Buxton and Lamb by any chance?'

If I'd wanted to appear one step ahead of my client, events had certainly played into my hands. Startled, Alice Haig said, 'How on earth did you know?'

'It may not be much consolation, but you're not the only person in town the Goldings have been leaning on. They're empire-building, Mrs Haig. You're supposed to be a vassal state.'

It would have been hard to imagine anyone less cowed than the woman currently gathering herself together to leave. 'In that case, I'm afraid they've picked the wrong person. And if they persist, they'll have a fight on their hands.'

When Alice Haig had gone, I made myself some tea, drafted a reply to Sidney Flint's letter, then typed it up onto headed notepaper which I'd had printed a couple of years before to use on such occasions. Thus the reply appeared to come from Fuselli, Crouch, solicitors and commissioners for oaths, whose office coincidentally shared an address with my own. Pretending to be a solicitor wasn't exactly professional behaviour, nor was it strictly legal, but it was effective and I got a kick out of it. Also, it enabled me to grade my response to a situation by choosing the most appropriate signatory. When heavy artillery was required, up stumped G. Fuselli himself, the senior partner. But since Tipton and Co. had had the gall to palm Sidney off with the understrapper C.T. Frazer, on this occasion I signed myself L. Grint, per pro U.U. Packer, the latter an employee so lowly that they didn't even make it to the list of partners printed at the foot of the page. If this caused the recipients to lie awake at four in the morning racking their brains for Christian names beginning with U, so much the better.

The job done, I banked Alice's cheque, drove home, took two aspirin, undressed, and dived under the quilt.

Although going back to bed had seemed like a good idea at the time, I hadn't reckoned on waking up to discover that it was already twenty to four, and I'd been due at Marine Lodge ten minutes earlier. An undignified scramble got me out of the flat dressed and refreshed, at least to the extent that I could pass for a healthy person as long as you didn't look twice. I threaded the

Minx through Boulevard traffic and turned right up Marine Approach towards the Promenade.

Originally, Marine Approach had been well named. A broad street of promising aspect, at its north end it had once broadened further and channelled the visitor between rows of oyster merchants and novelty shops, beneath the iron bridge which carried the Promenade, and out onto the beach with its bathing machines and donkey rides. To either side of this sunken highway, the road sloped gently up to join the Promenade. But when the sea had forsaken Southaven and a Marine Lake had been constructed on the foreshore, between the Prom and the retreating sea, this earlier approach had lost its purpose. It was decided about seventy years ago to bury the lower road and create a single sweeping avenue, rising unobstructed to the Promenade and the pier entrance. Local legend had it that the workmen had left the old shops untouched, exactly as they were on the day business had ceased for ever. As I drove up to the corner with the Grand Hotel Vaults on my left, it pleased me to imagine the ghosts of long-dead holidaymakers a few feet below me, tucking into their eternal oyster suppers.

I turned left past the Grand and left again between low hedges onto the forecourt of the Marine Lodge. Mine was the only car. If Alice Haig wanted to maintain the appearance of a thriving enterprise, this empty car park was hardly the best way to go about it.

As I mounted the steps towards the entrance, I could see figures moving in the cheerfully lit lounge to the left of me, and I fancied I heard Giles Rawley's rather penetrating voice. Any doubts were dispelled when I came into the lobby. Even at seventy-six, Giles could still pump out the decibels which had once carried his words up to the gods in many of the nation's theatres. Seeing no one at reception, I was about to head off down a corridor in pursuit of the lounge when Alice Haig appeared from a doorway behind the reception desk.

'Mr Rigby. I've been waiting for you.'

Her tone implied that I was late. I was. I said, 'We did say four o'clock, didn't we?'

She raised one pencilled eyebrow. 'Half past three. I hope you're not always late for appointments.'

'Must have got my wires crossed.'

Now she gave a distinct sniff of scepticism. It wasn't going to be easy to shoot things past Alice Haig. She said, 'It was fine to park on the forecourt today, you're here as Giles's guest. But if you come another time, it would be more discreet to use the staff car park at the back. The rear door is always open during the daytime.'

I said, 'The party seemed to be in full swing as I passed the window.'

'You're not too late to catch the presentation of the cake.'

'Sounds very grand.'

'I do hope Oscar's risen to the occasion. My chef, that is. I can't have him resigning again.'

As it happened, I already knew Oscar as well. Lena Golding had not one but two keen admirers from the Marine Lodge Hotel. Oscar would drop in at the Grand Vaults towards closing time most evenings, once he'd scrubbed the kitchen to his satisfaction. Though rivals for Lena's attention, he and Giles seemed to get on well.

I glanced beyond Alice's shoulder into what was clearly her office. I said, 'Could we take a moment to look at security?'

'Yes, that would be sensible.' We stepped in. There was a good lock on the door, which only a professional would have been capable of picking, but the filing cabinet and desk drawer were far less well protected. With persistence, even an amateur could have gained access to Alice Haig's papers.

I said, 'Who has the keys to this office?'

'Apart from me, only the reception staff and Graham, the night porter. But during the winter I mostly take care of reception myself.'

'In that case, I'd like to have a word with your night porter.'

Once again, alarm flamed up in Alice Haig's eyes. 'Please be careful, won't you. Graham can be very touchy. He's an insomniac, it's why he prefers to work nights.'

'If you don't mind my saying, your staff seem unusually sensitive.'

In customary fashion, Alice took a few moments before replying. 'Perhaps it's wrong to speak ill of the dead, but you must understand that my husband was a very thoughtful, generous man.'

I wondered if I'd misheard. 'How's that speaking ill?'

'Let me put it another way: he was a soft touch. He had a terrible habit of employing people who came to him with a sob story, then accommodating their every whim. I was forever reminding him that we were running a business, not a charity.'

'I'm surprised you've not fired them all and started again.'

'I did let a few go. But I find I'm not quite the rational actor I should like to be.'

'Rational actor?'

Alice smiled. This was an entirely new development, and her face stood transformed. 'I do apologize. It's economics jargon. I did a night class in economics when Ian was alive. Accountancy too.' Alice shook her head. 'I was a walking cliché in those days, a suburban housewife with time on her hands. I don't know how I put up with it.'

'Have you always been the book-keeper here?'

'I started about five or six years ago. It was just to save money, really. But that's why when Ian died I knew exactly how much trouble we were in. Apart from doing the books, though, I'd always kept my distance before – the hotel was Ian's affair, not mine. He never welcomed ideas or suggestions.'

If my view of Alice Haig was correct, I imagined this hadn't gone down well. 'I suppose he had his own way of doing things.'

'He certainly did. He'd been mismanaging it all for years, accepting credit from people who were never likely to pay, failing to keep in step with inflation. I don't know for sure, but I suspect he was within days of calling in the administrators. That's probably what gave him his heart attack.'

'How did you turn things round?'

'I sold our house in Crowburn Park and put all the money into the business. We live in one of the staff flats now, out at the back.' She waved a hand towards Wright Street, which ran parallel to the Promenade. 'Terrible for the children, no garden, all very cramped.

But I was determined to save the hotel.'

Alice glanced at the handsome long case clock standing in the hallway. 'They'll be home soon. Nigel's doing his mock A levels at present, I'd better show my face and see how he's got on today. But I'll introduce you to the gang first. There's no one staying apart from Giles's daughter and our four long-term residents.'

'Not great for your cash-flow.'

Alice frowned. 'There's no need to remind me. Twenty rooms, and only five occupied. We just have to cling on until the spring. Shall we go through?'

'One more thing: have you mentioned to anyone that I'm working for you?'

'I thought it better not to.'

'Good. Let's keep it that way, shall we? I'm just here as a guest of Giles today.'

Alice Haig led the way out to the lobby again, and round into the corridor I'd seen earlier. Released from navigational duties, I was now free to look around, and at once it became clear that the Marine Lodge was slipping into decline. The hall furniture looked comfortable enough but shabby, the elegant wallpaper had faded to a non-specific brownish colour, and in one or two places the carpet had been patched with brighter remnants of itself. It didn't take a business expert to conclude that the hotel needed substantial investment.

But it would be misleading if I didn't also record that I took a shine to the place, straight off. I've never been a big fan of hotels. Having survived considerable trials to provide myself with a roof and a bed, I couldn't see much point in paying good money to sleep somewhere else. Nevertheless, the Marine Lodge did have a certain homely charm, a welcoming lack of pretension. I wondered whether that afforded some clue as to the character of Ian Haig, deceased.

The lounge, when we reached it, boasted a rather grand pair of glass-panelled doors. Alice swung one open, ushered me into the room, and followed close behind.

All the occupants turned towards us as we came in. Simultaneously, their faces glowing with sudden delight, two of the men said, 'Alice!'

## *four*

As soon as I'd resolved that one of the speakers responsible for this stereophonic cry was Giles Rawley, and the other a Person Unknown of around fifty-five with a weakly handsome face and military bearing, my eye felt free to seek out the buffet table against the wall, where the still useful remnants of Giles's birthday tea stood arranged on plates and oval dishes. I'd eaten nothing since breakfast. With the first signs of returning health had come a return of appetite.

Person Unknown, who had the advantage over Giles in that he'd been standing near the door when we came in, while Giles occupied an armchair on the far side of the room, now stepped closer to Alice Haig, placed a guiding hand on her elbow and said, 'Are you joining us? Come and sit down.' I could see that this hand was two fingers short of the full set.

Alice frowned. 'I can't, I'm afraid. The children should be back soon and I need to talk to Nigel.' Person Unknown's hand still rested against her elbow. Conscious of this, Alice now moved to break the contact and turned to address Giles. 'I hope you don't mind, Giles. Really I'd have liked to help you celebrate.'

Giles dismissed this with an airy gesture which I'd seen him deploy before. 'Can't be helped, can it? You've got a hotel to run. And I see you've brought me Sam as a substitute.' Though he now regarded me warmly enough, there was no mistaking that in comparison with Alice I was not so much substitute as booby prize. To me he said, 'Haven't seen you in the Vaults this past few days.'

'I've had this thing that's going round. Happy birthday, Giles. Many of 'em, and all that.' This would have been the moment to hand Giles the present which I'd failed to provide.

Giles nodded acknowledgement. 'Good of you. Everybody, this is Sam. You know – Sam, my drinking companion from next door.' By next door, he meant the Grand Hotel. 'You've heard me speak of him, I think.'

A small, silver-haired woman in an expensive-looking mulberry suit now said, 'Ah, yes,' in a tone of relief, as if the mystery of my identity had been keeping her awake at night. In fact, around the room as a whole there was a general relaxation of puzzled expressions, one or two of which had quite nakedly been giving me the old 'Who the hell are you?'

Sitting on the settee alongside Mulberry Suit, a robust middle-aged woman with equine features said, 'I dread to think what you get up to, Dad. And at your age, too!' That gave me enough material to deduce that this must be Giles's visiting daughter Cordelia, whose presence I'd been told to expect.

Giles said, 'Sam will never tell, he's far too discreet.' Then to me he said, 'We have heard the chimes at midnight, though, haven't we?' He attempted a sly wink and laughed his usual rather forced laugh. I say attempted because Giles had a lazy eye and wasn't the world's sharpest winker, but the general idea still came across.

While I smiled back thinly, Alice Haig said, 'Better leave you to it, I'm afraid. Oscar should be along with the cake soon.' She turned towards the door.

Unknown Person objected. 'Must you really go? Wait for the cake at least!'

Giles said, 'Do shut up, Laurence. Give Alice credit for knowing her own mind.'

There was no effort at politeness in either the text or the delivery, and the Laurence character appeared duly stung, to the extent that his charming if lop-sided smile now froze.

The friction between these two men – these rivals? – was not lost on Alice Haig, and for a second or two I thought she was about to make some comment. But then she seemed to think better of it. Simply saying, 'See you all later,' she left the room, though not before she'd favoured Laurence with a smile. If she'd intended it to be confidential, she was out of luck. Giles noticed it, and it was plain from his scowl that he didn't much care for it.

A foreign-looking elderly gent with a refined air and sallow complexion now leaned some way towards me from his armchair, stretching out a formal hand. He said something along the lines of 'Aznavorian!'

Unsure what this could mean, I gripped the hand and shook it, not risking speech. But it must have been the bloke's name, because in what I took to be a competitive spirit Laurence now offered his hand as well and said, 'And I'm Laurence Glass.' While I grasped it, noting the odd sensation arising from the digit deficit, Glass was saying, 'Really Giles ought to be doing the honours, but we can't wait all day while he finds his manners. Do you know Miss Pyle?'

Mulberry Suit was being indicated. She smiled a smile too sweet for some tastes, gave me her surprisingly strong hand in turn, and said, 'Call me Rosemary. We're all friends here.'

When Giles's daughter had followed suit – her married name was Cordelia Lane – that completed the round of introductions. But it hadn't quite exhausted the list of those present. Standing beside Giles's chair and patiently watching proceedings through placid dark brown eyes was the bell boy Alice had mentioned earlier. He wore the traditional outfit with brass buttons and a short, bum-freezer jacket, and although it was extremely shabby and one size too small for him it did have the effect of emphasizing his pleasing physique. Caught between conflicting social imperatives I now gave him an encouraging smile without offering my hand, but he met even this limited advance by looking away.

Giles had now recovered sufficiently from his sulk to say, 'Come on now, Sam, get stuck in. The food won't eat itself.'

Grateful for this prompt, I approached the groaning board and said, 'Does anyone else want anything?'

'You just help yourself. We've got the boy here to fetch and carry for us.'

I began loading a plate with sandwiches and sausage rolls. Behind me, Cordelia was saying, 'Actually, Evan, if you wouldn't mind getting me one of those pork pies – '

But before the boy could comply, Giles said, 'Another? You've done nothing but stuff your face all day. Then you complain because you're fat!'

Evan now shifted from foot to foot in painful indecision. Miss Pyle said, 'Giles, don't be horrid. Let the girl eat if she wants to.'

The sallow man, who looked too birdlike and fastidious to eat much himself, said, 'Ignore him, Mrs Lane. You know your father enjoys his little joke.'

It was obvious that the wise thing for me to do now was avoid any involvement in the pork pie issue. Nevertheless I found myself suspending work on my own refreshments in order to place two of the pies, which represented little more than a mouthful each, onto a second plate, and hand it back to Giles's daughter. While she thanked me, Giles predictably said, 'Et tu, Brute? You might think on a chap's birthday his opinions would count for something.'

Laurence said, 'Sorry Giles, but it works in reverse with you. You must get so sick of sharing your opinions on the other three hundred and sixty-four days, we thought you'd appreciate a day off.'

'I see. So I'm not allowed to have opinions now.'

Her mouth full of pie, Cordelia said, 'Don't be crotchety, Dad. It's your birthday.'

Laurence said, 'Yes, cheer up, for God's sake. Hasn't Alice laid on this excellent spread for you? I'm sure she'd never do as much for the rest of us.'

Having poured myself a cup of tea, I lowered myself onto an upright chair near Miss Pyle. She said to me, 'Giles has always been Alice's favourite.'

The man himself said, 'Oh, piff,' and the airy dismissal was pressed into service again.

But Miss Pyle would have none of it. 'It's no use denying it, Giles. This little party speaks for itself! But we don't mind, do we, Sarkis?' Sallow Complexion generously indicated that this was true. Meanwhile Laurence, who I was willing to bet did mind, kept his counsel. Miss Pyle said, 'Besides, Giles is only resident for four months of the year, so Alice has to make a fuss of him while she's got him.'

Meanwhile I'd been tackling a couple of the sandwiches. They weren't bad, but the bread could have been fresher. When I sipped tea to help them down, I found that it was nearly cold. My own fault, of course, for turning up late. I swallowed and said, 'So the rest of you are all permanent residents?'

The bloke with the difficult name said, 'Miss Pyle and I came at about the same time – it's three years ago now.' Miss Pyle nodded warmly, suggesting that they'd been happy years. 'Of course, Alice's husband was running the joint then.'

Giles said, 'It's not a "joint", Aznavorian, it's an hotel. Speak English, if you know how.'

Seemingly unoffended, the sallow man said, 'Before Ian died we rarely saw Alice, did we, my love?' Miss Pyle nodded again. 'We were sorry to lose him, he was a very kind-hearted man. But Alice has been generous too, in her own way.'

Miss Pyle said, 'We're hardly a burden to her, Sarkis. Without us, the place would struggle terribly during the winter months.'

Giles huffed and said, 'Swings and roundabouts though, isn't it? She could make a fortune out of your rooms in the summer, but instead you cling on like leeches at your "special rate".' He intoned these words with particular distaste. 'Some of us have the decency to clear out in the summer and let her make some profit.'

'Only because you have long-suffering daughters.' This came from Laurence, who'd remained standing near the doorway, his hands locked behind his back. 'But for them you'd be stuck here full-time.'

As it happened, Giles had already given me the low-down on his annual migrations. He spent roughly four months of the year with each of his other two daughters, both of whom were married but childless, and the winter months here at Marine Lodge. This had been going on for about six years, ever since his wife had died and he'd fallen out with his housekeeper. Giles claimed that the latter had been responsible for tipping off hoodlums that his Sussex home contained a valuable coin collection handed down through generations of Rawleys. The coins had gone awol while Giles was touring in what he described as a 'vile and trendy' production of the Scottish play, featuring half-naked witches and a trampoline. Cordelia, however, was in no position to provide Giles with winter quarters, being married with four children and a cramped four-bedroomed house in Reigate. Giles was apt to view the son-in-law darkly, especially with regard to his business acumen, or lack of it.

Laurence's remarks displeased Giles. 'Stuck here? I am not stuck, as you put it. Marine Lodge is a very comfortable hotel, and outside Sussex there is nowhere in England I'd rather be than Southaven. I've passed some of the happiest times of my life here. Did you know that I was in rep here during the last war?'

Laurence Glass rolled his eyes.

Giles continued. 'The Little Theatre, a complete gem of a place. Marvellous company, people like Cyril Luckham, nothing they couldn't tackle. Packed houses, too. The town was bursting at the seams, with everyone looking for entertainment in the evenings. Wounded soldiers, civil servants – the Grand was commandeered by the government, you know, never found its feet as a hotel again until now.' Giles Rawley sighed complacently. 'I know there was a war on, but they were glorious days. I gave some of my finest performances here.' He turned to the sallow man. 'You saw my Vanya, didn't you? Aznavorian?'

'Eh?' Mr Aznavorian, who'd switched off when Giles began to talk theatrical history, now found himself obliged to switch on again. 'What's that you're saying?'

Piqued, Giles said, 'You saw me in Chekov, didn't you? During the war?' He'd raised his voice, and I realized now that Aznavorian must be hard of hearing.

Aznavorian said, 'Chekov, yes, absolutely right. A belter!' His expression clouded. 'Or was it Ibsen?'

'Listen, Aznavorian, we've had this out before. It can't have been Ibsen because I've never played Ibsen in Southaven. I've done Doctor Rank at practically every other damned theatre in the country, but not here. Get that into your skull once and for all.' Giles leaned a little closer to his target. 'If you ask me you're going senile. Much more of this and Miss Pyle will have to find someone else to pay court to.'

Not surprisingly, a silence followed this observation. Apart from Giles, who had sat back in his armchair complacently, and the boy Evan, whose demeanour seemed quite unaffected by events in the room, everyone else now began to study the ceiling, the floor, or the backs of their hands. This made a poor spectator sport, so I turned to Laurence and said, 'How about yourself, Mr Glass? Are you a permanent resident too?'

'It's Major Glass, as a matter of fact.'

'Oh – I didn't realize.'

'Doesn't matter. Not important. Ancient history now, in any case.'

Giles said, 'Answer the question, Laurence. Will you be staying, or not?' Then with renewed emphasis, 'We'd all *love* to know.'

Miss Pyle weighed in. 'You must have had time to think it through by now.'

'Well – it rather depends, doesn't it.'

As one, Giles, Miss Pyle and Mr Aznavorian all sighed an exasperated sigh. Aznavorian said, 'That's what you always say.'

Major Glass objected. 'I can hardly be blamed for affairs which lie outside my control.' Then to me he said, 'You see, I have a sister in Broadstairs – '

Miss Pyle said, 'How *is* your sister, Laurence?'

'She rang on Tuesday. A little worse, if anything.' Major Glass turned to me. 'My older sister is a chronic invalid, my brother-in-law looks after her. But now it seems he has a heart problem himself, a defective valve apparently. I could be required to take his place at any time.' I tried to assemble my sympathetic face. The Major continued. 'Tell me, Mr – '

'Rigby. Call me Sam.'

'Well – Sam – Giles has mentioned you, but I don't recall his saying what you do for a living.' He was giving me a look I couldn't quite read, but I suspected that among these well-dressed, well-fed people my appearance left some room for improvement. To them, I probably seemed to have more in common with the taciturn bell-boy.

Giles said, 'You see, Sam, I've not blabbed. Matter for you what you come up with. I always used to tell strangers I was a taxidermist. If you say you're an actor they invariably bore you with stories of their exploits in am-dram.'

Laurence said, a little doubtfully, 'So you're another actor?'

'No, I'd be hopeless. I'm a private investigator.'

To my left, Miss Pyle said, 'Really? How *too* intriguing!'

Giles said, 'Perhaps you should investigate what's happened to this bloody cake.'

Almost to herself, his daughter said, 'So impatient. You were always the same.'

Aznavorian said, 'It'll be along in a brace of shakes, Giles.'

Laurence Glass said, 'I have every confidence in Oscar. They train them well in the ACC.' If I remembered rightly, Oscar Hammond had been attached to the Catering Corps while doing his National Service, and had chosen to stay on afterwards. I didn't know how long he'd been back out on civvy street.

Giles's expression mellowed. 'Oscar's a good fellow really. No imagination, but sound. You heard about the people next door making him an offer?'

Evidently this came as news to everyone else in the room. I doubted whether Alice Haig knew about it either. Miss Pyle said, 'At the Grand?'

Giles nodded. 'Tried to lure him away with promises of improved pay and conditions. He's besotted with that tart of a barmaid so I'm surprised he turned them down.'

These were not the terms Giles employed to describe Lena Golding in her presence. The conversation had taken a useful turn, so I pushed it along. 'I expect you all saw that nonsense in the Gazette?'

'They're clearly trying to undermine Alice.' This came from Laurence. 'And what better way than by stealing her chef?'

Of course it was more than possible that it had been someone in this room who'd passed details of Marine Lodge's financial plight to the Goldings. Alice had been right, Evan didn't look sharp enough for such skulduggery, and Cordelia Lane was just visiting. But perhaps one of the others might have some motive for trying to ingratiate themselves with Alice Haig's new neighbours. I said, 'It must make you all feel very insecure.'

Aznavorian seized on the word as if it were his specialist

subject. 'Insecure? Why insecure?'

'If the Grand ever does absorb Marine Lodge, I doubt whether there'll be room for people like yourselves.' And as I said it, I wondered why any of Alice's residents would pursue a course of action which threatened to leave them homeless. I recalled what I'd asked Sidney Flint the day before. Perhaps one of these people had something to hide, some secret which the Goldings had unearthed in their customary style and were now exploiting. I studied the faces of my suspects: Giles Rawley, Laurence Glass, Rosemary Pyle, Mr Aznavorian. If the matter under discussion had caused guilt to stir within, it hadn't been enough to bring a blush to anyone's cheek.

Sensing activity on the other side of the glass-panelled doors, Laurence said, 'You see, I told you,' and held one of them open.

A wooden trolley now entered the room, topped by a square, iced cake on which blazed numerous candles. The vehicle was propelled from the rear by a substantial, red-faced man of about forty, wearing impeccably clean kitchen fatigues and a chef's hat. He said, 'Thank you, Major,' as he passed close to Laurence, and the latter seemed to mutter 'Corporal' before allowing the door to swing shut again.

Pulling up in the centre of the room, Oscar said, 'Happy birthday, Mr Rawley. Sorry I've been so long.'

Giles waved the airy hand again.

'Couldn't find the candles, could I? Knew I had the things – a place for everything, and everything in its place. Question was, *what* place exactly?'

Giles said, 'It looks magnificent, Oscar. Well done.'

Oscar beamed and said, 'Thank you, sir. Now I've found the blighters, do you want a crack at blowing them out?' Giles made to rise, but Oscar said, 'Don't get up, I'll come to you,' and wheeled the trolley in front of Giles's chair.

Cordelia said, 'Come on, Dad, make a wish.'

And Giles was visibly doing just that in his head, and preparing a massive intake of breath, when another voice said, 'Isn't anyone going to sing?'

It was clear from the speaker's shocked tone that he

considered blowing out candles without first singing 'Happy Birthday' to be a gross act of blasphemy. The voice was plain and flat, with stronger local inflection than anyone else's in the room.

Oscar gave Evan a look of unmixed hostility and said, 'What have I told you about speaking out of turn?'

Miss Pyle said, 'But Oscar, he's right, you know.'

Laurence said, 'Stand down, Corporal. Would you like to lead, Mrs Lane?' And in a very healthy tenor, Cordelia began to sing. We all pitched in. Any passing talent scout from the Huddersfield Choral Society would most likely have quickened their pace and fled the scene, but Giles looked pleased, and I thought I detected quiet satisfaction on Evan's impassive face. As the last note died away, Giles took aim and blew.

Immediately Cordelia said, 'Well done, Dad!'

But in fact one of the candles had remained obstinately alight. Giles Rawley gave it an unfriendly look and said, 'There's always one, isn't there?'

Laurence said, 'You must be losing your puff.'

The unfriendly look was transferred to the recent speaker. 'I'm losing nothing. Never been fitter. I dare say I could still tap-dance if my shoes hadn't fallen to pieces at Pitlochry Festival in '62. You look after your own health, Glass. If you ask me, you're looking a bit peaky these days.' And he snuffed out the final candle between his fingers in what was no doubt meant to be a marked manner.

Laurence held up conciliatory palms and smiled his charming smile. He was a good-looking bloke in his way, and there'd be nothing to wonder at if he had indeed managed to turn Alice Haig's head. 'Sorry, Giles, didn't mean to strike a raw nerve. Corporal, are you going to cut that thing up, or is it just for decoration?'

Oscar now removed several candles and with practised hand sliced into the cake, producing a number of rather small pieces. Either he had inside knowledge of the poor appetite of those present, or he'd spent much of his career stretching food as far as it would go and now found it hard to break the habit. As the pieces came ready he slipped them onto side plates and handed these to Evan for distribution. When he seemed about to stop at six, Giles said, 'What about yourself and the boy?' Oscar hesitated. 'Well, what's the problem?' And with a faux-suspicious twinkle Giles added, 'What exactly have you been putting in it?' When he twinkled like this he had a charm all of his own, and it took years off him.

Oscar's professional pride appeared wounded. 'It's nothing like that, sir. I wouldn't want to intrude, that's all.'

'Don't be silly, man, have some cake and sit down with us. That goes for you too, Glass. I'm fed up of you hovering over there as if the company's not good enough for you.'

Everyone now had both cake and a seat, with the exception of Evan, who remained standing while he ate. Although, as I've said, the slices weren't over-large, Evan might have done better not to try and scoff the whole thing in one. I recognized a kindred spirit. A childhood of not knowing where the next meal might come from had left me with a tendency of shovelling food down as fast as possible, before anyone could take it off me. As an adult I'd learned to show proper restraint in public, but perhaps for Evan the problem remained too recent and too raw.

Apart from a few complimentary remarks about the cake, conversation now gave way to eating. These remarks were well deserved. The rich fruit mixture benefitted, if I wasn't mistaken, from a healthy shot of brandy, a drink of which I knew Oscar to be especially fond and which had probably contributed some percentage of the colour in his face. Miss Pyle, a delicate eater, paused to recall how impossible it had been during and after the war to assemble the ingredients for a really good fruit cake, and after that the topic of rationing became general, exciting varied reminiscences.

But I soon noticed that Laurence, on an upright chair near the door, took no part in this, and instead was looking down at the untouched cake on his plate with a kind of horror. His face had blenched, and droplets of sweat stood out on his forehead. At last he tried to get a grip on himself, picked up the cake, and raised it towards his mouth, but his hand shook so badly that it fell from his grasp onto the carpet. He gave a sudden cry of dismay, a wild, uncivilised sound which broke into the polite talk around him and stopped it dead. Apparently no longer realizing where he was, Laurence Glass followed the cake onto the floor, took hold of it again, and once more tried and failed to eat it.

With surprising grace for a man of his girth, Oscar rose swiftly from his own chair, crossed the room and crouched beside the other man, slipping a protective arm around his shoulder. 'Major Glass! Major Glass! You're OK, sir, you're with friends. Major?'

Sarkis Aznavorian was shaking his head. Miss Pyle said, 'Oh dear,' and laid her plate aside.

Giles sat back and said, 'Then comes my fit again,' in a tone devoid of sympathy.

Cordelia said to him, 'What is it? What's he doing?'

But it was Aznavorian who answered, in a low voice, 'Major Glass was in Burma. A prisoner of war. Sometimes things remind him.'

Miss Pyle said, 'As often as not it's food, isn't it, Sarkis?'

Still holding the Major tight against his ample body, Oscar said, 'It's terrible what they done to him.'

Aznavorian said, 'The Japanese?'

'No, the army.' Then the Major seemed all at once to return to himself, and to become aware of the eyes which were fixed on him. With a look of deep shame, he freed himself from Oscar's embrace, stood up, and quickly left the room. Oscar said, 'Excuse me,' and followed.

After a brief silence, Cordelia said, 'Poor man.'

Evan moved towards the trolley and said, 'Who wants more cake?' He then seemed taken aback by the disapproving looks which came his way.

Aznavorian said, 'Not now, boy.'

Surprise was replaced by disappointment. There'd be no way now that Evan could justify cutting himself a second slice.

I said, 'Does the Major have these attacks very often?'

Giles said, 'Twice nightly, with matinees on Thursday and Saturday.'

Around the room, several people seemed to take offence at this remark, but it was Aznavorian who voiced it. 'That's a bit thick, Rawley. The man's an old soldier.'

'And what would you know about that? When you had your chance, all you did was show them your heels.'

Aznavorian blushed to the roots of his neat, iron-grey hair. 'I was unwell! My health would never have withstood active service. I found other ways to serve my country.'

'If it is your country.'

'Of course it is! I've lived here since I was four years old.'

'And done very well out of it, too. Your mysterious illness doesn't seem to have held you back.'

'I'm not ashamed to have been successful. I've never understood why you English always pretend to be worse off than you are.'

Giles glowed with triumph. 'There – what did I tell you? "*You* English"!'

Aznavorian flushed again, more deeply than before. 'Yes, I am Armenian, and proud of it! And if my poor wife and I had had children, I should have raised them the same way I was raised, to be proud of the culture they came from.'

'Why not go back, if it's so wonderful?'

'You know very well that's impossible. I'm as English as you are now.'

Giles smiled a smile of the utmost complacency. 'Sarkis, if you lived to be a thousand you'd never be as English as I am.'

Cordelia, who had perhaps witnessed similar scenes on other occasions in the past half century or so, had probably had enough of all this, because she now said, 'Come on, Dad. Time for your lie down.'

Giles Rawley examined his daughter without affection. 'But I'm not tired.'

'You always rest before your evening meal. It does you good, you know it does.'

Giles's tone had changed. 'It's my birthday. I might miss something!' Cordelia's manner had brought out the child in her father, an aspect of him which was seldom far to seek. I felt grateful. Though I knew from our sessions in the Vaults that Giles could be amusingly sharp-tongued when speaking of absent others, I hadn't quite realized that he could also shoot from the hip in their presence. It was good to be reminded that he had a more innocent side to his nature.

Cordelia persisted. 'You don't want to be too worn out to enjoy your evening. Besides, we were going to have a little chat, weren't we?'

'Were we?'

'About – you-know-what.'

The child faded from view. 'You've had my final word. If you don't like it, I suggest you get off home to that waster of a husband.'

Dismayed, Cordelia hung her head.

Catching sight of himself and not altogether liking what he saw, Giles covered his daughter's plump, pink hand with his own. 'I'm sorry, Cordy. You're a good girl, always have been. Perhaps you're right, perhaps I am a little tired. Would you all mind if I laid down the weary head?'

No one objected, and Giles stood up with no great difficulty. He was, as he'd said, a fit man for his age. Just then, Laurence Glass, looking much recovered, came back into the room. Seeing Giles on his feet, he said, 'Is the party over?'

We were all getting to our feet now. Giles ignored the question, and Laurence shrugged and moved past us to stand at the window. The rest of us shifted around to catch a final word with Giles Rawley. When my turn came, he said, 'Our usual tonight? Or are you still under the weather?'

As it happened, I was once more playing host to a headache, though whether caused by illness or the mismatched fabrics with which time and chance had covered the lounge furniture, I couldn't say. But headache or no, I needed to come over this way at some point, to interview Graham the night porter. A couple of drinks in the Grand Hotel Vaults would hardly slow my recovery, so I said, 'Well, since it's your birthday – '

Giles said, 'That's the spirit. I'll see you later. And thanks, all of you. It's been a quite lovely little party.' Followed closely by Cordelia, Giles made for the door. But there he stopped to address us again. 'You know, the man was right. It really is a stage, all of it,' and with a gesture he took in not just the room but the wider world beyond. 'One man in his time plays many parts. But of course, you'd know all about that, wouldn't you?' He seemed to have addressed this last remark to me, and for added emphasis he now winked one of his rather approximate winks. Then he turned on his heel and was gone.

## five

Out in the main hallway, I found Southaven's answer to Meg Richardson seated behind the reception desk. A couple of feet away from Alice, a slim, bespectacled youth with short mousey hair was leaning on one end of the counter, a foot drawn up behind him. He looked towards me as I approached, then sneezed into his hand and said, to no one in particular, 'I think I may be dying.'

Evan had remained in the lounge to clear up, and the residents had all headed off in the opposite direction from me, towards the lift and the stairs, so I saw no reason why I shouldn't stop for a brief word with my client. Alice Haig looked over my shoulder to check that she could speak freely, then said, 'Did you learn anything?'

'Possibly. It's too early to say.' I felt this neatly balanced the twin requirements of suggesting progress while discouraging any notion of a quick result. I hoped to be on Alice's payroll for a while yet.

The boy sneezed again, and this time withdrew a rather unsavoury handkerchief from his trouser pocket and blew his nose. Though we hadn't been introduced, I said, 'You've got that thing that's going round.'

The speccy youth, who I guessed must be Nigel Haig, seemed a little surprised to be spoken to like this by one of his mother's associates, but nevertheless replied confidently enough. 'The throat's the worst part. Or it may be the head, I'm not sure.'

I said, 'I'm just getting over the same pestilence. You can expect hell.'

Alice said, 'Mr Rigby – do you have to?' Then to the boy she said, 'I think you'd be better at home tomorrow. When's your next exam?'

'Not till Monday. I don't really need to go in.'

Having no very fond memory of exams or tests of any kind, I said to the boy, 'I hear you're doing mocks at present. How did it go today?'

'Not too bad. It was Maths, my best subject. But I was just telling Mum, I think I messed up this one question where you were supposed to imagine a figure in four dimensions.'

I said, 'Ah! A case for Professor Z Nussbaum.'

'You read New Scientist?'

I found the astonishment in the boy's tone wounding. 'Never miss it. Not that I understand a word of it, obviously.' And I tried for a Giles-like twinkle.

This attempt at levity caused the speccy youth to glare at me, but he was then overcome by a loose, rattling cough, indicating that the pathology involved not only the throat and head but also the chest. Alice Haig must have been feeling left out of the conversation, because she now intervened and said to me, 'What steps do you intend to take next?'

'Would it be all right to talk to your night porter today? Graham, isn't it?'

'Graham Leeds. He comes on at nine this evening. Do please try to be diplomatic.'

The boy said to Alice, 'Is he looking into all that business with next door?'

Alice said, 'Why don't you go and see if Bobby's back? And get yourself a hot drink.'

'By the way, we're out of aspirin.'

'Blast. I'll buy some in the morning, if I can get a moment.'

'Send Evan out for them.'

'He'd only come back with drain cleaner or something, you know what he's like. Oh, Nigel, could you put the oven on five for me? I'll be over as soon as I can.'

The boy said, 'OK,' gave me a nod, and walked off towards the back door, presumably heading for the flat which his mother had told me about. He'd not inherited her good looks, but then he also showed none of that constraint of manner which made his mother so prickly to deal with.

I said to Alice Haig, 'You've certainly got your hands full. Two boys as well.'

'What? Oh, no – Bobby's a girl. Roberta. Actually, she'd go mad if she heard me calling her Bobby, but I keep forgetting. She says people expect a girl called Bobby to be an out-and-out tomboy, which she most definitely isn't. But it seemed to fit her when she was five, and it stuck.'

'How old is she?'

'Sixteen, just a year younger than Nigel. I had them close together, to get the whole baby thing over with as fast as possible. Ian would have liked two more, but I know my limits.' Then Alice Haig seemed to recall that our relationship was supposed to be on a purely professional footing. Her guard came up again, and she said, 'Let me know how it goes with Graham.'

'What about the housekeeper?'

'Mrs Clark? You could see her in the morning if you like. Around nine might be good, she'll have had time to get herself organized.' The old anxiety overtook Alice Haig once more. 'But you *will* be careful what you say, won't you?' Then Alice caught sight of something behind me, and her face warned me to be silent.

'Sam?' I turned to find that Laurence Glass had come into the lobby, wearing a short overcoat and with a hat in his hand. 'You have some business with the hotel, do you?' It was pretty clear that the Major wanted to know what that business might be.

Wishing that Alice Haig and I had withdrawn our discussion to the privacy of the office, I couldn't quite think what to say. Alice herself filled the silence. 'Mr Rigby was just enquiring whether we had a table for Valentine's Night. I had to disappoint him. Going for a walk?' I thought she'd handled that rather well.

Laurence said, 'Yes, just a quick turn on the Prom while it's still daylight. I could do with some fresh air, been cooped up inside all afternoon.' He offered me his hand, the hand with the missing fingers. 'Nice to have met you, Sam. Good luck with the private eye game.' He nodded to Alice, then went outside. A blast of Irish Sea air took his place in the hallway.

I said, 'You've not confided in Major Glass about employing a detective, then?'

'Why would I do that?' The reaction was especially sharp.

I risked saying, 'You seem to be on friendly terms.'

'No more so than with my other long-term residents. I can't have them thinking that they're under suspicion in some way.'

Naturally, I didn't believe her. The woman had a soft spot for this Glass character, whatever she might say, but I was less certain that she'd gone so far as to admit it to the man himself.

Having wound up proceedings with Alice Haig, I exited the building and drove back to Leigh Terrace. Sidney Flint was just getting out of his beat-up old Jaguar as I approached along Preston Road. For a moment, I couldn't imagine what had brought him to see me for the second time in two days, but then I remembered that a late afternoon rendezvous had been my own suggestion. I slipped the Minx expertly into the tight space in front of the Jag, and landlord and tenant climbed to the top floor together.

When I'd lit the gas fire to ward off hypothermia, I showed Sidney Flint the letter I'd written, or rather which U.U. Packer had written as representing Fuselli, Crouch. To my surprise, he seemed at first to doubt the wisdom of employing solicitors who didn't actually exist to any great extent, but after a little persuasion he began to see the charm of it, and I wasn't sure that he didn't even crack half a leathery smile. He asked me again how I intended to convey the thing to the capital in mid-strike, but I repeated my performance of tapping the side of the nose and assured him that while second-rate investigators might be stumped by such a problem, S. Rigby would always find a way. At the same time I made a mental note to go crawling to Mark Howell and ask him for a favour. I knew that internal police mail would be going up and down the country unimpeded, and I hoped to convince him to let Fuselli, Crouch's missive hitch a ride on the next mule train out of town. Then, naming no names, I told Sidney that his was not the only local business to have received unwelcome correspondence from Shoreditch. I'd hoped that this might make him feel less anxious, but it was no very cheerful Sidney Flint who trailed out of the flat ten minutes later to the sound of my promise that I would keep in touch. Again I had the sense that he might be keeping something from me, some fact which left him especially vulnerable to bullying tactics. But since he chose not to level with me, he would only have himself to blame if things blew up in his face.

As soon as Flint had gone, I felt ill again. Finding myself suddenly devoid of company or of any purpose in life I immediately began to shiver, as a dull ache once more enthroned itself in Broca's area of the brain. I took a couple of Disprin and lay down for an hour without bothering to undress. Offered the chance of this brief, recuperative nap, the unconscious self seized it with both hands, and it was a fresher and a sounder Me who then returned to the living room to search for the telephone.

Considering that I'd used the device to speak to Aunt Winnie as recently as this morning, it was uncanny that it should once again have buried itself beneath several layers of old magazines like a wintering hedgehog. Nevertheless I found it, and within a few seconds heard my old chum Bernie Foster say, 'Yes? Who is it?' in her usual straightforward way.

I said, 'It's me. I hope you've been doing your job.'

She said, 'Of course I have. I just got off at six.'

Bernie was a nurse on the cardiac unit at the Infirmary. This, however, was not the job I'd had in mind. 'Not that job, your other job. You're supposed to be keeping an eye on Eileen Docherty for me.' Matt's girlfriend worked in orthopaedics.

'I am doing. I give you detailed reports every time we meet.'

'They've been tailing off lately. It's come to my notice that she's started toying with Matt's affections again.' And I told Bernie about the Valentine's Night dinner which was now not to be.

Bernie said, 'Perhaps she does have some sort of work thing, like she told him.'

'On a Sunday evening?'

'Or a family do, maybe. Could be anything.'

'I realize that. But what's the point of me having a mole on the inside if you can't tell me exactly what she's up to?'

I could imagine Bernie flaring up in her well-ordered flat at the other end of the line. She's always been an exceptionally fine flarer-up. When they make it an Olympic sport she'll be disappointed with anything less than silver. 'You're being ridiculous! I haven't been put on this planet to go round snooping on behalf of Sam Rigby.'

'I hope that's not a resignation speech.'

'Look – I don't mind keeping up with Eileen's news, but you've got to stop obsessing about her like this.'

'I'm not obsessing about her. I just happen to believe that she plays fast and loose with my assistant when she shouldn't. If he's going to be rendered unfit for work I want to be the first to know about it.'

Bernie said, 'Pah!'

Well, when you've got friends you have to expect these things. At least it wasn't 'Pooh!' I said, 'All right, I accept I may be taking rather a strong line. But you would let me know if there was anything fishy going on, wouldn't you?'

'Of course I would. How's tricks, anyway? I hear you've been pretending to be ill.'

The problem with news is that it can travel in both directions. 'I'm not pretending. I've had this thing that's going round.'

'Poor you. Would a little session in the Velvet Bar aid recovery, do you think?'

'Possibly. I can't do tonight, though.'

'Nor can I. Tomorrow? Saturday?'

Given my increased level of interest in the affairs of the Grand Hotel, I wasn't sure where I might best be deployed in the evenings ahead. I said, 'I've got a tricky case on at present. Can I phone you again when I know what I can manage?'

'Of course. Be my guest. Keep me dangling. Your life's far more important than mine. I'll just sit here and wait for your call.'

'There's no need to be sarcastic.'

'Fun though, isn't it?' I suppose Bernie and I have certain traits in common.

The call concluded, I checked my watch. Nearly seven thirty. If I was to spend a heavy evening interviewing night porters and admiring Mickey Golding's stupendously cute nose, I would need to eat first. I'd barely eaten at all for several days, and at Giles's tea party I'd held myself back in case he subjected me to the same barbed comments he'd used on his daughter. Now I wondered whether the Hen and Chickens might offer the best solution. The place had lodged in my mind when Matt had mentioned it during our morning conference, and stayed there ever since. Formerly a cavernous pub, it had been taken over by one of the national steak house chains, and comprised a bar area and two quite separate restaurants: downstairs, Rustlers, for the determined boviphile; and upstairs, Roosters, with a more varied menu. It was possible to eat relatively cheaply in the second of these options, especially if you were a parsimonious private investigator whose rent would fall due the following day. Having taken a little extra care over my appearance, in case Mickey was in the mood to look at me as closely as I always looked at him, I dressed warmly and let myself out of the flat.

Finding that my legs no longer ached, I'd decided that a little walk might do me good. The Marine Lodge, the furthest point on my planned excursion, was less than a mile from my door, and the Hen and Chickens lay directly in its path. Though the air remained chilly, the wind had dropped, and it occurred to me as I rounded the corner onto the Boulevard that it was almost a pleasant evening.

This impression was corrected some minutes later when I turned again to walk up Marine Approach. The street hosts a more or less permanent gale scything down off the Irish Sea, which now delved between the buttons of my faithful leather jacket and burrowed under the scarf at my throat. Snow began to fall.

Quickening my pace, I soon reached the Hen and Chickens, which stood not far short of the entrance to the Grand Hotel Vaults but on the opposite side of the road. The place wasn't busy, and upstairs in Roosters I chose a table with a view of the whole room.

The chicken cacciatore which I ate might charitably be called unremarkable. I suspected that the sauce had been cooked and bagged many miles from Southaven, and had got lost for a few days in transit. All the same, I enjoyed it, partly because I was breaking a long fast, and partly because the waiter, no longer a young man, introduced an unexpected and entertaining note of formality. Curious as to why he was treating me like royalty, I asked. It turned out that he'd worked all his life in posh hotels, before semi-retiring to Southaven for the climate (I know, I know), and he found that keeping up the old standards even in the humbler surroundings of the Hen and Chickens not only helped to pass the time but brought fat tips as well. I said I hoped he wouldn't be expecting a fat tip from me. Showing keen judgment, he laughed at this, with the result that in the end I felt obliged to give him a fat tip after all. His name was Alf. We parted bosom friends.

Outside, the snow had stopped without settling, but the wind was no less acute. I was reminded of a couple of evil January nights I'd spent in Frinton while doing my National Service. I crossed the street, above the remains of the buried oyster bars, and glanced in through the window of the Vaults. Mickey Golding, in his usual white shirt and tight black trousers (Matt had been no less than truthful about this), was clearing tables, with his back to me. It would still be a little early for Giles to appear, but for a moment I had the impulse to go straight in and enjoy a relaxed chat with Mickey while I could do so undistracted. Sadly, the work ethic from which I intermittently suffer chose to assert itself at this point, arguing that once I'd settled in the Vaults all hope of my pushing on later to talk to the night porter would be lost. Chastened, I continued up the slope to the Promenade.

Ahead of me, somewhere in the dark, a pile of twisted metal alongside the pier was all that remained of the Pier Pavilion, recently demolished after nearly seventy years of lending an oriental flavour to visitors' holiday snaps. Poorly maintained since the war, it had finally fallen victim to rainwater incursion and neglect. The Gazette had featured drawings of the hangar-like amusement arcade intended to replace it. Local members of the

Civic Trust, barely recovered after their long but doomed campaign to save the Empire cinema, were now back in the cockpit, boosting the flagging thesaurus industry as they bombarded the Gazette with letters decrying the proposed development as a blot, scar, or excrescence.

As it was so late, I didn't fancy following Alice Haig's suggestion of entering Marine Lodge by the back door. The entrance from Wright Street would be pretty dark, and I didn't trust myself to find it. So once again I walked in at the front, surprised to find the door unlocked at this hour. Sitting behind the counter of the reception desk, a stout man with a weak chin looked up in surprise. There was no other sign of life.

'Can I help you, sir?'

I said, 'It's Sam Rigby,' expecting that this would evoke recognition, but the weak-chinned man only stared at me, his colourless lips slightly parted. I tried again. 'Mrs Haig has employed me to find out how your new neighbours came into possession of damaging information about this hotel.'

The man said, 'Nobody told me.'

This was a bad start, but I pressed on. 'Do you think we could talk privately – in the office, perhaps? I'd rather the guests didn't see me and wonder why I'm here.'

The man now stood up and said, 'I'm sorry, sir, I'm not prepared to speak to you without Mrs Haig's authorization.'

This was commendable in him. And irritating. 'Can you put a call through to her?'

His head tilted suspiciously at this cunning ploy. 'A call?'

'Yes. A call.' And to avoid misunderstanding I added, 'Ring her.'

He looked down. I'd noticed an ancient-looking switchboard behind the counter when coming out of the office that afternoon. He looked up again. 'I don't like to disturb her. It's no use her paying someone to look after the place overnight if she's only going to get phoned up every five minutes.'

Again, commendable. I said, 'When was the last time you had to call her about something?'

The man now made an odd, crumpled face, indicating that

thought was going on. Then he let it go and said, 'August Bank Holiday weekend.'

'She'll have got over it.'

There was a brief pause. Then, recognizing that he'd been outsmarted by a greater intelligence, the man with the weak chin lifted the receiver to his ear and flicked the switch for Alice Haig's flat. In so doing he never took his eyes off me, clearly convinced that I might dash out of the building with the long-case clock under my coat at any moment. 'Mrs Haig? Graham here. Sorry to disturb, but I've got someone at reception says his name's Tim Digby.'

I took advantage of the continued visual contact to mouth the correct name, but the man ignored me and carried on.

'Tall chap, shifty-looking. He says he's working for you.' During Alice's response, which I couldn't make out, the night porter's eyes remained fixed on my face. 'OK. Yes, I will. Yes. Thanks, Mrs Haig.' He put the receiver down. 'Apparently you're on the level.'

I said, 'I know,' and indicated the office.

'Let me just drop the catch on the front door first.' Graham Leeds came out from behind the counter, crossed to secure the door, then led me through into the office and pushed the door to without fully shutting it. On a side table I noticed a flask, and a brown paper package which might contain sandwiches. Within reach of these stood a worn but comfortable-looking armchair on which rested copies of the Gazette and the Daily Express. This must be where the night porter would be passing the long hours of his lonely vigil.

He said, 'You'd better sit down.' But it was an upright chair he pointed to, while he himself, after laying aside the newspapers, sank into the armchair. Perhaps as the result of unbreakable association of ideas, he yawned.

I said, 'When you're on duty, do you ever leave this room unlocked and unattended?'

He shook his head. 'Absolutely not. Or – ' He made that face again. 'Not often. Perhaps occasionally. A couple of times a night, let's say. When I'm on my rounds.'

'Your rounds?'

'I walk about sometimes, check the public areas to make sure everything's as it should be. There's nothing happens in this hotel during the night without me knowing about it.' But as he said this, Graham Leeds's eyelids were drooping. If he found it hard to keep awake even with Sam Rigby for company, how likely was it that he could elude the enfolding arms of Morpheus when left alone?

I said, 'Mrs Haig mentioned that you're an insomniac.'

This woke him up a bit, though not much. 'Did she, now? Well, I'm surprised at her, to be honest. I'd have thought that was a private matter.'

I felt the need to apologise on Alice Haig's behalf. 'She's under a lot of strain just now.'

'We all are. It's one damn thing after another in the hotel business. Doesn't mean we go round shooting off about other people's problems.'

Alice had been right to call Graham Leeds touchy. 'I'm sure she meant no harm.'

Unruffling a little, he said, 'She's right, though, I do have trouble sleeping. Been the same ever since my wife died. She had this beautiful snore, very musical, a bit like a euphonium playing in the tenor register. You might think it would have disturbed me, but I always found it soothing. Now it's gone, I can't sleep.' He sighed wearily. 'I shall never hear that sound again, this side of the grave.'

Though aware of the risks, I said, 'So you don't try for a little nap here from time to time?'

Predictably, he took offence and said, 'Absolutely not!' again. 'Though of course, you can't help it if it just comes over you, can you?'

The post of night porter may not be an easy one to fill, but I couldn't help thinking that in Alice Haig's shoes I'd have given Graham Leeds his cards at the first opportunity and told him to hop it. I said, 'Do you have any dealings with next door yourself?'

'Like what?'

'Do you know anyone there, or go in at all?'

'I haven't set foot in the Grand Hotel since the New Year's Ball of 1959. A shocking price, we'd have been better off at home watching Kenneth McKellar.' At the memory of this financial catastrophe, he ran one finger round inside his shirt collar, which tended to bite into the folds of his neck.

'And in the last few weeks have you noticed anything unusual here? For instance, have you suspected that someone might have been in this office when they shouldn't have?'

He girned again. How this was meant to assist thought, I couldn't imagine. Then he put his lips, nose and vestigial chin back where they belonged and said, 'No.'

'You're quite sure?'

'Nothing gets past me, Mr Roby.'

I couldn't be bothered to correct him. Whatever he might say, I supposed that names weren't the only things that got past him, and that if someone had indeed wanted to look at Alice's accounts without permission, fear of discovery by the night porter would not have loomed large in their calculations.

I doubted whether Graham Leeds had anything more to tell me. Thanking him for his time, I asked if he'd show me out via the back entrance, so that I'd be sure of finding it on another occasion. A corridor of increasing obscurity snaked round past the back stairs and the kitchen, which was in darkness. Perhaps Oscar was already in the Vaults, savouring a slow brandy. Then the night porter unlocked the glass-panelled door, and I stepped out into the yard.

The Marine Lodge hotel had been formed many years since by knocking together three good-sized private residences, though doubtless these would have been in use as rooming-houses from quite early in their lives. Each one must have had its own outbuildings at the rear, but as they'd passed into single ownership it had become possible to rationalize this space. Just outside the door, I passed an old brick lean-to of uncertain function, probably a survival from the pre-hotel era. To my left, against the long, high back wall of the Grand Hotel garage, stood a row of parking spaces, currently occupied by only three cars. I guessed that one might be Alice Haig's and another the night porter's, but was mystified as to who might be the lucky owner of the sleek, black Armstrong Siddeley Sapphire which stood between them. This had been reversed into its space, and the enigmatic sphinx on its bonnet reflected light from a nearby street lamp. To my right, above a row of lock-up garages, stood the staff flats Alice had mentioned, one of which was now her family's home.

I continued onto Wright Street, and turned left there to walk past the much larger rear courtyard of the Grand Hotel. Ahead of me, a Daimler and a Mercedes were just leaving the yard. It seemed to be a big night for posh cars. They turned onto Marine Approach and moved out of sight, and as I arrived at the corner myself I began to realize that I still didn't feel especially chippy. My recuperation was in the fragile early stages, and for a moment I wondered whether to do the sensible thing, turn to the right, and head for home.

But then I would have to miss seeing Mickey Golding. Sweeping aside my lingering symptoms, I turned resolutely left, was temporarily knocked back as the pitiless onshore blast caught me full in the face again, then strode on up the slope towards the Vaults.

## *six*

Among the modest crowd of evening drinkers in the Grand Hotel Vaults, Giles Rawley stood out by his absence. It was now half past nine, and the man should by rights have been comfortably perched at the bar for the last half hour. Instead, two large and ugly strangers had taken over the stools normally adopted by Giles and myself.

Behind the bar, Mickey had noticed my arrival. He must also have noticed the displeasure on my face as I observed the unsightly interlopers, because as I approached the bar he said to them, 'Gents! I think you'll find the perfect table has just come free for you over there in the window.' He indicated the table he meant.

First Ugly Bloke now said, 'We tried it before. There's a draught.'

But Mickey said, 'Not at all,' seized hold of their drinks, and came out round the end of the bar. 'If you'd like to follow me.' He continued across to the window, put down the drinks, and made a show of ordering the table and chairs as if this was the most sought-after spot in the bar. The two men, wrong-footed by the pace of developments, now glanced at each other as if trying to decide whether to make an issue of this. Mickey straightened up beside the table and said, 'When you're ready.'

They were big men, while Mickey himself, though not without muscle, was a little below average height. I'm not sure I'd have risked picking a fight with them myself. But they concluded that it wasn't worth making trouble, descended gracelessly from the stools, and went over to the table. As I examined him more closely, First Ugly Bloke looked familiar, and when he caught me looking at him recognition seemed to dawn on his face too. I got the feeling he didn't like me very much.

Back behind the bar, Mickey began to pour my usual stout from the bottle. It would be the first alcohol I'd drunk for several days, but the advertisers assured us that it was Good For You and I was in the mood to take them at their word. Mickey said, 'Where's your friend?'

'Giles? I don't know. It was his birthday today, perhaps it's all been too much for him.' I'd now replaced the ample backside of First Ugly Bloke with my own less substantial ditto, and was wondering why the world seemed suddenly out of joint.

Mickey placed bottle and half-full glass on the bar in front of me and said, 'You're not smoking.'

And there was the explanation, in a few simple words. Normally I'd have lit up by now, but though my hands were protesting the lack of displacement activity, the rest of me still wasn't interested. I said, 'I've been ill,' and handed over the readies.

Feeding the till with my hard-earned cash, he said, 'What –

have you had that thing that's going round?' I nodded and he looked gratifyingly sympathetic. 'Oh, poor Sam! It's a little devil, so they tell me.' Then he leaned towards me and lowered his voice. 'I've missed you.'

I said, 'I think I've missed you too.'

This puzzled him. 'Only think? What's the matter?' The nose sat unbearably cute in the middle of his face.

I hadn't expected to catch Mickey alone, and I'd given insufficient thought to what I'd say to him about his family's behaviour towards my two new clients. It was too late for calm consideration now, so I plunged in. 'If you're the sweet, good, kind young man I've always thought you are, then I've missed you. On the other hand – '

Mickey saw that this was no joke. 'Has something happened?'

It would be a terrible shame to put my burgeoning friendship with Mickey Golding in jeopardy, particularly since I suspected, from the looks he quite often gave me, that it might soon pass beyond friendship to another stage. Until now, I'd allowed myself to believe that as the youngest son he'd more or less steered clear of his family's unpleasant habits. If I'd been deceiving myself, I needed to know the truth before things went too far.

'You could say something's happened, yes. Messrs Tipton, Buxton and Lamb have happened.' And I gave him a hard look he wouldn't have seen from me before.

'Who are they when they're at home?' If the innocence with which Mickey said this was genuine, then I had nothing to worry about. He had a habit of rubbing his nose, and he rubbed it now. It seemed to grow cuter with every rub, and I feared if he did this much more there could be consequences for public order.

I said, 'You've really never heard of them?'

'No. What are they, some new prog rock band?'

'Not exactly. I think they're your family solicitors.'

He dismissed this with a gesture he might have picked up off Giles Rawley. 'I don't know anything about all that stuff. I leave it to the others. My role in the outfit is entirely limited to catering and customer relations. And looking after the old girl, obviously. Me and Lena promised Dad we'd keep her out of trouble.'

'I'm afraid your mother may have other ideas. She's been using these Tipton, Buxton people to strong-arm her way into some local businesses. You must know this phoney tale about the Grand taking over Marine Lodge?'

'Phoney? I thought that was for real.'

I carefully decanted more from the bottle into the glass. 'Your mother, or those acting on her behalf, made the Marine Lodge a ridiculously low offer. They turned it down. Next thing they know, they're being paraded on the front page of the Gazette in their underwear. Now, does that sound like your mother's *modus operandi*, or doesn't it?'

'My mother's what?'

I'd forgotten that Mickey, in contrast to Matt, had attended a Church of England school, and that Latin was thus a closed book to him. But at least it was beginning to look as if the Goldings' casual attitude to the law was equally beyond his ken. I took a first sip of the drink, and liked it. I said, 'Well, I suppose we can't choose our family, can we.' In a million years I'd never have chosen mine. I smiled a warm smile, intended to show that Mickey was forgiven for whatever it was that he hadn't done.

A little confused, but also evidently relieved, he smiled back.

Suddenly I remembered that I'd agreed to dig some dirt on Mickey's family for Alice Haig. Faced with Mickey himself in the flesh, this began to seem like a shabby idea. But I said, rather lamely, 'Anything new in the hotel game?'

Mickey wiped down the counter, removing beer and cigarette ash left behind by the Ugly Blokes. 'Not much. The old girl's a bit pissed off, though.'

'Because?'

'She's spent a fortune kitting out a casino space here, and they've just rejected her licence application. They're saying three casinos in town would be one too many.'

I ran up a sceptical eyebrow. 'Why would they do that? It's true we've already got two casinos, but they're both run by the Malones. You'd imagine some competition would be welcome.'

'I know. But the Malones objected, and the magistrates think they've got a point. Mum says they're hooligans.'

'The magistrates?'

'No, the Malones. She also calls them amateurs, losers, and bird-brained Johnny-come-latelys.'

'Sounds like she knows them well.'

'She doesn't, though. She invited them over for a chat but they just ignored her.' Another customer came to the bar, and Mickey moved along to serve them.

I had a suspicion the Malones might live to regret their high-handed attitude. But this mention of invitations had reminded me of something else I'd wanted to talk to Mickey about. Unfortunately, now it came to the point the idea seemed less of a breeze than it had done in the quiet of my own home. My plan was to take over Matt's redundant Valentine's Night booking at the Hen and Chickens, and ask Mickey if he'd like to join me. But what if he met this invitation with the same disdain that the Malones had shown to his mother? I'd been greatly enjoying my flirtation with Mickey in these past few weeks. If I pushed the thing too far and he turned me down, the fun would be over.

But still, when Mickey had finished serving the new arrival and come back to join me, I risked saying, 'How does your weekend look? Have you got your usual Sunday off?'

He wrinkled his nose. I wished he wouldn't. 'Carlo wants me to work.' Carlo was the hotel manager, a Welsh-Italian with the looks of a veteran street fighter. 'We're going to be busy in the restaurant Sunday 'cos of Valentine's Day. And we're switching all the tills to decimal, he wants experienced staff on duty.'

'Bad luck it happens to be your day off.'

He nodded. 'Mind you, if I'd had any decent Valentine offers myself I'd tell Carlo where he could stick it. Can't let work ruin your life, can you?'

There was a short, uncomfortable silence while I failed to shoot for this open goal. After a while, it became a long uncomfortable silence. Mickey cracked first. He said, 'When are you going to come for that swim with me? You keep wriggling out of it.'

'Like I said, I've been ill.'

'All right, what about tomorrow then? I'm in the pool eight

o'clock every morning except Sunday. Got to do my lengths, it's the only proper exercise I get.'

I said, 'I can't really make tomorrow, I'm seeing someone.' I was supposed to be paying a visit to the housekeeper at Marine Lodge at around nine. Strictly speaking I could easily have been out of the pool and ready for action by then, especially since the swimming baths were handily situated on the corner opposite the Grand at the top of Marine Approach. But the fact was, I'd felt nervous about this idea of Mickey's ever since he'd first brought it up. It would be the first time we'd met elsewhere than in the Vaults.

He said, 'All right then, make it Saturday.'

I was just trying to dream up some fresh excuse to forestall opening this new chapter in our relationship when the door swung open and Giles Rawley came in. As Giles approached the bar, looking tired as it seemed to me, Mickey said, 'Many happy returns, Guv'nor!' and set about preparing Giles's scotch and soda.

Giles said, 'Too kind, too kind,' unwound his scarf, and took the stool next to mine. Normally given to the dignified straight back, on this occasion he allowed the spine to curve from weariness. He said to me, 'Have you been here long?' I pointed out the limited inroads I'd made on the glass in front of me. He understood and said, 'Wouldn't want to leave you all by yourself with this alarming young man for too long. But where is everybody? Where the devil's Oscar? He said he'd buy me a drink. More to the point, where's my lovely Lena? Has she forgotten what day it is?'

In Oscar's absence, I paid for Giles's drink, and he blustered gratitude. Mickey said, 'Carlo's got Lena covering the cocktail bar. Hold the fort a minute, I'll fetch her.' And he made his exit via the inner door which led up to the hotel. Most of the hotel's customers chose to drink in the cocktail bar or the lounge bar, and in reality the Vaults operated almost as a separate business tacked on at the side. According to Mickey, when Lou Golding had resurrected the Grand she'd decided to keep the Vaults going for the sake of local PR. Most of its clientele would have little use for the hotel proper, but she wanted us Common Folk to take a positive view of the Grand and all its dealings.

I said to Giles, 'Trouble getting away?'

He sighed. 'How sharper than a serpent's tooth it is to have a thankless child.'

'Cordelia?'

'My wife wanted to call her Jean but I wouldn't listen. I should have known there'd be trouble. Cheers.' He drank off half the scotch and soda. Giles was no big drinker, but he looked about ready for it.

'I thought Cordelia was meant to be the good daughter.'

'She does try, bless her. But when it comes to men she lacks judgment. My son-in-law isn't exactly the King of France.' Giles sighed and shook his head. 'Let's talk about something else, shall we?' He looked round. 'Still no Oscar. I'm afraid he rather let himself down at dinner.'

'How do you mean?'

Giles neatly mimed toping from a bottle. 'The brandy again, I should think. But I thought he made a really fine job of that cake this afternoon.'

'I'd never seen him in action before.'

'Laurence Glass was right, they train them well in the Catering Corps. So what did you think of my fellow-inmates?' Before I could answer, Giles's face came alive, and he said, 'Oh – here she is! I thought you'd forgotten all about me!'

These remarks were addressed to Lena Golding, who was entering from the hotel. Apart from the nose, there wasn't much to tell you at first glance that she and Mickey were twins. She was shorter, and had dyed the dark hair blonde. But she possessed all of his cheek and more, and her voice was his too, transposed upward. She said, 'How's my favourite film star?' and kissed Giles full on the lips. I wondered how it might be to experience this sort of attention from her brother.

Giles said, 'The first decent birthday present I've had.' He no longer looked so weary, and his posture had improved.

Lena said, 'Many of 'em, you old goat.' She pinched his nose. He patted her bottom, through the short black skirt. She smacked his cheek, but lightly. 'Now don't go taking liberties, or I'll have to withdraw your privileges.'

'Which are?'

'Do you see me giving the other customers a big fat kiss? Does Sam get one when I see him?'

Giles objected. 'I doubt whether he wants one.'

Lena smiled at me and said, 'Got your card marked, hasn't he?' Then to Giles she said, 'So did they give you that party next door?'

'They did. Delightful. Though of course I'd have enjoyed it more if you'd graced it with your presence.'

Lena appeared doubtful. 'I can't imagine a Golding would be terribly welcome at Marine Lodge today. It's thanks to us the whole town knows they're on their beam ends.'

I decided to interrupt this love-in. 'The big question is, how did you Goldings come to know about it?'

Lena looked at me sharply. Giles said, 'What a curious thing to say.'

The street door opened, and a group of eight or nine young men filed noisily into the bar and headed our way. Lena's face switched automatically into professional mode. She walked round behind the bar and said to the first of the men, 'What'll it be?'

With Lena now out of earshot and our own conversation masked by the din being kicked up by these newcomers, Giles said to me, 'Magnificent, isn't she?'

'A handful, certainly.'

'I thought I was all for the quiet life in my old age, but Lena's made me wonder.'

It was pure nosiness, but I said, 'What about Alice Haig? I couldn't help noticing you and Major Glass both playing up to her.'

Giles gave me a keen look. 'Alice Haig is in a different league. If I'd been younger I'd have proposed to her long ago, but what use can she possibly have for an old relic like me?'

'Come on, Giles, there's life in the old dog yet.'

'I'll try to take that as a compliment. But still, not enough life for Alice. She doesn't need any more burdens than she already has. I do admire her though, Sam. Clear-headed, careful with money, eminently practical – she's like the wise daughter I never had. So naturally, when someone like Glass comes sniffing around – ' Giles left the thought incomplete. 'What did you think of him – Glass, I mean?'

'Couldn't make him out, to be honest.'

'Really? You're supposed to be a private investigator, I'd have thought you could read a man like him with your eyes shut. And what about the others?'

'Miss Pyle seemed very nice.'

'Rosemary Pyle is a gold-digger and a Jezebel.'

'What?' I hauled up both eyebrows this time. 'She seems completely harmless.'

'Seems is the word. Sticks to Aznavorian like a limpet, and do you know why? Money. She's running out, he has it by the cart-load. I think she has some idea that he'll marry her, but he's far too shrewd for that. Armenian to his finger-tips, and tight as a duck's arse. Buys her presents, of course. You'll have noticed that suit she's always showing off – he bought it for her. But get him to hand over the purse-strings? Never.'

Mickey returned at this point. Ignoring us as he passed behind the bar, he lightly held Lena's arm and addressed some remark to her ear. She stopped pouring in mid-pint, gave Giles a dazzling smile and said to him, 'See you later, big boy. They want me out front.' She went back into the hotel.

Mickey had taken over from her, but now toggled the lever he'd been operating and said, 'This Red Barrel wants changing. Sorry lads, won't be a minute.' The lads in question were the two or three young men Lena still hadn't served. They now grumbled about being abandoned, but pointing out that the keg wouldn't change itself Mickey lifted the trapdoor in the floor at his feet and disappeared into the cellar. I'd nearly finished my drink and I hoped he wouldn't be long.

Giles said, 'I realize you like him, but he's not really in Lena's class, you know.'

Privately, I thought it was the other way round. To change the subject, I said, 'So what exactly have you got against the Major? It's obvious you don't think much of him.'

Rather cagily, Giles said, 'True soldiers don't show their battle scars. Look at Coriolanus. He was so loath to parade his wounds for the plebs that it cost him the consulship of Rome.'

'If you're talking about that turn the Major had, it didn't look to me like he had any choice.'

'We all have a choice, Sam. I saw things in the first show I can never forget, and I try, believe me. You have to keep it down.'

I said, 'I never knew you fought in the first war.'

'What did you think I was doing – concert parties on the Maginot Line? Well, I'm sorry I mentioned it, it's best forgotten. But when I see Laurence Glass – ' A rare look of indecision appeared in Giles Rawley's eye. He said, 'If you swear you won't tell Alice, I'll let you in on something.'

Suddenly a booming voice from the street doorway said, 'All right now, ladies and gents, if you'd all stay where you are, please.'

Giles and I turned to find out who'd been responsible for this announcement, and Giles said, 'My God, it's Jack Warner.' A burly uniformed officer of advancing years stood blocking the exit to Marine Approach.

One of the young men now asked me what was going on. Not wanting to put myself forward, I said, 'Ask Dixon of Dock Green over there,' which he then did.

The constable eyed him with marked disfavour and intoned, 'This is a raid pursuant to the Gaming Act of 1968. We have reason to believe unlawful gaming is taking place on these premises.'

This caused something of a sensation. While the effects were still rippling around the bar, Mickey came back into view, observed the altered scene, and asked the officer for an explanation. He repeated his earlier line, word for word, then fell silent. Shrugging his shoulders and clearly taking the disturbance in his stride, Mickey shut the trapdoor and went on pouring beer. As he did so, he found a moment to glance in my direction and wink at me in a highly congenial manner.

I looked around gauging reactions. It seemed to me that the Two Ugly Blokes were particularly displeased at having their evening overseen by Lily Law. In fact Vaguely Familiar Ugly Bloke had gone so far as to turn up his collar, though whether this was an attempt to conceal his identity or whether there really was an evil draught at the table in the window, it was impossible to say.

Giles said, 'How thrilling. I haven't been caught in a police raid for years.' Raising his voice, he said to Mickey, 'Is it true? Do we find ourselves in the midst of irregular dealings?'

Mickey, his usual relaxed self, smiled and said, 'Don't be daft. It's probably some sort of misunderstanding.' And to me he added, 'Unless it's those Malones trying to score a point.'

DC Mark Howell now entered the bar from the hotel. He'd replaced his usual anonymous brown suit with a bright sports jacket and a tie bordering on the psychedelic. He called out to the constable, 'Anything here, Bradshaw?'

'No, sir.'

'Don't let anyone leave.' Mark turned to go. I wanted a word with him, so leaving Giles with Mickey, I crossed to join him.

Behind me, the booming voice said, 'Stay in your seat, sir, if you would!'

But by now Mark had spotted me. He smiled and said, 'It's all right, Bradshaw, he's with me.' As Mickey called last orders, Mark took me out into the corridor on the hotel side of the door, which led up a few steps to the ground floor toilets. There he came to a halt.

I said, 'Let me guess: you've had an anonymous tip-off.'

Mark said, 'I might have known you'd be here. Never far from trouble.' But he seemed pleased to see me. Things had been this way with Mark since before Christmas, and if anything he became friendlier every time I bumped into him. I was baffled by this, but also cheered. Mark's attempt to conceal his sexual preferences from everyone in the local police force had long obliged him to hold me at arm's length, and I didn't much like being sacrificed to further his glittering career. Back in the summer it had looked as if Mark might be promoted to Detective Sergeant, though still only in his late twenties, but then, unaccountably, nothing had come of that. Meanwhile he and WPC Cilla Donnelly, whose motives were similar to his, had pretended for months to be in a relationship. Their latest wheeze was to make out that the relationship was on ice because Cilla had caught Mark cheating – all needlessly baroque and absurd – and they hoped to sustain this stand-off for as long as possible.

Personally, I thought it feeble of Mark to let himself be reduced to such play-acting. From time to time I said as much, and he resented it. But lately I'd begun to think he resented it less.

He said, 'I was wanting a word with you.'

I said, 'And I with you. Do you want yours first?'

'Perhaps not while I'm on duty. I'm off all weekend – are you busy?'

'Working on a couple of things. Cup of tea would be nice, though.'

'Say, Saturday afternoon?'

I said I'd phone him if there was going to be any problem with that, and then laid out my own difficulty of conveying Fuselli, Crouch's letter down to Shoreditch, suppressing as I did so any reference to this shadowy legal organization. Mark was eerily happy to help. 'Bung it in an envelope with my name on and drop it in at the station in the morning. I'll make sure it goes tomorrow.' He gave me one of his best smiles.

I said, 'What's with the tie?' I took the object in question between my fingers. 'A bit flamboyant, isn't it? You'll be getting comments.'

But at that point another uniformed constable came in sight and bore down on us. I let go of the tie. The officer said to Mark, 'No sign of anything. We've searched top to bottom.'

Mark said, 'We might as well clear out then. Just a wild goose chase.' The man left us.

I said, 'Do you want my opinion on this?'

'Not really.'

'I think it's the Malones throwing their weight about. It's not enough that the Goldings had their licence application rejected, the Malones want to rub their noses in it.'

'You seem well versed on the background. Between ourselves, the Super's worried that Southaven may not be big enough for both families.'

'And how is your friend the Super?'

Mark's face clouded. There's some possibility that my tone may have been offensive. 'He's not my friend.'

The previous year, Mark had become a freemason, and he now hob-nobbed on a regular basis with the likes of Superintendent Sturges. Mark was sensitive to any mention of this.

I said, 'Not your friend? You've wasted your sub, then.'

'I wish you wouldn't do this.'

'Do what?'

'You can be so nice when you want to.'

'Really?' It was news to me.

Mark looked up in my face. He was on the short side for a policeman, and if he'd had Giles Rawley's job they'd have had to stick his co-star in a trench. He sighed. 'What am I going to do with you? Come on – let's go and relieve Constable Bradshaw.'

Back in the bar, Mark called out, 'Thanks for your patience, everyone. You're free to go now.' The delivery lacked Bradshaw's carrying power, but it served its purpose. Mark nodded to the constable, who left via the street door. Then Mark patted me on the shoulder and said, 'Saturday afternoon – don't forget,' and was about to turn back into the hotel when he caught sight of Mickey Golding watching him from behind the bar. Their eyes locked.

I couldn't recall when I'd ever seen two people take an instant dislike to one another without a word being spoken, but I was seeing it now. Mark and Mickey stared long and hard, gripped by a horrified fascination. Superficially, you might have supposed they were similar. The height was similar, the colouring too, and while Mickey went in for the cute nose, Mark notoriously sported a pair of elfin ears picked from the same catalogue. Mark had a slight edge in years, and Mickey in weight, but otherwise they seemed cut from the same cloth. It was evident from the look they were exchanging that they themselves saw things very differently. From the back of my mind, some voice of inner wisdom counselled me to do all in my power to keep these two people apart.

Finally, when the hostile glare had continued for so long that I'd begun to think of stepping in, Mark turned and went, apparently having forgotten that I was there.

I took my seat again. There was a fresh bottle on the bar. Giles said, 'I thought you'd probably want another.'

'You shouldn't have. It's your birthday, I ought to be paying.'

'Don't be silly, you know you're very welcome. It's not as if I haven't got it.'

The question of just how much money Giles Rawley did have remained unresolved for me. On the one hand, I doubted whether he could have grown rich from his work. He'd had supporting roles in a few popular British films, but the repeat fees couldn't have added up to much. Giles was never a leading man; the lazy eye had probably put paid to that. From what I'd seen of him, he very much took care of the pennies, and he'd told me that he always chose a modest room on the top floor at Marine Lodge in order to keep down his expenses. But on the other hand, the importunate behaviour of Cordelia wasn't the only clue which had sometimes led me to think that Giles might have a fortune stashed away.

Mickey relieved the evening's final customer of their cash and declaimed, 'Time, please! You've had your lot, ladies and gents.' He began to clear glasses from the bar, among them Giles's.

I said, 'Giles, aren't you having a last one yourself?'

'No, dear boy, I've had enough for today. There was wine at dinner, all very nice, but you know I'm not a great fan. I can hear my bed calling. My bed and my book.' Giles's reading habits were similar to my own. I'd been known to bump into him coming out of the library with the full allowance of books under his arm while I was going in.

A few customers were preparing to leave, but for the most part the denizens of the Vaults were the sort who clung on until the last second of drinking-up time, and would have stayed half the night if they could. Giles began replacing the scarf which would stand between his wrinkled throat and the night's bitter blast.

I said, 'I hope you've enjoyed your birthday.'

'They're a mixed blessing at my age. I find myself looking back, and it's unwise.' He gave a weak smile. 'It always seems to me that I haven't done much with my life.'

I wondered what view he might take of my own non-existent achievements. I said, 'Rubbish! I should think you were hardly ever out of work.' Giles was no household name, but as a reliable character actor he'd always been in demand.

'You're right, of course, and I'm not saying that wasn't gratifying.' A rare dreamy look came in his eye. Giles's attention had turned inward, slipping away from the Grand Hotel Vaults to rejoin his younger self somewhere, proud, ambitious, the world all before him. 'But you see, I was never any good. Oh, I held up my corner all right, I realize that. I *looked the part*.' He said this with extreme distaste. 'But I wanted to act, I wanted to be up there with the greats.' He lowered his eyes. 'I simply never had the talent.'

My experience of dealing with artistic types has been limited. I'd once done a night class in life drawing, so I knew how it felt to discover that I entirely lacked what it took to turn life into art. But I didn't think this sad story would do much to console Giles in his present mood, so I buttoned the lip and let him carry on.

He said, 'Still, work isn't everything, is it.' He looked up again, back with us in the Vaults now. 'I'm hoping I might be able to do something for Alice Haig. God knows she deserves it. And I suppose the grandchildren might make something of themselves, even with that ghastly man Lane for a father. So it's not all doom and gloom.' He got down from the stool. 'Sorry if I've been a touch maudlin. Comes over me sometimes. Shall I see you tomorrow?' I said I hoped so. Then Giles Rawley said goodnight to Mickey, and walked out into the darkness.

Back in the fifties I'd seen Giles play a university professor in a Christmas ghost story on TV. It wasn't a huge part, but he was good in it, and it stuck with me. I'd always meant to tell him. This recent monologue on the subject of his supposed failings might have been the perfect moment, but once again I'd let it go by. As he passed out of sight I was saying to myself, 'Tomorrow. Definitely tomorrow.'

## *seven*

Though I was almost the last to leave the Grand Hotel Vaults, Mickey Golding's responsibilities restricted further conversation between us. Nevertheless, he did find a moment to ask me, 'Who was that bloke you were with?'

'What bloke?'

'The copper. The one with the jacket.'

I'd been right about Mark's new look attracting comment. 'That's DC Howell. We were colleagues back in the day.'

'Colleagues? Is that all? You looked pretty chummy to me.' But at that point Carlo came through from the hotel to see how Mickey was getting on with clearing the bar, so the lie I'd been preparing went unspoken. Then just as I was about to leave, Mickey said, 'Tomorrow night?'

'Possibly. I might be going to the Velvet Bar but I could drop in here on the way.'

'If not, I'll see you Saturday morning.'

'Why, what's happening?'

'For God's sake, Sam! We're going swimming, remember?' And he leaned closer. 'What's the matter? Don't you want to see the goods before you sample them?'

I was still mulling over this remark an hour later, as I sat up in bed making further progress with the tale of Ishmael, Captain Ahab, and the Great White Whale. Only one construction could be put on it: it looked as if Mickey intended us to get better acquainted at no distant date. The nose was far from being his only attractive feature, but although I felt pleased, I was anxious too, and the day's revelation that Mickey's mother apparently saw Southaven as an extension of the East End of London had done nothing to settle my nerves. Still, I knew that if Mickey stuck to his guns I wouldn't resist him. Who could say what might already have happened by Valentine's Night?

I shifted my attention back to Melville's narrative. I was on something of a Melville kick, brought on by a passage I'd come across in Bradley's *History of Southaven*, a book which I'm never not reading; it lies around the place waiting to be picked up in odd moments, and when I finish it I start again, like painting the Forth Bridge. Bradley has a chapter on the town's literary connections. These include the fact that the American author Nathaniel Hawthorne spent the best part of a year here during the 1850s, when he held the post of American consul in Liverpool, commuting in and out of the city by train. My interest aroused, a couple of years back I'd had a go at *The Scarlet Letter*. I had to renew it at the library four times before I finished it, and that was the end of my Hawthorne phase.

But my most recent trawl through Bradley had brought up a fresh name: Herman Melville. What I'd failed to notice on previous readings was that Melville had paid Hawthorne a two-day visit here in November 1856, when they'd walked on the dunes together and enjoyed a cigar while sheltering from the usual inconvenient wind on what Hawthorne's journal called 'this bleak and blasty shore'. Well, I'd never read a word of Melville; Hawthorne's name stood on the title page of *Moby Dick* as dedicatee; and the upshot was, that's where I'd elected to make a start on his works.

And I didn't mean to stop there, either. I'd got it into my head that Melville was going to become my new Favourite Writer, so at the library I'd taken down from the shelves not only *Moby Dick*, but also *Redburn* (because it was set partly in Liverpool – not quite Southaven, but close enough to be interesting), and *Billy Budd, Sailor*. Both these latter volumes were now biding their time on my bedside table. I was saving my fourth ticket – they only let you have four books at once in case the surfeit of culture kills you – for *The Confidence-Man*, purely on the strength of the title. They'd had to order it from another library, and I was waiting for the notification.

Just as Ishmael was sizing up his chances of getting a decent night's sleep at the Spouter Inn, the phone rang.

Presumably, if I were what Alice Haig might term a Rational Actor it wouldn't vex me so much whenever the phone rings, since after all this ringing represents a key aspect of the service I'm paying for. But vex me it does, and the present instance formed no exception. Only the hope that it might be Matt making his promised report lifted my mood sufficiently to persuade me that I should leave Ishmael to take care of himself and bowl through into the living room. Once there, I flicked on the light and made a dive for the phone, before whoever it was lost heart.

The pips sounding at the other end increased the likelihood that this must indeed be Matt, calling from some benighted Manchester kiosk. They stopped, and Matt said, 'Sam?'

I said, 'It's very late.' I hadn't meant to sound unsympathetic, but when you've been sitting in a warm bed with a good book and some third party breaks in on the tryst, kind words don't trip readily from the tongue.

Annoyed, Matt said, 'You told me to report back! I've had to walk for ages to find a phone where the coin-box wasn't full.'

'I don't get you.'

'It's the strike, there's no one emptying the damn things. I'm stuck out here earning money for us, and all you can do is complain!'

For one reckless moment I considered apologising, but once you start to give ground there's no saying where it might end. 'What news of Gordon Asprey?'

'His wife's right. He's got a woman there with him.'

'Blonde hair?'

'As expected. So far I've only had a glimpse of her closing the curtains, there wasn't time for a photograph. I stood under a tree across the road all evening hoping they'd go out, but no such luck. I'll have to try again tomorrow.'

'How are the digs?' Perhaps this show of concern might make up for my earlier remark.

'Aagh! The place is filthy! There was a dead mouse under the bed.'

'It's the live ones you've got to watch out for.'

'Can't say I'm all that keen to turn in. It's not as if it's any warmer than the street. What about you, what's been going on?'

I told Matt about Marine Lodge, and the connection with Sidney Flint's problem. He said, 'Commercial espionage, that's what it is. Everyone's doing it these days, I read about it in the Mirror. Have you worked out who the rotten apple is yet?'

'The night porter's best placed in terms of opportunity. But he doesn't seem like the type.'

Thanks to the miracle of telecommunications, Matt's snort travelled the forty miles between us with force undimmed. 'Doesn't seem like the type? I see you're applying the full scientific rigour of the patent Rigby Method.'

I smiled a private smile. Such were the pleasures denied to me when Matt went away on a job. I said, 'If you were here, I'd put you over my knee for that.'

'You'd have to catch me first. Anyway, it looks like I'll be stuck here another day or two, until I can get some snaps of the mystery woman.'

'Don't be too long, will you.'

This was the sort of thing I always tried not to say to him. But it was late, I was tired and not very well, and I'd said it. Matt said, 'Missing me, are you?'

And that's when I remembered about my plan for Valentine's Night. I said, 'I was going to ask you something. Did you ever cancel that booking you'd made for Sunday evening at the Hen and Chickens?'

'Eight o'clock in Rustlers. I suppose I should, shouldn't I. Valentine's Night, I expect they've got a waiting list.'

I said, 'Hang onto it. I've had an idea.'

The pips went. Matt tried to talk through them, but I couldn't make out what he was saying. Then the connection was broken. Either he'd run out of coins, or yet another coin-box was now full and out of commission.

I went back to bed and rejoined Ishmael in the Spouter Inn, but since the phone call Melville wasn't capturing my interest. I turned out the light and lay down. In the darkness, my thoughts reeled forward to my Saturday swim with Mickey Golding, and to whatever might happen between us afterwards. But once again a third party interrupted the tryst. I found myself imagining how Mickey might look when he grew older. What if the cute nose got left behind in the middle of a ravaged, wrinkled face below receding hair? Which is where Matt barged in. He'd be a looker all his life, would Matt. There was nothing cute about him, nor was his father in Wormwood Scrubs, or his mother sending out threatening letters to the citizens of Southaven. No doubt about it, Matt was a catch.

But Matt was going out with Eileen Docherty, and Mickey Golding wasn't.

Anxious to dispel the impression of poor time-keeping which I'd given Alice Haig, I cleverly set my alarm for seven thirty. Unfortunately, after it went off so did I, for another forty-five minutes. This resulted in another undignified scramble to get out of the house. I lost further time by forgetting the letter from Fuselli, Crouch to Messrs. Tipton, Buxton and Lamb, and having to go back up three flights of stairs to fetch it.

At the police station, the desk sergeant was of a vintage to remember me, and also the scandal linking my name with Mark Howell's which had cost me my job. He greeted me cordially enough, but when he saw the name on the outer envelope his left eyebrow set off in a northerly direction, and I could see him asking himself what business the very proper, stainless and unsullied DC Howell could possibly have with a Known Homosexual.

I lost time again by visiting the newsagents for cigarettes. The old urge was back. Sam Rigby was restored to health.

The morning felt unexpectedly mild and benign, with the sun now chasing off the infernal darkness imposed upon us by governments messing with the clocks. A walk round to Marine Lodge would be pleasant, but it was already five to nine and my only chance of being punctual was to take the Minx. The traffic was heavy, and by the time the one-way system had obliged me to drive most of the length of the Boulevard in order to approach the hotel from Wright Street it began to look as if walking might have been the quicker option.

As I turned into the back yard of Marine Lodge, I saw two

figures beside the Armstrong Siddeley I'd noticed the night before. Sarkis Aznavorian was just opening one of the rear doors, to place a brown carpet-bag carefully on the seat. Miss Pyle stood at the front of the car, idly stroking the sphinx mascot with a gloved hand. I parked beside a blue Mini which hadn't been there the previous night, and stubbed out my cigarette. As I got out of the car Miss Pyle recognized me and said, 'Sam!' I wished her good morning. She said, 'I thought you'd have had enough of us old crocks yesterday.'

If the point of using the hotel's rear entrance had been to avoid coming to the notice of the residents, the policy had clearly failed. Hoping to forestall questions, I said, 'You look as if you're off somewhere.'

Aznavorian had now come round to join Miss Pyle. He said, 'They're promising us a decent day, we thought we'd take advantage. A day trip to Lytham. Rosemary likes it there.'

I said, 'That's a very fine car.'

'My pride and joy, bought it for a snip a few years ago. I keep it back here because of the salt in the sea air.'

'You're right to protect it, it's a piece of history.'

Aznavorian nodded a worldly-wise nod. 'The market in luxury vehicles is dying. You see they've nationalised Rolls Royce now? A Tory government, at that – you'd never credit it!'

Miss Pyle, who'd been visibly engaged in thought, now said to me, 'I suppose Alice Haig has asked you to investigate the break-in.' She smiled that sweet smile of hers, the one I didn't trust.

Though it was, of course, the first I'd heard of any break-in, I seized this gift gratefully. 'That's right. I'd better go and find her.'

'She was at reception just now, talking to Laurence Glass. He's leaving us for a while – it seems his brother-in-law's been rushed into hospital.'

Aznavorian said, 'The sister can't be left on her own.'

Miss Pyle said, 'Are we ready, Sarkis?'

'Eh? What's that?'

'I said, are we ready to leave?' This repetition was delivered sweetly enough, but in very large block capitals. Miss Pyle's tolerance of infirmity had its limits.

'Oh, yes, just about, my love.'

I wished them a pleasant day, and left them. As I walked towards the rear door I heard the engine fire up, then subside to an easy purring. I turned to watch as the vehicle glided forward and went out onto Wright Street.

The back door stood open. Someone had been making a mess of the lock, and the door frame had splintered.

I set off towards reception, but as I passed the sliding door to the kitchen I noticed Alice Haig in there. She stood at a metal work-top in the middle of the room, wearing a striped chef's apron and scraping marmalade from a small serving pot back into a jar. Worry often clouded her expression, but I thought it looked worse than usual this morning. She looked up and said, 'Mr Rigby! To be honest, I'd forgotten you were coming.'

Also present was young Evan, who'd taken up a rather attractive pose leaning against the door to the dining room. It would be hard to say what function in the hotel's life he was meant to be fulfilling. My entrance made no impact on him of any kind. The face remained impassive and he didn't budge an inch.

I said, 'Miss Pyle tells me you've had a break-in.'

'There's nothing missing, as far as I can see. But it's obvious who's responsible.'

'You suspect it's to do with next door?'

'First all that drivel in the Gazette, and now this.'

'Did your night porter not hear anything?'

'Apparently not. Admittedly, Graham's hearing isn't what it was. The first we knew about it was when I came in at seven to relieve Graham and make a start on the breakfasts.'

'I'd imagined Oscar would take care of breakfast.'

'Not during the winter, except when we're very busy. He comes in mid-morning.'

'Have you called the police?'

'Yes, of course. But when I said there was nothing missing they seemed to lose interest. They're sending someone out later to discuss security with me.'

'You're sure the residents aren't missing anything?'

'I've asked them all. Well, all except Giles. Giles is not a morning person, Mr Rigby. He'll probably drift down for his breakfast at about half past. I didn't want to wake him specially just for this.' Alice Haig, who'd persevered with her sticky task at intervals during this exchange, now slammed the marmalade jar down heavily onto the metal work surface. 'Oh, damn those Golding people! And they'll not stop at this, will they? Who knows what they might do next. We've got to start fighting back, Mr Rigby, before they cause untold damage.'

My eye strayed from time to time to Evan. He was jailbait, obviously, but they couldn't bang you up just for looking. Besides, I'd been wondering whether these remarks about the possible deeper significance of the break-in had aroused any show of interest in him, but no, his pose hadn't shifted, and he appeared barely cognizant of what we were talking about. It struck me that if the Goldings wanted to bug the Marine Lodge Hotel, they could choose few hidden microphones more effective than this strangely inert youth. Was Evan really as stupid as people made out? Something definitely went on in that handsome skull of his, as we'd seen when we neglected to sing before Giles blew out his candles. Was he absorbing every word we said here in the kitchen, to pour them out later to some representative of the Goldings' nascent empire?

I said to Alice Haig, 'I hear you're losing Laurence Glass.'

Momentary alarm crossed her face, but then she recovered and said, 'Oh – yes, he'll be away for a while. His sister's neighbour rang while he was taking that walk yesterday afternoon. Laurence is upstairs packing a bag, his train's at eleven.'

I glanced across at Evan again, and said to Alice, 'Do you think we might – ?'

She didn't take the hint. 'Might what, Mr Rigby?'

'Perhaps there's something else Evan could be doing.'

Light dawned. 'Yes – of course. Evan, could you run across to Whitakers and pick up some aspirin for me?'

Standing almost to attention now, Evan said, 'I've got no money.'

'Get some from the flat, it's not locked. Nigel will tell you where, he's at home today. He's probably still in bed.'

'Yes, Mrs Haig.' Obediently, Evan set off on his errand.

I said, 'He seems willing enough.'

'If only he had a bit more about him. But then I suppose he wouldn't be available to work here for such a modest wage.'

I was wondering how easily Evan could gain access to the hotel when there was no one around. 'Does he live in?'

'He's got the flat next to ours. He had to share it in the summer, but he's on his own just now. The state of the place sometimes, you wouldn't believe it! Mrs Clark goes in and tidies up, but for a quiet boy he's got an uncanny knack for creating mess in double-quick time. Now, what was it you wanted to say to me?'

I told Alice Haig about the developing conflict between the Goldings and the Malones, and about the police raid at the Grand the previous night. She said, 'At least the Goldings are not having it all their own way.'

'The Malones aren't just going to lie down and let themselves be walked all over. But if they really want to take on the Goldings, they need to raise their game.'

'Why's that?'

'The Malones are small time. They've always stuck within the law, give or take. And they've had no real competition – they're lazy, badly protected. You could do worse than help them out a little.'

'I don't quite see – '

'I'm not sure I'm clear about it myself yet. But if we can stoke up the war between the Goldings and the Malones, it might get Goldings off your back for a while, until we can come up with something more decisive.'

Alice Haig chewed this over. She looked suddenly smaller, and perhaps I was seeing her as she truly was, a sheltered, middle-class Southaven woman out of her depth. But she rallied, squared her jaw, and said, 'And how do we achieve this "stoking up"?'

'Leave it to me. I had an idea during that raid. The Grand Hotel may be about to have an extremely unsuccessful Valentine's Night.'

Briefly it seemed as if Alice Haig might smile, but then her face reset itself along the old lines. I said, 'Perhaps I should get on and talk to your housekeeper.'

'Mrs Clark, yes. I'll come with you. She's upstairs somewhere.'

We headed out through the sliding door towards the back stairs. As we reached them, three screams, wild, unconstrained, found their way down to us from above.

Alice Haig said, 'Mrs Clark!' and started climbing at a good rate. I managed to overtake her on the stairs, but at the first floor I stopped. A neat but heavy woman, face white with terror, came thumping down from the floor above. The sight of a stranger only made matters worse, and she was on the point of turning to run back the way she'd come.

But then Alice caught up with me and said to the housekeeper, 'What is it?'

Wide-eyed, the woman said, 'Sir Giles!'

To the best of my knowledge, a grateful nation had so far failed to honour Giles Rawley with a knighthood. But it seemed an inappropriate time to discuss this, so I just said 'Where?'

Alice said, 'Number twenty-one, second floor front.'

Catching a strong whiff of starched linen, I pushed past Mrs Clark and continued upwards. At the half-landing I glanced back, to see Alice Haig coming after me. I called out, 'Stay with her!' then turned and ran on.

The door of room twenty-one stood open. I stopped on the threshold. A bundle of fresh, white towels had been dropped near the door, perhaps by the fleeing housekeeper. The window opposite gave a fine view across the Marine Lake to the sea beyond, where for once the tide pressed in close against the sea wall. Under the window, the mirror of an old mahogany dressing-table reflected a three-quarter bed projecting into the room.

Someone shouted, 'What the hell's going on?' Coming towards me from the direction of the main staircase was Laurence Glass. 'I heard someone screaming.'

I said 'Don't come any closer.'

'Who the devil do you think you are, to tell me what I can't do?'

Major Glass kept coming. I turned and squared up to him.

'This is a crime scene.'

'Don't be ridiculous, man.' He'd drawn level with me now, and when he came to a halt in front of me I began to hope that he'd go no further. But inevitably he looked into the room, caught sight of the mirror, and saw what I'd seen myself. 'Good God!' He pushed me out of the way, with a strength I hadn't expected, and strode into the room. 'Rawley!' He stood by the bed, distraught, hands pressed against his temples.

Reluctantly I followed Laurence Glass into the room. 'Come away now, Major.' His breathing was short. He couldn't take his eyes off the sight in front of him. 'Major Glass – you need to leave the room.' I could see that he was sweating heavily. 'Major!' He twisted round to look at me, but there was no hint of recognition. Then the eyes turned up in his head, he clutched at his chest, and in a moment he came down, hitting the floor like a sack of coals.

'Laurence!' From behind me, Alice Haig hurried into the room. Kneeling alongside the Major, she said, 'Laurence, can you hear me?' He stared straight ahead of him, breathing a fast, rasping breath, one hand still tight against his chest. 'Oh God, he's having a heart attack! Get an ambulance!'

It was only when she turned to direct those words towards me that Alice Haig saw Giles Rawley lying in the bed, his head a bloody pulp, a hammer on the counterpane beside him.

# THE SECOND BOOK

## *eight*

A murder can really take the shine off your morning.

I'd been looking forward to getting my teeth into the case of Alice Haig and the leaked accounts. Instead, I was closeted in the lounge of the Marine Lodge with my least-favourite policeman, Detective Inspector Henry (known as Harry, when his back was turned) Hargreaves, who'd decided to make use of the place as his temporary incident room. He'd brought along all the props associated with his chosen vice, leaving the hotel to supply only the ash tray. As a result, the lounge had already taken on the distinctive Hargreaves aroma of pipe smoke and old tweed.

We were seated at opposite ends of the buffet table which had so recently hosted the late Giles Rawley's birthday tea. Covered yesterday by an immaculate white cloth, in its nude state it revealed the faded quality shared by all the furniture in the building. A recent layer of polish failed to hide the ringed stains left by generations of careless guests. Hargreaves's mug of tea was currently adding another.

If I seem to have taken an undue interest in the historic surface of the lounge table, that's because it was the safest spot to rest my eyes when not giving evasive and unsatisfactory replies to the DI's questions. If I looked at the man himself, I had to resist a powerful urge to shove his pipe right down his throat. But if I glanced out into the room I could be sure to meet the satirical eye of WPC Cilla Donnelly, to whose lot it had fallen to take notes. She seemed to find my combative relationship with the veteran detective hilarious, for reasons known only to herself.

The great man was talking. 'Let me be clear about this. The deceased was already known to you prior to your engagement by Mrs Haig?'

'We'd been drinking pals ever since the Grand Hotel reopened.'

'I wouldn't have thought you'd have had much in common.'

'You know what they say – opposites attract.'

Hargreaves exercised his eyebrows and gave the stem of his pipe a reflective chewing. Then he said, 'And he left the Vaults at – what time, did you say?'

'Closing time. I stayed behind for a last one, but he wanted to get to bed.'

'He didn't give you the impression that he expected to meet with anyone when he returned to the hotel?'

'No.'

'Or that he felt himself to be in any kind of danger?'

'No. He was unusually – I don't know, wistful perhaps. Melancholy.'

'Do you think something might have happened to cause that?'

I shrugged. 'It was his birthday. He'd been thinking about the past, that's all.'

Hargreaves leaned back in the chair and continued chewing the now dormant pipe while subjecting the ceiling to close examination. It must have inspired him, because after a while he said, 'Now, Samuel, I hope you won't take this the wrong way. No doubt when Mrs Haig supposed that you, as a private investigator, would be able to mount a more discreet inquiry than the proper authorities, her confidence was well-placed. But I can't help noticing that within hours of your accepting the commission, one of her guests has been bludgeoned to death.'

'That's ridiculous! You're not suggesting I had anything to do with this?'

'Why not? It was the same with that business last summer. I told you to keep your nose out of it but no, Samuel Rigby knew better, as he always does. Next thing, we were knee-deep in corpses.'

Foolishly, I allowed my eye to stray in the direction of Cilla Donnelly. Though her pencil was poised efficiently enough, the rest of her could hardly have appeared more thoroughly entertained if she'd been sitting on the front row at the annual Pavilion panto. I'd have to have a word with her about this afterwards.

'So you think that just because I've started asking a few questions, we can expect a murder spree?'

'You see, I told you not to take this the wrong way, and you've ignored my advice as usual. I'm only saying that it seems like a remarkable coincidence.'

'And that's all it is. I don't see how Rawley's death can have any connection whatsoever with my investigation.'

'Had it not occurred to you that the victim himself might have been the source of this leak of information?'

The correct answer was that it had only occurred to me the moment Hargreaves suggested it. I was so busy thinking how annoying it was when Hargreaves got ahead of me like this that I neglected to reply. Hargreaves said, 'No, I can see that it hadn't. Quite what Mrs Haig believes she's paying you to do, I can't imagine.'

'Rawley would never have got involved in anything like that. He had – a particular regard for Mrs Haig. Why would he want to destroy her business?'

'Did he have any sort of special link to the Grand, beyond enjoying these regular night-caps you've told me about?'

I didn't want to mention Lena. It would look bad, and in any case I felt reasonably sure that whatever attraction Giles may have felt for her would hardly have been enough to lead him to betray Alice Haig. Only reasonably sure, though; Giles had that child-like side to him, and I guessed that Lena could be pretty persuasive when coming to the aid of the Family.

I said, 'No. The man you want to talk to is Oscar Hammond.' I told Hargreaves about the Grand's attempt to purloin Alice Haig's chef. Perhaps they'd made him another offer too, one which he'd accepted.

Unconvinced, Hargreaves relit the pipe, so that fresh clouds of smoke circled his impressive head. He looked like Helvellyn in the rain. He said, 'Was Rawley a man with enemies, would you say?' Once again I didn't answer immediately, and before I could do so the DI added, 'Why do I always feel your replies lack candour? Tell me, Samuel – what time is it?'

I eyed him suspiciously. This must be some sort of trick.

'There! You see? Instead of simply consulting your watch and telling me, you're calculating how little you can get away with revealing. I don't know why I waste my energy on you.'

Cilla Donnelly was smirking. It was a bad habit and I wished she'd give it up. I said, 'If you must know, Giles Rawley wasn't universally popular. He had a sharp tongue. But I can't think that anyone hated him enough to – to do that.'

'No feuds with the other residents?'

I thought of his rivalry with Laurence Glass. 'Not as such. Friction, that's all.'

Then Hargreaves said, 'Very well. You can go.'

'What?' The surprise had forced my voice up an octave or two. I climbed the stave and fetched it down again. 'Already?'

'Naturally if you think of anything else which might have a bearing on the case, you'll let me know.'

'Of course, Harry, er, Henry, straight away.' I pushed back the chair and stood up, trying to keep the thrill of liberation from registering on my face.

'And Samuel – ' Hargreaves leaned back again and regarded me coolly from beneath the upper slopes. 'If by any chance it should occur to you to engage in some form of parallel investigation – '

'I wouldn't dream of it. Unthinkable. It's out of the question. Scout's honour.'

'You've said similar things to me before, I seem to recall.'

'That was different, I felt I had a responsibility. But this time I won't come anywhere near it. I swear.'

For a few seconds Hargreaves studied me in silence. Then he shook his head with an expression of disappointment and said, 'Send in that housekeeper, would you, if she's fit to talk to me now.' I nodded to the man, then nodded to Cilla, who nodded back. When we were all done nodding, I bolted for the open spaces.

The police had arrived with admirable swiftness once they'd realized we weren't just worried about a break-in any more. The ambulance arrived at the same time, turning into the back yard just as the first police car was disgorging its team on the forecourt. Laurence Glass, still conscious and still in pain, was soon stretchered out of the building, and Alice Haig had the presence of mind to send with him in the ambulance the bag which he'd originally packed for Broadstairs, so that he wouldn't want for pyjamas or other essentials. She'd have gone along with the Major herself, but for the stern words of the officer temporarily in charge of the scene. Nobody was to leave the building. Another officer was dispatched to search along the Promenade for Cordelia Lane and curtail her morning walk. Word was sent to the Blackpool force to look out for the Armstrong-Siddeley and conduct it back to Southaven immediately. Before long, Hargreaves arrived, with Mark Howell in support, and they'd already spent half an hour upstairs before the scene-of-crime boys turned up. I'd have liked the luxury of that half hour myself. Because of Laurence Glass's attack, I'd not been able to devote much attention to the state of the room, beyond gaining a broad impression. If I wanted more information later, I'd have to ask Mark for it, and history taught that my request might not be warmly received.

Eventually Mark had been left in charge of the crime scene – as far as I knew, the body was still up there – while Hargreaves had set up his incident room and begun the interviews. From courtesy, he'd started with Alice Haig. Next he'd asked for the housekeeper, since it was she who'd discovered the body, but having been told that she was still in shock he settled for me instead.

While Hargreaves was establishing the incident room, Alice Haig and Oscar, who'd arrived a little early for his shift, had been equally busy creating its counterpart, a sort of refugee centre in the dining room where tea, coffee and biscuits were available, along with the companionship of other souls affected by the morning's horror. Two tables had been pushed together, and I returned from my interview with Hargreaves to find that an unlikely group had assembled around them. Her eyes red from crying, Cordelia Lane looked as if without the support of the table she'd slip immediately to the floor. Mrs Clark sat stiff and upright, apparently revived now, but gripping a mug of tea with both hands for whatever comfort that might bring. Alice sat near Cordelia, taut with anxiety. A little disengaged from the women and with his chair well back, Oscar had folded his hands over his generous belly and was twiddling his thumbs distractedly. And standing mute by the window, Evan watched everything, displaying not the least sign that the vicious murder in room twenty-one had touched him in any way.

There was one notable absentee from this gay gathering. Alice had telephoned Graham Leeds at his home to ask him to return to the hotel, but the call went unanswered. As soon as a plod could be spared from front-line duties, Graham would be hearing a knock at his front door.

True to form, Evan had ignored me as I'd come in, but the other four all looked up, perhaps hoping that I'd brought good news. Death being a one-way ticket, there was little chance of that. I said to Mrs Clark, 'He's ready for you.' When she seemed about to abandon the tea, I said, 'Take that in with you. You might find it helps.' Once the housekeeper had left us I said to Alice Haig, 'A word?'

I thought I recognized some brief flash of guilt in the look which met this simple request, but if it had been there at all, it passed. Once more in command of herself and of the situation, Alice led me out into the corridor and down to her office behind the reception desk. A uniformed officer had been stationed just inside the front entrance to the hotel, and to prevent his over-hearing anything I pushed the office door shut behind me.

I said, 'Any news of the Major?'

'I rang ten minutes ago. He's stable. They're not saying if it was a heart attack or not, but he doesn't seem to be in any immediate danger.'

'You must be relieved.'

No doubt Alice Haig understood very well what I was implying, but she said, 'You were right about the Detective Inspector.' I'd forewarned her that Hargreaves took no prisoners. 'Another ten minutes and I'd have confessed to anything.'

'He's hardly likely to suspect you of any involvement.' I should have added 'yet', but I didn't want to upset her.

She scoffed loudly. 'That's not how it felt!' Alice Haig lowered herself into the old office chair behind her desk. 'Sit down, Mr Rigby, won't you.'

I tried the armchair where I suspected Graham Leeds snoozed out much of his employment. It was every bit as comfortable as it looked, but I couldn't relax. My mind had been on red alert since the first moment I'd seen the framed reflection of Giles's body on the bed. Now the unwelcome memory of that image left me disinclined for honeyed words, and I said to Alice Haig, 'If you didn't kill Giles Crawley, why are you feeling so guilty about it?'

I'd hoped to provoke a response, and I got one. 'Guilty? That's absurd!' She looked guiltier than ever.

'Mrs Haig, what is it that you've done? You might as well tell me. Hargreaves is bound to find out eventually, and perhaps we can start some damage limitation first.'

That Alice Haig took time to reply was hardly unusual, but I'd never seen her chew her lip before. Inevitably, this reminded me of Matt. All morning I'd been thinking that I must summon him back from Manchester as soon as possible. Without his quick and unpredictable intelligence, how could I possibly investigate Giles Rawley's murder? After what Hargreaves had said, you may be thinking that I'd be ill-advised to follow any such course of action. But there are some things you just have to do, whether they bring the bonus of crossing Harry Hargreaves or not.

Eventually Alice said, 'I should never have asked him to do it.'

'Do what?' But then the pieces suddenly slotted together in my mind. I don't know why it had taken so long; Matt would have got there in half the time. 'No – let me guess. As soon as the first letter came from the Goldings' solicitors, you asked Giles to do some snooping on your behalf.'

'Not snooping, Mr Rigby. That's such a distasteful term.'

'All right then, prying. Spying. Poking around.'

'I merely asked if he wouldn't mind passing on to me anything he happened to learn during his evenings at the Grand.'

'Only he took the request more seriously than you'd intended.'

Alice winced at this idea, and turned to look at the wall calendar. Either she'd not found the time to fill in the forthcoming events of 1971, or it was set to be a quiet year. She said, 'I know he asked the staff a lot of questions. Apparently he'd become quite friendly with the daughter – '

'Lena.'

'That's right. I'd started to worry that he might make himself unpopular. And of course, once those lies appeared in the Gazette I realized that I'd have to employ a professional and tell Giles to let the matter drop. But what if I was too late? What if Giles had discovered something and they decided he had to be silenced?'

On their own patch in the East End, the Goldings could get away with some pretty nasty behaviour. They had the protection of friends in high places. But was it likely that they could so quickly have found similar benefactors here in Southaven?

I said, 'So you think this is somehow the work of the Goldings?'

Alice Haig looked at me as if I was an idiot. 'You have some other idea, do you? Perhaps you think Rosemary Pyle got up in the night, took a hammer from her make-up case and ran upstairs with it? Of course it's the Goldings! They've brought their horrible, violent ways up from London with them. As soon as I heard that the Grand had been taken by outsiders, I knew no good would come of it. But this is so much worse than anything I'd imagined! A murder, here at Marine Lodge! It would have broken Ian's heart.' She paused for breath. Her normally rigid perm had begun to work itself loose, and she had to brush a stray curl out of her eye. 'Who will want to come here now? We'll be ruined. I may as well hand over the keys straight away.'

This was not what I'd expected from the once-militant Alice Haig. I said, 'Of course, you may be right. The Goldings may have done this, and your hotel may be ruined. But on the first point, if Giles really had turned up something juicy I expect they'd have leaned on him or tried to buy him off, not caved his skull in with a hammer. And as for the business angle – I suggest you wait and see what happens when the news gets out.'

'I don't understand.'

'I've only heard the phone ring twice all morning. I suspect it'll be a very different story tomorrow.'

'You mean – we might actually benefit – ?' Alice looked

uncomfortable about this.

'But you need to focus on the present just now, and let all of that take care of itself. Have the next of kin been informed?'

'Not yet. Mrs Lane said she would phone her sisters as soon as she felt up to it.'

'How about Giles's solicitor?'

Alice Haig tilted her head. 'I'm sorry, Mr Rigby, you're a little ahead of me. I don't quite see – '

'The first thing DI Hargreaves will want to know is what's in Giles's will. As a matter of fact, that goes for me too.'

'I hardly think it's any of your business.'

I said, 'It wasn't so much *my* business I was thinking of.' And I gave her the Rigby stare, calculated to unnerve even the most hardened desperado. It certainly unnerved Alice Haig.

'Are you saying I'm likely to be a beneficiary?'

'Don't you already think so yourself? Listen – I'm putting two and two together and I may be making the square root of nothing. But I've got a hunch that Giles was loaded, and that he intended to see you right.'

Alice looked away, uncomfortable again, and began fiddling with the double string of pearls around her neck. She said, 'You know, he did once tell me that I mustn't worry about the future, he was sure I'd be fine. I realize that's the sort of thing people say, but it was the *weight* he gave it, if you know what I mean.'

'But if that's true, I'm afraid you've got a little problem: Henry Hargreaves.'

Alice looked blank. 'You must think I'm very stupid, Mr Rigby, but I don't seem to be keeping up with you today.'

Which was right, she wasn't. Violent death had broken in on Alice Haig's narrow world and dulled her reason. I said, 'To be fair, Hargreaves isn't one to jump to conclusions. But if it turns out that Giles has left you a substantial sum, you're going to find yourself right up there with the Goldings at the top of his list of suspects.'

'But that's insane!'

'He's a policeman, he's trained to follow the money. Until we find out who killed Giles Rawley you'll have Hargreaves sticking to you like fly paper.'

'We?'

'I'm sorry?'

'You said, until *we* find out.'

'Oh, yes, that.' I tried to look competent. 'I was wondering if you might want to extend my remit.'

'You mean, employ you to mount a parallel investigation?'

I could have wished Alice hadn't hit on the DI's exact phrase, but this was no time for squeamishness. 'That's right. With luck I'll have you off the hook in no time.' I threw in a reassuring smile.

Alice was silent, clearly giving thought to my attractive offer. It was true that she didn't have much evidence of my skills as yet, so she was largely flying blind. On the other hand, in the present situation she was alone and vulnerable. She might have hoped to count on Giles for support, or perhaps on Laurence Glass, but Giles was dead, and Laurence lay in the Infirmary dealing with troubles of his own. Eventually she said, 'Very well, Mr Rigby. But for heaven's sake, be discreet!'

I wasn't sure how I could achieve that in the circumstances, but I said, 'Of course, of course. The same terms as before, if that suits you. I might as well start right away, unless you need me here for anything.' I got up out of the chair. It took effort, and I couldn't blame Graham Leeds if he opted to stay in it most of the time.

Alice was frowning. 'I believe I'm still grounded within the hotel. You couldn't just do something for me?'

'Whatever you like.'

'I've not been able to look in on Nigel. He wasn't well enough to get up this morning, and since Evan took him those aspirin he's been all on his own. Could you just slip in for a minute and tell him what's happened, and say I'll be there as soon as I can? The flat isn't locked.'

Alice too was on her feet now, and we moved towards the door. I remembered something I'd meant to ask her. 'When Mrs Clark met us on the stairs, she said, "Sir Giles." What was that all about?'

Alice Haig brushed away the pesky curl again, displeased by it and by my question. 'It's a piece of nonsense, Mr Rigby. Of all the times for her to choose – You see, it was a sort of nickname some of the staff gave him. Someone had heard him complaining about theatrical knighthoods being handed out to all and sundry, and of course it sounded like the worst sort of sour grapes. Ever afterwards they called him Sir Giles behind his back. Poor Giles, I hope to God he never knew.'

We said our farewells out in the corridor, and Alice Haig set off towards the dining room with renewed purpose. As I passed the kitchen I could see Oscar preparing sandwiches. I stopped for a moment and said, 'I don't suppose you'll have many takers for those.'

He looked up. 'I felt I had to be doing something, that's all. I was going mad just sitting there. It makes no sense, does it? He was an old soldier, like the Major. You know he was at Ypres? That's what I can't get out of my mind. He survived that bloodbath, and then this goes and happens to him. It's all wrong! If it wasn't for men like him, we'd none of us be here at all.' Oscar paused to wipe sweat from his brow. 'And you know what gets me the most? No one ever cares what happens to you afterwards. Now the Provos are using us as target practice in Northern Ireland. Training can't prepare you for what it's like, there'll be kids coming out of the army in a year or two with their minds in tatters. They'll need help, but they'll not get it, any more than the Major did.'

I guessed that the chief object of Oscar's concern for the damaged ex-serviceman was probably Oscar himself, but if all this had any link with Giles's death, I couldn't see it. I said, 'Had you noticed any change in him lately?'

'You saw him yesterday yourself – the same as ever, wasn't he? A real gent, was Giles Rawley.'

It would have been helpful if Oscar Hammond could have solved the case for me in the first ten minutes of my taking it on, but apparently he was as much in the dark as I was. I turned to leave, but a thought struck me. 'Oh – by the way, Oscar, where did you get to yesterday evening? Giles was expecting to see you in the Vaults.'

If Oscar had ever decided to take up playing poker, he'd have lost his shirt in minutes. The man had been cursed with a very readable face, currently open at the chapter on awkward secrets. He looked away for a second, but when his glance settled on an open bottle of brandy further along the worktop he quickly looked the other way. He said, 'I was tired, wasn't I. It had been a long day.'

'So when you'd finished doing the dinners here last night, you went straight home?'

'Yeah. Needed my beauty sleep.'

'And that's what you're going to tell Detective Inspector Hargreaves?'

'Of course.'

'He won't believe you, Oscar.'

'What are you talking about? I was at home all night!'

I shook my head and tried to look sympathetic. 'He's a terrible man is Hargreaves, leaves strong men weeping. Where were you really?'

Oscar picked up the bread knife he'd been using when I'd come in. He didn't actually threaten me with it, but nevertheless it was clutched tight in his hand as he said, 'I don't have to talk to you. I've got these sandwiches to make. Just clear off, all right?'

I beat a tactical retreat.

The back yard of the Marine Lodge was something of a sun-trap, open to its late-morning rays and well-protected from the nagging breezes endemic to that part of town. An early promise of spring blessed the mild air. Two men were busy loading something into the back of a police vehicle, the something which had until recently been Giles Rawley. I crossed to the nearest of the staff flats, the one with Haig written above the doorbell, and let myself in.

## *nine*

The staff flats occupied two upper stories above the row of lock-up garages which I'd noticed before. To judge from the flaking paint on their doors, these garages were either little-used or unloved, but sturdy padlocks suggested that some of them at least contained objects worth securing. Beside each pair of wide doors stood a narrow one giving access to the floors above via a stairway which turned back on itself. At the first floor, the door to the Haigs' flat proved to be unlocked, as Alice had said it would. I stepped inside, calling out, 'Hello?'

A voice similar to that of the boy I'd met the previous day replied, 'Who is it?' Similar, but not identical; the voice had lost its shine.

'It's Sam Rigby.'

'Who the hell's Sam Rigby?'

Guided by the sound, I climbed a further, narrower flight of stairs. 'Are you up here, Nigel?'

'Yes, worse luck.' Tracing this last remark to a room on the right, I gave the door a push and walked in. Nigel Haig had been semi-recumbent in the single bed, but now heaved himself up to lean against the headboard. His hair was matted with sweat, and the room smelled of boiled invalid, an effect caused by the electric convector heater which was replicating conditions tropical enough to give Laurence Glass one of his flashbacks. Nigel Haig said, 'Oh, it's you.' I'm not the sort who lights up the room when he walks in, but even so I've known people sound more pleased to see me. 'Mum told me all about you. You're some sort of gumshoe.'

'She's a bit stuck over at the hotel just now, she said she'd come and check on you as soon as she could.' I took another look at the patient. 'I see you've reached the near-death stage.'

'I've got a temperature of a hundred and two. Though I think this thing may be bust.' He picked up a thermometer from the bedside table, examined it mistrustfully, put it down again next to his glasses, then examined me instead. His eyes were watery and an unhealthy flush covered his pale cheekbones. He said, 'If you're going to interfere with me, I should warn you I haven't had a bath for three days.' And while I was trying to locate the power of speech he added, 'You are queer, aren't you?'

'Am I?'

'You've got to be. All that horrible chumminess at reception yesterday, it was embarrassing. I don't think Mum noticed, but she never notices anything unless it's about work.'

'Perhaps I'm just naturally friendly.'

'Friendly, my arse. You're exactly like our old geography teacher, Bummer Harris. He was besotted with my friend Paul Whitehead, everybody knew about it. He always did that revolting chummy thing too, like he was your best mate. Grotesque. Anyway, get on with it if you're going to do it, I want to get back to sleep.'

I said, 'You're bored, aren't you?'

Nigel now took up a school textbook from the bedspread, examined it just long enough for me to see the word Physics, then put it down again. He said, 'A bit, yeah. I was trying to revise for Monday, but I've got a splitting headache. All these books, and I don't think I could read to save my life.' Nigel's was one of the few rooms I'd ever seen outside a library which could have competed with my living room for book density, and I found the effect pleasing. The difference was that here they were all meticulously arranged on the metal shelves which filled most of the wall space. A small wardrobe or tall-boy and a very tidy desk with attendant chair formed the only other items of furniture.

I said, 'Did you take the aspirin Evan brought?'

'Yes, but they don't seem to make any difference. I couldn't believe he actually brought the right thing! That boy is as thick as a brick.'

'So everyone seems to think.'

'You don't agree?' Nigel's eyes narrowed. 'Oh, I get it. You fancy him, don't you. Ugh! Even my sister says she wouldn't say no. He can probably have any girl he wants.' Nigel Haig crossed his arms and sulked.

'Are you not lucky with the ladies, then?'

'"Lucky with the ladies"? I didn't know people still talked like that. Presumably you've not read *The Female Eunuch*?'

'I did start it, but I dropped it in the bath.'

Conversation was now suspended while Nigel gave himself up to a bout of coughing. He searched for a tissue beside the bed and spat into it a quantity of thick brown catarrh. Then he threw the tissue in the direction of a waste bin by the desk, and missed. He said, 'God, I wish I was dead. Aren't bodies foul?'

I couldn't let that pass unchallenged. 'I rather like them myself.'

'Only when it's Evan's kind of body. I bet you don't like mine, do you?' Nigel's pyjama jacket stood open enough to allow a partial view of his chest, very white and flat. I took refuge in silence. 'No, of course you don't. Nobody ever fancies me, not even rabid homosexuals. I'll be eighteen in April and I'm still a virgin. Can you wonder I get depressed?'

'I'm sure someone must fancy you, Nigel.' Off the top of my head I couldn't quite think who that might be, but still.

'They don't, though. Bobbie got all the looks. Have you met Bobbie yet? You should see the tits on her, and she hasn't even finished growing. I wouldn't care, but she's clever as well. She's even got Grade 8 on the viola. All I can do is differential calculus.'

'The world will always want mathematicians. Physicists too.' I thought I'd better be even-handed about it.

'Only for our brains. If you're trying to get into some girl's knickers, Maxwell's Equation is a complete waste of time.'

In fairness to Nigel Haig, I could still remember well enough how it was to be seventeen and biologically condemned to think about sex every waking moment. Consequently, despite the fact that he was feeling annoyingly sorry for himself I felt sorry for him too. Perhaps what he needed was a change of subject. I said, 'I didn't just come to see how you are. Can I sit down?' He seemed to take the question as rhetorical, so I moved the chair from by the desk and parked my backside. I said, 'There's been – an incident.'

Immediately Nigel sat forward, his sexual worries forgotten. 'Is

Mum all right?'

'Yes, your mother's absolutely fine. But I'm afraid Giles Rawley's dead.'

'What, Sir Giles? That creep?' I must have looked puzzled, because he went on. 'You should have seen the way he used to look at Bobbie.'

'Does your mother know about this?' Apparently my mind had set off down a certain track.

'Doubt it. She likes the old bastard anyway.'

'And did he ever – ?' I couldn't think of a diplomatic way to complete the question.

'Did he ever try it on? You'd have to ask Bobbie, there's stuff we don't tell each other. She kept out of his way, though, I know that much.' To himself, he added, 'So that explains why there's been all this racket in the yard.'

Though Nigel Haig had not belonged to Giles's fan club, I still felt concerned as to how he would take my next piece of news. After all, the Marine Lodge hotel was Nigel's home, almost as much as the flat itself. Unable to think of a less dramatic way of phrasing it, I said, 'The fact is, Nigel, Rawley was murdered.'

His eyes widened. 'No! Amazing! Perhaps Bobbie did it. Was it poison? Girls always use poison, don't they.'

If Nigel had been fonder of the deceased, I might have censored the details at this point. But I said, 'He was attacked with a hammer. It was pretty bad.'

'Where?'

'In his room.'

'How do you know it was a hammer?'

'The murderer left it behind.'

'I wonder if it's ours.'

The apparent improvement in Nigel Haig's health in the past minute had been remarkable. Probably at least half his symptoms were down to boredom. I said, 'What do you mean?'

'Well, does anyone recognize the hammer? My dad's workshop is right by the back door.'

'That lean-to?'

'He was a wizard at DIY, he did all the repairs in the hotel.' I thought this might explain one or two deficiencies, but I kept that to myself. 'He used to say he'd picked it all up off someone called Barry.'

'Barry Bucknell?'

'You knew him as well? Anyway, we've kept everything just how it was when he died. If there's a hammer missing, there'll be a space where it should be hanging up.'

'Do you know if he had anything like a jemmy?'

'What's a jemmy?'

I was appalled. What were they teaching youngsters in schools these days? 'Or a crowbar, something like that? The back door of the hotel was forced open during the night.'

'He had all sorts of stuff. Do you want me to show you?' And he moved to throw the sheets aside.

I put a hand on Nigel's arm. 'You're staying where you are. You're ill.'

'That's not fair! I'll miss everything.'

'If there's a key to the workshop, you could tell me where it is.'

'Won't the police want to go in there first?'

I admired the boy's perceptiveness. 'They will indeed. But we can't have everything we want in life, can we?' I'd have followed this up with a roguish twinkle, but I didn't want another lecture on chumminess.

Nigel smiled a grudging smile. 'You know, you're not too bad, as perverts go. The key's tucked behind a little pile of bricks to the left of the door. Are you going to try and find the killer?'

'Your mother has asked me to investigate.'

'I could help you.'

'I've already got an assistant.' I didn't mention that Matt was thirty miles away. 'Besides, you're in bed with this thing that's going round.'

'I'm feeling a lot better.'

'Look, I tell you what. I promise I'll keep you up to date with what I'm doing. How's that?'

He looked disappointed. There was a danger he might sulk again.

'Now, is there anything you want before I go? Some food?'

'I can't eat.'

'Nice cup of tea?'

Nigel said yes to that, with the air of one accepting a very poor consolation prize. I went down to the cramped kitchen, made a mug of tea with two sugars as requested, and took it back upstairs. Spectacles on his nose, Nigel was having another crack at the physics textbook. I put the tea on the table and said, 'I'm sure they won't keep your mother much longer.'

During my brief absence, the temporary energy boost brought about by news of Rawley's murder had apparently subsided, and Nigel looked every bit as ill now as he had done when I'd first arrived. But he still managed to say, 'You will come back, won't you?'

'Of course I will.'

I could see he didn't believe me. He performed a long sigh of self-pity and said, 'Now go away and let me die in peace.'

I headed for the door, but turned there and said, 'Don't worry, you'll be over this before you know it. I was still in terrible shape yesterday morning, but look at me now.'

He did, then said, 'You look dreadful.'

There was no answer to that, so I left him to cook in his own germs.

Out in the yard again, I noticed something about the modest lean-to which had previously escaped me: there was a small, square window in its south-facing wall. I crossed the tarmac and peered in. Though my shoulders were blocking out some of the sunlight, a work-bench could plainly be seen on the wall opposite. Anyone who'd approached this window in daylight as I was doing would have a pretty fair idea of what lay within. No doubt at some times of day it might even be possible to see whatever was hanging on the back wall, though most of it currently lay in shadow.

I moved round to the door, at right angles to the hotel's rear entrance. As Nigel had said, a pile of bricks could be found to one side of this, but I had no need to rummage behind them for the workshop key since it already showed in plain sight, sticking out of the keyhole. Quickly scanning the yard for keen-eyed police officers, I depressed the door handle with my elbow, hoping that this might leave any fingerprints on its surface relatively undisturbed. The door swung open and I stepped up into the interior. Rather than use the light switch to my left, I simply waited for my eyes to grow accustomed to the contrasting glare and gloom of the scene before me.

Meanwhile, my sense of smell was experiencing a rare treat. Above background notes of damp brickwork and something which may have been oiled cloth, a warm, complex aroma of old wood rose to the nostrils, carrying with it hints of childhood memory. As my sense of sight caught up, the likely origin of this smell now appeared. Suspended from nails and hooks on the wall to the left of me, a finer array of carpentry tools than I'd ever seen gave testimony to the late hotelier's passion, many of them boasting handles of antique wood which were objects of beauty in themselves. Awls and adzes, planes and pliers shared the space with a wide variety of drills, screwdrivers, mallets, chisels, wrenches, and everything necessary to the carpenter's craft. Small drawers in a unit beyond the work-bench must have been home to screws, nails, washers, and who knew what else. And it was clear that Nigel's father hadn't been content to rest at acquiring carpentry skills. Scattered here and there around the workshop were drums of cable and twine, short lengths of copper piping, grouting tools, buckets for mixing plaster, in fact just about anything which might have been required for conducting day-to-day repairs in the adjoining building.

But I'd not come here to admire Ian Haig's commitment to order and industry, impressive though that was. Glancing down to my left, I earned my first reward. A short, cat's-paw jemmy lay out of place on the work-top. If I'd wanted to break into the hotel, this might have been the very tool I'd have chosen. It looked as if the intruder had first entered the workshop and picked out the jemmy, used it to prise open the hotel door, then returned it without bothering to put it away properly. Had they then removed a hammer from the wall? Keeping my hands to my sides to avoid disturbing anything, I moved a little further into the room, giving myself the best possible view of the wall and its contents.

In fact, two or three hammers remained in place, alongside a selection of hatchets. A couple appeared to have some specialised use which I couldn't guess at, and to their right hung a great sledge-hammer. You could have caused serious mischief with this, but it would have been difficult to swing around in a smallish and low-ceilinged room. Between this giant and the two fancy hammers, a pair of nails close together suggested a missing object in the sequence. They'd have made an ideal resting place for the hammer which had killed Giles Rawley.

I heard someone step in through the open door. Mark Howell said, 'Thinking of taking up woodwork?'

I'd rather not have seen the man at this precise moment, but I replied affably enough. 'We did it at school. I was quite good as a matter of fact. My tea-pot stand was a thing of wonder.'

'Perhaps you should switch careers. Good carpenters are as rare as hen's teeth.'

I thought I detected an outbreak of tone in Mark's delivery. 'I've already got a career.'

'You won't have, when Hargreaves discovers you're investigating this murder.'

I regarded Mark more closely, seeking evidence that he shared the Hargreaves perspective on my activities. Finding none, I said, 'Shouldn't you be chasing me out of here? Or arresting me on a trumped-up charge?'

Mark now went so far as to touch my sleeve. I won't say he was doing this in full public view, but several resident spiders probably talked of little else for days. He said, 'It's the natural order, isn't it? Hargreaves warns you off, you defy him. I wouldn't have things any other way.'

I said, 'I suppose you've had a pretty rough morning.'

Mark looked away. 'It's the worst I've ever seen. Someone really hated that man.' His eye settled on the work-bench. 'Just a minute – this jemmy – '

'I had the same thought. Shall we try it?'

Mark took latex gloves from his jacket pocket, slipped them on, and took the jemmy outside, with me following behind like an eager apprentice. The claws seemed to match the damage to the rear door's frame perfectly. Mark said, 'I'll have to get the team out here. You'd best make yourself scarce.'

'I think there's a hammer missing.'

'In there?' I nodded, and Mark took a look for himself. Out in the sunlight again, he said, 'Could be, couldn't it. Was the key in the door like this?'

'Yeah. Apparently it normally lives behind those bricks. Either someone already knew that, or they got lucky.'

Mark said, 'It wouldn't take luck, that's the first place you'd search. So, someone found all the equipment they'd need out here, broke into the hotel, went up the back stairs – '

'What did the doc say about time of death?'

'Two or three in the morning. I can't understand why the night porter didn't hear this door being forced.'

'He's a bit deaf. In any case, he sleeps half the night, as far as I can make out. No sign of him yet, I suppose?'

'We sent a man round, but he doesn't seem to be at home. How did he get on with Giles Rawley?'

Though I'd already enjoyed the luxury of interviewing Graham Leeds, it now transpired that I'd been asking all the wrong questions. 'I haven't a clue. But he doesn't look much like a homicidal maniac, if that's what you're thinking. Besides, why would he come out here and pretend to break into the hotel?'

Mark shrugged. 'Make it look like an outside job. Hargreaves says the owner here is convinced her new neighbours did it.'

'The Goldings.' I needed to make the best use of Mark while I had him. 'Listen, Mark – what's the official line on Southaven's new first family of crime? Are we meant to be worried about them, or does the Super just think they're a shot in the arm for the local economy?'

Mark frowned, a fact which did him credit. He may only have been a Detective Constable, but it was heart-warming to note that he felt a responsibility towards his adopted home town and its citizens. 'Like I said before, the Super's not happy. What are the Goldings really doing in Southaven? Obviously Frank Golding's a major-league villain, but if they can turn a perfectly good dishonest penny in the Smoke, why up sticks and resettle in a place like this? It's an affluent town compared to some, but it's not exactly Eldorado.'

'Perhaps that's the point of the hotel. Perhaps they plan to make the money come to them.' Mark made a face, clearly unconvinced, so I added, 'Or perhaps Lou Golding really does want nothing more sinister than sea air and a quiet life.'

'On balance I'd say we're giving them the benefit of the doubt up to now. After all, Frank Golding's two older boys are the ones to watch, and they've stayed put in London. Some people think there'll be trouble here with the Malones, but there hasn't been so much as a black eye on either side yet.'

'If it was the Malones who tipped you off about illegal gambling at the Grand, you can expect some kind of retaliation.'

'I know, I know. But we can't go round expecting the worst all the time. They may decide there's room enough in town for both of them.'

'My gut instinct says that's bollocks.'

Mark smiled. 'You and your famous intuition. Have you never heard of logical deduction? Anyway, I suggest you disappear before I call in the forensic boys. Oh, by the way, I did send off that letter for you.'

I said, 'Why are you being so nice to me? You're making me nervous.'

'Because you're nice to me, that's all. Are we still on for that cuppa tomorrow afternoon?'

Pleasant as it is to be treated kindly by ex-lovers, I've never liked surprises. 'When am I going to get the bill?'

He looked astonished. 'Bill? What bill?'

'You want something, don't you? Everything comes with a price tag.'

Mark said, 'Always the same suspicious mind. Now go away, before Hargreaves comes prowling. And try to keep from under his feet, he's in a rotten enough mood these days as it is.'

In an ideal world, I'd have liked to go back into the hotel, chuck Hargreaves out of the lounge, and conduct some interviews of my own. It baffled me that the police were given precedence in cases such as this, when what was plainly needed was the clear eye of the unprejudiced outsider. I knew from my years on the force that the business of acting like a policeman takes up most of your energy, leaving only a small fraction for fighting crime. Yet DI Hargreaves had been entrusted with the case, while I was condemned to skulk in car parks.

Still, such was the way of the world. Leaving Mark to summon the crime scene boffins, and finding myself hungry for the first time since I'd caught sight of the image in Giles Rawley's mirror, I decided that if any skulking was to be done it might as well take place in the Grand Hotel Vaults, which served a tolerable ploughman's lunch.

Two minutes later I paused by the bar to greet Lena Golding. She said, 'Nice to see you looking better.'

'Someone just said I looked dreadful.'

'Obviously blind. You having the usual?'

From her manner, I presumed Lena had not yet heard the news of Giles Rawley's death. It would be better kept quiet until the police chose to release the story. I said, 'And a ploughman's while you're at it. I'll be back in a tick, got to pay a visit.'

I pushed my way through the door on the hotel side and out into the corridor. The gents toilets here were mainly used by customers of the Vaults, there being more impressive facilities elsewhere on the ground floor, so it wasn't unusual to find that you had the place to yourself. However, someone with cat-like tread must have followed me in, because when I'd finished off and was just zipping up, an unpleasant voice close behind me said, 'You're not welcome here.'

Resisting the temptation to turn round and find out who this party-pooper might be, I rebuckled my belt and said, 'That's odd. I always find the staff very friendly.'

'You'll get out now if you know what's good for you.'

I've never had much idea what's good for me, but I felt that that was a private matter between myself and whatever maleficent deity had devised my life to date. I said, 'What if I've decided I like it here?' And then I did turn, since I was getting a bit fed up of talking to the wall.

The voice, I now discovered, was the property of First Ugly Bloke. He stood just two feet away, reinforcing his message with a cold glare. A little to the north of my kidneys, activity stirred in the adrenal glands, and in the same moment memory stirred too. According to my brain's memory centres, there was a clear association between adrenalin flow and the repulsive face now before me. Catching up at last, I said, 'How's your friend's head?'

The site of our previous convocation had been a patch of waste ground in Bolton Street formerly occupied by the old railway engine sheds, and the meeting had been called so that First Ugly Bloke and two of his mates could give me a damn good kicking. If they'd seen the state I was in next morning they'd probably have been well satisfied with their work, but I was guessing that all First Ugly Bloke remembered about it was that I'd left one of his chums with a nasty crack on the head. These things rankle, but even so I was surprised by the vehemence with which he now grabbed my shoulders and shoved me back against the urinal. One foot went into the gully. I was just thinking how lucky I was not to have struck my head on the wall when I heard the cistern flush above me and a damp sensation spread down the back of my left leg. Then First Ugly Bloke's forehead darted towards me, smashed into my own, and propelled  the back of my head into the wall it had just avoided. I said, 'Ow.'

As I think I mentioned, First Ugly Bloke was a big chap, at least my height and very much heavier. Last summer he'd been working for a loan shark by the name of Joe Braithwaite, or Slasher to his intimate friends, so I knew he must have had plenty of experience in the world of rough and tumble. The wise thing now would be to play the coolest of cool hands, since I was clearly not the favourite in this particular race. What's more, I detest all violence, unless of course I happen to be in a bad mood at the time.

But whether it was the blow to the skull, or the creeping dampness about the trousers, I suddenly found myself in a very bad mood indeed. With my shoulders pinned right back, my options were limited. I spat in the man's eye.

Cleverer souls than First Ugly Bloke might have spotted the flaw in his approach to this inconvenience. He wiped the eye clean with his right hand. Consequently, I was now free to offer a spirited left hook to his jaw. This left hook of mine is pretty useful, especially when I'm in thrall to wet-trouser rage, and less substantial thugs than First Ugly Bloke would probably have gone over backwards at this point. So I was disappointed to gain no more than the removal of his hand from my other shoulder, but beggars can't be choosers and at least that allowed me to dodge past him and set a rapid course for the door. He turned, more nimbly than seemed fair, and came after me, but then I heard a cry, followed by the pleasing sound of eighteen stone of ill-will hitting the deck.

I risked a backward glance. A trail of water on the floor tiles marked my route from the urinal, and it was this which had undone my attacker. No doubt if I'd been of a more caring nature, I'd have paused a moment and found a phrase or two with which to point the moral, which I feared he might be too stupid to arrive at unaided. Instead I left him struggling to right himself like a woodlouse, and squelched out of the door back into the hotel.

## ten

There were several reasons why I didn't turn right and head back into the Vaults. Although the bottle would by now be standing on the bar, and the ploughman's would be ordered, I was suddenly feeling the dizziness and nausea resulting from twin blows to the skull, and the sight of a lump of cheese might have tipped me over the edge. In addition, I didn't want to have to explain to Lena what had just happened. I felt confused as to exactly whose warning First Ugly Bloke was passing on to me. Perhaps he'd merely spoken in his own behalf, motivated by his pal's broken head, but in that case he'd phrased the threat very oddly. Could he be working for the Goldings now? Until I'd sorted this out, it seemed unwise to sit and chat with Lena Golding. And thirdly, it was likely that First Ugly Bloke, once he'd achieved the vertical again, might follow me into the Vaults and take up from where he'd left off.

But my main reason for slinking off without ceremony was simply that when a cistern has just discharged its contents down your leg, it dulls the appetite for social life. So, as the door of the gents toilets swung shut behind me, I turned instead to the left. Adopting an air of urbane insouciance, I crossed the plush lobby of the Grand Hotel and revolved my way out through the door onto Marine Approach. Once beyond the impressive cast-iron portico I was obliged to duck down as I passed the windows of the Vaults in case Lena happened to be looking out, but then I was in the clear and making for Wright Street and the Minx. Perhaps by the time I saw Lena next I'd have worked out a plausible explanation for my disappearance.

Half an hour later, suffering no worse after-effects from my encounter with Southaven's premier bruiser than a slight headache, I picked up the telephone in my office and put a call through to Matt's hotel. A subordinate answered, but although she seemed willing enough, my request over-stretched her limited powers. As I waited for her to fetch the proprietor I glanced out past the naked trees to the sunlit upper stories opposite. During the summer months, leaves prevented proper study of the Boulevard's architecture, but at this time of year there was a possibility that I might notice some curious feature for the first time – a hexagonal attic window, perhaps, or an area of decorative tiling. The builders of ninety years ago had thrown pretty well everything they'd got at the Boulevard, and though sometimes I couldn't be sure that I liked it there was no denying the thrill of discovery when some unexpected touch of Moorish influence suddenly emerged amongst the predominant Gothic and Italianate.

'Hobhouse.' A voice, at last.

'Ah, Mr Hobhouse, my name's Rigby, Sam Rigby. Can I leave a message for one of your residents?'

'Which resident would that be?'

'Mr Standish.'

'Certainly you can. I'll get a pen. Oh, there's one here. Fire away.'

'If you could just ask him to return to Southaven immediately.

It doesn't matter if he hasn't finished the job yet, this takes priority.'

There was a pause while Hobhouse set to work. 'Return – Southaven – Just a moment, the damn thing's run out. Be with you in two shakes!'

A clunk now informed me that the proprietor of the Mafeking Court private hotel had put down the receiver. As Matt had said, it was a very cheap hotel, and perhaps it was too much to expect that the boss should have ready access to functional writing equipment. I tried to ease the tedium of a longish wait by resuming my architectural studies, but the mood had passed. Sensing discomfort, I flexed my toes in the shoes I'd changed into earlier. They were my smart pair, kept in reserve for the kind of high-toned events to which I was never invited, and though several years old now they'd never truly been worn in. Still, at least they were dry, as were my trousers. I'd been in and out of Leigh Terrace in no more than ten minutes, and I was beginning to regret that I hadn't eaten two fish paste sandwiches instead of just the one.

'Sorry about that.' Hobhouse was back. 'Mrs Hobhouse wanted a word about the stair carpet. You wouldn't believe what residents drag into the building with them, and because they mostly go straight upstairs it all ends up on the carpet, doesn't it? I'm trying to persuade Mrs Hobhouse that we should be done with the carpet altogether and keep to the bare boards, but she just says 'What about the noise, John, what about the noise?' Have you ever run a hotel, Mr Wrigley?'

'It's Rigby, Sam Rigby.'

'Well, don't. It's far more bother than it's worth, let me tell you. And then the ingratitude of the average member of the British public defies belief. The things I've had said to me at this counter, I'd blush to repeat them.'

Hoping that he wouldn't go on to repeat them all the same, I said, 'Did you find a pen?'

'What? Oh, yes, I did. Now, what was the message again?' So I told him, and with no more than two or three interruptions while he attended to crises which had arisen at his end of the line,

Hobhouse wrote it all down.

I said, 'Thanks for that. Sorry to have taken your time, but it's important.'

'You're very welcome. We always like to go the extra mile at Mafeking Court. Mind you, there's not much chance he'll get the message.'

I could feel wobbly things happening in my body. 'I don't understand.'

'Mr Standish checked out this morning.'

All along, an inner voice had been telling me that no good would come from the direction of the man Hobhouse, but this still came as a shock. 'Checked out?'

'Straight after breakfast. In fact, I don't believe he even ate breakfast, he seemed in a hurry to leave. An extremely pleasant young man, I dealt with him myself. He particularly wanted me to know that in all his life he'd never had a night's sleep to compare with the one he'd experienced last night. I was quite touched, to be honest. Not that he left any form of gratuity, but I suppose times are hard, aren't they.'

'Did he say where he was going?'

'No. But if he does happen to come back for any reason, I'll give him your message straight away.'

I rang off and did some pacing. This, of course, is where having unobstructed floor space comes into its own. A confirmed pacer, I find the restrictive environment at Leigh Terrace something of a challenge. Only at Crowburn Estates can I really let rip. In the early months I'd worried that I might be disturbing the Old Man, whose office lies beneath my own, but it turned out he was far too deaf to notice the rhythmic thuds above his head.

What was Matt up to? For a moment my spirits had risen at the idea that he must have made a breakthrough in the Gordon Asprey case the previous night, and left Manchester this morning with the evidence safely on film and a satisfied smile on his face. But if that was so, he'd have been back in Southaven several hours ago, and I'd have heard from him by now. It seemed more likely that the punishing conditions at Mafeking Court had got the better of him, and he'd decided to find somewhere else to stay. In which case I had no way of contacting him.

I stopped pacing, sat down at the desk again, and had a word with myself. It was no use over-reacting like this whenever young Standish went AWOL. I was perfectly capable of handling the Giles Rawley affair on my own. After all, I'd been working alone for seven years before Matt turned up, and there'd been several occasions when the business had even begun to show promise. I needed to get a grip.

Retrieving my contacts file from the cabinet, I made another call. After a couple of false starts, I was soon talking, for the first time in half a dozen years, to Detective Sergeant Charles 'Chubby' Fallon of the Metropolitan Police.

'Sam! Well, you've made my day. I was telling Melanie about you only last weekend, but I never thought I'd be hearing from the man himself. What's up? Keeping out of trouble?'

This was the second time today that a member of Her Majesty's CID had been nice to me, and you might suppose I'd have welcomed this unreservedly. Sadly, there was a dark side to being singled out for Chubby Fallon's attentions. When we'd been colleagues of unequal rank on the Southaven force, Fallon had displayed a habit of doing me favours which I'd neither requested nor desired, but which in time he would inevitably call in. Somehow he arranged it that most of us stood in his debt one way or another, so that when he needed a blind eye to be turned to some irregularity he could always rely on us to cover for him. Towards the end, rumours were going round the station that he was protecting certain local interests in exchange for cash, but if anyone had conclusive evidence of this they were too much in hock to Fallon to risk producing it.

Then, just when things were starting to look difficult for him, he'd met a London girl on holiday, married her, and taken a job with the Met. Two years ago, they'd sent him under cover into the Golding organization, and now Frank Golding was behind bars.

I said, 'Yeah, I'm fine. No change really.'

'Still sleuthing?'

'Like a man possessed. By the way, congratulations for that nifty bit of work with Frank Golding.'

'You heard about that?'

'This may be Southaven, but national newspapers do occasionally get through. You must have been pleased with yourself.'

'Well – ' Fallon didn't sound pleased with himself at all. His voice became confidential. 'As a matter of fact, Sam, I'd been hoping there might be a promotion in it. I'm forty-three, if I don't get DI in the next year or two it may never happen. And Melanie's a wonderful woman, but there's no denying she has expensive tastes.'

I tut-tutted sympathetically. 'Any idea why they're not playing ball?'

'Nothing I'd care to discuss over the phone. Anyway, I don't suppose there's any hope of you coming up to town? You owe me a beer, if I remember rightly.'

'That's not true, I owe you six or seven. You thought it might be amusing to get me drunk on my birthday and see what happened.'

'What did happen?'

'Nothing, or I'd never have heard the last of it. If you want a return match you'll have to come up here, I'm afraid. You know my views on London.'

'I'm surprised at you. It's paradise for queers these days, there's new clubs opening all the time. We raided one just last week.'

'You call that paradise? And you try to make out you're broad-minded!'

'It's not me, Sam, it's the job. People can do what they like as far as I'm concerned.'

This was all interesting enough in its way, but it wasn't Chubby Fallon who'd be paying my next phone bill. So I said, 'Speaking of which, what exactly do the Goldings like to do now that Frank's cooling his heels?'

It may have been my imagination, but I thought Fallon hesitated before replying. 'Why the sudden interest in metropolitan crime? Southaven not lively enough for you?'

'I suppose you know Lou Golding's living here now? She bought herself a hotel.'

'Is that right? I don't really keep up with the family news since my cover was blown.'

'Really? Not even for old times' sake?'

'As it happens I think I did hear that Lou had moved out of town. Have you met her yet?'

'No. But I know the twins.'

'Lena and Mickey. Sweet kids, I thought. Seemed a bit out of place in their dad's empire.'

'So you wouldn't have any clue why their mother chose Southaven for her new base of operations?'

'I'm not sure I like the way you say "operations".' To do the man justice, I had possibly coloured the word a little. 'Can't a woman buy a hotel these days without criminal intent?'

'What's she like?'

'Lou Golding?' Chubby Fallon thought this over for a moment or two. 'Let me put it this way: if I had to choose between meeting Lou or Frank up a dark alley, I'd pick Frank any day.'

'And how about the other boys? Are they keeping busy?'

'Like I said, I don't know much about it any more. But it's no secret they've been developing gambling interests.'

'Casinos?'

'Not just that. There's only so much money you can make in the legitimate game. The big cash is in private clubs.'

'You mean, unlicensed places? Surely they just get closed down?'

Fallon chuckled. 'If we can find them, yeah. The whole reason these places exist is because wealthy punters want a chance to play outside the law – high stakes, fancy rules, winner takes all. It's a closed world, we never get a look-in.'

'I don't suppose Lou's involved in anything like that? She tried to open a casino at the hotel but they turned down her licence application.'

'I'm sure it was all above board. She won't want no hassle with Frank inside. It's the boys you've got to keep your eye on now. Frank Golding was old school – robbery, extortion, that kind of thing. The boys want to modernise, bring the whole machine up to date. But tell me, Sam – apart from knowing the twins, what's your interest in all this?'

I thought it better not to name names, so I just said, 'Lou Golding's been putting pressure on a couple of my clients. She's trying to acquire property without the bourgeois formality of paying for it first.'

'Are you sure? I'd have expected her to be keeping a low profile.'

'Listen, Chubby, what do you know about a firm of solicitors called Tipton, Buxton and Lamb?'

Fallon laughed. Whenever he did this, it usually turned out to be at your expense somehow. He said, 'Why, were you thinking of making a will?'

'Not really.'

'I would, if I were you. That is, if you intend to have dealings with Tipton and Co. They smooth the way for some of the nastiest villains in the East End.'

'Including the Goldings?'

'Maybe. Now, if that's all, I'd better be getting back to the job.'

This came abruptly, but I had no particular claim on Fallon's time so I said, 'Thanks, Chubby, you've been a great help.'

'Who's this Chubby you keep on about? No one calls me that here. I've slimmed down, doctor's orders. Weight training, squash with the DI three times a week.'

This surprised me. I found it hard to picture the man without the excess weight he'd formerly carried. But that wasn't the only thing which had changed. I said, 'You realize you're losing your accent? You've gone native.'

'Have I? Well, you know how it is. You adapt to what's around you. Anyway, I'd best be off. Lucky you caught me today, me and Mel are off skiing tomorrow.'

'Aviemore?'

'Don't make me laugh! Chamonix, we go every year. But listen, Sam, seriously now – don't mess with the Goldings, all right? I wouldn't like to see you get hurt.'

'I never knew you cared.'

'I don't. But if you fetch up on some tip with your throat slit, who's going to buy the beers next time I'm in Southaven?'

'You'll be back then, will you?'

'Course I will. My grandad sold oysters up near the Prom, the place is in my blood. Ta-ta for now. And give my love to that bastard Hargreaves.' He rang off.

I pushed my chair away from the desk and stared at the phone. It stared back. Perhaps if I examined it long enough it might provide the key to that puzzling call. About half way through, I'd started to wonder if it hadn't been a big mistake talking to Chubby Fallon. He was always a dark horse, and now he'd spent months under cover with the Goldings. What if he'd gone native there, too? What if every word I'd said was going to be passed on?

But if that was true, why tell me so much about the latest exploits of the Golding boys? He'd given me exactly the lead I needed. Perhaps the raid at the Grand Hotel which Mark Howell had led the previous night had been justified after all, and somewhere in the building Lou Golding had managed to establish a private gambling club so well hidden that it could continue to do business right under the watchful eyes of Southaven's finest. If so, and if I could prove it, then I would have the upper hand, and Alice Haig and Sidney Flint would have nothing more to fear. Of course, it would mean failing to report criminal activity, and the law might take a dim view of that if it ever came to light, but I'd have to cross that bridge when I came to it.

The more I thought about it, the more Fallon's behaviour made sense. If he was still on the Goldings' payroll – and someone must be shelling out for those skiing holidays – then he would have to dish selective dirt on them from time to time to avoid his chums in the Met becoming suspicious. And like he'd said, there was no secret about the Golding boys' gambling operation, or the dodgy solicitors come to that. Any of his colleagues could easily have given me the same information.

What didn't make sense was this: if Fallon had gone native in Frank Golding's criminal network, why did he have Frank put away?

Despite prolonged study, the phone on my desk seemed unable to answer this question, or any other for that matter. My brain was hurting, so I decided to employ it on a more routine task, and spent the next hour typing notes of what had happened at Marine Lodge, keeping strictly to the facts and postponing any form of speculation. I then took out fresh paper and wrote by hand a list of everyone I could think of who might have been involved in Giles Rawley's murder, no matter how unlikely a culprit: the Goldings, or someone acting on their behalf; Alice Haig; Laurence Glass; Sarkis Aznavorian; Rosemary Pyle; Oscar Hammond; Graham Leeds. Then, a little reluctantly, I added Cordelia Lane to the list. I paced for a while, then sat again and wrote three further names for the sake of completeness: Nigel Haig; his sister Bobbie; and finally Evan Bickerstaff. Mrs Clark the housekeeper would have featured too, but apparently she and her husband had been up half the night nursing their precious cat, which had bowel trouble and wasn't expected to survive.

Even without Mrs Clark it was a very long list, and I found myself heaving a deep sigh. Any one of these people would have been physically capable of the murder. If Rawley had been sleeping at the time, stealth and accuracy would have been far more important than brute strength. A single, fluid motion could have carried the murder weapon in a sweeping arc above the murderer's head, building momentum as it travelled. Aimed correctly, the first blow would surely have been fatal. But it was clear enough from the state of the body that other, vicious blows had followed. Either the murderer hated the victim, as Mark had suggested, or they took pride in seeing a job well done.

If I was to keep an uncluttered view of all these people, I knew I'd have to confront my prejudices first. In my years on the force, time and again I'd seen suspects fingered for no better reason than the prejudice of the investigating officer. In the present case, who exactly were my inner judge and jury itching to send down?

I didn't like Cordelia Lane. My reluctance to write her name had stemmed simply from unwillingness to shatter Giles's illusion that his daughter was a 'good girl'. Of course, there'd been plenty of tears that morning, but I thought Cordelia was a manipulative piece of work who couldn't wait to get her hands on her father's money.

I didn't like Laurence Glass either. He was a ladies' man, and the way he carried on around Alice Haig turned my stomach. He'd had a bad war and I should have felt sorry for him, but I didn't.

And finally, I didn't like First Ugly Bloke. He was violent and stupid, and every time I'd met him to date I'd had to wash my trousers afterwards. If Lou Golding had told him to kill Giles, I had no doubt that he could have done it without compunction and then gone straight home and slept the innocent sleep of babes.

Now I added 'First Ugly Bloke' to the list alongside 'someone acting on behalf of the Goldings', and drew boxes around his name and Glass's and Cordelia's. Then I sat back and admired my work. I felt a lot better for making my feelings about these people explicit. Unfortunately, the fact that I disliked them didn't make them guilty, or get me any closer to solving the crime.

I locked up the office, briefly considered calling in on Aunt Winnie and Uncle Fred, but then let myself out via the front door of the building instead. It was possible that my aunt had forgotten how I'd spoken to her on the phone the previous morning, but I didn't feel up to finding out. I collected the Minx from the back yard and drove home. The earlier promise of spring had now passed, and a cloudy sky heralded rain. I parked in front of Leigh Terrace, then walked around the corner to buy fish and chips. I was about as hungry as it's possible to be without actually eating your own arm.

Having eased the pangs by scoffing selected chips on my way back to the flat, I struck a blow for civilisation by transferring everything that remained onto an actual plate and eating it with an actual knife and fork. I'd have considered dining at the kitchen table, too, but for the fact that I was just in time to catch the TV news. With a tray on my knees, I watched while both the national news and Look North neglected to mention the death of Giles Rawley. Perhaps the police had been tardy in releasing the information. Though Giles was never a household name, his face would have been familiar enough to many people, and I felt convinced that his murder wouldn't go unreported in the national media.

While I was dumping the plate in the sink and making a mental note to wash it up at some point, together with the various other items which had somehow collected there since Matt's last visit to the flat, there was a distinctive knock at the door. This listless, trailing motif, like the last stirrings of a sick death-watch beetle, announced the weekly appearance of Dennis the rent boy. I let him in, and we moved into the sitting room to conduct our business.

If anything, Dennis was looking even less robust than usual. The pale, hollow cheeks seemed paler and hollower, and two fresh pimples had erupted on his chin. His hair drooped in an oily slick over one eye. Dennis liked to start work at the top of the building and continue downward, and he was still wheezing asthmatically from the long climb. As a rule I didn't attempt conversation with him, since experience taught that he would sooner have his toe-nails ripped off than engage in small talk, but nevertheless I said, 'So how are you these days, Dennis?'

He looked suspicious. In a quiet monotone he said, 'All right.'

'I'm not detecting your usual zest and sparkle. Feeling peaky at all? You realize there's a thing going round? I've had it myself, and believe me, you don't want it. And here you are, out without a scarf! It's madness.' Of course, if Dennis had worn a scarf it might have suggested that he or someone else cared about him, and his image would have been ruined. Only a thin raincoat with one button missing protected him from the elements.

Dennis made no effort to respond to this show of concern for his health. Realizing that my conversational gambit had failed, I fell silent, and Dennis then said, 'Haven't you got the money?'

'What makes you say that?'

'When people haven't got the money, they talk instead.'

'I was being friendly Dennis, that's all. Perhaps you'd like to sit down. I could make you a cup of tea if you want.' He looked suspicious again, so I abandoned the idea of tea and said, 'Nearly finished for today?'

'I'm just starting.'

'A good time to catch people at home, Friday tea-time. I expect you'll be going out on the town afterwards, will you? Meeting friends? Going to the pictures?' And it seemed unlikely, but I added, 'Seeing – a girlfriend, perhaps?'

Dennis said, 'I need to get on.'

'Naturally, yes. The money's just here.' It was Sidney Flint who'd been responsible for this latest doomed effort to draw out Dennis's sociable side. Until I could neutralize the Goldings, Sidney remained vulnerable, and I'd not liked the defensive way he'd responded when I asked if he was hiding anything. As a result, I found myself curious about Sidney's world. Dennis fitted into that world somewhere, but how?

I fetched the envelope containing my rent from the mantelpiece. It was my practice to set aside the rent money quite early in the week if possible, since childhood experience had induced in me a horror of homelessness. Now I crossed back towards Dennis, but instead of handing over the envelope I held it up by one finger and thumb and said, 'How long have you known Mr Flint?'

'Mr Flint?'

'Your employer. Tall bloke, yellow skin. I'm doing a job for him at present and it would help if I had a little more background information. I was just wondering how long you'd known him.'

'Mr Flint doesn't like me talking.'

'You'll not get into trouble, Dennis, I promise. Sidney particularly told me that I could count on your full cooperation.'

'He never said anything to me.'

'I expect it slipped his mind. He's trying to resolve a very difficult matter at present, I'm sure you wouldn't want to stand in his way.'

'I'd never do that. But – '

'So how exactly did you come to work for him?'

Dennis was eyeing the envelope hungrily, not, I imagined, from cupidity, but rather from a deep desire to regain control of his evening. But still he managed to say, 'I suppose I've always worked for Mr Flint.'

As this was the first personal question I'd ever known Dennis to answer, I allowed a brief pause in case the event should be marked by an earthquake, a thunder-bolt, or a plague of frogs. When none came, I said, 'Always?'

'They used to send us out to do odd jobs for people.'

Hoping to reduce the distracting influence of the envelope, I let my hand fall to my side and put an extra couple of steps between myself and Dennis's waif-like figure. 'When you say, "they" – ?'

'The home. I was in care. Cheshire House.'

I knew the place, further out of town along Preston Road. 'And Sidney was one of the people you were sent to?'

'Then when I left at sixteen, he took me on full time.'

'Where were you living then?'

'A bed-sit in one of his properties, not far from where Mr Flint lives himself. It made it more convenient if he needed me at short notice.'

'And now?'

'Now what?'

'I mean, where do you live now?'

'Oh, the same. I've never left.'

I moved even further off. My mind was busy, but I couldn't quite make out what it was up to. I said, 'I expect Sidney is a reasonably good employer?' Actually I expected nothing of the kind, but I felt that I was walking on eggshells here.

'The best. I never want for anything.'

It would be going too far to claim that this reply was made with real vigour or animation, yet some such force did seem to lie behind it. In my own experience, Sidney Flint was a miserable, tight-fisted rogue who could have gone on to play Scrooge without rehearsal, but it was evident that Dennis saw things differently. I might be baffled, but I would have to accept that his loyalty to Sidney was quite genuine.

Noticing my lapse into silence, Dennis seized the day. 'Can I have the money now?'

There was no point in pushing my luck, but I was just about to hand over the envelope when memory kicked in. 'Hang on a moment – I'm giving you too much. There's four pound ten in here.' I took out the ten bob note, meaning to replace it with five shillings in change.

'But that's correct.'

'Not any more. Sidney and I did a deal, he's knocked off five bob.'

Once again Dennis said, 'He never said anything to me.'

I wished devoutly that Dennis and Sidney would learn to communicate a little more. 'You see, Dennis, I'm doing this job for him at a special rate, so he said he'd reduce my rent.'

Dennis said, 'That doesn't sound very likely.' Inconveniently, that was true. 'You'll have to take it up with Mr Flint. Give me the full whack now, and if he agrees then I'll just collect four quid next time.'

With heavy heart I passed the envelope to Dennis, who checked the contents, pocketed it, and signed my rent book. I had a strong suspicion that Flint would find some way of dishonouring his side of our bargain, while still obliging me to honour mine.

Only when Dennis had drifted out of the flat to resume his round did it occur to me that I should have called Sidney in Dennis's presence and clarified the whole affair. Though it was too late for that now, I rang him anyway. He was disposed to be helpful. 'Of course, Sam, I'll mention it to the lad before next week, never you fear. I've always been one hundred per cent straight in my business dealings, and I'm too old to change now. How've you been getting on about these Tipton people?'

'The letter went off today.'

'Not by courier, I hope?' The note of alarm in his voice was pitiful.

'It won't cost you a penny, Sidney. By the way, I've checked up, and I'm pretty certain Tipton's are acting for the Goldings.'

'Criminals on my back after all these years! I blame that Wilson chappie, worst prime minister we've ever had. No wonder there's a crime wave! Heath's got his work cut out, and that's a fact.'

'Cheer up, Sidney. I'm starting to get an angle on the Goldings. If things go our way, they might soon be in no position to make threats. But listen – and don't take offence again, I'm only doing my job – are you absolutely sure they've got nothing on you? I can't help you if you don't square with me.'

There was a brief silence. Then, in a low voice, Sidney said, 'I'm beginning to wish I'd never placed this matter in your hands. My word is my bond, it always has been. If you can't learn to believe what I say, I may be forced to terminate our arrangement.' He hung up on me.

I had mixed feelings about this. On the one hand it suggested that I might no longer be Sidney Flint's best friend. On the other, at least now I had a shrewd idea what his weak spot might be.

## eleven

It was around seven fifteen when I tried the back door of the Marine Lodge and found it unlocked. With admirable efficiency, Alice Haig had already got someone in to effect a temporary repair. How she'd felt able to deal with such mundane matters on a day of high drama like this, I could only imagine.

After a quick call to Alice to check that the police were now off the premises, I'd decided to walk over to the hotel, enjoying a placid cigarette as I went. The evening was cold but fine, and the onshore breeze down Marine Approach seemed no worse than usual. The walk had helped me to clarify my thoughts, and as I stepped into the back corridor I was looking forward to this first opportunity of interviewing suspects in the case of Giles Rawley's murder.

Oscar Hammond was in the kitchen, just where I'd left him at lunchtime. The trolley stood near him, and he was in the process of pouring custard from a pan onto portions of what might have been fruit pie or crumble in three separate bowls. I waited until this delicate operation had been completed before saying, 'Evening, Oscar. Could I have a word?'

He looked up at me without warmth, then across towards the dining room door, which had been wedged open. 'Not a good time. I need to finish off these dinners.'

'Of course. What if I come back in an hour or so?'

'Suit yourself.' He took the pan to the sink and ran water into it. I noticed the brandy bottle on the work-top again, though in truth I couldn't be sure that it was still the same one.

Leaving Oscar to his work, I went on through to the lobby. There was no one at the counter, but a light showed round the office door. I knocked. Alice Haig said, 'Yes?'

She was seated at her desk, the account books open in front of her. Her face was flushed, and the tight perm had once more begun to slip its moorings. 'Oh – Mr Rigby, come in. Sit down, won't you. What an extraordinary day! I'm not sure whether this is a dream or a nightmare, but I'm certain I can't be awake.'

These unusually fanciful observations from Alice Haig added to the impression that she was in no ordinary state of mind. I said, 'What time did the police leave?'

'About six. It was such a relief to have command of my own hotel again. That man Hargreaves spent the entire day issuing orders like a little Hitler. If he'd stayed a minute longer, we'd have come to blows.'

I knew the feeling, but decided it might be unprofessional to say so. 'Did everyone turn up eventually?'

'I'm sorry?'

'Graham Leeds? Mr Aznavorian?'

'Oh, I see. Yes, they did. Apparently the police found Graham in a betting shop on Mission Street.' Alice Haig's delivery of the words *betting shop* left little room for doubt as to how she viewed these fairly recent additions to the town's life. 'I had no idea he went in for such things, it quite shook me.'

'Did he have anything new to tell us? I thought he'd be on duty now.'

'The Detective Inspector kept him waiting a long time before talking to him. Afterwards he was practically falling asleep where he stood. I sent him home to get some rest and said he could come back at midnight. He seemed terribly upset about everything, and he kept apologizing as if I must somehow think Giles's death was all his fault, just because he'd not happened to hear anything. As a matter of fact, he offered his resignation.'

I hoped Alice had seized this chance to be rid of a liability. 'So you'll be looking for another night porter?'

She looked guilty. 'Well – no. I couldn't let Graham go, could I? He's been here such a long time, and since he lost his wife I think he rather depends on the job to give shape to his day. I'm sure Ian would have kept him on.'

Privately, I reflected that if the Marine Lodge was to survive, Alice Haig needed to make up her mind whether she was a hard-headed businesswoman or a sentimental fool in thrall to her late husband's memory. I said, 'You look as if you could do with a rest yourself.'

'It's out of the question, someone has to stay on the desk through the evening. I was forced to ask Bobbie to make something for Nigel's tea, and she's pretty hopeless in the kitchen.'

'Couldn't Oscar have rustled something up?'

'Oscar likes to keep a strong professional boundary, and I must say I agree with him. It would never do to have him start cooking for the family as well as the guests. Oh, I meant to thank you for looking in on Nigel earlier. What with one thing and another, I've still not been up to see him. He's picked a very bad time to be ill.'

From anyone else, this remark could have been taken as humorous, but it was possible that Alice Haig genuinely believed her son to be acting out of bloody-mindedness. I said, 'And how's the other patient?' Alice pretended not to understand, so I said, 'Major Glass.'

'I'm told he's stable. He's in no danger. They're not even sure that it was a heart attack, it may have been more of a nervous thing. The Major has a history – '

'I know.' For some reason, I didn't want to hear all about the poor Major and his terrible experiences. I tried changing the subject. 'Did the police catch up with Mr Aznavorian?'

'As a matter of fact, they didn't. You'd think that car would stick out like a sore thumb, but perhaps the police aren't very observant these days. He and Miss Pyle came back at about four o'clock, still blithely unaware that anything had happened. And I don't think they were of any more use to DI Hargreaves than Graham had been. They both said they'd neither seen nor heard anything of interest last night.'

All the same, I was looking forward to questioning them. There was the small matter of the bag which I'd seen Aznavorian loading into the back of the car, and then of course I'd never trusted Rosemary Pyle's rather saccharine demeanour. Perhaps Giles's lurid view of her had been correct, though why she might want Giles dead I had no idea.

'By the way, Mr Rigby, you were right about the will.'

Alice Haig had dropped this statement into the conversation gingerly, as if unsure whether she should be voicing it aloud. Her eyes roamed freely, settling anywhere but on my own. I said, 'How right, exactly?'

'Giles named me as the chief beneficiary. They phoned the solicitor this afternoon. It's all very awkward.' And now she did look at me, but I couldn't read her expression. There was vulnerability in it, and alarm, but I thought perhaps I could see calculation too.

'Awkward? I'd have thought you'd be pleased.'

'And I am, of course, in a way. As far as the business is concerned, this changes everything.'

'Do you know how much you can expect?'

'Not yet. But it seems Giles had inherited a lot of property from his father, in Hove I think, and it's likely to be worth a good deal. He owned shares, too, and government bonds. Astonishing, he never expressed any interest in that sort of thing.'

'Some people don't talk about money.'

'You're right, Giles would have considered it vulgar. But there it is, just the same. I'll be able to pay off all the debts. We can invest in the hotel again, do all the work that's been neglected. We could even think of expanding.'

I couldn't help noticing the use of the plural pronoun, but I didn't want to interrupt Alice Haig in full flow to ask for clarification.

Still seeming flushed and excited, at least in comparison with her usual stiffness and reserve, Alice Haig went on. 'But where you had it absolutely right was the effect that this would have on the Detective Inspector. He called me straight back in and went over everything I'd told him before as if he didn't believe a single word of it.'

'I'm afraid you've got an excellent motive and no alibi.'

'Where else would I be at two in the morning but tucked up in bed? And of course no one can vouch for that. If Nigel had only been as ill as Mrs Clark's cat, I might have been up and seeing to him, but the children have always tended to nurse themselves through their illnesses.'

'So the fact is that you could easily have slipped out, broken into your own hotel to make it look like an intruder, and murdered Giles with the hammer which you knew could be found in your husband's workshop.'

This time I had no difficulty in reading Alice Haig's expression, in which coldness and hostility formed the key elements. 'You're beginning to sound like that awful man Hargreaves. But how did you know about the hammer?'

'Were you able to identify it?'

'Yes, I'm sure it was one of Ian's. I've often seen him use it. The Inspector got a lot of mileage out of that, and he simply wouldn't let go. By the end of the interview I'd started to believe that I must be mixed up in this horrible murder somehow after all.'

It may not have been diplomatic, but I smiled. 'You've got to hand it to him. There's nobody can touch Hargreaves when it comes to piling on the pressure.'

'Then I came out of the lounge and walked straight into Cordelia. She looked daggers at me.'

'Why? I don't understand.'

'It was the first time I'd seen her since the details of the will had emerged, she'd been up in her room telephoning. She said I'd manipulated a fragile old man and I should be ashamed of myself.'

'Fragile? That's hardly right, is it? But you've not told me what was in the rest of the will.'

Alice collected her thoughts. 'Well, it was embarrassingly simple. The other two daughters each receive a relatively small cash legacy. They're both very well-placed, of course, Giles knew he didn't have to worry about them. Then Cordelia's four children receive similar sums, to be held in trust until they're twenty-five.'

'He's making them wait, isn't he?'

'But you realize why that is? Giles wanted to give them every chance to be beyond their father's influence when they came into possession of the cash. Giles was dead set against Howard Lane.'

'What about Cordelia?'

'She gets nothing. Not a bean.'

I whistled. Though I understood that Giles had been no angel, the gesture seemed cruel nevertheless. 'Presumably he was afraid that giving money to Cordelia was no better than giving it to her husband directly.'

Alice Haig leaned back and drew a deep breath. 'Well, there you have it, Mr Rigby. Apart from a bequest to the Actors' Benevolent Fund, everything else came to me.'

'Do you know when Giles made the will?'

'That's the remarkable thing. It was last week.'

I sat forward. 'Then his solicitor's in Southaven?'

'No, in Sussex. It was all done by post.'

'There is no post.'

'Then I suppose they must have used a courier.'

'Yes, at vast expense. Which tells you how much importance Giles attached to it. I would imagine someone here must have witnessed the thing.'

'Perhaps so. I hadn't thought of that.'

'Do you know what was in the previous will?'

'I only know what the Inspector told me.'

I found myself getting to my feet. There was such a rush of activity in my brain that if I hadn't displaced some physical energy there might have been another Windscale. 'I need to start work. They should have finished dinner by now.'

'Miss Pyle and Mr Aznavorian usually take coffee in the lounge. I've no idea what Cordelia will be doing. She seemed to be on the telephone for most of the afternoon.'

'Has she been in touch with the sisters?'

'Yes, they'll be joining her in Southaven as soon as they can.'

I said, 'More guests for the hotel, at any rate.'

'Apparently they're staying at the Grand.' She managed to make the Grand sound like the last place on earth any reasonable person would wish to stay.

I said, 'A bit of a low blow.'

'Cordelia told me to my face that Marine Lodge wasn't quite up to the standard her sisters are used to. She and I have always got on reasonably well, but I think that's history now.'

Alice left her chair and followed me to the office door. I said, 'Any chance I could have a quick look at Giles's room?'

The familiar look of anxiety settled on Alice's face, no doubt reinforced by the pummelling she'd received from Harry Hargreaves earlier in the day. She said, 'It's all locked up, I'm not to allow anyone in there.'

'But I need to view the crime scene.'

'I would have thought you'd seen more than enough this morning.'

'I wasn't in the right frame of mind.'

'If that man Hargreaves finds out – '

It depressed me to consider how often Hargreaves had obstructed my investigations in the years since I'd left the force. In the present case, everything depended on whether Alice Haig was more afraid of Hargreaves or of being sent down for murder. It could go either way. I said, 'But he won't find out, will he? I'll not touch anything, I just want to refresh my memory about the layout.'

Alice still looked doubtful.

I said, 'The way things are, Hargreaves won't get off your back until you're serving life in Holloway.' And I held out my hand.

Without another word, Alice went back to her desk, removed the key to room 21 from a drawer, and crossed to give it to me. I nodded and went out into the lobby. There was no sign of life, so I moved on quietly round to the back stairs and climbed to the second floor. When I'd unlocked the door I took the key out again in case anyone came by, then went into the room, pushed the door shut behind me and switched on the harsh centre light.

The towels which had been lying on the floor that morning had been taken away, and the sheets on the bed had been removed, together with the body itself. Otherwise everything remained as I'd seen it before. In the corner ahead of me, an old armchair stood placed to catch light from the window, and a newspaper, somewhat disordered, had been draped over one arm, waiting for Giles to finish reading it. The other arm carried some items of underclothing. The dressing table was furnished with an old-fashioned toilet set of hairbrush, hand mirror and clothes brush, which kept company with a large number of personal items – several pairs of cufflinks, Giles's watch with its brown leather strap, a few copper coins and so on – which had been set down tidily on the mahogany surface. A fancy ball-point pen lay next to a wooden rack which held hotel notepaper and envelopes. In the next corner, a pair of trousers on a hanger had been suspended from one handle of the ornate wardrobe, which failed to match the dressing table or indeed any other furniture in the room. Bedside tables flanked the bed. One held a telephone, the other a lamp, an alarm clock and three library books in their plastic covers. Top of the pile was a biography of Edith Evans, but dried blood on the spines prevented me from reading the titles of the other books. A large volume of Shakespeare's complete works peeped out from the shelf beneath. There was more blood on the bedhead, and splattered upward on the wall behind. On the floor near my feet, Giles's slippers remained where he'd left them when he'd got into bed. His dressing gown hung from a hook behind the door.

For a moment I closed my eyes and tried to picture the man whose last home this had been. He soon stepped forward, a Scotch and soda in his hand, his eyes regarding me humorously (though the lazy eye never quite participated fully in the actions of its neighbour), and some apt quotation from the Bard on his lips. 'One man in his time plays many parts.' True enough, but I'd meant to ask Giles why he'd chosen to direct that remark so particularly to me, as he was leaving his birthday tea party. Too late to ask him now. I opened my eyes again, found the room much as I'd left it, and decided to get out quick, before the rising temptation to ransack every last drawer for evidence became too great to resist.

After returning the key to Alice Haig, who was taking a telephone booking at the reception desk, I went in search of the three remaining guests of the hotel. The dining room stood empty, with the door from the kitchen now closed. I passed along the corridor. Through the glass panels of the lounge doors I could see Rosemary Pyle and Sarkis Aznavorian, seated in armchairs to either side of a coffee table which hosted their empty cups. Though a copy of the Times lay on Aznavorian's knee, he'd not been reading it. The two friends were deep in conversation.

They looked up as I came into the room, now restored to its usual arrangement after serving as Hargreaves' HQ. Rosemary Pyle's face instantly adopted the smile which was her calling card. 'Mr Rigby! How nice.'

'Sorry to disturb. Would it be a good time to ask you both a few questions?'

Aznavorian said, 'Questions! There seems to be a bull market in questions today.' He didn't sound very pleased about it.

'Now, Sarkis,' said Miss Pyle, 'that's hardly Mr Rigby's fault, is it? Why don't you sit down, Mr Rigby? Alice warned us that we could expect a further interrogation.'

Still determined to be churlish, Aznavorian said, 'I expect you'll want to pick us off one at a time.' He'd seemed affable enough at the tea party, even when under attack from Giles Rawley, and the change in him surprised me.

I drew up a chair and made a third at the coffee table. 'It might save time to see you both together.'

'That's something, at any rate.' Aznavorian now set aside the newspaper, as if puzzled as to how it had found its way onto his lap. 'Rosemary and I have no secrets from one another.'

'How was your day out?'

'Eh?'

I'd temporarily forgotten that Sarkis Aznavorian was hard of hearing. 'Did you enjoy your trip to Lytham?'

'Oh, yes, yes. Didn't we, my dear? It was a corker. Cracking day for it, too.' Aznavorian's frequent resort to slang seemed odd in one so fastidious. Perhaps he'd adopted the habit long ago, to help mask his immigrant status.

Miss Pyle said, 'But then to come back to such terrible news – '

Aznavorian shook his head. 'I'm not sure I'll be able to sleep tonight. I've always felt safe here, but now it makes you wonder.'

'I can't imagine we're in any danger, Sarkis.'

'That's because of the life you've led. If you'd once been hounded from pillar to post like I was – '

'You were very young, dear. I'm surprised you remember.'

Aznavorian turned his head away from us, absorbed in some private reality. 'It's more the feelings that have stuck with me. That, and the fact that I could see my poor mother was terrified. I don't think she ever got over those years.'

Not wanting to be left out, I said, 'This was before you came to Southaven?'

'I was just a slip of a thing. We moved two or three times because of the persecution, but my father decided we wouldn't be safe until we got right out of there.'

'Where was this?'

'I was born in Burgas, on the Black Sea, then we moved to Plovdiv. Bulgaria, you know. It's behind the Iron Curtain today, that's why I can't easily go back. Anyway, there was an Armenian family we knew who got out ahead of us and wrote to us from Southaven, the Kouyoumdjians. In 1902 my father sold up and we came and joined them.'

Miss Pyle, who'd been showing a proprietorial interest in Aznavorian's biography, now said to me, 'They were Michael Arlen's people.'

Apparently this was supposed to mean something. I said, 'I'm afraid you've lost me.'

'These Koumou – ' She came to an awkward halt.

Aznavorian glowered at her. 'Kouyoumdjian. I don't know why you struggle, it's a perfectly simple name. Michael was originally Dikran Kouyoumdjian.'

'Did you say Arlen?' I still couldn't place the man.

'You mean, you've not heard of him?'

Miss Pyle said, 'Oh, dear. He's dropped *right* out of fashion since the war.'

Aznavorian said, 'It's a crying shame,' and rapped his knuckles on the chair arm grumpily.

'You must know *The Green Hat*, Mr Rigby?'

'That does ring a bell.'

Miss Pyle said, 'It was his first big success. They filmed it with

Greta Garbo, if you remember.'

Kindly, Aznavorian said, 'I think you'll find that was before Mr Rigby's time, my love.' Then to me he added, 'How about the Falcon? Did you see any of those films?'

'With George Sanders? Yes, when I was a boy. My mother used to work at the Empire.'

'Well, that was a Michael Arlen character.'

'So Arlen was from Southaven?'

'They lived just along the Prom here. We used to play together, though he was a couple of years older than me. But we always kept in touch after he left.' Taking a break at last from the bad-tempered scowl he'd worn through the interview so far, Aznavorian gave a contented smile. 'They were good times, at least until the war came. Bulgaria went in with the Germans, everyone thought we were spies. Even if my health had been tip-top, they'd never have wanted me in the forces.'

'Can I ask what line of work you went into?'

'I've always liked old things, Mr Rigby, things that connect you to the past. My father was a furniture maker, real quality stuff, not the rubbish you get nowadays. I followed him into the business, but what really interested me was antiques, and that's the road I took after my father died. General antiques at first, but then I began to specialize in rare books.'

'Sarkis's business has taken him all over the world.' Again the note of pride from Miss Pyle.

He nodded acceptance. 'That's true, my love, it has. But you always come back to Southaven in the end, don't you? There's a pull to the place, I can't account for it.'

Talking about the past seemed to have soothed Sarkis Aznavorian's mood. Hoping that I wasn't about to unsettle him again, I said, 'I'm afraid I'm going to have to ask you about last night.'

'I don't see why Alice can't leave it to the police. I didn't much care for the chap who interviewed me, but he seemed to know his job.' Aznavorian glanced across at the table where this inquisition had taken place.

'Mrs Haig feels that anything which might speed up the

process – '

'Yes, all right, I know. We've got to catch whoever it was before the Marine Lodge goes down the plughole, taking us all with it. But I don't see what I can tell you that's likely to help. I've got room 11, it's the one directly underneath Giles's. But I never heard a thing. I'm actually a little deaf, Mr Rigby, though you may not have realized it.'

'A pleasant room, is it?'

'One of the best in the hotel. Rawley used to complain that I was hogging a good room which Alice could have made better use of, especially in the summer. But I pay for the privilege.'

'Which rooms do the rest of you have?'

Miss Pyle said, 'The Major and I are on the second floor, at the opposite end of the corridor to Giles. And Mrs Lane has room 14, on the first floor.'

Aznavorian said, 'A nice room, that. And not cheap. Of course, Rawley's paying.'

'And how about yourself, Miss Pyle? Did you notice anything at all unusual last night?'

'I believe that yesterday I did ask you to call me Rosemary.' The smile again. I felt instinctive resistance to getting too familiar with this apparently harmless woman. It may have been unreasonable of me, but I didn't trust the smile, and I didn't trust the mulberry suit either. I said, 'In the circumstances, Miss Pyle – I mean, since I'm working for Mrs Haig now – I'd prefer to keep things on a more formal footing.' I was taking a leaf out of Alice Haig's business manual, and it felt like a smart move.

Miss Pyle tried to conceal disappointment. 'As you wish. Well, I'm afraid it's exactly as I told the Superintendent.'

'Actually he's a Detective Inspector.' Why I was so concerned to correct Miss Pyle, I couldn't have said.

'Is he?'

'He's been stuck at DI for years. If you call him Superintendent you'll upset him.'

Miss Pyle raised two expressive eyebrows. 'Who would have thought these matters could be so delicate? Whatever his rank, I had to confess to him that I'd slept soundly last night, as I usually do. I'm rather a heavy sleeper as a matter of fact, it would take an elephant to waken me. Everything seemed to be just the same as usual. Although – '

'Yes?'

'Well – there was something, before I'd actually drifted off. When the door to room 21 opens, I can just hear it from my own room. My light was out by then and I didn't look at the clock, but I heard Giles come upstairs, then ten or fifteen minutes later I heard him go out again. He might only have gone down the back stairs to the kitchen, because in a short while he came back. If it was him, of course. At the time I never imagined it could be anyone else.'

'Did you hear anything after that?'

'No. And I was glad, because sometimes he had nightmares, you know.'

'Rosemary – '

'It's all right, Sarkis, Giles has gone now. It can't hurt him.' She turned to me. 'He used to scream in his sleep until it woke him up.'

Aznavorian said, 'He never liked to talk about it. I'm afraid we went behind his back and asked Mrs Lane. Apparently he was always the same, even when she was a girl. No one was supposed to mention it.'

Miss Pyle cut in. 'But Cordelia's mother told her that Giles used to dream he was back in the trenches. Imagine!' Her eyes were wide with the horror of it. 'To live with that for more than half a century! At least it's over and done with now.'

Aznavorian said, 'It helped me to understand why he was always needling me about not fighting. He could be cruel sometimes, but I tried to bite my tongue.'

For a while none of us spoke. My mind was trying to come to terms with this new information about the man I'd known merely as an entertaining drinking pal. Then I said to Miss Pyle, 'So after he'd finally come up to his room, you definitely heard no more from him?'

'That's right. I'm sure whoever did this awful thing must have used the back stairs, because there's a floorboard outside my door which goes off like a gunshot when anyone steps on it.'

I was wondering how to phrase my next question without giving away more than I needed to. If the contents of Giles's will were not yet common knowledge, I didn't want to be the first to spill the beans. I said, 'Was either of you aware that Giles had made a new will recently?'

Aznavorian said, 'Yes, of course. We witnessed it, didn't we, my love?'

So that was one puzzle solved. 'Did he happen to say anything about it?'

'Not a dickie bird. He just asked us into his room one afternoon last week.'

'And you can't think of anything that might have prompted him to take such a step?'

'Without knowing what he'd altered, it's hard to say.'

Miss Pyle had been brooding, but now she said, 'You know, I wondered at the time whether it had anything to do with that young man who came to see him.'

I may not have trusted Miss Pyle, but I had to admit she was giving good value during this interview. I said, 'What young man was this?'

'You remember, Sarkis, don't you? It would be about two weeks ago, just after lunch. We were on the front step there, trying to judge whether we'd be able to walk to the bank and back before it started raining, and he pulled onto the forecourt on that lovely motor-bike.'

'Ah, yes, the boy with the motor-bike.'

'He got off and came towards us, and I remember thinking he looked just like James Dean.'

'Who is James Dean, my love?'

'Oh, Sarkis, really! You must try to keep up. He's a very handsome young film star, or he was. Such a tragedy. Anyway, we said good afternoon to him and he went in, but then there was nobody on reception so he came straight out again and asked us whether Giles Rawley was staying here, because he had something for him. We told him which room it was – Giles had gone upstairs after lunch – and he went back inside. That was the last we saw of him. When we returned from the bank, the motor-bike had gone.'

'And did you mention it to Giles later?'

'Of course we did. We wanted to be sure the young man had found him. But though Giles thanked us, it was *quite* obvious he wasn't going to say what it was all about.'

Aznavorian said, 'He may not have said anything, but you could tell it had bothered him.'

I said, 'You don't just think this was a courier from his solicitor in Sussex?'

Aznavorian thought this over. 'No, I don't. Whatever it was had come as a complete surprise to him. I think it was something personal.'

An attractive thought presented itself. 'Did you happen to mention any of this to DI Hargreaves?'

Rosemary Pyle put her nose in the air. 'I disliked the Detective Inspector. If he'd wanted to hear everything I could have told him, he shouldn't have been so rude.'

Despite my reservations about Miss Pyle, I felt she showed the right spirit when it came to dealing with Hargreaves. I said, 'Would you recognize the young man again?'

Miss Pyle said, 'Oh, yes. A very striking figure. He was from somewhere down south, to go by the voice. It might have been Sussex, of course, where Giles hailed from. And I'd know the motor-bike too, it was one of the new Japanese bikes.' My usual mask must have slipped at this point, because she went on, 'Don't look so shocked, Mr Rigby. There's no reason why a woman can't be interested in machines.'

'Of course, of course.'

'They were always a passion with my father, and I just picked it up. Did you know he was Manager of Corporation Tramways here? But I suppose trams were before your time, like Greta Garbo. They were such a delight, you young people have no idea what you've missed.'

Tentatively, Aznavorian said, 'I'm afraid buses were always likely to be more cost-effective in a place like Southaven.'

Miss Pyle rounded on the source of this ill-advised remark. Sparks flew between her trolley mast and the overhead wire, and her cheeks reddened dangerously. 'In their last full year of service, the trams were more profitable than they'd ever been! The problem was simply lack of investment, resulting from all those silly diktats coming out of Whitehall telling local councils that buses were the future. Nonsense! They were just new and fashionable, that's all. Destroying the tram system was sheer vandalism. We'd soon get rid of our summer traffic jams here if we had the trams back again.'

I said, 'Did it mean your father was out of a job?'

'He was almost due to retire in any case when the service ended in '34. I gave up my teaching post here and we moved back to Berkshire, where he'd grown up.'

'You were a teacher?'

'I taught Classics in some of the better girls' schools. But then my father became frail, and I stopped work to look after him until he died, a few years ago. That's when I came back here. Sarkis is right, Southaven always draws you back somehow.'

I glanced at my watch, wondering whether Oscar Hammond would be waiting to talk to me. Noticing this, Miss Pyle said, 'Oh dear, I'm rambling on, aren't I?'

Though she'd not addressed the remark to him, Aznavorian said, 'Not at all, my love. I'm sure Mr Rigby's very interested.'

I said, 'If you do think of anything that might help to identify the man who came to see Giles, could you let me know? Mrs Haig will tell you how to contact me.'

Aznavorian said, 'Meeting concluded, is it? To tell you the truth, I could do with forty winks. It's been a busy old day.'

I said, 'That's all for now. Thank you, you've both been very helpful.' I got up, and replaced the chair where I'd found it. Then it occurred to me that I'd forgotten to ask the most important question. I said, 'By the way, may I ask what was in that bag you took with you today?'

Aznavorian said, 'Bag? What bag?'

'When I was parking in the yard, you were just putting a brown bag on the back seat of your car.'

Aznavorian looked mystified. 'I don't remember any bag. Rosemary, did we take a bag with us to Lytham?'

'A bag, dear? No, we certainly didn't.' Miss Pyle turned to me. 'You must have been mistaken, Mr Rigby.' And she smiled the sickly smile.

## *twelve*

Though I'd allowed the two friends to believe that I accepted their version of events, I emerged into the corridor convinced that the vanishing bag might prove highly significant. From the spatter of blood and gore around Giles's bed, it seemed impossible that the murderer could have escaped unmarked. If this was an intruder, they would have carried the blood outside with them. But if it had been someone in the hotel, the bloody clothes must either have been hidden or taken out of the building somehow. The brown bag I'd seen that morning could have been perfect for the job. I was pretty sure that Hargreaves's team had found nothing in the hotel, because an arrest would almost certainly have followed.

The grandfather clock was striking nine as I came into the lobby. A very smart-looking young girl with a mass of dark hair was talking to Alice Haig at the reception desk. Alice was saying, 'I can't understand why you have to dress up just to stop in and watch television.'

'What, so I'm supposed to sit around in that horrible uniform?'

'And you know I don't like you wearing make-up. You're too young!'

'I'm sixteen. All the other girls wear it.'

I said, 'Hello.' The girl glanced round for a moment to check whether I was of any use or interest, decided I wasn't, and turned back again.

Alice Haig said, 'Mr Rigby, how are you getting on? This is my daughter Bobbie, by the way.'

'Mum!'

'I mean, Roberta. This is Mr Rigby, who's looking into poor

Giles's death.'

Bobbie Haig then looked me rapidly up and down and said, 'Nigel told me about you.'

I said, 'Good things, I hope,' not that I considered it likely.

But Bobbie had already turned to her mother again. 'Are you going to come and look at this washing machine, or aren't you? I've tried everything I can think of.'

'Can't it wait until the morning?'

'I need something to wear at Julia's tomorrow afternoon. All my decent stuff's in the wash.'

'I don't see why you have to make such a song and dance about it. What's wrong with what you're wearing now?'

'This? Ugh!' Personally I couldn't see any problem with the narrow brown skirt and orange jumper, provided you liked orange. Bobbie said, 'It's old! And everyone's seen it before.'

Alice Haig said, 'Mr Rigby, do you know anything about washing machines? We have an intermittent fault.'

Bobbie said, 'But mum, you already know how to fix it, you've done it twice before.'

Apparently inured to such but-mumming, Alice said, 'I have to look after the desk.'

Although I was anxious to get on and talk to Oscar Hammond, at the same time I felt it might be prudent to help a client in her hour of need. I said, 'I could hold the fort for you, if you like.'

'Would you do that?' Alice Haig's grateful tone suggested that in recent times offers of help had been hard to come by. 'If there are any calls, just take the number and say I'll ring them back.' To her daughter she said, 'Come along, let's get this done. And as soon as you've hung it all to dry, I want you going to bed, is that clear?'

'Oh, mum, it's the weekend! Why can't I stay up late?'

Alice and Bobbie Haig moved off towards the back door. I heard Alice say, 'I suppose next you'll be catching this cold off Nigel, and I'll have *two* invalids on my hands,' and then they were gone.

Blessed silence fell. I stepped round behind the counter, and with my sleeve wiped off the mark left by Bobbie Haig's fingers.

The old clock ticked. There was a smell of polish and boiled cabbage, which probably exuded from the carpets in the evening when other activity had slowed. Presumably this was the sort of atmosphere in which Graham Leeds fell asleep at his post on a nightly basis, and you couldn't blame him, especially if he'd spent half the day in the betting shop. I began to wonder if I might have time to slip into the office and go through the account books before Alice Haig returned.

When the phone rang, it scared the living daylights out of me. I don't know why they can't start quietly, to give you a chance. I picked up the receiver and a voice said, 'Lionel Green, Southaven Gazette. Could I talk to Alice Haig, please?'

'Mrs Haig's busy. What's it about?'

He laughed. 'What do you think it's about?'

'Sorry, I didn't realize it was a guessing game.' I'm not particularly fond of journalists, but then they don't usually like me either so we're all square.

He didn't rise to the bait. 'Could you get Mrs Haig to call me back?' He gave the familiar number of the Gazette's news-desk, but I didn't bother to write it down. If the Gazette wanted to grill Alice about Giles's murder, they could at least pay for the call.

I'd barely put the phone down when it rang again. I said, 'Marine Lodge!' Actually, it may have been more of a bark. My telephone manner has sometimes attracted criticism.

'Rod Furnival, Daily Mirror. Am I speaking to the manager?'

'What would you say if you were?'

There was a brief pause before the voice answered. 'I'd say, How well did you know Giles Rawley?'

I said, 'I'm just the boy who cleans the boots. You'll have to try again in the morning.'

'You don't sound like the boy who cleans the boots.' It might have been interesting to learn on what evidence he'd based this remark, but I never found out because at that point I cut him off. These two calls suggested that the police must now have released the information about Giles's death. If they'd done so early enough to catch the 9 o'clock news, Alice might soon find herself under siege. As a precaution, I walked over to drop the catch on the front door, so at least no one could walk in uninvited. Just as I was settling in behind the counter again, the phone rang a third time. I picked it up and said, 'Dogs' home.'

'I beg your pardon? Isn't that the Marine Lodge Hotel?'

'Depends who's asking.'

'It's Howard Lane here. I want to speak to my wife.'

I said, 'Ah, yes, I'm sorry Mr Lane. We're being plagued by nuisance callers this evening. Understandable, given what's happened.'

'Look, can you just put me through?'

I'd hoped for a quick exchange of pleasantries, enough to give me some sense of the man's character, but all I'd picked up so far was that he had scant patience with hotel receptionists.

The question now arose as to whether I could indeed put Howard Lane through to Cordelia, assuming she was in room 14 and hadn't left the hotel for any reason after dinner. The ancient switchboard reminded me strongly of the one in use at the police station during my first months there as a raw cadet. One of the girls – actually, she was nearing retirement – had taken a maternal interest in me, or at least I'd hoped it was maternal, and had shown me how the system worked. The whole lot had been ripped out soon afterwards and replaced by something more up to date, but now I was looking down at its brother, or perhaps its distant cousin. I said, 'I'll try her room for you,' put the incoming line on hold, and dialled 14. When this didn't work, I tried dialling 114 instead. The ringing tone was soon interrupted by Cordelia Lane's voice. 'Yes?'

'I have a call for you, Mrs Lane. Putting you through now.' A couple of flicked switches later, husband and wife were in communication.

This seemed like a heaven-sent opportunity, so if it was wrong of me to listen in on the conversation then heaven had only itself to blame.

'Hello, darling, it's me.'

Cordelia Lane struck a rather homely figure, and to hear her thus addressed proved that you don't have to be Brigitte Bardot to inspire endearments. But I felt that Cordelia rather spoiled the effect when she now said, 'Don't you *darling* me!'

'Now, Cordy, listen – '

'Where the hell have you been? I've had nothing but stone-walling from Berthe, and when I tried you at work they said you'd not been in for two days. I've been worried sick!' Perhaps the notion I'd somehow picked up of Cordelia being under her husband's thumb needed adjustment.

'I'm so sorry about your father.'

'Berthe told you, did she?' I was guessing that Berthe must be the family's au pair.

'Do you need me to come up? You only have to say.'

'You know I don't like leaving Berthe to manage on her own. The children take advantage, and her cooking's as bad as her English. I suppose you never came home at all last night?'

'Mr Rigby, what are you doing?' I'd been so absorbed in this fascinating exchange that I hadn't noticed Alice Haig's return.

'Oh – just checking that I'd put it through all right. Mr Lane rang for Mrs Lane.' I laid aside the headset. 'Washing machine behaving now?'

'You just have to pull the knob out and push it in again. Bobbie's a very bright girl but not remotely practical.'

'Does she always do her washing on Friday evening?'

Alice Haig said, 'Whyever do you ask?'

For someone I took to be pretty smart, Alice Haig's intelligence seemed to come and go in a puzzling manner. Perhaps as a mother it hadn't occurred to her that Bobbie could be washing Giles Rawley's blood off her clothes even as we spoke. But Alice was paying me, so I just said, 'No particular reason. The phone's been busy, by the way. There've been a couple of calls from the press.'

'Already?' And she looked towards the door.

'Don't worry, I dropped the catch. Is the back door locked?'

'Not yet. I'll do it when you leave, I'm sure none of the guests will be wanting to go out now.'

'I still need to talk to Oscar.'

'He's already gone, Mr Rigby. He seemed in rather a hurry.'

Oscar Hammond was proving difficult to pin down. 'Would it be all right if you gave me his address?'

'Of course, in the circumstances. He's just at the other end of Wright Street, in that little terrace. Number thirteen.'

'I'll be off, then. And, Mrs Haig – I'm sure you don't need the advice, but if you'd rather not speak to the press then don't.'

Alice Haig's expression soured. 'After that nonsense in the Gazette, I'm not taking a very positive view of journalists at present. I'll simply refer them to the police.'

'One more thing. Were you thinking you might try to visit Major Glass at some point?'

'How does that concern you, Mr Rigby?' The expression was now admirably inscrutable. 'I may go and see him and I may not, but I hadn't planned to inform you of my decision.'

This had been pitched somewhere between frosty and downright rude, and I chalked it up as further evidence of Alice's tender feelings towards the Glass character, whose bland good looks appeared to me to be his sole recommendation. No doubt some exasperated component of Alice's nature was wondering what had become of her usual robust, sensible self. I said, 'Well then, perhaps I'll bump into you at the Infirmary. I hope you manage a quiet night.'

The far from quiet day had taken a visible toll. Alice's normally rigid coiffeur constantly sprang breakaway movements and had to be swept back into line. There were dark patches beneath her eyes. Nevertheless, and perhaps feeling somewhat penitent after her cool response to my question about the Major, she now found the grace to say, 'Thank you for your help today. It was a stroke of luck, happening to find you at such an awkward time.'

This isn't the sort of thing I hear very often, and I waited a moment for her to take it back. When she didn't, I nodded briefly, and left her. The phone was already ringing again as I moved off down the corridor.

Out on Wright Street, I faced a dilemma: whether to turn to the right and look for Oscar Hammond at home, or to the left, and seek him in the Grand Hotel Vaults. Although he'd failed to appear in the Vaults the previous evening, I thought it unlikely that he'd miss the chance of Lena Golding's company twice in a row, so I duly turned left. But when I reached the Vaults a couple of minutes later, a glance round the crowded bar revealed no trace of outsize ex-army cooks. Reaching for a glass, Mickey Golding said, 'Pint?' But I declined. If I settled in the Vaults now it would soon be too late to make a civilised visit to Oscar's home address. Mickey said, 'In that case, I'll see you in the morning.'

I wasn't going to pretend I hadn't understood. Somehow, Mickey had cornered me into rising early and taking vigorous exercise, two things I usually went to great lengths to avoid. Perhaps Alice Haig wasn't the only one letting unsuitable men distort their customary behaviour. I said, 'What if I produced a doctor's note?'

'Don't be daft, you'll be fine. I'd have thought you'd be looking forward to it.'

'I am. This is my looking-forward-to-it face.'

Relentless, the man pressed on. 'Eight o'clock in the plunge pool, then?' By way of assent I shook my head wearily. I'd meant to nod but it came out wrong. Then Mickey glanced at the clock and said, 'Still no sign of Giles.'

In the madness of the day, I'd lost sight of the fact that Giles Rawley's violent end must still be unknown to most of Southaven. I moved closer to the bar, so that I could speak to Mickey privately. 'There's bad news. Giles is dead.'

'What?' Mickey looked puzzled, but when I told him what had happened the colour drained from his face. 'It ain't right. Who would do that to old Giles?'

For some reason I didn't want to tell Mickey that I'd been employed to help find the killer. But then, perhaps the reason was obvious. Like Alice had said, perhaps Giles had unearthed some truly spectacular dirt on Mickey's family, as a result of which he'd had to be silenced. Mickey's reaction to the news seemed innocent enough, but with the Golding family honour at stake I couldn't rule out that Mickey might know more than he was saying. 'The police are on it. They'll find the bloke, I'm sure.'

'A bunch of local plods? That old chum of yours last night didn't look like he could catch a cold, never mind a murderer. Case like this, you need the Met.'

'Listen, I've got to go. We can talk about it tomorrow.' Mickey looked disappointed, but I raised a valedictory hand and went out into the street.

During the two minutes I'd been in the Vaults, it had started to snow. The previous day's Gazette had indeed forecast 'snow furries', but even as you attempted to picture these cuddly organisms you found yourself wondering for the umpteenth time whether some frustrated copy editor might be having fun at the readers' expense. Standing on Marine Approach as the soft flakes drifted down, I suddenly lost interest in the trek up Wright Street to Oscar's home. He'd surely keep for another day. What I really needed to do was go back to the flat, in case Matt was trying to call me from wherever it was that he'd moved on to after fleeing the Mafeking Court Hotel. But a different prospect was taking shape in my mind. Perhaps it wouldn't do any harm to enjoy a couple of sedate pints in the Velvet Bar with Bernie Foster, and put the day's events behind me.

I rang her from the call box across the street. Naturally, she gave me a hard time for expecting her to drop everything and rush to be at my side. I'd have done no less myself. But I could tell she was pleased really, and twenty minutes later we were enjoying the first of what turned out to be several glasses. The atmosphere around us was highly convivial. There's nowhere else to go in Southaven if you're reckless enough to fancy people of the wrong gender, at least, not indoors there isn't, and a fair smattering of the usual boys and girls were in attendance, despite the uncertain weather. My 'flu symptoms now barely perceptible, I added enthusiastically to the pall of cigarette smoke which hung in the air, and searched among the familiar Friday night faces for any sign of new ones. Finding none, I was free to give all my attention to Bernie.

The first drink was indeed quite sedate. Since Bernie worked in the cardiac unit at the Infirmary, I asked if she had news of Laurence Glass. Apparently, checks had revealed no problem with his heart, and it seemed that what I'd witnessed in room 21 had been nothing worse than an anxiety attack, albeit a severe one. The Major had now been moved upstairs to the general ward. He remained somewhat fragile, and the plan was to keep him in under observation over the weekend.

We then dropped all talk of work, and ordered the second drink. This may have been reasonably sedate too, but as time and further alcohol went by, a change came over us. By eleven o'clock, silliness had broken out.

Like many well-ordered people, Bernie is particularly charming when in thrall to silliness. The neat suit and perfect brogues stand suddenly in sharp relief when their owner is pretending to be a goldfish. And yet the quiet voice in my ear, so rarely off duty even after a great many more drinks than I'd just consumed, kept warning me that far from being charmed by Bernie's performance I should have been treating it with the utmost suspicion. Something was going on. All this larking about was intended, consciously or otherwise, to throw me off the scent. The more Bernie clowned, the more suspicious I became. When I could stand it no longer I found myself grabbing her wrist and saying, 'Come on now, Bernie – what's wrong?'

She looked astonished. 'Wrong? Nothing's wrong.' She pulled away from my hand.

'You're behaving strangely.'

'And you're talking nonsense.'

'Wait a minute, I know what it is – you're seeing someone new, aren't you?'

Bernie is normally the coolest of customers, but at that moment her eyes betrayed her by failing to meet my own. 'No I'm not.'

'Yes you are. It's snowing outside, but you've got a marked spring in your step. You were even nice to Leslie when you came in.' Leslie Lush was the resident barman, usually regarded as the cheese to Bernie's chalk.

'I'm always nice to people.'

'Who's the lucky girl?'

'I've told you, there is no lucky girl. Honestly, Sam, you're impossible sometimes. Perhaps if you got yourself a lucky boy you might start making more sense.'

'As a matter of fact – ' Too late I realized that I didn't particularly want to tell Bernie about Mickey Golding yet. She seized the moment.

'As a matter of fact, what? Has someone finally recognized your unconventional appeal?'

I wasn't sure how to take that. 'You realize you sound Irish sometimes?'

'I am, on my mother's side, as you well know. But don't change the subject. I demand to be brought up to date immediately.'

Concluding that silence was no longer an option, I told Bernie what little there was to tell. Her response wasn't exactly what I'd expected. She said, 'And does Matt know about this?'

'What difference does that make?'

'I bet he doesn't like it.'

This was true, he didn't. I said, 'It's none of Matt's business.' Bernie smiled and looked enigmatic. I said, 'You're smiling and looking enigmatic. Stop it.'

'Of course it's Matt's business. The two of you are joined at the hip.'

'That's ridiculous.'

Bernie ignored this intervention. 'You'll end up together eventually, it's obvious. He's just taking his time.'

I didn't know why, but I felt panic rising. 'Please, Bernie – you haven't said anything to Eileen?'

'About what?'

I was thinking of last summer and that moment under the lime trees. 'Eileen has no idea, she mustn't find out about Matt's history.'

Bernie looked offended. 'She won't find out from me. But this isn't about her, is it? It's about Matt.'

'You think he's just stringing Eileen along?'

'Isn't that what *you* think?'

Somehow we'd moved a long way from goldfish impressions. 'I don't know what I think.'

'Of course you do. You're just waiting for Matt to sort it all out in his head. In the meantime you try to keep yourself amused with the likes of this Mickey person – who, by the way, is quite clearly a disaster in the making.'

'Thanks a million.'

'Don't mention it. What are friends for?'

I drummed my fingers on the bar. When Bernie states her view, argument can't shift her. Besides, there was a chance that she was right. I tried a lateral manoeuvre. 'Have you seen Eileen?'

'Not since Wednesday.'

'So you still don't know why she's wrecked Matt's plan for Valentine's Night in such a heartless fashion?'

'You mean you're not pleased?'

I tried to understand this, but failed. 'Explain.'

'You're always pleased when something comes between them. This show of concern about Eileen breaking Matt's poor little heart isn't fooling anyone.'

Matt had made a similar point on his way out of the flat the day before. It was unpleasant being ganged up on like this, as if I couldn't be trusted to fathom my own motivation without the help of a vast squadron of assistants, confidantes, and other well-wishers. But reasoning once more that if that was how Bernie saw things argument would be futile, I let the matter drop.

All the same, it came back to me as I was sitting up in bed an hour later, reading Melville again. As they shared a cold bed in the freezing Spouter Inn, Queequeg kept throwing his brown, tattooed legs over Ishmael's, and in many respects conditions were not that different in my own bedroom, except for the lack of warming South Sea Islanders beneath the continental quilt. Was I really glad whenever the good ship Matt-and-Eileen drifted close to the rocks? And if I was, would that be so wrong? Whatever he might say, I didn't believe that Matt was truly happy. Why shouldn't I think he'd be happier with me, despite the ructions there'd be in his family if he took that road?

No, I wasn't going to let Matt or Bernie make me feel guilty. The pressing issue now was, where on earth had Matt disappeared to, and would he reappear in Southaven in time to help me with the case of Giles Rawley, late of this parish? My enquiries so far had thrown up a few hints to be pursued, but nothing whatsoever in the way of a theory. I needed to bounce ideas around, I needed fresh thinking. In short, I needed Matt.

Now Ishmael and Queequeg were sharing an affectionate

midnight pipe. There was nothing to stop me fetching my cigarettes and lighting up, but I felt it wouldn't quite be the same.

The alarm clock trilled exuberantly at a quarter past seven the following morning. I not only cursed it, I picked the thing up and hurled it across the room, as if the decision to wake me at this unnecessary hour on a bitter February morning in order to go and splash around in cold, chlorinated water had been made unilaterally by the clock itself. In reality I grasped full well that responsibility rested with its owner and no one else, not even Mickey Golding. If Mickey wanted to persist in inviting me to engage in unnatural activities then he had a perfect right to do so. It should have been my place simply to say no, firmly and kindly, and perhaps in time to help him see the error of his ways. Instead, unbelievably, I was getting out of bed and stumbling towards the bathroom.

As a sop to my *amour propre*, I'd invented a pat justification for this mad adventure. It's well known that exercise stimulates the brain. The plan now was that within a couple of hours of climbing out of the pool I would either have solved the riddle of Giles Rawley's murder or, at the very least, identified some new track-way through the dark forest of my investigation. And perhaps this might turn out to be true, but just now I was mostly thinking of the way Mickey Golding looked at me sometimes, of the cute nose, of the neat backside in the tight black trousers, of the unknown possibilities which lay ahead. As I munched on a slice of Mother's Pride, these thoughts, together with the toast and tea, brought transformation to the reluctant, clock-throwing Rigby seen earlier. By the time I left the flat, a miracle had occurred. I was genuinely looking forward to the swim, and to whatever might follow.

With my kit in a canvas bag over one shoulder, I walked briskly through a thin wind up Marine Approach. I could have brought the Minx and parked it on the Promenade, but I'd decided that would run counter to the spirit of the occasion. A warmish front had moved in overnight, causing yesterday evening's half inch of snow to melt away. At the top of the hill, Sir George Cattermole's imposing statue of Queen Victoria gazed out over the ruins of the Pier Pavilion towards the distant sea. I quite liked it myself, but I've heard complaints that if you stare at it for any length of time the old girl seems to be holding the orb and sceptre far too casually, as if looking after them for a friend who's just popped out to powder her nose. These ruins, so poignant to anyone who'd known the Pavilion in its glory, sought to impress a desolate, backward-looking stamp on my early morning mind, but I resisted. This was to be no day for regrets. A brighter future beckoned, a future of exercise and affectionate pipe-sharing. I turned right onto the Promenade, then, at one minute past eight, turned right again through the door of the Southaven public baths.

The Victorians had done all in their power to lend some kind of distinction to what was after all a humble leisure activity. Sandstone, marble, and a laudably irresponsible attitude to blending architectural styles, had provided a context in which even the most well-heeled of visitors need not be ashamed to frolic in the shallow end.

But I'd been admiring the entrance lobby for no more than a second or two when a far more arresting image passed through each lens, to be smartly inverted and thrown onto the associated retina. Standing near the till was Mickey Golding, apparently deep in conversation with the boy Evan Bickerstaff.

How well did these two know one another? What could they possibly have to talk about? And was I looking at the smoking gun with which the Goldings were threatening Alice Haig's business?

## thirteen

I advanced on the two men and made my presence known.

This was the first time I'd seen Mickey in civilian clothes. I knew that, while his sister had a room of her own in the staff block behind the Grand Hotel, Mickey himself preferred to travel in and out from his mother's house in Welldale on a much-loved if not very powerful motorbike, and in keeping with this he wore a short black leather jacket over his denim shirt and jeans. The shirt featured pop studs, and the jeans, every bit as tight as his black work trousers, were circled by a broad leather belt with a buckle of an interlocking Celtic design. A smart new duffel bag over his shoulder completed the picture. You may wonder how I managed to take in so much detail, but even at eight o'clock in the morning Mickey Golding repaid close study.

'Hey, Sam! Bang on time as well, I'm impressed.' Mickey was looking annoyingly healthy and wide awake, as if he'd already taken his swim and was just leaving.

I said, 'I see you know young Evan here.' Evan's brown coat and patterned jumper seemed homely alongside Mickey's stylish ensemble.

'That's right. Another pool regular, aren't you?' Evan nodded. 'Though not as regular as me.'

Evan protested. 'I come afternoons sometimes, when you're not here. That's when I get my time off. But it's busier then, I prefer it first thing.' This was the most I'd ever heard Evan say at a single utterance.

Mickey said, 'You should badger the old cow to give you mornings.'

'She likes me to be around at breakfast. But there's hardly anyone in the hotel today, she let me go for a while. I wondered if I'd see you.' I thought I detected some kind of tone in this remark.

'Never miss, if I can help it.' Mickey turned towards me. 'Are you ready for this? Feeling keen?'

'Yes. Slightly.'

'An early morning dip's the best thing in the world. Let's not keep the young lady waiting any longer.'

The girl on the till had indeed been watching us from behind half-lowered lids throughout this exchange. She appeared to have been dragged from her bed very recently, and the resentment lingered. Once in receipt of our cash, she handed over three cubicle keys on wristbands. Mickey checked them, then said to the girl, 'Adjacent cubicles, please, if you can.' The girl took the keys back and duly replaced them. Then Mickey led the way down the stairs to the biggest of the three swimming baths, the plunge pool.

Several early swimmers were already in action. One side of the pool had been given over to those doing lengths, while a young family were enjoying aquatic larks at the shallow end. We searched out the cubicles numbered on our key. I've once or twice visited more modern pools with designated changing rooms, but this was not the Victorian way. Here, separate walk-in cubicles surrounded the pool on three sides. Mickey selected the one in the middle, while Evan and I split off to either side. But as I was pushing the door shut behind me, Mickey pushed it open again. He came in, closed the door, and said, 'You're in a grump. What's up?'

Though these spaces had been designed quite generously for the solitary bather, they were a little on the small side for two. This was as close as I'd ever been to Mickey Golding, and I found the unexpected intimacy so soon after breakfast unsettling. Perhaps this caused a delay in speech, because Mickey now followed up his preamble by adding, 'Well?'

I said, 'I'm not exactly in a grump.'

'Then you're doing a good impression.'

'I just hadn't realized you were on terms with Evan Bickerstaff.'

'Bickerstaff? Is that his name? You northern types don't mess about, do you?'

I wasn't sure how I should be playing this. Mickey had assured me that he knew nothing about the events which had caused Alice Haig's financial plight to be aired in the Gazette, but assurances aren't proof. As a complicating factor, I wanted to believe him. But this only made me doubly suspicious when I discovered that Mickey had a contact at Marine Lodge after all, and not just any contact, but quiet, insignificant Evan, the definition of the perfect mole. I didn't know if it would be wiser to reveal what I suspected or instead to say nothing now and keep a closer watch on Evan in the future. But it was very early in the morning, and Mickey was standing so close that I could feel his breath on my face. I threw caution to the winds and said, 'Someone's been passing details of the Marine Lodge's finances to your family. Until this morning, the only link I'd found between the two hotels was that Giles and Oscar both fancied your sister.'

'Remarkable girl. People know class when they see it.'

'Then I stroll up here today and find you and young Evan enjoying a cosy moment.'

'Wait a second – you're jealous, aren't you?'

'Why would I be jealous?'

'Oh, Sammy, Sammy!' Mickey ran a gentle hand down the front of my chest. 'Evan's just a boy. A very sweet boy, I'll grant you, and I'm not sure he ain't got a bit of a crush on me. But I'm in the market for a man.' And once more he gave me the sort of look which had led me into my present predicament.

I tried to ignore the look, the hand, the pop studs, and the many other allurements which Mickey offered. I said, 'I need to be sure you're being straight with me.'

His attitude changed instantly. 'Yeah? And why should I, when you're not being straight with *me*?'

It was the first time I'd seen this new, no-nonsense Mickey. Unfortunately, he was every bit as attractive as the flirtatious Mickey I was familiar with. As far as I could tell by the dim light in the cubicle, his eye flashed steel. I said, 'What are you talking about? Of course I'm being straight with you.'

'Bollocks. You never told me you were working for old Ma Haig.'

Oh, that. 'Should I have done?'

'I thought we were friends. Now I can't help wondering if you've just been using me all along.' And a third Mickey came into view, one whose feelings could be hurt.

I heaved a deepish sigh. I hadn't realized I'd been holding so much tension. I said, 'How did you discover Alice Haig was employing me?'

'I picked it up from Oscar last night. He assumed I already knew. I pretended I did, but I don't think he was fooled. It was humiliating, if you must know.'

'Listen, Mickey – until two days ago I'd never even met Mrs Haig. She approached me because of that story in the Gazette, she needed to find out how your mother's solicitors came to be so well-informed about the Marine Lodge's financial situation. It's not my fault your family has a certain way of doing business. So don't blame me, OK?'

I was just feeling pleased with this latest gambit when there was a knock at the door. Evan said, 'What are you doing?'

I said, 'I'll be out in a minute.'

Evan said, 'OK,' and I heard bare feet moving away. There was a splash as he entered the water.

To Mickey I said, 'We'd better get ready.'

'You doing anything after? We could go for a coffee if you like.'

I hadn't expected this. 'So you're still speaking to me?'

Mickey gave me a searching look. 'I wish I knew if I can trust you. You've got round me somehow, and I don't like it. But I can't seem to help myself.' He looked aside for a moment, then turned back, gave me the briefest of brief kisses on the lips, and left the cubicle.

It transpired that Evan Bickerstaff was a very strong swimmer. In the water, the passive, inert young man whose presence at the Marine Lodge could so easily be overlooked was replaced by an active force of nature, his practised stroke matching speed with elegance. Now I could understand how he'd acquired the classic physique which so contradicted his mask-like facial features. Up and down he went, utterly at home in the water, oblivious to everything around him.

By contrast, Mickey's approach savoured more of enthusiasm than technique. You could always tell where he was in the pool by the amount of surplus water being thrown in all directions. An elderly woman who'd been doing lengths in a restrained breast stroke actually stopped and trod water for a while so that she could watch his whirlwind progress, then shook her head and carried on. He even broke with protocol by speaking to other pool users as he went. I heard, 'Brisk today, ain't it?' 'Sorry, was that your leg?' and, to the elderly woman, 'I like your cap,' amongst other throwaway remarks. I found myself wondering whether he talked during sex. At first he'd tried to remain close to me, keeping up a sociable banter as he did so, but for the sake of a quiet life I'd allowed myself to fall half a length behind. Though hardly a crack swimmer and using far less energy than Mickey, I then maintained a similar rate. But I tired first, and after about fifteen minutes I stopped at the shallow end, leaning back against the pool's edge, and wiped water from my face and eyes. Here, Evan came and joined me. He watched Mickey's antics with his usual blank expression, but didn't speak. Our elbows were touching. The biceps bulged in his upper arm, like an egg in a snake.

I said, 'Quite a character, isn't he?'

Evan said, 'He's different from people round here.'

This was on the button, and went some way to accounting for Mickey's attractiveness. I said, 'A bit of a shock, what happened to Giles Rawley.' I wasn't sure whether I'd ever find a better moment to talk to Evan about the murder. He seemed so much in his element here, and I suspected that once back on dry land the old Evan would reassert himself and the shutters come down again.

'He was a good bloke, Sir Giles. Gave me tips, and that.'

'You didn't hear anything the night he was killed? Doesn't your flat overlook the yard?'

'My bedroom's round the other side. It'll be some madman, won't it?'

'You must see all sorts of things at Marine Lodge. You can't think why anyone there would want to kill Giles?'

'Like who? They're all ancient anyway.'

'I hear Bobbie Haig didn't think much of him.'

'But Bobbie's not going to smash his head in with a hammer, is she?'

While Evan might be a man of few words, it seemed that if you could once get him talking he did talk sense. I said, 'Mrs Haig's got a problem on her hands. Someone's been passing sensitive information about Marine Lodge to Mickey's family.'

'I know. There was that thing in the Gazette.'

'Any idea who it might be?'

'I've been asking myself the same question. If it's one of the staff, we're going to get the sack, aren't we? And the residents wouldn't do it either, because they don't want to be kicked out on the street. It's got to be someone from outside.'

'But how could they get into the office?'

'It's obvious, isn't it? They've put something in that flask Graham brings with him every night, and knocked him out. They had a plot like that on *Paul Temple* last week.' And having solved the mystery for me, Evan now disappeared below the water, pushed off with considerable power, and surfaced several yards out, transformed once more from man to fish. Inspired by the ease of his movements, I had another go myself, trying to imitate the curve of his hand as it dipped into the water, and the strong backward sweep of his arm. But Evan rarely turned his head to breathe, while I had to break my rhythm between every couple of strokes. If I ever took this up seriously, the fags would have to go.

Out on the Promenade twenty minutes later, Mickey and I said goodbye to Evan Bickerstaff and watched as he trailed listlessly in the direction of the Marine Lodge and servitude. Mickey said, 'What do you reckon? Has that boy got the hots for me or am I imagining it?'

'It's always hard to tell what Evan's thinking.'

'Nice body. I wouldn't chuck him out of bed.'

'He's under age though.'

'Is he?'

'Nineteen.'

'It ought to be the same age for everyone, it ain't right. We gotta make them change the law.'

'How, exactly?'

'There's people in London doing demos and such-like. I got a mate does it, I was gonna get involved. But then we moved up here.'

The tone of disappointment was unmistakable. I said, 'There's a lot to recommend Southaven.'

Mickey frowned. 'Trouble is, people here don't know how to have a good time.' The frown showed his nose to particular advantage.

I said, 'Some of us do.'

'Yeah?'

'Are you still on for that coffee you mentioned?'

'Lena's covering for me till twelve.'

'That gives us three hours. My place?'

'Is it far?'

'Not for a top athlete like you. We could go the pretty way round.'

Which we did. This just involved using the Promenade rather than the Boulevard, and to be strictly accurate on such a grey morning there was nothing very pretty about it at all. A line of gulls perching on the bar which jutted out into the Marine Lake had a hunch-shouldered look, while an Airedale terrier taking its mistress for a walk faced bravely into the stiffening breeze, determined to set her a good example.

Mickey said, 'Did you hear any more about Giles?'

'No. And I've not seen this morning's papers yet.'

'It made the front page of the Gazette. My mum has it delivered, likes to know what's going on in the town.' He summarised the story. It seemed that the Gazette knew far less about it than I did, but I didn't point that out. Then Mickey said, 'He was a game old bird, wasn't he? I'll miss him.'

The conversation lapsed. A distant cargo ship, perhaps en route for Glasgow, formed the only visual relief from the grey of sea and sky. After a while Mickey said, 'It ain't exactly the East End.'

'Surely you can't be homesick? February's miserable everywhere.'

'Maybe, but you forget about it when you're strolling up Shoreditch High Street. It gets rubbed in your face a bit here. And the weather! I ain't never been so cold.'

'Why don't you wear a jumper like everyone else?'

'They look old-blokeish, don't they? No offence.'

'I'm sorry if Southaven isn't quite what Sir is used to.'

'Come on, Sammy, don't get sensitive.'

'You realize the only person who calls me Sammy is my mother?'

'I'd like to meet her.'

'People who haven't met her often think that.'

'She can't be any more of a challenge than my old girl.'

I was remembering what Chubby Fallon had said about Lou Golding and dark alleys. 'Your mother has quite a reputation.'

'Yeah? Well, she's worked for it. Business is a tough line for a woman, people think they can take advantage.'

I said, 'Business?' and then regretted it.

'What do you mean, "business"? Just because my dad got mixed up in a few dodgy deals – '

'Let's not talk about it, OK? We're going to find it hard to agree.'

'That's not fair, you're casting aspersions. The Goldings are legitimate business people, we always have been.'

'Of course. Don't let's argue.'

'Well I didn't start it.'

'No. I'm sorry.'

We turned inland, in the direction of Preston Road and home. The breeze was behind us now. After we'd walked in silence for a while, Mickey said, 'Did you enjoy it, then? The pool?'

'A lot more than I'd expected. Thanks for the suggestion.'

'It was just an excuse to get you out of your clothes really.'

'And?'

'I'm not serving you beer any more, it sits round your middle. You obviously don't get enough exercise.'

'Exercising on your own is boring.'

'Then you'll have to exercise with me, won't you? We'll have those few extra pounds off you in no time.'

'The problem is, I'm not much of a morning person.'

'I don't mind when we do it, Sammy. Or how, for that matter.'

'It's good of you to be so flexible.'

'My pleasure. I'm sure we can think of something.'

Then we were silent again, but the quality of the silence had changed. For my part, this was because I'd already thought of something, and was imagining it in vivid detail. You may object that it was only a matter of hours since I'd told myself how much happier Matt would be with me than with Eileen Docherty. But I'd wakened at four in the morning, reflecting that while Matt persisted in his error my own opinion counted for nothing. The relationship may wobble from time to time, but there was about as much chance of Matt ditching Eileen as there was of Pan's People joining the Royal Ballet.

Besides, Mickey was gorgeous, and showed evidence of hurling himself at me. It would be rude to step out of the way.

We now crossed over the Boulevard, where the first of the Saturday shoppers were heading towards the bigger stores. I said, 'See, it may not be Shoreditch but we have life here too.'

'If you say so. That Roxy place is a terrible dump, ain't it?'

We were just leaving this former cinema behind on our starboard bow. It was now a casino, run by the Malones. I said, 'It's top notch inside. You may be viewing it with the eye of prejudice.'

'Yeah, well, those Malones had better watch out, that's all I'm saying.'

'You shouldn't talk like that so close to the police station.' We were opposite the fire station now, with the cop shop just around the corner. 'Some people might interpret it as a threat.'

'You'd have thought the Malones would welcome a bit of honest competition. They've had it too easy, that's what it is.'

We reached Leigh Terrace and made our way up to the top floor. The unaccustomed exercise had done odd things to my legs but I was trying not to let it show. When he saw the bucket on the landing, Mickey said, 'Problem with the roof?'

I turned the key in the lock. 'Problem with the landlord. But don't worry, your mother's trying to fix it for me.'

Mickey followed me into the narrow hallway. 'I don't get you. What's my mum got to do with it?'

'I think she's trying to buy my landlord out. I'd have thought she'd have her hands full with the hotel. Leave your bag here, if you like.'

Mickey put down the duffel bag alongside my canvas bag, and we moved through into the living room. He said, 'It's all about business with her, always has been. She don't rest up much. Business, and the Church. It's a bit parky, ain't it?' He rubbed his hands together.

I picked my way across the floor to turn the gas fire full on, hoping the meter would last out. 'The Church? Is she religious?'

'Gets on my wick, as a matter of fact. Hey, this place is pretty good. Why do you keep your books on the floor?'

'I don't mean to, it just happens. Matt normally tidies up after me, but he's out of town.' I hadn't meant to bring Matt into the conversation, either. Mickey had only met him once, but that had been enough for him to draw certain conclusions.

'Ah yes, your faithful sidekick with the brown eyes and the steady girlfriend. Are you positive there's nothing going on between you two?'

'I told you before.'

'No, well, I suppose he is a bit young for you.'

'Not that young. He's twenty-two.' Or at any rate, he would be in a few weeks' time.

'Twenty-two? Practically pensionable.' Mickey took off the black leather jacket and searched in vain for somewhere to put it.

I said, 'Let me take that. Coffee?'

'Strong and black would be brilliant.'

'Sugar?'

'Not for me. Rots your teeth, doesn't it?'

I returned from jacket-hanging and coffee-making to find Mickey on his haunches, investigating my record collection. I said, 'Put something on, if you like.'

'A bit early in the day. I don't see any classical stuff.'

I set the coffee mugs down on the little table. 'Are you a fan?'

'My mum's got me into it. She likes the Russians – Rimsky-what's-his-name and all that lot.'

I said, 'You surprise me.'

He looked round. 'Think we're ignorant, do you? There's brains in my family, let me tell you. Lena's even got A levels. She's done all her chef's exams too, but Carlo likes to keep her front of house.'

'What about you?'

He got up and moved to the settee, such as it was. 'I left school to pursue career opportunities.'

'Like working for your dad, I suppose.'

'He's got a lot of businesses, he needs top-grade staff. Stop hovering and come and sit down.' He patted the seat beside him. 'You can turn that fire down a bit as well.'

I pulled off my sweater and joined Mickey on the narrow settee. We raised our drinks. Mickey said, 'Here's to health and fitness. And friendship.' We drank, then both of us settled the mugs on our knees, where they steamed peacefully. Mickey looked around him appreciatively. 'You've fixed up a good life for yourself, haven't you? Thriving business, cosy little flat in the middle of town. Now you just need someone to share it with.'

My left hand rested on my thigh. I was having the devil of a job restraining it from settling on Mickey's thigh instead. I said, 'Are you offering?'

Mickey said, 'I don't know whether you'd accept. You keep giving me mixed signals.'

I thought about this. 'You know you're supposed to be working tomorrow? What if I told you I've booked us a table for dinner?'

'It's Valentine's. You must have been planning ahead. Where is this table?'

'Hen and Chickens.'

'Roosters or Rustlers?'

'Rustlers.'

Mickey took another drink, then said, 'Are you sure Southaven's ready for two blokes eating together on Valentine's Day?'

'We can find out, can't we. What do you say?' Then I gave up the unequal struggle and let my left hand have its way.

Mickey glanced at the hand, hesitated for a moment, then put the mug on the table in front of him. Sensing possible developments, I did the same with mine. Mickey said, 'This is what I say,' and swung gently round to kiss me on the cheek. Encouraged, I did some swinging round of my own, drew him towards me, and gave him a different kind of kiss altogether.

I said, 'Sorry about the mixed signals.'

He said, 'I like the way you're putting me straight.'

I said, 'You smell salty.'

He said, 'So do you.'

I kissed him again. This time I also let my right hand do what it had been wanting to do with the pop studs on Mickey's shirt, then slipped the hand inside. Mickey grunted. His left hand was sliding up and down my back. Not for the first time, I wished I had a longer settee. Bringing in my spare hand, I got the rest of the studs unpopped and began to push Mickey's shirt back over his shoulders, hampered by the fact that at the same time he was fiddling unsuccessfully with my own buttons. I said, 'Let me do it,' and quickly took off the shirt. Then I eased one arm beneath his legs, and with my other hand at his back I carried him bodily across to the bean bag, and laid him down against it. My back gave me gyp for days afterwards, but it was worth it.

Mickey said, 'You're stronger than I thought.'

I said, 'Ssh,' and lay down next to him, running my hand over his chest and belly. I had my eye on the Celtic belt buckle, and the interesting area of Mickey's jeans just to the south of it. Then it wasn't just my eye, my hand had joined in. Mickey grunted again. I began to undo the belt.

We both heard the sound at the same time, the metallic scrape of a key in the lock of the flat door.

I said, 'Shit!' and rolled away from Mickey as if he'd been electrified. He seemed bewildered, so I said, 'Get dressed!' It's possible my tone was less than friendly.

The outer door opened and slammed shut. From the hallway Matt shouted, 'Get up, you lazy sod! It's half past nine! I've brought food.' And he must have turned into the kitchen.

I tried to button up my shirt with the ten thumbs currently in my possession. Mickey reached for his shirt and began fastening the pop studs. His belt still hung open. Quietly I said, 'Your belt!'

With no great haste, Mickey attended to it. He whispered, 'You told me there was nothing between you two.'

'There isn't. It's just – awkward.'

From the doorway, Matt said, 'Sorry, didn't mean to barge in.' I couldn't tell how much he'd seen. He stood there a moment flexing his moustache, then went back to the kitchen.

Mickey said, 'I don't understand.'

'It's hard to explain.'

'Who's in charge here, you or him?'

'I'm sorry, Mickey. I'll make it up to you.'

'See what I mean? Mixed signals.'

'I really like you, honestly. Can you come back tonight, after work?'

'Hadn't you better clear it with your boyfriend first?' He was making for the door.

'Please don't go.'

Mickey turned and said, 'You need to sort this out, Sam Rigby. Otherwise it's no deal.' I followed him into the hallway, where he stepped over Matt's holdall, found his bag and jacket, and let himself out onto the landing.

I said, 'I'll come and see you in the Vaults this evening.'

He was at the top of the stairs now. He said, 'Do what you bloody well like,' then clattered down out of sight.

In the hallway, I faced the stretch of wall less compromised by coat hooks and useful shelves and banged my forehead against it. Then I took a couple of restorative breaths and strode into the kitchen.

Making toast, Matt said, 'Nicky not staying, then?'

I couldn't be bothered to correct him. 'He has to go to work.'

'I take it he spent the night.'

'As a matter of fact we've only just come in. We went swimming.'

Matt looked up from spreading butter. 'I could have sworn you said you went swimming.'

'Very droll.'

'Was that after he spent the night, then?'

'He didn't spend the night. And I don't see why you're interested, anyway. Is some of that toast for me?' Something had given me an appetite.

Matt handed me a slice and said, 'I bought eggs and bacon.' A grocery bag stood on the drop-leaf of the cabinet, next to a fresh copy of the Saturday Gazette.

'The cheap stuff, I hope.'

'The best. We're celebrating.'

'We are?'

'I cracked the case.' Looking extremely pleased with himself, Matt bit into his toast, then added, as far as I could make out, 'I'll do the fry-up in a minute.'

I fetched my coffee from the living room, leaving Mickey's abandoned mug to cool all by itself. Matt and I sat at either end of the kitchen table. I said, 'So you've solved the problem of Gordon Asprey and the long blond hairs.'

'It's a good one this, you'll like it.'

'Proceed.'

'Right. Well, there I was last night, stood across the street from Asprey's flat and freezing my bollocks off – '

'Just a minute. Where did you get to after you quit the Mafeking Court? You don't look as if you've slept much.'

'Never mind about that. I was standing there thinking it was going to be like Thursday all over again. It had got near ten o'clock and they'd shown no sign of going out, though I'd seen the woman when she closed the curtains, just like the day before. Then a taxi pulled up and I had the camera ready, not that I thought there'd be much chance of getting a decent shot because it was too dark. The woman came out on her own. She got into the taxi and it took off. I hadn't heard what she'd said to the driver because there was this bloke on my side of the street just kick-starting his bike. Well, I'd had an idea during the night, when I was tossing and turning in that miserable excuse for a bed.' He looked me in the eye. 'Next time I'm going to pick the accommodation myself.'

'Of course, be my guest. Money's no object. In fact, why not do everything yourself, then I can retire to the country and breed whippets.'

When I'd first known him, Matt would have risen to this, but as it was he ignored it and pressed on. 'Like I say, I'd come up with a theory, but to test it out I needed to follow the taxi. So I asked the bloke with the bike if he'd give me a ride.'

'I hope you didn't pay him.'

'For God's sake, Sam! I have never met anyone so tight in my whole life. Have you never heard of spending money to make money?'

'Yes, I have. And I've also heard of spending money to wind up in the insolvency court.'

Matt tut-tutted. 'It's no wonder you're always teetering on the brink.'

'Teetering? Who's teetering?'

'Do you have to interrupt all the time? I'm losing my thread.'

'Taxi. Motor-bike. Compliant member of the public.'

'How do you know he was compliant?'

'In my experience, people usually give you what you ask for.'

'Perhaps they'd do the same for you if you weren't so prickly. Anyway, yes, he said where do you want to go, so I said follow that cab, and he laughed, and then I said no, really, and he said hop on. We caught up with the taxi in no time. That bike was fantastic. You should have seen us go!'

'Now you're interrupting yourself.'

'My prerogative. Who's telling this story, anyway?'

'At this rate we'll be eating that fry-up for lunch.'

'Shut up and let me get on.' Matt wriggled in his seat now, clearly warming up for the main event. 'So after about ten minutes the taxi pulled up outside a bar in the city centre, down some back street near the canal. The woman got out and I waited a few moments then followed her into the bar. I couldn't see her at first and I was afraid I might have lost her – there was another entrance at the far side. I bought a drink and hung around, hoping she'd turn up again. Then I saw her coming out of the toilets. She went and joined this group of women at the far end of the bar.'

'A girls' night out.'

'By now I was pretty sure my theory was correct, I just had to get closer to make certain. I took my drink and walked right past these women so I could have a good stare.' Of Matt's many irritating qualities, a marked self-satisfaction when proved right stood near the top of the list. He was rapidly inflating with it now. 'Turned out I'd been spot on. Guess who she was?' He beamed at me with the utmost complacency.

I said, 'Gordon Asprey.'

Deflation was immediate. You could hear a faint hiss as smugness leaked out into the atmosphere. Matt said, 'I hate you.' All things considered, I thought this showed admirable restraint. 'How did you know?'

I shrugged my shoulders. 'It was obvious from the start. I did think of suggesting it to Beryl Asprey, but she'd never have believed me. Besides, we needed the work.'

Matt gave me a look unmixed with fondness. 'I've just spent

two days freezing to death in the street!'

'Did you get any pictures?'

'Nothing useful.'

'Never mind. Your eyewitness account should do the trick.'

'Are you saying you want me to phone her?' Matt looked alarmed. The conversation would no doubt prove awkward.

Though Matt needed to learn all aspects of the business, I decided to spare him this particular trial. Perhaps it hadn't been strictly necessary to send him out on surveillance in the middle of February. Almost contrite, I said, 'Leave it to me. I might wait until Monday so we can charge her for another couple of days. What did you do after you'd rumbled him? If you checked into the Midland I might have to punish you severely.'

Matt said, 'I found somewhere,' then got up and moved to the cabinet to empty the bag of groceries.

I said, 'You're being evasive.'

'No I'm not.'

'You're performing displacement activity with bacon.'

Suddenly, he turned on me. 'Look, never mind where I stayed, all right?' And I was just trying to decode his complex and unsettling facial expression when the phone rang. He seized this opportunity. 'Aren't you going to answer it?'

Naturally I'd have preferred to let it ring and continue questioning my supposedly faithful sidekick while I had him on the ropes. But a sense of my wider responsibilities intervened. Back in the living room, I lifted the receiver.

'Mr Rigby?'

Recognising the voice, I said, 'Mrs Haig. Everything under control over there?'

'As a matter of fact I'm at the Infirmary. It's Laurence. Something's happened.'

There was no mistaking the change in Alice Haig's usually business-like delivery. 'You sound upset. What's the matter?'

'Yesterday, Laurence had one of his – one of his turns, when they brought his evening meal. Afterwards they put him in a side room on his own, for the sake of the other patients. But someone's attacked him in the night!'

'Is he OK?'

'He's shaken but – yes, I think he's all right. Mr Rigby, can you get over here? I'm awfully afraid they were trying to kill him!'

## *fourteen*

I decided to take Matt with me.

Of course, there was always the risk that once inside the Infirmary he would slip away to fawn over the woman Docherty, but if that could be prevented I'd be able to start introducing him to the players in this unhealthy game. I needed to learn how much, if anything, Matt knew about Giles's death. I'd seen the newspaper on the kitchen cabinet and assumed that, dyslexia or no, he must at least have run his eye over the front page, given his well-known appetite for local news.

I'd hoped to discuss the matter during the long descent to the street, but when I mentioned the newspaper a regrettable incident occurred. It was Matt's fault. For what felt like the thousandth time, he fielded his threadbare gag about the Gazelle, and I don't know why but this time I snapped. I roundly forbade all further mention of this harmless ungulate, on pain of severe consequences. At this point, Matt should have read the warning signs. Instead, he asked me who I thought I was to be giving him orders, adding that if he wanted to say Gazelle then he would say Gazelle, threats notwithstanding. To prove the point, he said Gazelle, not just once but repeatedly, Gazelle, Gazelle, Gazelle, over and over again. When we reached the ground floor hallway and he was still saying it, I shoved him roughly against the wall and raised my fist.

Time froze, the brown eyes wide with alarm.

It was unnerving beyond belief. How could this have blown up out of nowhere? Why did I feel that it wasn't just about some irritating joke?

Then the pathetic moustache quivered a little, and when I saw it my anger leached away. I backed off and turned my head aside, staring at the floor. It was filthy. The whole building was filthy. Perhaps Lou Golding would put a bomb under it and make everything right.

Matt said, 'You were going to hit me.'

I said, 'No. Never.'

I heard him move. When I looked up, he was already at the front door. I followed him outside and down the steps to where the Minx was parked on the street. Three young Jews passed on their way to *shul*. Matt waited for me to unlock the passenger door, then got in. I walked round the front of the car, climbed in, and drove off.

We travelled half a mile without speaking. Then, staring rigidly ahead, Matt said, 'I suppose it was only a matter of time.'

I knew what he meant but I said, 'What was?'

'When I saw you get heavy with that bloke out at Otterdale last summer, I remember thinking it would be my turn some day.'

'Look, Matt, I'm sorry, OK?' We were caught in traffic. Around us, people were going about their usual business. Matt and I should have been doing the same, but we weren't.

'There was a kid called Casey in the second form at Our Lady, used to bully the smaller kids. Is that what you were like?'

'I don't remember.'

'Four of us got together and beat the crap out of him.' Then the bottleneck eased and we were on the move again, passing by the redbrick bulk of the toffee factory. My mother had started a new job there about four weeks earlier, and I hadn't seen her since. This usually meant that she'd found some new man to subsidise her existence, and so had less need to call on me.

We turned onto Ormskirk Road. Matt said, 'I thought you liked me.'

'That's got nothing to do with it.'

'The look on your face – '

'This isn't fair! You're milking it. I don't know what came over me, it just happened. I've said I'm sorry, now can we forget about it?'

We pulled onto the Infirmary forecourt. I found a parking space, switched off the engine, and sat in silence for a few seconds. Then I said, 'Are we all right? You don't have to come in with me if you don't want to.'

'I'm not staying out here if there's something going on. What's all this about?'

I gave Matt a sketchy outline of events in the past forty-eight hours. He didn't even know that Giles Rawley was dead. It puzzled me that Matt should have bought a Gazette and then failed even to glance at it. He must have been too busy mulling over what had happened in Manchester, but the case of Gordon Asprey was surely too prosaic to have gained much traction in his mind. I wondered again where he'd spent the night.

When I'd crammed Matt with the basic information he would need, we crossed the draughty forecourt and went inside.

The lobby of the Infirmary doubles as the waiting area for Accident and Emergency, but trade was slack that morning, with only a couple of prospective customers occupying the canvas-backed chairs set out there. At the desk, the receptionist was chewing the fat with a tall nurse whose back was turned to us, but it was a back I knew well. Despite the shocking presence of a skirt below it, it belonged to Bernie Foster. I said, 'Good morning, Nurse Foster.'

She turned and said, 'Weird, I was just going to call you.' Then seeing Matt she added, 'The wanderer returns.'

Matt said, 'I got an early train.' He always seemed a little intimidated by Bernie, preferring the skirted incarnation we were seeing now to the suited and brogued one he'd met occasionally elsewhere.

I said, 'We're on our way up to see Laurence Glass.'

'You'll have to get past Sister Wolfe first.'

'She won't stand a chance against the Rigby charm. Apparently someone's had a go at the Major during the night.'

'I'd heard. The police are here.'

My heart sank. 'Not Hargreaves, for God's sake.'

'No, it's that smart one who got you fired.'

'Mark?'

'The same.' Discretion had prevented her from referring to Mark as my ex-lover in front of the receptionist. It seemed impossible that her colleagues could be in any doubt as to where Bernie's inclinations lay, yet like most people in most jobs she did nothing to confirm their suspicions. She said, 'When you're done, can you come back down to the cardiac unit? I want to check something with you.'

We left Bernie at reception and took the lift to the first floor. This wasn't from laziness but because in the Infirmary I can never find the stairs. Having spent several weeks here the previous summer, Matt must have got to know his way around pretty well, but I didn't feel like consulting him. Stifling air met us as soon as the lift doors opened. I have a theory that hospitals generate special air in the basement, low on oxygen but high on spirit-crushing odours such as urine and carbolic soap, then pipe it round the rest of the building. We turned left and then right for the men's ward, which occupied one wing of the building at this level. As we came up to the double doors, they flapped open, and Mark Howell emerged, looking a bit yellow. Bodily functions were never Mark's strong point. Unusually, his mood appeared to lift when he saw me, yet another example of the odd behaviour which I'd detected from him in recent times. He said, 'Sam! Still on for that cuppa this afternoon?'

I'd forgotten all about our tea date. I said, 'I've been looking forward to it. Fourish at mine?'

'No, let's do it properly. How about the Swiss House, on the Boulevard?'

'You don't think it's a bit – ?' I couldn't find the word.

'A bit what? We'll be fine, I'll see you there. I suppose you're here to see the Major? Nasty stab wound, he was lucky.' Then Mark turned to Matt and said, 'I haven't bumped into you lately. Sam treating you all right, is he?'

I broke in and said, 'Any news on the investigation?' At one time, Mark would have refused to answer, but given the present state of relations I doubted if that would apply.

He said, 'Not really. If it's someone from outside we've got a tough job on our hands. The crime scene gave us virtually nothing, not even a set of unexpected prints.' He glanced back over his shoulder in the direction of the ward. 'And now this happens.'

'Any idea who it was?'

Mark shook his head. 'The Major's a fresh air fiend, some bloke got in through the window. It was too dark to see the face, apparently. Must have been pretty agile, there's a convenient tree out there but you'd need to be fit to climb it.'

'The weapon?'

'As a matter of fact, we found it near the bottom of the tree. Ordinary outdoor knife, pretty cheap I would say, the sort you could get anywhere. He must have dropped it climbing down and not hung around to look for it.'

'What if they come back and try again?'

'We're going to post someone from uniform by his door.'

'Wouldn't they be more use outside?'

'Not if the assailant decided to slip into the room from the corridor. Anyway, Glass agreed to keep the window closed in future.' Mark straightened his tie, then brushed from his sleeve some invisible object which was causing him offence. 'Right, better get back to the station, Hargreaves is on the warpath today. You know he's thinking of retiring?'

'News to me.'

'Well it hasn't dulled his sarcastic streak, I can tell you that much. Good luck getting round the ward sister. A word of advice: don't try charm, she's immune.'

Mark set off towards the lift, or perhaps the stairs if his geography was better than mine, and we stepped through the double doors into the ward. We were in a corridor with rooms to either side, one of which probably housed the Major and a distraught Alice Haig. Beyond this corridor lay the open ward. Experience taught that it would be wise to seek out the ward sister before taking action of any kind, and we found her at a desk in her office, the last room on the right, which looked onto the ward through an internal window. When I appeared in the doorway, she said, 'Who are you?'

At least she'd started with an easy one. 'Rigby, Sam Rigby. I'm here to see Major Glass.'

Very deliberately, she looked up at the wall clock, then back to me. 'Visiting time is from three to four.'

'I believe a woman named Alice Haig is with him. Mrs Haig asked me to come.'

'Mrs Haig is not in charge of this ward. Major Glass has experienced an assault, he needs to rest. Instead we've had an endless succession of policemen here since four o'clock this morning. I was about to ask Mrs Haig to leave. Normally there would have been no question of allowing her access to the patient in the first place, but since the Major has no family here and since he and Mrs Haig are engaged – '

'What?' The skeleton featured in a large anatomical chart on the wall had suddenly developed a severe case of St Vitus' dance.

Sister Wolfe ignored my interjection and went on. 'I suggest you leave and come back at three o'clock. Good morning.' She returned to the study of a ledger on the desk in front of her.

Though the situation looked grim, I wasn't quite ready to admit defeat, so I was still lurking in the doorway when Matt pushed past me and advanced into the office. He said, 'Sister Wolfe?'

I was just reflecting on the aptness of the ward sister's surname when she looked up, smiled warmly, and said, 'Matthew! How lovely.' This marked change in her vocabulary caused me to look at her properly for the first time. She was, it turned out, no termagant, but a pleasant-looking silver-haired woman with appealing dimples in her cheeks. She said, 'Have you been down in A&E?'

'Not today. I'm with him.' He jerked a thumb backwards.

Sister Wolfe gave herself up to astonishment. 'With Mr Kirkby?'

I said, 'Rigby, Sam Rigby.'

Matt said, 'That's right. He's my boss.'

Now Sister Wolfe sat up a little, the better to digest this extraordinary information. She said, 'And what is it that you do?'

Matt said, 'He's a private investigator. I'm his right-hand man.'

'You must find that extremely interesting.'

Matt said, 'Not really. And the pay's terrible.'

'Then why do you stay on?'

'I'm indispensable. I wouldn't want to let him down.'

It seemed that Sister Wolfe and my second-in-command had forgotten that I was standing just a few feet away. To refresh their memories, I spoke. 'We're investigating the murder of Giles Rawley.'

This struck a chord. 'That poor man! I saw it on the news. He was always so good in *Emergency Ward Ten*.'

As it happened, I thought Sister Wolfe was probably mixing Giles up with someone else, but this seemed like a bad time to correct her. 'I'm helping the police. We need to find the murderer as soon as possible. The Major had a room on the same floor at the Marine Lodge, his testimony could be vital.'

The ward sister wrestled with her professional conscience. 'Surely a few hours won't make any difference? The Major will still be here at three o'clock.'

'There's a dangerous lunatic at large who thinks nothing of smashing in an old man's skull with a hammer. Time is of the essence.' I'd always wanted to say 'Time is of the essence' at some such charged moment. It wasn't the sort of thing you could drop into general conversation.

Sister Wolfe sighed. 'I suppose the circumstances are quite exceptional. It's the second door on the right. But do try not to overtax him.' Then to Matt she said, 'How is your mother?'

'Fraught. My little sister's getting married next month.'

'Which one is that?'

'Marie.'

'Oh, yes, little Marie. You all grow up so quickly! Shall I tell Nurse Docherty you were here? I don't think she's in again until Monday.'

'It's all right, I'm seeing her tonight. Then of course she's got that thing tomorrow, hasn't she?' And Matt looked intently for Sister Wolfe's reaction.

'What thing is that, Matthew?'

I said, 'Matt, come on. We need to keep moving.'

Sister Wolfe said, 'No more than twenty minutes, please.'

Reluctantly, Matt followed me out into the corridor. When I

thought we'd passed beyond earshot of the office, I said, 'You seem very intimate with Sister Wolfe.'

'She used to go out with my Uncle Pat, years ago.' The Standish clan had tentacles in every corner of the town's life. Matt had always known that he was part of a larger whole, and in some ways I envied him this reassuring embrace. At the same time, it would make life more difficult if he should ever decide to be more open about his feelings for men. It had been easy for me. I only had a handful of relatives, and they'd all been disappointed in me already.

Matt said, 'Did you see how she looked when I mentioned tomorrow? She knew nothing about it, you could tell.'

'If it bothers you so much, you're going to have to confront Eileen.'

'Have you ever tried confronting Eileen? She'd have me tied in knots before you can say Leslie Crowther.'

We were outside the door of the Major's room. I said, 'Do you think you could put Nurse Docherty out of your mind for a few seconds? We're trying to catch a killer.'

Piqued, Matt said, 'Yes, all right. But you've got to admit the whole thing's fishy.' Hoping that a change of scene might do him good, I knocked, and we went in.

Alice Haig was just pulling on the pea-green coat I'd seen before. I introduced Matt to her and the Major, and she said, 'I do hope I haven't over-reacted, asking you to come over here like this. I was still quite shocked when I rang you, but I suppose the police do have it all under control.'

This was Alice Haig in a nutshell. Someone had just tried to murder her fiancé, and she was worried about over-reacting. I said, 'I needed to talk to the Major anyway.'

'I really must get back to Marine Lodge. I've left Graham looking after the desk when he should be at home by now. You were right, Mr Rigby. The telephone has never stopped ringing, and I've booked every table in the dining room for the entire weekend. How can people be so ghoulish?'

'I still haven't talked to Mrs Lane. Would it be all right if we call in when we've finished here?'

'Of course. Cordelia's mostly kept to her room. When I do see her, she gives me the most outlandish looks, as if I'd engineered the whole business about the will just to spite her.'

'By the way, I hear congratulations are in order.' Mention of the will had caused me to reflect that if Alice and the Major had become engaged while he was still alive, Giles might have been less generous with his bequest.

Laurence Glass said, 'Has that ward sister been gossiping? It's barely two hours since we closed the deal.'

Alice said, 'Please don't spread it around the town, Mr Rigby.'

Glass said, 'People will have to know, Alice.'

'I haven't had time to settle into the idea myself. I don't want people showering me with questions.'

I said, 'I wish you both the very best.' Privately, I thought Alice was making a mistake, and I could only imagine what Bobbie Haig and, in particular, her brother Nigel would have to say about it.

Alice said, 'I really must go. I'll see you at the hotel. Nice to have met you, Mr Standish. And Laurence – do be careful, won't you?' Then she kissed the Major rather primly on the forehead, and left the room.

On Sister Wolfe's evidence, you'd have expected to find Laurence Glass in a state of total nervous collapse. Instead, he sat propped up in the bed, exuding health and vigour. A bandage passed around his chest beneath his armpits, leaving the rest of his torso exposed, and it now became apparent that the Major's very correct, conservative clothing had concealed the body of a sometime man of action.

Trying for a tone of blokeish empathy, I said, 'You're a dark horse, Major, I had no idea.'

Laurence Glass gave a weak smile. 'When I asked them to call Alice, she was here in minutes. I was terribly touched. Of course I'd been wanting to say something to her for a long time, but everything is so public at the Marine Lodge. Mr Rigby, would you mind – I really am extremely warm, do you think you could open that window for me? I hardly think anyone's likely to chance their arm against three of us.'

I crossed to raise the window, which, as a product of late

Victorian civic architecture, allowed generous space for the ingress and egress of anyone up to no good. It looked out to the side of the building. The tree which Mark had mentioned continued upwards to the height of the second storey, and despite what Mark had said it would have made an easy enough climb for anyone who'd practised in childhood. The shift from the branches to the window-ledge looked tricky at first sight, but poking my head right out I could see not only various footholds afforded by decorative brickwork, but even a handy drainpipe which might have been placed there specifically with climbers in mind. We weren't looking for Spider-Man, just an ordinary human being with a steady hand and eye. A line of conifers had been planted along the perimeter wall, screening the building from the side street beyond, but one of the street lamps stood in a gap between these trees and could have lit the attacker's ascent.

I turned back into the room. Matt was saying, 'So you didn't get a look at his face?' I was relieved by this evidence that at least one small section of Matt's brain remained unconsumed by thoughts of Eileen Docherty.

The Major shook his head. 'It was dark, and everything happened very quickly. The police asked whether I could even be sure that it was a man, and I had to admit I couldn't.'

I said, 'You seem remarkably cool about the whole thing.'

'Do I? Perhaps you're forgetting my history.'

'Is there any reason you can think of – '

'Why someone would attack me like this? On the face of it, no. But after what happened to Giles, one begins to wonder.'

'Along what lines?'

'Rather obvious ones. The only thing Giles and I have in common is that we were both soldiers. For whatever twisted reason, someone bears a grudge.'

There was of course one further link between the two men, in their shared feelings for Alice Haig. But I just said, 'At any rate, you seem to have been very lucky last night.'

'If it was luck, Mr Rigby, it was the luck of the devil.'

'What makes you say that?'

Major Glass reflected for a moment. 'During the war, I worked on the Burma railway. Conditions were appalling, you can't imagine it if you weren't there. One of the worst things was the arbitrary cruelty of the guards – Koreans, most of them, no sense of honour, though in a way you could hardly blame them because the Nips treated them like dogs. The point is, we never knew when these – these animals were going to burst in and drag us all off our mats. Sometimes they just began to lay about them for no reason at all. We were far too weak to do anything about it, half dead from hunger and physical exhaustion, not to mention the diarrhoea. That's what did for a lot of us, you know. We'd shipped out to the Far East expecting to fight a decent war, but instead there we were, shitting ourselves to death.'

Our reaction to these words must have registered somehow, because the Major now said, 'I'm sorry, I realize it's not very pleasant. I was only trying to explain why I got into the habit of sleeping with one eye open. Ready for anything, you see. You might think I'd have got back to normal after the war, but if you've been through something like that it never really ends. You may try to forget it, but you can't. I still sleep extremely lightly, and so I'd become aware of someone in the room with me perhaps a fraction of a second before he struck. I tried to move out of the way, and the knife just went in here.' With the opposite hand, he indicated the area above his right pectoral, now covered by the bandage. 'Quite a shallow wound, he must have been put off his stroke. With my being in hospital he may have thought that I'd put up no resistance, but actually I was perfectly well, as I've been telling anyone who'll listen ever since they brought me in here. Now apparently I'm to be imprisoned until Monday morning at the earliest.'

I said, 'Was there a struggle?'

'Not really, no. I'd love to have got my hands on the blighter, but by the time I'd fought my way out of this bed he was half way through the window. Why do nurses have to tuck the sheets in so tightly? They seem to think they're wrapping parcels. I looked out, but I couldn't see anything. Then I called for help.'

At this point there was a knock at the door, and WPC Cilla Donnelly came into the room. If she was surprised to find that the

Major had company, she didn't show it. She said, 'Major Glass?'

'That's me.'

'WPC Donnelly, sir. I'll be outside your door from now on if you need anything.'

'Poor girl, you'll be bored to death, won't you? I told that plain-clothes officer, the one with the loud jacket, it's quite unnecessary. The fellow won't dare come back, and anyway, if he does I'm ready for him.'

Cilla said, 'We generally advise against people taking the law into their own hands, sir.' The open window caught her eye. 'Didn't you undertake to keep that window closed?'

'It's a hundred degrees in here! Do you want me to boil to death?'

'If anything happens to you while I'm on duty, I could lose my job.'

While the Major was thinking this over, I moved back to the window and said to him, 'Shall I?'

Clearly reluctant, he said, 'Yes, go ahead. Can't have the constable thrown out on her ear, can we.'

I lowered the sash and fixed the catch in place. To the Major, Cilla said, 'Thank you very much, sir.'

The Major said, 'Get them to fetch you some tea, or something.'

Acknowledging this kind thought with a nod, Cilla left us. The Major said, 'Robust-looking individual. Have to admit I'm in two minds about allowing women to serve in the police force. It'll be the army next, won't it?'

I said, 'Can I ask you about the night of Giles's death?'

'Fire away. Not much I can tell you, I'm afraid.'

'So you didn't hear anything, even though your room is on the same floor?'

'I didn't say that, but what I did hear doesn't amount to much, that's all. I'm generally awake quite late. To be honest I find it difficult to drop off, and I don't look forward to trying. In fact I often walk up and down for a while if I can't sleep. But on Thursday night I was still dressed, just glancing at the financial pages, when I heard Giles leave his room. It may have been around midnight, I'm not sure, but I noticed it because it was unusual. As a rule, once he'd come up to bed, that was it. There's not much to go downstairs for, after all, unless you're desperate for a confab with our rather peculiar night porter. I wondered if there might be something wrong, and I listened out for him to come back again. I doubt whether he was gone more than five or ten minutes.'

Matt said, 'Can you be sure that the person you heard coming and going was Giles Rawley?'

The Major raised his eyebrows. 'I hadn't thought of that. No, I can't.'

'And did you hear anything afterwards?'

'I didn't, but that's suggestive in itself. I don't know if anyone's told you, but the poor chap used to have nightmares. I often heard him cry out, but not on Thursday night. Presumably he couldn't, because he was already dead.'

Something about the way Laurence Glass said 'the poor chap' had stuck in my throat. I said, 'There was no love lost between you and Giles Rawley, was there?'

'I don't know what you mean.'

'Come on, now, Major. I saw Giles in action on Thursday.'

The Major tried to smile, without much success. 'He could be sharp with just about anyone.'

'But especially you.'

Laurence Glass stroked the blanket in front of him with his right hand, the hand with the missing fingers. 'It was all about Alice, really. Giles was reasonably civil towards me when I first arrived, but then I think he could see that something was developing between Alice and myself. He was possessive of her, when he had no right to be.'

'That must have annoyed you.'

'Annoyed is too strong.' The Major leafed through his vocabulary in search of a better word. 'I was *disappointed* to be denied his friendship. At his best he could be excellent company, and we were both veterans, after all. I can't claim to have much in common with Aznavorian or Miss Pyle, though Sarkis and I do chat about business sometimes.'

'Business?'

'The army was my first love, and I stayed on as long as I could after the war. But there were limits to what I could do, because of this.' He held up the damaged hand. 'Eventually the frustration got the better of me, so I took off and set myself up in business instead. Did rather well for myself as a matter of fact, travelled a lot, just like Sarkis did. We chat about our globe-trotting past.'

Though the clothes I'd seen the Major wearing might once have been expensive, they were no longer new. In addition, he was over-wintering in one of the cheaper rooms in a relatively cheap hotel in an unfashionable resort. I said, 'What happened to all the money?'

This question, or the tone in which I'd asked it, seemed to rankle. The Major said, 'You don't pull your punches, do you, Mr Rigby?' The weak smile came again. 'I suppose you're within your rights. My own fault for talking up my success. But at first the business really did do well. I've never had a family or anything like that, so of course I had little call to spend what I'd accumulated. But then – ' The Major looked away, towards the window and the world outside. 'I'd been managing to suppress the flashbacks for many years. Suddenly – and I don't know to this day why it was – they returned, with ten times the force. One moment I might be in the middle of some business lunch with important clients, and the next I'd find myself back there in the jungle, sweating, covered in vermin, vomiting my guts out into some god-awful latrine. I couldn't go on like that. I began to withdraw from contact with people. I'm ashamed to say I sought the help of a psychiatrist.'

I glanced across at Matt, wondering how he was responding to all this, but I couldn't read his expression. To the Major I said, 'And that's when the money stopped piling up.'

'I'm no longer fit for work, I've been ordered to rest. I have a certain amount of capital, and I eke it out as best I can.' He smiled at me again. 'So now you know.' And in that smile I saw the full depth of his humiliation, the once-proud military man brought low.

There were questions I'd still have liked to ask Laurence Glass, but now that I'd seen that broken smile I hesitated to push him any further. In fact I was just wondering whether to wrap up the proceedings when Matt said, 'How did you lose those fingers?'

One of the key qualifications for being British is that when you see a person lacking some body part you must on no account ask what became of it. Though the Standishes were as British as fish and chips, they were strangers to any such compunction. Rueful, the Major raised his hand and examined it. 'These?' he said, referring to the fingers as if they were still present and correct. He turned to me. 'If I tell you, you won't say anything to Alice, will you? I told her I lost them trying to fix a Jeep in '47.'

Though I didn't actually reply, the Major seemed to think it was enough to have made the request, and continued. 'It was during the war, of course. I was Company Sergeant then, I wasn't promoted to Major until afterwards. I had a good friend in the company, James Hazeldine, a Norfolk man through and through. Somehow we managed to do everything together, he was sent up-river to Kanyu camp with me, we worked together every day on that wicked, pointless railway, and I'm not exaggerating when I say that but for him and his solid English humour I think I'd have been driven mad. Nothing in life had prepared me, you see, nothing at school, nothing in my military training. It was as though you'd suddenly found yourself stationed in hell. Well, as I say, we did everything together, and I'm afraid that included falling ill together. Poor James had beriberi, his lower body was horribly swollen, there was no question of him working in that state. And I'd become hopelessly weak myself. It was the diet, just a tiny portion of rice and anything we could grow or scavenge to supplement it, but there was less opportunity for such things up-river and we all suffered in consequence. I'd begun to lose my eyesight, and to some extent my hearing, so from the Nips' point of view I was wasting valuable space. James and I were lucky, they decided we could join a group of sick men being sent down-river to Chungkai, where nutrition was slightly better. Of course, this wasn't kindness. It simply meant we'd be more likely to recover, in which case we'd be put straight back on the job.

'I sat next to James on the boat. He was giving me a commentary on the sights we passed along the way, with his usual tart observations thrown in. Then we got talking about what we were going to do after the war. Normally we didn't think that way, we took each day as it came, but somehow this boat trip had given us hope. We said we were going to do this, and we were going to do that, and naturally food played a disproportionate role in all our schemes. But finally James said he hardly cared what he did, provided he need never have dealings with any more of these stinking, slitty-eyed pigs as long as he lived.'

Here the Major paused, reached for a glass of water on the unit beside him, and drank, as if trying to drink down the mounting agitation in his voice. Calmer, he replaced the glass and went on.

'Those were the exact words, I'll never forget them: stinking, slitty-eyed pigs. James obviously hadn't meant the guard to hear his little outburst, and in any case most of them had only the most basic English. But I'm afraid luck was against him that day. The guard had been sitting behind us, and now he came forward and stood in front of us and said, "Who say this thing?" I tried to stop him but James just lifted his hand a little, like this, and then suddenly the guard scooped him up in his arms – he weighed next to nothing, of course – and threw him overboard. He started screaming, there was no question of him being able to swim in his condition, and I tried to stand up and get to the side. That's when the guard took my hand – '

Again the Major paused. He bowed his head for a moment, and his left hand covered his right protectively on the blanket in front of him. After a few seconds' silence, he looked up.

'He took hold of my hand, slipped his knife from its sheath, and sliced off the fingers – one, two, as if he were cutting bread – and then he called for the medical orderly who was travelling with us, and went and sat down again.

'I don't need to tell you that in a place like that the wound could easily have killed me, and in fact when we reached Chungkai I was on the edge for a couple of days, actually hoping that this would be the end. But I recovered. With the hand strapped up I was no use for heavy work, so I was sent back to Changi to sit out the rest of the war. You could say James saved my life.' The Major paused a third time, but went on almost immediately. 'It was my fault that James died. If I'd not been so hard of hearing at the time he could have spoken more quietly and the guard would never have picked it up.'

While telling the latter part of his story, Laurence Glass had directed his gaze at the walls, or the bed-linen, or anywhere at all in the room other than his two silent listeners. Now, though, he looked directly at Matt, gave the weak smile again, and said, 'Well, you wanted to know. And if you were wondering exactly why I can't sleep at night, it's because I'm back in that ruddy boat, and I can hear James screaming and there's absolutely nothing I can do about it.'

Then he fell silent, and seemed to turn in on himself, as if unaware of our presence. After about ten seconds of this, I began to consider a variety of wholly inadequate remarks, but was rescued from making any of them by the Major stirring himself and adding, rather more steadily, 'Old Giles Rawley told me there was a new Burma Star group starting in Southaven, and he couldn't understand why I didn't want to go along. Can you imagine anything worse than getting together with a bunch of veterans, all falling over themselves to pretend everything's all right now?'

I suspected this might be misrepresenting the activities of such a group, but while I was considering this the door swung open without preliminaries, and Sister Wolfe was amongst us.

'Now, Mr Rigby – I believe I did say twenty minutes.'

I looked at my watch. 'Good heavens, I didn't realize. He's all yours, Sister.' I turned to the Major. 'Thanks for your help, Major Glass. I hope you don't get too bored. If you need company, you'll find WPC Donnelly quite a fair conversationalist.'

His face was turned away from us and I thought he would make no reply, but when we reached the door he said, with sudden animation, 'Not a word to Alice! War is a man's game, Mr Rigby. It's better kept that way.'

We were in the lift before either of us spoke. Matt said, 'He's about the same age as my dad.' Matt's father worked for the council inspecting drains and sewers, one of those jobs whose usefulness is inversely proportional to its appeal.

For a moment I struggled to grasp the significance of Matt's remark, but as we stepped out into the ground floor corridor I said, 'Do you know what kind of war your father had?'

'Not really. There's a picture of him in uniform on the sideboard, my mother likes it. He was in North Africa, but he never talks about it.'

A quarter of a century had passed, but the war was still all around us, even in a place like Southaven. 'Perhaps you should ask him.'

'He's got no time for the Germans, I know that much, but he says he agrees with Ted Heath, we ought to go into the Common Market to stop it all happening again.' Points of agreement between Matt's father and the prime minister were rare. A couple of weeks earlier, we'd bumped into him on the Boulevard, and he'd pinned me to a lamp-post for a quarter of an hour while he delivered a lecture on the evils of the Industrial Relations Bill.

Back in the reception area, I remembered Bernie's request to drop in at the cardiac unit. I'd have preferred to get straight over to the Marine Lodge, and I briefly considered telling Bernie at a later date that the whole thing had slipped my mind. But since it hadn't, and since I was at least mildly curious to know what she wanted, I said to Matt, 'I need to pop back and see Bernie. Are you coming?'

But Matt took the keys and went off to wait in the car. He was still angry with me, I could tell, and I hadn't the first idea how to start putting things right.

I found Bernie in conversation with the ward sister at the foot of a bed with drawn screens. Reflecting that their hyperactive floral pattern was enough to make anyone ill, I presented myself, and Bernie said, 'It's a matter of identification, that's all.'

Indicating the screens, the sister said, 'She was brought in around midnight. She gave her name as Elizabeth Grable.'

I said, 'Betty Grable.'

'Yes, and of course we picked up on that but she insisted. The important thing was to make her comfortable, so we dropped the whole question and carried on. Then this morning Nurse Foster came in and thought she recognized her.'

Bernie said, 'I can't be sure, Sam. It's been a long time.' And she drew back the screen.

The frail, elderly-looking woman in the bed had been asleep, but now her eyes slowly opened. In a thick voice, my mother said, 'Sammy? Is that you?'

## *fifteen*

It was about five weeks since I'd last seen my mother. Aunt Winnie had run into her on the Boulevard just after New Year, and had been alarmed by her general condition. Personally I'd not felt too concerned, as I knew that my mother took celebration of Jesus's birth very seriously and often didn't recover until the spring. Nevertheless, I drove out to Marshfield to check up on her. She'd been renting a tiny fishermen's cottage in Duck Lane for the past six months, a lengthy tenure by her standards. I'd found her quite pale and probably underweight, but in good spirits, anticipating her new job at the toffee factory with enthusiasm because she knew a couple of the girls who'd be working on the line with her. She relieved me of five pounds and a pack of cigarettes, and I left feeling reassured.

Now here she was in a hospital bed, rail thin and old before her time. The ward sister said, 'She's rather groggy, I'm afraid. We had to give her a sedative.'

I said, 'Hello, Mum. How are you feeling?'

My mother said, 'Have you got a little ciggie, Sammy love?'

'You won't be able to smoke in here.'

'I'm going home in a minute. There's a taxi coming.'

Bernie Foster said, 'She's confused. She needs sleep as much as anything.'

The ward sister said, 'If you come into the office I can take down some details. You can see your mother for a minute or two afterwards.'

My mother's eyes had already closed again. Bernie went to attend to another patient while I followed the sister to her lair, a good match for Sister Wolfe's hideout on the general ward upstairs. Introducing herself as Sister Redman, the sister said, 'So – not Betty Grable after all.'

'Her name's Shirley, Shirley Rigby. What happened? What's the matter with her?'

'A policeman found her last night, collapsed on the pavement on Marshfield Road. At first he thought she'd been drinking, but when he looked more closely she was obviously having some kind of attack.'

Knowing my mother's habits, I said, 'She might have been walking back from the Coach and Horses in Merechurch. She rarely misses a Friday.'

'The house doctor thinks she's had a mild heart attack. Is there any history of heart trouble?'

'No. She's always been strong as an ox.'

'Perhaps you haven't looked at her lately, Mr Rigby. She isn't as strong as an ox any more. The likelihood is that her poor health will have brought on this episode. Does she drink very much?'

Aware that people have different standards, but that I was talking to a medical professional, I said, 'Possibly. And she smokes.'

'We'd gathered as much. It all places a severe strain on the heart. We should know more next week, when we can run tests.'

Having supplied the details required for Sister Redman's paper-work, I went back to my mother's bedside. She was asleep. Her skin had a yellowish tinge, and grey showed through her hair at the roots. I sat down and watched the slow rise and fall of her chest. After a while I placed my hand over hers, where it rested on the blanket. We weren't much given to displays of physical affection, but I didn't think she'd mind.

We'd been going on like that for a couple of minutes when my mother's eyes opened. She tilted her head towards me and focused on my face. Then she said, 'Your father was here,' withdrew her hand from mine, and fell asleep again.

*

I called Aunt Winnie from the payphone in the reception area. Unfairly, she suggested that none of this would have happened if I'd just kept a proper eye on my mother, though Winnie knew full well that an audience would only have encouraged her. Then I called directory enquiries, followed by the toffee factory, which I knew still worked a Saturday shift. There I learned that after an unreliable start my mother had been off sick for the past fortnight. I felt a flush of anger. If she really was sick, why couldn't she have let me know? Given her cavalier attitude to the truth, I might never discover what had actually been going on.

Out in the Minx, Matt greeted my return without warmth. Apparently he meant to go on giving me a hard time, but as I'd crossed the forecourt I'd come up with a plan: do nothing. There had to be at least some possibility that if I ignored the problem it would go away.

I told Matt about my mother, and to give him his due he did make some grudging pretence of sympathy. He'd still not met her, but his mother knew mine by sight and reputation and wasn't much impressed. From Kathleen Standish's point of view, my mother represented yet another reason why her precious son would be better off not working for me. I had no doubt that the old scandal of Shirley Rigby and her bastard child remained fresh in Ma Standish's memory.

Matt then sought further details in the case of Giles Rawley's murder, and in particular whether I had anyone fingered for it. I led with Laurence Glass, partly to allow Matt the pleasure of pointing out that unless we had two murderers on our hands the Major was unlikely to have tried murdering himself. Second on the list came Cordelia Lane, but while I mistrusted her dutiful daughter routine I could think of no reason why she might want to harm Laurence Glass, on top of which I doubted whether she'd do much good up a tree. Finally we had to consider the Golding connection, whether in the repellent shape of First Ugly Bloke or some other minion of that empire. Giles had been nosing into the affairs of a family with a history of violent crime, and now he was dead.

Matt said, 'The person with the strongest motive is still Alice Haig.'

I demurred. 'We can't be sure of that until we know everything about these people. We need to keep asking questions. Besides, why would Alice pay me to investigate a murder she'd committed herself?'

At the Marine Lodge, there were no spaces left in the staff car park at the back, where the black Armstrong-Siddeley dominated a collection of humbler vehicles. We found a lucky spot on Marine Approach and returned up Wright Street on foot, to enter the hotel by the back door. It was almost noon, and a complex aroma of roast meats told us that Oscar must be hard at work.

I risked glancing into the kitchen. Two sous-chefs, young girls I'd never seen before, were busy prepping vegetables, while Oscar himself tasted the contents of a large saucepan from a wooden spoon. His face registering uncertainty, he added salt. The brandy bottle stood near him on the counter. Then he saw me in the doorway. He said, 'You pick your moment, don't you?'

I hadn't intended to question Oscar at this point, but the man was right there in front of me. I said, 'Still sticking to your story?'

'What story's that, then?' Admirably professional, the two girls ignored us and worked on.

'You say you went straight home from here after dinner on the night Giles was killed.'

'I don't just say it, I did it. Now clear off, we're expecting mayhem any minute.'

'One more thing – when the Grand tried to steal your services from under Mrs Haig's nose, who actually made the approach?'

'I'm warning you, I want you out of here. My girls are under enough pressure as it is.'

'Last night, someone with a knife tried to turn Laurence Glass into cutlets. Was it you, Oscar?'

The man now bore down on me. There was no shortage of him, and I felt my body's emergency services rush to their posts, with all leave cancelled. At the last moment I took a step backwards, causing Matt, whose foot had carelessly got underneath my own, to say, 'Ow!' Then Oscar slid the door shut in front of my face.

We found Alice Haig at reception, directing would-be diners towards their troughs. Evan Bickerstaff loitered near the grandfather clock. Despite our elbows having become close pals earlier that morning, he'd now returned to his previous pattern of ignoring my presence. However, he didn't ignore Matt, and neither did Matt ignore him. The signs were not large, but they were there: the eyes met, separated, and met again, after which both parties studiously avoided further contact.

The diners went on their way, showing an unusual interest in the walls and ceiling, as forming part of the set on which Giles Rawley had met his end. Alice said, 'You can't miss it, can you? Naked prurience. We've even had people in for morning coffee, and no one ever comes here for morning coffee in February. How did you find Laurence?'

'Sturdy. I don't think you need to worry about him.' There was a badly-folded copy of the Gazette on the counter. I said, 'Anything in the paper?'

'Yes and no. The cheek of it! They make a serious mistake, which could wreak untold damage on my business, then have the audacity to print a tiny apology on page 7.'

I tried to look sympathetic. 'That's the press for you.' More diners were arriving. 'But business doesn't seem to have suffered too much, does it?'

'We can hardly thank the Gazette for that, can we? Now – were you planning to speak to Cordelia?' Alice's expression sought to cushion me against disappointment.

'Why, has she gone out?'

'No, I think she's in her room. But when I got back to the hotel earlier she was down here having coffee. She told me to my face that I'd cheated her out of her inheritance. Apparently I'd poisoned Giles against her husband. Of course I had no idea what she was talking about, and it was extremely awkward – there were half a dozen people listening, all hugely enjoying the spectacle, but she didn't seem to care. I doubt whether you'll find her very receptive to your questions.'

The new arrivals were clamouring for pre-prandial sherries, so

Evan led them off towards the lounge. Matt watched him go. I said, 'Receptive or not, I've got to talk to her. Can you put a call through? It's getting busy down here, we might be better going up to her room if she doesn't mind.'

The call was made, with considerable tact on Alice's part, and a reluctant Cordelia Lane summoned Matt and myself up to her billet. As we made for the stairs, a middle-aged waitress bearing menus nearly collided with us in the hallway. I was getting my first glimpse of how Marine Lodge must function during the holiday season, where each meal marked another performance in the theatre of hotel life. Giles Rawley himself would have made a magnificently imperious *maître d'*, if the actual theatre hadn't claimed him first.

On the stairs, I said, 'That was Evan Bickerstaff.'

Matt feigned ignorance. 'What was?'

'The boy whose backside you were studying. Everyone seems to think he's stupid.'

'And is he?'

'Perhaps you could make it your business to find out. He has ample opportunity both for Giles's murder and the attack on Laurence Glass. As for motive – '

'I wasn't studying his backside.'

'No, of course you weren't.' I knocked on the door of room 14, and a voice invited us in.

Cordelia Lane said, 'I don't know where we're all going to sit.' She was in no brighter mood than Alice Haig had intimated.

I said, 'My assistant generally prefers to stand,' and introduced Matt. Cordelia didn't so much as glance at him.

'You'd better sit here by the window, Mr Rigby.' She removed her handbag from an upright chair. The furniture here seemed far superior to the selection of oddments I'd found in Giles's room on the floor above, and the large window admitted a generous helping of February light. It was, as Sarkis Aznavorian had said, a pleasant room. 'I don't understand why you want to talk to me. It was bad enough being interrogated by that vulgar policeman, on the very day I'd lost my poor father, without having to go through it all again on the whim of that woman.' She settled into a comfortable armchair on the opposite side of the window. In the corner of my eye I could see Matt asking himself whether it would be all right to perch on the end of the bed, and deciding that it wouldn't.

'I thought you'd always got on well with Mrs Haig.'

'Up to a point, yes. But I realize now that I've been deceived.' Cordelia was embracing the role of Wronged Party with considerable vim, having clearly inherited something of her father's gift. 'While I've been showering her with gratitude for making a friendly winter home for my father this past few years, she's been working tirelessly to destroy my future.'

Matt said, 'I'm sorry, Mrs Lane, but I've been out of town until this morning and I've not caught up with all the facts. Would you mind telling me about Mr Rawley's will?'

Cordelia Lane now examined Matt for the first time. On the odd occasions when I wanted to look harmless I really had to work at it, and I found the ease with which Matt could pass himself off as an innocent young man caught up in unpleasant events distinctly annoying. Nevertheless, I had to admit the trick was useful. Given Cordelia's present mood, the question of how to approach the delicate subject of the will had stumped me.

But apparently Cordelia had no intention of allowing herself to be tamed without a struggle. 'It's quite extraordinary to have to discuss such things with strangers.'

Matt said, 'I know, and I don't like asking. But we need to see every side of the picture if we're going to catch your father's killer.'

'Surely it would be better left in the hands of the police?'

I said, 'Be honest, Mrs Lane – exactly how much faith do you have in the abilities of the local force?'

Here, Cordelia Lane's expression spoke for itself.

I pursued my advantage. 'Detective Inspector Hargreaves is shrewd and systematic, and he understands the criminal mind. What he can't understand, because he doesn't try, is cultured, intelligent people like your father.'

She studied me doubtfully. 'Whereas you do?'

Fortunately, Matt cut in on a different tack. 'I'm still in the dark. Was it a very big estate?'

I now saw that I should have kept plucking the pecuniary string all along, because Cordelia instantly spun round to face Matt and said, 'Of course it was! Alice Haig will be a wealthy woman, while I'm left scratching in the dirt. It's wickedly unfair! He knew I was hard up, it's not easy when you have four children at home and a husband determined to live beyond his means.'

I said, 'What does your husband do, Mrs Lane?'

'He works for an art dealer up in London. He's no great expert, but I've heard his employer say that Howard has one of those faces which sell pictures. All an act, of course.'

Matt said, 'Did the will come as a surprise? Were you expecting to do better?'

'You make it sound as if I were waiting eagerly for my father to die. He could be difficult, perhaps hurtful at times, but he was my father and I loved him. I thought he'd be with us for years yet.' Tears stood in Cordelia's eyes. As a precaution, she withdrew a handkerchief from the sleeve of her cardigan.

I said, 'But you'd always believed that Giles would leave you comfortable?'

'Until I came up for this visit, yes. Oh, it was dreadful!' And now she dabbed at her eyes with the handkerchief.

'He told you he'd changed his mind?'

'It was worse, far worse!' Cordelia took a moment to collect herself. 'He said he wanted me to leave Howard! Leave him, and have nothing more to do with him. Of course, I asked what had brought this on. My father had never been fond of Howard, he couldn't see Howard's strengths like I do, but this felt like something different, something new. But he wouldn't tell me why, and I said he could hardly expect me to walk out on my husband of twenty years for no reason at all. He said there was a very good reason, but for my sake and the children's he preferred not to share it with me. So I told him there was no question of my leaving Howard, and that's when he brought up the subject of the will.'

Cordelia Lane fell silent, and turned to look out of the window, perhaps hoping that the grey prospect might calm her. But she seemed no less upset when she turned back and resumed her story. 'My father said he'd recently changed his will, leaving a little in trust for the children but nothing for Howard and myself. He said he'd done this in anger and hadn't slept properly since, and that if I would just do as he asked me then he'd gladly restore my own part of the inheritance. I'm afraid I lost my temper with him, Mr Rigby. My father could be terribly obstinate, and he just wouldn't see that this demand was wholly unreasonable. Then in the heat of the argument he let slip that he'd found something out.'

Matt said, 'Something about your husband?'

'Yes, of course! And I pressed him and pressed him, but he absolutely wouldn't say what it was.'

I said, 'Did you argue about this on the night he was killed?' Cordelia looked at me narrowly, so I added, 'He hinted at family strife when I saw him that evening.'

The eyes refilled, the handkerchief was redeployed. 'If only I could take it all back! The things I said to him! And I never saw him alive again!'

Now Cordelia cried in earnest. I couldn't feel much sympathy. I've always preferred people who wait until you've gone before turning on the water-works. Matt saw his opportunity and finally sat down on the bed. When it seemed possible that Cordelia might be over the worst, I said, 'Do you know any young men with motor-bikes?'

Cordelia sniffed and dabbed. 'Motor-bikes? What are you talking about?'

I told her about Giles's mysterious visitor with the Japanese machine. 'Is there anyone like that in your family? Or perhaps someone your husband works with?'

'Not that I know of. You think it was this man who brought my father the information about Howard?'

'It rather looks that way, doesn't it?'

There was a brief pause while this sank in. 'Oh, dear. I thought it must all be some invention of Alice Haig's. I've just accused her of the most dreadful things.' She relived the memory, then said, 'Oh, dear,' again.

I said, 'How much did you tell DI Hargreaves about the will?'

'By the time he interviewed me he'd already spoken to my

father's solicitor, I could hardly pretend that nothing had happened. As far as I recall, the only thing I didn't mention was my father's impossible ultimatum. You and Howard are the only people who know about that.'

Among the extensive cast of characters who've set up home in my mind over the years can be found a version of Alice Haig's night porter, in charge of alerting the front of the mind when something's not quite right. Most of the time he dozes harmlessly, an abandoned newspaper just slipping from his knee, but for some reason Cordelia Lane's remark woke him up. Noticing this, I said, 'You told your husband?'

'Of course I did. I telephoned him that same day, the day I arrived here. I won't repeat what Howard said about it.'

'He was angry?'

'He has a lively temper. I almost regretted telling him, but a good marriage is based on trust, Mr Rigby. Howard and I have no secrets from one another.'

I wondered whether this was true. It seemed that Howard Lane had gone missing for at least twenty-four hours, leaving the children with the new au pair. People rarely like to discover that you've been eavesdropping on their telephone conversations, so I had to phrase my question carefully. 'Do you know where your husband was on Thursday night?' I could see from the look on Matt's face that he didn't think I'd phrased it carefully enough.

Some colour rose to Cordelia Lane's cheeks. 'What a very strange question! He was at home, of course.'

This falsehood wasn't enough to clarify whether Cordelia actually knew the truth or not, but if she did she certainly wasn't going to share it with me. Deciding it might be wise to hit reverse, I said, 'And did you notice anything unusual that night yourself? Perhaps something different here at Marine Lodge after Giles walked round for his drink in the Grand Hotel?'

Cordelia considered this carefully. 'I had my usual coffee after dinner with Miss Pyle.'

'Just Miss Pyle?'

'Mr Aznavorian excused himself, he had something to attend to.'

'But you don't know what?'

'I'm afraid not. Then I went up to my room. It seemed a perfectly normal night. I think I may have wakened at one point and heard the Major walking about in the room above me.'

'Can you be sure of that?'

'It happens nearly every night. He has difficulty sleeping, he says it helps if he gets up for a while. So no, nothing unusual at all. I was quite wakeful myself, because of the awful row I'd had with my father, but I just stayed in bed running over it in my mind.'

Here, a more systematic investigator – Harry Hargreaves, for example – would have asked where Cordelia Lane had been the previous night while someone was puncturing the Major just above the right nipple, but I was put off by her poor suitability for arboreal stunts. For the present, Cordelia probably had no more beans to spill, so Matt and I left her to repair her make-up. I had the impression that, however upset she might have been, and whatever terrible things might have happened at the Marine Lodge during the last thirty-six hours, Cordelia Lane was looking forward to her lunch.

In the corridor, Matt asked if there was any chance that he could see Giles Rawley's room. But I felt that Alice had been reluctant enough to give me the key the first time I'd asked, and it might be wiser not to push my luck.

I wasn't quite sure what to do next.

Then, just as we got back to the reception desk, where Evan once again lurked impassively while Alice Haig spoke with someone on the phone, the door opened to admit a lively draught followed by Miss Pyle and Sarkis Aznavorian. I introduced them to Matt, and said, 'Have you been out working up an appetite?'

Rosemary Pyle said, 'Precisely so, Mr Rigby. We've had pleasanter walks, though, haven't we, Sarkis?'

'Eh? What's that, my love?'

'It's not much of a day, is it?'

'Oh, no, no, it's February through and through. Not especially cold, but that wind finds every gap in your clothing.'

Miss Pyle said to me, 'Have you found out who that young motorcyclist was? I'm beginning to feel guilty that I didn't mention him to the police.'

I knew the feeling. In fact I'd as good as decided to pass the information to Mark Howell when we met that afternoon. 'No news yet, I'm afraid. By the way, Mr Aznavorian – what was it that you had to do which kept you from your after-dinner coffee on Thursday?'

He looked perplexed. 'I think I had it as usual, didn't I?'

Miss Pyle intervened. 'No, Sarkis, don't you remember? We were off to Lytham next morning and you wanted to top up the oil in the Armstrong.' Then she turned to me and added, 'It's a beautiful car, of course, but immensely thirsty.'

Aznavorian said, 'That's right, I remember now.'

I said, 'Wouldn't it be rather dark for a job like that? Why not leave it until the morning?'

He shook his head. 'That wouldn't do at all. Rosemary doesn't like to be kept waiting – do you, my love?'

'Now Sarkis, that's nonsense and you know it is.' Miss Pyle smiled her slippery smile, to cover the heat which her friend's amiable sally had generated. Then she looked at her watch and said, 'Come along, now – lunch. We mustn't be late, particularly with its being so busy today.'

'Very good, my love.' And the couple left us.

Matt said, 'She seems very nice.'

I said, 'Don't be fooled. Giles warned me about her. Did you notice that smile? I wouldn't trust her as far as I could throw her.'

'You're always so negative about people. Why can't she just be a sweet old lady?'

'Because she's too sweet to be wholesome. And I don't think for a second that Aznavorian's after-dinner activities had anything to do with the car. They both lied to me about that brown bag I saw them with on Friday morning, and they're lying about this as well. If only they were younger.'

'I don't get you.'

'Well, I'd feel I could pile on the pressure.'

'You mean, slap them around a bit?'

Matt looked me in the eye, and though it was an awkward moment and I couldn't think of a useful riposte, nevertheless I looked him in the eye right back again. The brown eyes may have been charged with an unusual degree of anti-Rigby sentiment, but I was fond of them. Besides, being on the receiving end of Matt's disapproval had a charm all its own. The contact made, neither of us seemed prepared to break it, and things could have gone on like this for some time if Alice hadn't piped up from the reception desk, the phone call now concluded. 'That was Graham, the night porter. Quite ridiculous! He said he'd rather not come in tonight – as if I could possibly find someone at such short notice!'

Moving back towards the desk, I said, 'Couldn't Evan cover for him?'

'Evan can't be expected to work a twenty-four hour shift. And I shall need him on his toes for the Valentine's Day rush tomorrow.'

Though standing only a short distance away, Evan gave no sign that we were talking about him. I said, 'What was Graham's problem?'

'Nothing at all. He says he's unwell, but it's not true, he was fine when he left here at seven this morning. Anyway, I think I've talked him round. Really, staff can be an absolute nightmare sometimes.'

No doubt much more might have been said on this topic, but at that point the saga of relations between the Marine Lodge and its overweening neighbour unexpectedly began a fresh chapter. I heard the door open behind me, and Alice's expression when she saw the newcomer caused me to look round, just as the inevitable blast of winter air was reaching the reception desk.

The stranger halted just inside the door to take her bearings. She was a short but powerful woman in late middle age, wearing a scarlet trouser suit topped by a pale fur jacket. Then, glancing neither to left nor right, she crossed the hall towards us, and as she did so an invisible red carpet seemed to unroll itself beneath her feet. At the desk she stopped and said, 'I'm looking for Alice Haig.'

Alice said, 'I am Alice Haig.'

The other woman now subjected Alice to unhurried scrutiny. Most people would have found this unsettling, and perhaps made some nervous remark, but Alice stood her ground.

Then, apparently satisfied with the result of her survey, the woman said, 'My name is Golding. Let's take a little walk.'

## sixteen

For some reason I'd always pictured Mickey Golding's mother as a rather tall woman with a Roman nose. Alongside my disappointment at her actual height, I now had to deal with the shocking fact that her actual nose was the image of Mickey's, and by far her least authoritative feature. But while Mickey's character had developed along the accommodating lines suggested by the nose, his mother's presence in the lobby of the Marine Lodge hotel radiated an uncompromising power. There could be little question that here stood the mastermind behind the unpleasant solicitor's letters which had so shaken the worlds of Sidney Flint and Alice Haig. If those letters fell within her conception of legitimate business practice, I could only guess what else it might stretch to include.

Alice, her hair more than ever resembling the helm of some Amazon warrior, said, 'I have a hotel to run, Mrs Golding. I'm afraid I don't have time for little walks.'

'Not even if I make it worth your while?'

Alice hadn't expected such a speedy rejoinder, and took a moment to digest it. 'How? How can you make it "worth my while"?' There was no missing the scornful quotation marks.

'I got a proposal to put to you.'

'If it's anything like the proposal I received from your solicitors, you'll be wasting your breath.'

'My thinking's moved on.'

'Then perhaps you'd like to join it. If you'll excuse me, I have work to do.' And Alice turned her attention to the bookings ledger on the desk.

As grand gestures go, this was effective in its way, but still not enough to deter Louise Golding. 'Don't make the mistake of thinking you can push me aside. When I moved to this town, the rules changed. You can either deal with that, or go under. Now, which is it to be?'

Lou Golding had been obliged to deliver this speech to the Amazon helmet, but when it was over Alice slowly raised her head. 'Perhaps in London you were able to make people dance to your tune. You'll learn that in Southaven we have our own way of doing things. You may find it quaint, but you can either deal with it, *Mrs* Golding, or go back where you came from. Please make sure you close the door properly on your way out.'

To my surprise, this did temporarily silence Alice's unwelcome visitor. That artful stress on the title, *Mrs*, subtly suggested that Frank Golding was not the only person of that surname who might be locked up if they stepped out of line. I won't go so far as to say that Lou Golding appeared uncomfortable, but she had at least stopped talking.

Her progress in one direction blocked, Lou Golding looked around for inspiration. What she found instead was me. Her eyebrows drew together a little, and she said, 'Would you by any chance be Sam Rigby?' I owned up, and the eyebrows relaxed. 'My boy Mickey happened to mention you. Is it true that you're working for Mrs Haig?' I replied that she would need to ask Mrs Haig that question. 'Oh, so you are, then. In that case you might be able to help me. Do you know some way I can persuade her that I've come here in good faith?'

'I do, yes.'

Lou Golding seemed to expect me to go on, but I thought I'd make her work for it. Something about her style had got the wrong side of me. Eventually she said, 'Go on, then, what you got in mind?'

I said, 'It's very simple. You'll kick yourself when I tell you.'

Losing patience now, Lou Golding said, 'This ain't some bloody parlour game!' I noticed Alice shaking her head over this abuse of the language.

I said, 'Mrs Haig's right, we do things differently here. You could start by apologising to her.'

Lou Golding seemed baffled. 'Apologise? What the hell for?'

'For sending her threatening letters. For having a malicious story printed in the Gazette.'

Alice now broke in. 'And for having the sheer brass neck to come into *my* hotel and address me as though I were some peasant woman on your estate.' She turned to me. 'Thank you for your contribution, Mr Rigby, but I'm quite capable of fighting my own battles.'

'It don't have to be a battle.' This came from Lou Golding. 'I may have misjudged you, Mrs Haig, and if I have then I'm sorry, all right? And for the rest of it – I ain't learned to talk the lingo round here yet, maybe I need to smooth off a few rough edges. It's a culture shock after Shoreditch, I'll tell you that for nothing.'

Though to some degree mollified by this assurance that she wouldn't be charged for Lou Golding's observations, Alice said, 'Not a battle? We're competitors in a cut-throat trade, how can it be anything else?'

And to look at the two women, you'd have said that this was a battle which Lou Golding had already won. The scarlet trouser suit announced her victory, the fur jacket announced it, and so too did the earrings, pearls set in a circle of tiny diamonds. But she said, 'There's a time to fight, and a time to cooperate. Us hotelier types don't just stab each other in the back, do we? We form associations, we have great beanos with dances and speeches and all that malarkey. We're both businesswomen, we both know what it's like to try and make your way in a man's world. You and me got a lot in common.'

'I hardly think so.'

Lou Golding's expression clouded with disappointment. 'This ain't the welcome I was expecting from a nice little northern town. I was told people were friendly here. I was told they'd give you the shirt off their backs.'

'I shouldn't imagine you need the shirt off anyone's back, Mrs Golding.'

'But at least you might hear me out. What harm would it do? A little ten-minute turn on your lovely Promenade, that's all I'm asking.'

Though ordinarily no great fan of wealthy criminals, I'd found my sympathies shifting during the latter part of this scene. Perhaps Lou Golding was right. It couldn't be denied that she owned the big hotel next door; Alice would have to engage with her sooner or later. And perhaps Alice had been thinking along similar lines, because she now said, 'Evan – can you manage the desk for a while?'

Without speaking, Evan detached himself from the grandfather clock to go behind the counter, while Alice Haig disappeared into the office and re-emerged with one arm in the sleeve of the pea-green coat. Sweeping past Matt and myself without remark, she continued to the door and held it open. Lou Golding nodded to me, drew herself up to her full five foot nothing, and went outside with Alice following. The draught eddied round the lobby, dislodging a couple of publicity leaflets from the counter. Matt bent down to pick them up.

Again the question arose of what to do next. While the back of my mind was debating it, I said to Evan, 'So that was Mickey Golding's mother.'

Evan said, 'Do you think that fur is real?'

'No doubt about it. Probably torn from the living mink with her own fair hand.' A message came through from the working party down in the hippocampus. I said, 'Evan – is Nigel Haig still confined to barracks?'

'Yeah. I went in earlier to fetch him a newspaper.'

It was over twenty-four hours since I'd promised Nigel that I'd keep him up to date about my investigation. 'Any reason why I shouldn't drop in and have a word?'

Evan's blank face indicated that such questions exceeded his remit. I said to Matt, 'Do you want to come and meet Alice's kids?'

He looked shifty. 'I think I'll stay here.'

'Stay here and what?'

'Help Evan. There might be a sudden rush.'

'In which case you could do what, exactly?'

There was only a brief hesitation. 'I could show guests to the dining room.'

'You don't actually know where it is, though, do you?'

But before Matt could respond, Evan said, 'It might be useful. I may get stuck on the phone.' As he said this, the telephone rang, and at the same time a party of four arrived, anxious because they were late for their lunch booking. Matt tried to look official, but his coat spoiled the effect. If he'd only had a bum-freezer jacket and a silly hat, he and Evan could have gone on as Tweedledum and Tweedledee.

Resigned to the situation, I set off alone for the back exit. By now, Oscar had reopened the sliding door to the kitchen, and one glance was enough to tell me that the mayhem he'd predicted earlier had arrived at full throttle. Cooking for one has its disadvantages, but I could see no attraction at all in the hellish scene before me. Oddly, Oscar himself seemed more cheerful now, as if the pressure had taken his mind off other things. Not wanting to risk a repeat of our earlier spat, I carried on out into the yard, found the entrance to the Haigs' flat unlocked as before, and climbed the stairs.

A voice from the middle floor called out, 'Mum, is that you?'

It wasn't, so I said, 'It's Sam Rigby.'

The voice said, 'I'm in the kitchen.' I tracked it down, and found Nigel Haig in pyjamas and dressing gown stirring a pan of baked beans on the stove. Just as I walked in, two slices of rather burnt toast ejected themselves from a fancy toaster on the counter.

I said, 'You're out of bed. And you look marginally less ill.'

'The funeral's been called off. I had one of the worst nights of my life, then slept for a couple of hours, and when I woke up the whole picture had changed. Do you want some of this?' He indicated the saucepan.

'I don't like to deprive you of your lunch.'

'Doesn't matter, I can't eat it all anyway. Bung a couple more slices in the toaster.'

I followed these instructions while Nigel buttered the original slices on a plate. I said, 'Is Bobbie not around?'

'She's gone to some do at her friend Julia's. You've never heard such a fuss. "Oh, my hair! Oh, my clothes! Oh, I'll never be ready in time! Oh, oh, oh!" Girls are insane.'

'But you like them anyway.'

'I didn't say I like them, I just fancy them. At least if you prefer boys you don't have to put up with all that silliness.'

'I don't think women are any sillier than men.'

Nigel looked at me without respect. 'You must know some very silly men.'

'Would you call your mother silly?'

'That's different, she's old. Shit!' Conversation had distracted Nigel from his bean-watching duties, and they'd seized the opportunity to stick to the bottom of the pan. He spooned some out onto the plate. 'Do you want these?'

'You look hungry. I'll have the second lot.'

I pulled another plate from the dish-rack while Nigel sat at the kitchen table and made a start. He said, 'Food! I'd forgotten what it was like.' When my own toast liberated itself from the machine I buttered it, scraped the remaining beans out of the pan and put it to soak, then joined Nigel at the table. We ate in silence. Finally, Nigel pushed his empty plate aside, wiped his mouth and said, 'Have you worked out who did it yet?'

'No.'

'Why not? I suppose you've been too busy accosting men in toilets.'

I was pleased to mark this return of Nigel's caustic side, largely absent so far from today's performance. Nevertheless I ignored the comment and said, 'Did you know Major Glass has been attacked?'

'Evan told me. Apparently my mum took off to see him at the hospital. Between you and me, I think something's going on there.'

Much as I'd have liked to witness Nigel's reaction to news of his mother's engagement, it wasn't my place to break it to him. I said, 'Someone must have a motive for wanting to kill both Giles Rawley and Laurence Glass. Any ideas?'

Nigel considered the problem. Then he said, 'This is hard, isn't it? At least with Maths you know where you are.'

'Didn't you say you've got exams on Monday? You should probably be revising this weekend, not trying to solve crimes.'

This provoked alarm. 'I can do both! You just need to give me more facts, that's all. Have you talked to everyone in the hotel?

And what about the murder scene? You must have found some clues.'

I hadn't got all day, but I tried to give Nigel a reasonably comprehensive digest of the facts to date, including the detailed description of Giles's room which he'd requested. In a further departure from the previous day's pattern, when eventually I prepared to leave the boy looked actively disappointed. I offered to wash up, but he insisted that Bobbie would do it when she came in. I was half way out of the room already when he called me back. 'I meant to tell you. Evan said a peculiar thing this morning. He put the Gazette down on the table here with the story about Sir Giles on the top, and he said did I think it was right to keep secrets for people.'

'It all depends, doesn't it.'

'That's what I told him. Just because someone asks you, that doesn't mean you've got no choice.'

'Presumably you squeezed him for details?'

'A waste of time, he just went blank like he does and walked out, all dark and mysterious. To be honest, it's a feather in his cap as far as I'm concerned. I never realized he actually thought about things.'

I thanked Nigel for lunch and headed back into the hotel, wondering again whether we underestimated Evan Bickerstaff at our peril. The diners were beginning to leave now, and I heard one or two remarks which would doubtless have brought a glow of satisfaction to Oscar's jowly features. For Alice's sake, I was pleased that guests who'd come here to snoop at the scene of a murder talked only of the food as they left.

Alice herself had so far not returned. This surprised me. I'd expected her to allow Lou Golding no more than the suggested ten minutes, just long enough to give respectful ear to whatever Lou might be proposing and then turn her down flat.

As soon as he saw me, Matt, who'd been cosying up with Evan behind the counter, hurried out into the lobby and grabbed my wrist, eyes eager with communication. The sight of this more familiar Matt, as opposed to the finger-wagging impostor who'd followed me round all morning, greatly lifted my spirits. He said,

'We've got to go up to Rawley's room!'

'Why? What's happened?'

'I've had an idea. When we met Mark at the hospital this morning, he never mentioned the cops finding any sort of note or letter, did he? There's got to be a chance that the message our biker friend brought the other week is still up there. If it was sensitive, Rawley might have hidden it.'

Though a question mark hovered over Evan Bickerstaff's mental acuity, there was no such doubt about Matt's. I just wished he'd save it all for the work rather than applying it to his boss's behaviour as well. Trying not to show too much enthusiasm, I said, 'Unlikely, but perhaps we'd better take a look. Evan – the key to room 21, please. And where can we find rubber gloves?'

At first, Evan refused to comply, stating that it was more than his job was worth. Matt gave him a flash of the brown eyes in full pleading mode, and said, 'We'll take full responsibility, Evan, I promise.' When Evan still hesitated, Matt added, 'What do you think Giles would have wanted you to do?' Which apparently was the correct button to press, because moments later, keys in hand, we were advancing up the back stairs to the first floor cupboard where Mrs Clark stowed all the cleaning equipment. A minute later still, our hands encased in rubber, we slipped quietly into room 21 and closed the door.

Matt stopped to take a general look around. He said, 'Not up to much, is it?'

'It's all right. The view's good.'

'But I mean, if you had as much money as Rawley did, would you choose to stay in a place like this?'

I'd asked myself the same question. 'I'm not sure he thought of the money as his. He'd inherited it, and he meant to pass it on to people who deserved it, but in the meantime he was happy to live off his earnings.' The room remained just as I'd left it the night before, the newspaper still waiting for Giles to pick it up again. 'Besides, I've got a feeling this room reminded him of his touring days. Anything too posh would have spoiled the illusion. Not a great place to hide something, is it?'

Matt said, 'He'd only be thinking of the chambermaid, not

Special Branch.'

'In which case, why didn't the police find it? If there's anything here to find, that is.'

The only answer was to search for this note, or letter, or whatever it might be, ourselves.

If you've ever tried turning over a room while wearing rubber gloves a size too small for you, you'll be aware that it presents difficulties. Pockets in particular resist giving up their secrets. After a couple of minutes, Matt threatened to remove the gloves and work nude, on the grounds that the police had probably finished with the room and wouldn't be back. Here was yet another example of the Standish recklessness, and I urged restraint. After another couple of minutes I was coming round to Matt's point of view myself, but obviously I couldn't admit it. We worked on clumsily. We went through every drawer. We went through every item of clothing in the wardrobe, both on the rail and on the shelves, not omitting the trousers hanging from the door. We looked on top of the wardrobe, under the bed, behind the curtains. We checked the notepaper rack. We pulled out all the drawers to see whether anything had been taped to the back of them. We looked in the pockets of Giles's dressing gown. We didn't find a thing.

Downhearted, we paused to take stock. And that's when I noticed that my assistant's normally dark complexion had taken on a greenish hue. I said, 'Are you all right?'

He said, 'It's grim, isn't it.'

And I suppose it was. The blood I could cope with, having become pretty much inured during my time on the force. More testing was the strange, sad smell of a life nearing its end, now suddenly snatched away. But subtler, insidious, was the aftershock, the last waves of the eruption which had wrecked the peace of this room in the small hours of Friday morning. Would Alice soon try to book the room out as usual? With the same lost furniture? With the same bed?

I said, 'Don't think about it. We've got a job to do. And we seem to have scored a fat zero.'

Matt turned his head towards the more crowded, and bloodier, of the two bedside tables. He said, 'I'm afraid I was leaving that for you.'

So far our search had been conducted well away from the spatter of blood and gore at the head of Giles's bed. Now it struck me that the three library books should have been the obvious starting point for our investigation. The supposed note could easily lie somewhere between their pages. I crossed the room, laid each book gingerly on the bed, then went through them leaf by leaf. Dried blood from their spines dropped onto the mattress. I swept the reddish-brown flakes onto the carpet. Then I replaced the books exactly as I'd found them, with Edith Evans uppermost.

Matt said, 'What about the Shakespeare?'

The bard's works had been sheltered from the drenching suffered by the books on the open table above. I slid the volume off its shelf and put it on the bed.

Matt said, 'Cordelia. Try *King Lear*.'

The letter, a single closely-written sheet with its envelope now missing, had been tucked between the pages of the final scene. Every speech of Lear's was annotated, with underlinings, commas for the breath, and brief remarks in the margin. As far as I knew, it was a role Giles had never played, but if he'd been asked he was certainly ready.

I unfolded the letter and took it to the window for better light. Matt stood beside me, silently mouthing the words.

A Brighton address stood at the top of the page, and below it a date in January. The handwriting posed challenges at first, but I soon got the hang of it. The letter read:

*Dear Mr Rawley,*

*If you're reading this it's because I've passed away. They told me months ago it would finish me off, only I didn't believe them, but I do now because you can tell when you're on the way out and I am. I'll give the letter to my grandson Timothy to give to you, he's an honest lad and doesn't know what's in it and if you could find it in your heart to do me a last kindness*

> *then please don't tell him, he's got a soft spot for his old gran and if he knew the truth it would kill me.*

I could see a flaw in the writer's thinking there, but I let it pass and read on.

> *It's about that coin collection of yours, the one that got stolen. You'll recall that at the time I swore blind I had nothing to do with it and it hurt me very much the way you never believed me, I'd been a good housekeeper to you ever since your poor wife died and then that was how you went and repaid me. With the trust all broken between us it was plain I couldn't continue in my place but still I was very angry when you let me go. However now that I'm not long for this world I can't bear to leave things at such a sorry pass, your friendship always meant a great deal to me. So to get it all out on the table you might as well know that you were right, it was me that let that swine into your house while you were away, I only did it for the money, he'd heard me on the phone complaining I was up to my ears, he was very persuasive, O that man can turn on the charm when it suits him, but though he looked like making thousands off the deal himself I never saw more than two hundred miserable pounds for all my efforts, and I hope the good-for-nothing creep gets what's coming to him when I'm gone. I'm talking about Mr Lane, your son-in-law.*
>
> *That's all I wanted to say. It's a great weight off my mind to have put this right with you at last, which I would have done sooner if you hadn't been so horrible to me with all your nasty accusations. Now if I have to die, I can at least die with a clear conscience.*

> *Hoping this finds you as it leaves me, I remain*

> *Your obedient servant*

*Dolly Sprague*

*PS If you could spare Timothy something towards his petrol, I'd be very much obliged.*

Oddly dispirited by these posthumous lines, I handed the letter to Matt and sat down on the end of the bed. He put the letter on the dressing table, then sat down next to me. One of us sighed, but I wasn't sure which. Eventually I said, 'Quite a character, this Dolly Sprague.'

Matt said, 'Sounds like she was queuing up to die with her hat on.'

I was bemused. 'What on earth does that mean?'

'Couldn't tell you. It's one of my mum's.' He waved a hand in the direction of the letter. 'Not much of an apology, is it?'

'She's just trying to stitch up Howard Lane, now the law can't reach her any longer. No wonder Giles got so upset.'

Matt chewed his lip for a while, then said, 'Do you think Cordelia knows what her husband's been getting up to?'

'No. Do you?'

'No. She doesn't reckon he's a saint, or anything, but this is going to come as a shock. What'll you do?'

'Give the letter to Mark. The police need to follow it up.'

Matt tapped my shoulder with the back of his hand. 'Just a minute – what if Rawley had confronted Howard Lane about this? Rawley could easily have phoned him.'

'And what if Howard didn't like what he heard and thought Giles needed silencing? We've no idea where Howard was on Thursday night.'

Matt said, 'So why aren't you rushing out of here to talk to the cops?'

I'd been thinking about Laurence Glass. 'Do we know of any link between Howard Lane and the Major?' Matt didn't answer. 'It must be Giles's killer who was at the Infirmary last night. If that was Howard Lane, there has to be some connection.'

Matt said, 'Maybe the cops can dig something up,' but he

sounded less than confident about it. Personally I didn't know what to think. My brain said it had been a long day already, though it was barely three o'clock. There were too many suspects in the case, there was too much I didn't know. I began to wonder if I could do with a holiday, but it was hard to tell because I never took them.

And all the time part of me wasn't thinking about the case at all.

I rested an exploratory hand on Matt's leg. Even through latex, I felt the heat. He could have moved the hand if he'd wanted to, but he didn't. I said, 'I would never hurt you. You've got to believe that.'

For a while he didn't speak. I was very aware of his breathing in the hush of the violated room. Then he said, 'You don't know yourself. You're scary, but you don't realize.'

'Scary? Are you saying I scare you?'

'I just think I need to be careful.'

'Look, Matt – I slipped up badly today, I admit it. But that's just one time – one time in all the months I've known you! Now it seems like you're never going to let me forget it.'

'You can't undo a thing like that.'

'No?' I moved closer to him. Though for weeks I'd been desperate to avoid saying what I was about to say, I said it anyway. 'And you can't undo the lime flowers either.'

He looked at me as if I'd spoken in Swahili. 'The lime flowers? What are you on about?'

'Don't pretend you've forgotten. That day on the Boulevard last summer. No one forgets a thing like that.'

Matt turned his face away from me. After a while he said, 'I didn't know they were lime flowers.'

'You said you wanted to be with me! I've had to live with that every day since.'

'Maybe if I wasn't with Eileen – '

'Fuck Eileen!' I withdrew my hand and the rest of myself and got up to look out of the window. The unvarying February sky reached to infinity. It was impossible to believe the sun would ever shine again.

Matt said, 'In any case, I thought you were with Mickey now.'

At least he'd had the grace to get the name right for once.

'That's right, I am.' Which was almost true, though hardly a racing certainty after this morning's debacle.

Matt said, 'Well then.'

I carried on looking out into the world. The world felt like home, I knew how it worked, I knew how to behave in it. I didn't know how to behave in this room.

But then I was back on the bed, sitting sideways, and I'd taken Matt's hand in my own. I don't know if you've ever tried to play a scene like this with your hands encased in Marigolds, but I have to tell you it's not easy. I pressed on regardless. 'Leave her, Matt. She's not right for you.'

'I can't.'

'She's stringing you along. I don't know why you can't see it.'

'I care about her.'

'You care about me.'

'It's not the same.'

'We could be happy.'

'I'm happy now.'

'You're not!'

'Don't tell me what I am.'

'Perhaps I know better than you do.'

'I'm not leaving Eileen, that's the end of it.'

'Why? Because you're afraid people will talk?'

'I love her!'

'You've never loved her.'

'That's not true.'

'Isn't it?' I hesitated for a moment, then pulled him towards me and kissed him. He went with it cautiously for a few seconds, but then I felt him turn up the dial.

Suddenly he pulled away. 'You bastard!'

Someone rapped loudly on the door. 'Mr Rigby! Mr Rigby, are you in there?'

I'd brought the key inside with me, so I had to get up to admit Alice Haig. Meanwhile Matt had sprung off the bed to take a position as far away from me as possible. I think if he could have climbed into the wardrobe, he would have done.

Alice swept into the room under full sail and said, 'You've had two full days to work on the case, but you've given me absolutely nothing! That woman knew all there is to know about Marine Lodge, while I had nothing whatsoever to come back with. You gave me your word that you'd make enquiries, then that was the last I heard about it. Are you afraid of these Goldings, is that it? Or has she bought you off already, like she buys off everyone else?'

'That's unfair.'

'You left me defenceless out there. I felt as if I'd been thrown to the chickens.' Alice probably meant lions, though perhaps she had some history with chickens which I wasn't aware of.

'I have been trying, Mrs Haig, but then you wanted me to look into Giles's death as well.'

'If you couldn't manage both, you should have said so. I suppose you haven't even identified the source of the leak yet.'

'As a matter of fact, I think I have.'

This brought Alice Haig up short, and I have to confess I was relieved. The spectacle of Alice in attack mode made great viewing, as long as you weren't the one under attack. 'Then who is it?' As she spoke, she seemed to become aware at last of the two pairs of rubber gloves, but with laudable restraint she passed no comment.

'I'd prefer not to say yet.'

'Hah! You've got no idea at all, have you?'

'The fact is, when I do tell you you won't like it. I need one more night to be sure. You'll know in the morning.'

Reluctant to appear in any way placated, Alice said, 'But will it leave me in a stronger position with Mrs Golding? That's what I want to know.'

'It would do if she had any shame.'

'Which I'm prepared to bet she doesn't.' Alice came further into the room and looked around distractedly, as though she'd forgotten recent events which had put its occupant in the morgue. 'But Mrs Golding is not without other qualities. She's far more dangerous than I'd realized.'

For the first time it occurred to me that Alice Haig's animus towards Lou Golding might be tinged with admiration. I said, 'Our home-grown villains don't match up. There's a lack of ambition.'

'She seems obsessed with control. You know she didn't employ

Southaven builders when she refurbished the Grand? She brought her own crew up from London and had them camping out in the hotel. That's how she is. Now she wants to control me as well.'

'Can I ask what the proposal was that she put to you?'

Alice winced as if shrinking from a fly-blown corpse. 'That's neither here nor there. I refuse to be controlled, Mr Rigby. In time she'll come to see that I can't be won over.'

'So you turned her down, presumably.' Alice's eyes darted away from mine. 'What – you didn't turn her down after all?'

Alice moved to the window and looked out, as I'd done myself a few minutes before. I wondered what she was hiding from me.

She said, 'I told Mrs Golding that I would consider her offer.'


## seventeen


The Alpine café and patisserie is one of the Boulevard's most venerable institutions, occupying a prime location at the heart of the town. Having been established in the 1930s, supposedly after its owner took a walking holiday in Switzerland, it had since gone from strength to strength while other, less eye-catching businesses had faltered all around it.

I say supposedly because there circulated an alternative version of the foundation myth, in which the nearest the owner had ever come to Switzerland was an encounter with a fondue set down Portobello Road. Whatever the truth, the Swiss theme was dutifully reflected in all aspects of the café's presentation. I'd made the rare mistake of arriving a couple of minutes early, and as I took my seat in the raised area at the back, behind the busy patisserie, my ear was assaulted by bold cries from at least a dozen mechanical cuckoos, lunging out from behind rustic shutters to announce the hour of four. Though the first few had more or less synchronised their performances, their colleagues sought to correct them at intervals over the following minutes. To add to the horror, some of the newer clocks offered musical selections too. As the tones of *Edelweiss* died away somewhere to my left, the clock above my head declared improbably that it loved to go a-wandering along the mountain track.

A glum-faced waitress in a dirndl skirt approached my table, but I shooed her away, alarmed at the sight of her lace bonnet with its built-in blonde plaits wired to turn up at the ends. If Mark didn't arrive in the next ten minutes I meant to make a dash for it, so there was no point in wasting good money on a drink I might not have time to consume. More than usually disenchanted with the human species, I fell to studying the pictures on the walls. Several featured views of the Matterhorn. Mountains possess unusual power for the people of Southaven, a place so flat that candidates for the driving test have to use railway bridges when executing their hill start, and I succumbed to the familiar sense of awe. For the town's Miss Pyles, there were photographs of narrow gauge railways. Between these compelling images hung a variety of painted cow-bells illustrated in folk style. Critics who knew the word could be heard to complain that the whole effect reeked of kitsch, though personally I felt that marks should be awarded for taking a truly terrible idea and pursuing it without mercy of any kind. It almost disappointed me that the place wasn't overrun by dwarves masquerading as the Gnomes of Zurich, with tiny bells upon their tiny hats.

I'd sent Matt home. I couldn't hope to get any sense out of him after my dire misjudgement on the dead man's bed. There was now so much tension between us that I half wished I'd thumped him properly that morning and got rid of him for good. Once we'd returned Alice Haig to reception and got clear of the building, Matt had seemed less angry with me than I'd expected, but I couldn't see what right he had to be angry at all when I'd only done what he wanted me to do in the first place. Not that I cared. No one likes being called a bastard, bastards especially, and if my assistant intended to call me a bastard whenever I searched out his weak spots then he wouldn't remain my assistant for very long. Now we were approaching Saturday night, his hallowed night out with Eileen, and I was glad to have him temporarily out of my hair.

After ten minutes I weakened and ordered a pot of tea. The waitress then barked 'Cake? Tart? Scone?' Given to prolixity myself, I had to admire her verbal economy, but I still turned the offer down. When she'd removed her glum face to the kitchen I realized that I was simply too angry to eat cake: angry with Matt, angry with Alice Haig, angry with Mickey Golding, and above all furious with myself for mishandling every situation that came my way. Why, when there was a right thing to do and a wrong thing to do, did I invariably select option two?

I was just concluding that I did it on purpose and that my whole life had been dedicated to self-destruction when some of the cuckoos began to celebrate the quarter-hour and Mark Howell strode up to the table. He unbuttoned his mackintosh, hung it carefully over the back of the chair opposite me, and said, 'How are you? You're looking good.'

Though in most respects a more than competent detective, Mark was too apt to base his personal opinions in prejudice. If he'd actually looked at me, the evidence would have declared plainly that he was about to take tea with a sort of ill-tempered Mount Etna which had barely recovered from a recent bout of 'flu. I didn't say anything, and he sat down. 'Have you ordered?'

'Just tea.'

'What have you got there?' I'd taken Dolly Sprague's letter from my pocket. Now I pushed it across the table, and Mark unfolded it. But before he could get stuck in, the waitress appeared and hovered wordlessly. Her bonnet had somehow rotated through forty-five degrees, so that one plait hung down over her eye before heading skywards. Mark said, 'Russian tea, please, and a selection of cakes.'

I said, 'You'll be eating them on your own.'

'Nonsense, you love cakes.' The waitress scribbled on her pad, then slipped it into her lace-trimmed pocket. As she moved away she straightened the bonnet, and the plaits jerked back into line.

I said, 'Why did we have to come here? I told you, we could have met at my place.'

'Don't you like it here? I suppose you'd have preferred a burger and that awful soapy coffee at the Wimpy bar.'

'They don't have clocks.' For the moment, an absence of clocks formed my principal requirement in a venue, with an absence of cow-bells running a close second.

Mark said, 'People come from miles around to see this place.'

'Not twice, they don't.'

Now Mark finally looked at me, in a perfunctory sort of way. 'Are you in a bad mood?'

'Yes.'

'Then snap out of it. Honestly, you're like a spoiled child sometimes.' And he returned his attention to the letter. Though his taste in tea-shops might be suspect, I felt certain that Dolly Sprague would draw out Mark's better side. The first evidence of this came when he reached the bottom of the page and immediately started in at the top again. This supplementary reading complete, he said, 'Where did you get this?' I told him. 'What? You've been in that room? Hargreaves'll burst a blood vessel!'

'You'll have to say you found it yourself. Miss Pyle told me yesterday about Giles being visited by a young man on a motor bike. Naturally I passed this fact on to you, and you decided to go over the room again.'

'I can't believe we didn't find this yesterday. One of the uniform boys definitely looked through those three library books.'

'Perhaps he didn't like Shakespeare.' I'd been put off the man myself back at school, when staffing issues had led to us studying *A Midsummer Night's Dream* two years running. There's only so much Bottom a boy can take. But wise souls had since guided me back to the plays, and now I didn't mind them too much provided the curtain came down in time for last orders.

Mark said, 'Did you already know about this business with the coin collection?' I told him what I'd heard from Giles, how the theft and the subsequent loss of his housekeeper had been the spur which initiated his peripatetic way of life. I also mentioned how I'd inadvertently caught the opening of a charged phone conversation between Cordelia and her husband. Mark said, 'You realize that if Rawley spoke to Howard Lane about this letter, then Lane has a motive for murder?'

'And potentially no alibi.'

The waitress now returned with a tray, from which she off-loaded our teas, a plate of four assorted cakes on a doily, two side plates, paper serviettes, and a scrawled chit by way of a bill, all without saying a single word. Whether she'd exhibited this Trappist behaviour since her youth, like Evan Bickerstaff, or been reduced to it by having to wear fake plaits to earn a living, it was impossible to tell. As she left us, Mark said, 'I'll be getting this, by the way.'

'I should hope so. Have you seen how much they charge?'

Mark glanced at the chit. 'It's not too bad. The cakes look nice, anyway.'

As the plate had made its appearance, I'd suddenly found myself thinking that perhaps a morsel of cake would be acceptable after all. Attention focused in particular on the Swiss chocolate éclair, though there was little chance that I'd be the one who got to eat it. Of the two of us, Mark had always possessed the stronger will, even back in the days when I was a fairly experienced police officer and he was just a cute cadet.

Mark added sugar to his Russian tea, stirred it with the long spoon provided, and said, 'Tuck in. Have that éclair if you want.'

This direct gambit in the matter of the éclair unnerved me. Part of me knew that the thing to do now was grab it and stuff it down with all possible speed, but I also knew that if I did so Mark would say something like, 'You polished that off fast enough, didn't you?' and thereby gain the moral advantage. So I said, 'We could cut it in two.'

Mark said, 'It'd be a shame to spoil it. If you cut them, the cream goes everywhere.'

I said, 'You have it, then. I'll be all right with this sponge.'

Mark said, 'Are you sure?' and transferred the éclair to his plate. I watched it go with numb resignation. If I could just have accepted once and for all that I was a sponge person, it would have saved me an awful lot of suffering. I poured some tea from the little pot. It was piss-weak but I didn't dare start complaining in case it set me off about the éclair as well. Mark said, 'That's rather on the pale side, isn't it? You want to swoosh it round a bit.'

I swooshed it round a bit and poured some more. 'What are you going to do about Howard Lane?'

Mark took a sip of the Russian tea and said, 'Not my call. But I'd expect Hargreaves to get Sussex police onto it. They'll need to talk to the biker boy as well.'

Mark picked up the éclair and bit into it. Cream gushed out onto his chin. I said, 'I hope you're enjoying that.'

'It's excellent. Are you sure you don't want some?'

'I couldn't possibly.'

'Suit yourself.'

I tried the sponge instead. It wasn't bad, but it wasn't the éclair. I said, 'What's this about Hargreaves retiring?'

Mark dabbed his chin with the serviette. 'He hasn't spoken to me himself, but people say he's cheesed off with all the reorganization.'

The Southaven force was nearing the end of its days, being in the process of absorption by the county constabulary. It wouldn't make much difference to the rank and file, but senior officers like Hargreaves were having to adjust to a new chain of command. I said, 'You know what's really kept him at work?'

His mouth full of éclair, Mark said, 'No, what?'

'Mrs Hargreaves. I get the feeling he spends as little time at home as possible.'

'To hear him talk though, you'd think she was a marvel.'

'She is. She drinks even more than my mother.' With a sharp stab I remembered that my mother was currently lying in the Infirmary drugged up to the eyeballs. Aunt Winnie would have seen her at visiting time, so I could expect a report later. For some reason I didn't want to tell Mark about it, so I said, 'If Hargreaves is threatening to retire, he must be seriously fed up.'

Mark said, 'I don't think he fancies having to run all his decisions past County. The Super's not happy either, but I think he'll stick with it for now. Oh – I know what I was going to tell you. Guess who I saw in Marine Approach a couple of weeks back.'

'Valerie Singleton?'

'No, Chubby Fallon. At least, I think it was him.'

'But you couldn't be sure because he wasn't chubby any

longer.'

Pleasingly, this caused astonishment. 'Have you seen him too?'

I explained how I'd telephoned Chubby the previous day, in the course of my enquiries. 'But I thought he'd not been to Southaven for ages. Where exactly was he?'

'On that corner by the Grand. He disappeared down Wright Street.'

It was hard to avoid concluding that Chubby must have been heading for the staff entrance to the hotel. This was food for thought. While I mulled it over, a dissident cuckoo claimed that it was eight o'clock, found itself performing solo, then withdrew to take advice. I said, 'I don't like this.'

Mark said, 'You should have had the éclair,' and swallowed the last mouthful.

'I'm talking about Chubby Fallon. We don't see him for years, then suddenly the Goldings move here and he decides to pay the town a visit.'

'What are you saying?'

I didn't know, but perhaps if I carried on talking I might find out. 'Why did Lou Golding choose to come to Southaven, of all places?'

'The sea air?'

'She's had inside knowledge from day one. And she's throwing her weight around as if she's immune from the attentions of the law.'

'You think someone's protecting her?'

'Chubby Fallon's on her payroll, I'm certain of it. She gets the idea to move away from London, open up a new branch of the business, maybe leave her older boys to manage their home patch. Chubby suggests Southaven. Not only does he know the place like the back of his hand, he's got something on virtually every serving officer in the local force. She can do whatever she likes and you can't touch her.'

Mark idly picked up the slice of Battenberg which I'd earmarked as my next choice. 'So where does Frank Golding fit into all this?'

'He doesn't. He's an old school thug, a bit of an

embarrassment, so Lou got Chubby to sort him out, have him put away. We just assumed Frank was head of the organization, when all the time it's been his wife.'

Mark chewed cake, then said, 'Do you think they've got anything on the Super?'

Since joining the funny-handshake brigade the previous year, Mark had clearly begun to see Superintendent Sturges no longer as some remote divinity but as a vulnerable mortal. I said, 'Who knows? He always seemed pretty straight to me, but Fallon's got a nose for these things.'

'And Hargreaves?'

When I'd been a cop myself, I'd have staked my life on Harry Hargreaves's integrity. In fact if he'd had less of it, he might have been promoted above DI. These days I didn't feel so certain, but that was only because I didn't feel certain about anything any more. 'Chubby would have a tough time getting anything on Hargreaves. But you can't rule it out.'

Mark sighed. The cheerful detective constable who'd so recently breezed into the Alpine café had taken leave of absence. He said, 'What do you suppose Chubby's got on me?'

We both knew what Chubby Fallon had on Mark, at least in outline. Perhaps Fallon had taken the trouble to add names, dates and places to the vague suspicions about Mark's sex life which had always shadowed his career. I didn't bother to spell that out. I said, 'You could get the upper hand if you wanted. Times are changing. Apparently there's all sorts going on in London these days.'

'Since when did Southaven take any notice of London? Besides, this is the police we're talking about. We're not exactly in the vanguard of social reform.'

Intuition prompted me. 'Mark - you've never explained the reason for this tea party. Is something going on?'

He looked shifty. 'Not exactly.' Then he made a face, while he reconsidered this response. 'Well - yes. Yes, it is. I wanted to ask for your help.'

Mark didn't often ask for my help, or anyone else's for that matter, so he had my full attention. 'What's the problem?'

'It's not really a problem. Though I suppose it is. Or it might be.' It was rare to see Mark struggling to express himself like this. 'Cilla started it. You know she's been seeing this woman in Preston? It's been going on for months. Well, Carol wants to move to Southaven. They're going to live together.'

I could see the whole picture immediately, but I let Mark tell it his own way.

'You can't keep a thing like that secret for long. Everyone's going to realize that Cilla and I were never actually an item. She's going to wreck my alibi.'

I said, 'Has she thought this through?'

'Yes, every inch of the way. The force would have no legal or disciplinary justification for acting against her, and she's got allies, she's popular with some people. There are just a few diehards who'd try to drum her out, but she thinks she can win.'

'So what about you?'

Mark hadn't finished the Battenberg yet, but still he pushed his plate aside. 'You've been telling me for years that I should either stand up and be counted or ditch the job and start again, and I've been telling you for years that I can't ditch the job because I'm a policeman, and that's the end of it. But the fact was I never had the guts to stand up, and anyway I thought they'd just find some excuse and kick me out the first chance they got. This thing with Cilla's made me think again.'

'You're going to come clean?'

'I'm worn out with it, Sam. I've got to stop lying, it's twisting me inside out.'

I regarded my former lover with awe. Signed up from the cradle as a conformist, he was about to risk standing out from the herd, and I could only guess at the struggle it must have taken to bring him to this point. I wished he'd been able to share more of it with me, but that was never Mark's way.

At the same time, I was wondering whether he'd mind if I finished off the Battenberg. Otherwise there was nothing left but a shrivelled custard tart, and I've never liked custard tarts.

I said, 'You know I'll back you up on this.'

Mark said, 'Actually, I had something specific in mind. I want to make a gesture, to convince myself that I can do it. I get scared sometimes, but then other times I think ahead, and I get this wonderful sense of freedom, like nothing I've ever felt before. I want to try and weight the scales on that side. So I thought perhaps if I did something positive that people would talk about, something I could feel proud of – '

'I still don't see where I come into all this.'

He looked shifty again. 'I know it's a long time since we – you know, since we had our thing, but I wanted to show you that you're still important to me. To be honest, I'm – well, I'm ashamed of how I treated you when they chucked you out of the force, making out like I hardly knew you let alone cared about you – '

'Forget it, Mark, it's history.'

'Let me finish. I realize there's no way I can properly make it up to you, but I wondered if, just as a sort of – gesture – you'd let me take you out to dinner. And be seen with you. The word would get round and everyone would know what it meant. I could really use the moral support, Sam. I'll understand if you say no, but if you can bring yourself to say yes it would mean a lot to me.'

For the time being I couldn't bring myself to say anything at all. It was true that after our relationship ended I'd mooned about for ages like Saint Sebastian, another arrow piercing my flesh every time Mark ignored me in the street. So in a way I was glad that he often made it easy to forget that he was a good soul underneath it all, always assuming that he was. Whenever he was nice to me, I could feel the old wounds ripping open.

But I had to say something, so I said, 'I hope you're going to take me somewhere decent.'

Mark smiled. 'You'll do it then? I've booked us a table at the Hen and Chickens.'

'When?'

'Tomorrow at 8. I know it's Valentine's, but I presume you're not doing anything.'

This hurt a little, but I let it go. In my mind, I replayed the unfortunate scene from that morning, when Mickey had so baldly stated his terms and then walked out. Since then, far from trying to detach myself from Matt I'd only gone in deeper, and though the consequences had been disastrous I could see no hope of rescuing my relationship with Mickey in time for dinner the following night. I said, 'Roosters or Rustlers?'

'Roosters. They do a nice chicken cacciatore. Have you ever been?'

For some reason I said, 'Me? No. OK, then, you're on.'

Lowering his voice, Mark said, 'I could kiss you.' But he didn't. Instead, he spied the neglected Battenberg, and scoffed the lot.

Though afternoon tea with Mark Howell had turned out to be far pleasanter than I'd expected, several influences conspired to cut the occasion short. I wanted to get over to Crowburn House and see what Aunt Winnie had to say about my mother. Mark felt obliged to hurry back to HQ and act on the information provided by the late Dolly Sprague. But above all, I'd noticed that five o'clock was looming, and I could sense platoons of songsters limbering up for another display. I wasn't alone in this. All around us, customers appeared desperate to settle up and flee before the nightmare began. Mark was having trouble attracting the glum waitress's attention, and I'm sorry to have to admit that I left him to it and scarpered.

Outside, the cloud blanket had thinned now, and it looked as if we were in for a cold, clear evening. I crossed the Boulevard and walked round to the back of Crowburn House to knock on the door of Winnie and Fred's flat. Over another cup of tea I learned that they'd driven up to the Infirmary together in the old Anglia, but that Fred, who'd spent rather too much time in hospitals on his own account, had then concocted some excuse to wait in the car while Winnie attended to the serious business of the afternoon. Aunt Winnie could tell me nothing new. My mother had slept for most of the time, and had seemed confused during the brief moments when she was awake. I promised to go and visit her myself the following day, then made my apologies and went upstairs to the office.

A lot had happened during the twenty-four hours since I'd last entered this sanctuary. My head was a muddle of new facts and new interpretations. Cordelia and Howard Lane had stepped forward as key players, the murderer had attempted to strike a second time, and I'd begun to see the Golding family in a different light. I could never be as systematic as Mark Howell, but I could at least try for greater clarity, and in my case that usually involved typing up my notes. With such limited patience as I could muster, I set about it. By the time I'd finished, I felt not just clearer but calmer too, and I even had the rudiments of a plan.

I'd been neglecting Sidney Flint, so the first thing I did was to call him. He began by complaining that I hadn't been in touch lately, but in fact I don't think his heart was in it. After all, he'd heard nothing more from the Goldings, and his whole purpose in employing me was to get the Goldings off his back. From that perspective things didn't seem to be going badly, and in order to leave Sidney enjoying this fool's paradise I was forced to conceal any suggestion that the Goldings were even better situated to dominate Southaven's business life than I'd realized before. I had a hunch they might be running an illegal gambling operation from the Grand Hotel, but if they enjoyed protection from on high it would be no use my threatening them with exposure. Besides, the police had searched the place from top to bottom on Thursday night and come away empty-handed, so where was this gambling den supposed to be? I resolved to do some more digging. Unfortunately, the obvious place to start was with Mickey, last seen dumping his shares in Sam Rigby on the open market. I would have to go and grovel to him. If I went over to the Vaults now it might still be fairly quiet and I could hope for a less interrupted conversation. But then I thought again of his manner when he'd left me that morning, and my resolve evaporated. Perhaps I'd talk to him later, when I'd had a drink somewhere else first.

Fobbing Sidney off with bland reassurances, I ended the call, tidied up after myself, and then went home.

When in recovery from a serious illness, nutrition is of the first importance. Among the food Matt had brought in that morning, I discovered some boil-in-the-bag kippers. While their visual appeal may have been low, nutritionally they scored straight A's, so I put water in the kettle, peeled a couple of largish potatoes and retrieved half a bag of Surprise Peas from the back of the cabinet.

The eventual result might have disappointed Philip Harben, but he wasn't hampered by a limited budget, limited ambition, and a crippling belief that there was no point in cooking anyway because it would only have to be done again the next day. I wondered how Saturday dinner was going at the Marine Lodge, and whether I would ever find a good moment to interview Oscar Hammond. Perhaps he'd be in the Vaults later on when I dropped in to see Mickey, and I'd be able to kill two birds with one stone.

The food eaten, I took the rare step of washing up immediately. Though he disapproved of my tendency to hurl everything in the sink and leave it indefinitely, Matt had only encouraged it by doing the washing up himself whenever he came round. I didn't know whether what we'd experienced today might be a temporary falling-out or something much worse, but I felt it could do no harm to remind myself how to wash dishes.

When the usual urge struck, I went to the leather jacket for my cigarettes. Then it occurred to me that I hadn't smoked a single one since before my early morning swim. I'd not tried giving up since at least October, and perhaps I was due for another go. I took the cigarettes out and put them in a drawer. You may object that I should have chucked them straight in the bin, but I hate smoking cigarettes that taste of fish.

I took a quick bath, shaved for the second time that day, dressed with some care, then risked looking in the mirror. I still wasn't ready to face Mickey Golding. There was someone else I needed to see that evening, but it was probably too early to catch him, so instead I fell back into the familiar arms of the Velvet Bar. Once there, my mood gradually improved. Someone with no sense of humour kept selecting *Ernie, the fastest milkman in the west* on the juke box, but I managed to smile when it came round for the third time and suppress the insistent fantasy of shoving the culprit through a plate glass window.

I'm not sure how many bottles I put away, but when I spilled out onto the Promenade at around ten o'clock the night smiled back at me with teeth like new-cut diamonds. The air was so crisp it crackled as I walked, and I could feel the alcohol of human kindness coursing through my veins.

I was looking forward to a friendly chat with Graham Leeds, the night porter at the Marine Lodge Hotel. Friendly, gentle, patient – those were my watchwords. There'd be no need whatsoever to slap the man around.

## *eighteen*

As I turned into the back yard of the Marine Lodge, I saw Oscar Hammond leave the building, still costumed for the job and looking like a pantomime character in search of a stage. We met in the middle of the yard and I said, 'How was dinner?'

'Busy, but I like it that way. I've left the girls to clean up.'

I could smell the brandy on his breath. 'Will you be in the Vaults later?'

'Probably. Why?'

'You were going to tell me where you really went after you left here on Thursday evening.'

His mood, amiable enough so far, now chilled. 'The Vaults can get a bit mad Saturday nights. I might just change out of these things and stop at home.'

Oscar Hammond was up to his old tricks. 'For God's sake, Oscar – why do you keep playing hard to get like this? I'm trying to find out who killed Giles. Don't you care?'

He wrinkled his nose at me. 'You love it, don't you? Snooping around, asking your shabby little questions, pointing the finger – well I've had enough of that kind of thing.'

'When? In the army?'

He sneered. 'Never give it a rest, do you? What happened to me in the army's got nothing to do with Giles's death, OK? I've seen things and I've done things, but it's all in the past. This is my life now – ' And he looked around him, his arms spread wide to embrace the scene. 'Southaven, and this hotel. I don't know anything, I've got nothing to tell you, and if you don't like that you know what you can do. Now leave me alone.' He continued past me, taking care to brush against my shoulder as he went. I saw him turn right, presumably heading for number thirteen.

In our various fixtures to date, Oscar retained an unbroken record of success. It had been obvious from the start that he was hiding something, but I still had no clue what sort of something that might be. Even so, his dark references to the past set me thinking. Laurence Glass had suggested that the murderer might bear some grudge against old soldiers, and if that was true then perhaps Oscar himself could be at risk. But he was a big man in the prime of life, and there was probably no need to worry.

Passing the open door, I could see the girls hard at work restoring the kitchen's pristine cleanliness. I felt a moment's pride for having tackled the mess in my kitchen sink, though now I came to think about it I'd left some mashed potato in a pan on the stove, and I'd also forgotten to take the rubbish downstairs when I came out. Matt always cleaned up more thoroughly than I did. I wondered how his night with Eileen was going, but then I tried to push Matt out of my mind. He took up too much space there. For the present, I had other fish to fry.

Seemingly lost in thought, Graham Leeds stood at the far end of the reception desk with his back to me, and when I said, 'Hello, Graham!' in a very loud voice, he jumped. Such are life's pleasures.

Turning, he said, 'Oh, it's you. There's no need to shout, I'm not deaf you know. Well, perhaps a little bit.' As he made this concession, the weak chin withdrew beneath his jaw in a manner which I couldn't have copied even if I'd wanted to. 'If you're after Mrs Haig, you're too late, she's up at the flat. Goodnight, madam, goodnight, sir.' This was directed towards an over-dressed couple as they passed us on their way to the front door. When they'd gone, Graham said, 'I think that's the last two non-residents out of the lounge. You'd think people had no homes to go to, the time they can linger over a cup of coffee.'

I said, 'Many staying tonight?'

'A fair few, another six or seven rooms on top of our regulars. There's some gone out for the evening, so I can't lock up yet.' He frowned. 'If you've not come to see Mrs Haig, what *do* you want?'

'A friendly chat, Graham.'

He looked appalled. 'Are you another one that's got no home?'

'Perhaps we could go into the office. It's cosy in there.'

Graham glanced towards the front door. 'But I might be needed.'

'You are. I need you.'

He ran one finger round inside his shirt collar, the way I'd seen him do before. 'I'm a busy man, you don't seem to realize.'

'Why did you try to get out of tonight's shift?'

'I, er – I wasn't feeling well.'

'You look fine now.'

'It was a false alarm. I thought I'd got that thing that's going round.'

'So, nothing to do with feeling guilty, then?'

'Guilty? Why would I feel guilty?'

'How long have you had this gambling problem?' He looked towards the door again. I said, 'If you're hoping for salvation, it's not coming.'

'I don't want to talk to you, I've got nothing to say.'

Well, I was a bit fed up with people not wanting to talk to me. I said, 'Get in the office, Graham.' And when he didn't move, I said, 'Now!'

I followed Graham Leeds into the office and shut the door behind me. He crossed to the far side of the room, where he stood at bay with the old filing cabinet behind him. The flask, sandwiches and newspapers were all in evidence as before. I said, 'The gambling. When did it start?'

'I don't know what you mean.'

I looked up to the ceiling for strength, then back to the chinless wonder six feet in front of me. 'Is it since your wife died? Are you lonely, is that it?'

'It's no business of yours.'

'Then these new betting shops open, and you think, I know, I could have a little flutter on the gee-gees. But it gets out of hand. You can't seem to stop yourself. Eventually you're betting money you haven't even got.'

'I'm not doing anything illegal.'

'Then someone approaches you, offers to help you out. Hard cash in return for information. It would be easy for you, you're on your own here all night.'

'This is nonsense. You're talking through your hat!'

'Who was it that approached you, Graham?'

'I tell you, there was no one. It's lies, everything you're saying!'

But it wasn't lies, he knew it wasn't lies, and he knew I knew it wasn't lies, so between us we had the whole thing sewn up. Sweat beaded his forehead, and he kept trying to look over my shoulder, as though calculating his chances if he broke for freedom. When I took a couple of steps towards him, he tried to back further into the filing cabinet. He was within easy reach now. It would be difficult to imagine a more annoying face, and I began to consider slapping it, and slapping it hard.

Then I recalled my watchwords: patient, gentle, friendly. I said, 'You seem a bit nervous, Graham.'

'You've been drinking, haven't you?'

This was fair comment. 'I find it dulls the pain. Why won't you tell me what I need to know?'

He made a face. It wasn't quite one of the impressive girns he'd performed on the Thursday evening, but it was part of the way there. 'I will do, if you stand back.'

A little surprised by this change of heart, I stepped away. 'How's that?'

His eye measured the distance between us. 'Why not go over there?'

Eager to oblige, I moved towards the armchair as indicated, where the prime minister grinned up out of the Daily Express. But before I could quite settle in this new location, Graham Leeds bolted for the door, with the litheness of a man twenty years his junior. Disappointed in him, and in the slipperiness of human nature generally, I hastened to cut off his retreat. Grabbing him by the shirt front, I shunted him backwards to the filing cabinet and rammed him up against it. He was whimpering now, and trails of sweat like tears ran down his cheeks. I said, 'You stupid man.'

He said, 'I'm on tablets! If anything happens, it'll be your fault.'

'For the last time, who approached you at the betting shop?'

'They'll kill me!'

'Not if I get to you first.' I raised one knee and leaned it gently against his balls. 'I want names, Graham.' He squirmed a little but said nothing, so I leaned in harder.

'Aagh! That really hurts!'

'I don't like to do this, Graham, but you're forcing my hand.' I pushed again.

'Cess! They call him Cess!'

'Cess? Do you think I'm stupid?'

'No, really, I swear! A fat man, looks like an all-in wrestler.'

This description could easily have fitted First Ugly Bloke. I said, 'He works for the Goldings, right?'

'Yes.'

I withdrew the knee and relaxed my grip. 'Why don't you tell me what happened?' But to my amazement, Graham Leeds said nothing. That's when I finally slapped him. God knows he'd been asking for it.

He said, 'Ow!' and then, 'There was no need for that.'

'I'm impatient to hear your story. I expect it's a winner.'

'Then stop hitting me and I'll tell you.'

Sadly, after his earlier chicanery I couldn't trust Graham to keep his side of the bargain, so I manoeuvred him across to the armchair, pushed him down to sit on Ted Heath's face, then perched my backside on the edge of the desk and waited. Graham drew a handkerchief from his trouser pocket and wiped his brow with it. He said, 'It was a few weeks ago, just after New Year. I'd seen him in the betting shop before, he's connected with the management somehow.'

I could guess how that might be. It had already occurred to me that Lou Golding would be unhappy if she thought any gambling operation could go ahead in Southaven without paying tribute to her.

Graham Leeds went on. 'He came up to me and said his boss wanted a word. I told him to sling his hook but he got nasty, so I caved in. We drove out to Welldale to this posh house, Mrs Golding's place. I had to wait for her, it seemed like ages. Then she swept in. She was nice as pie, full of promises of how generous she'd be if I'd just collect some information on Marine Lodge's finances. I said I'd never do anything that might hurt Mrs Haig, but she said Mrs Haig would be grateful in the long run, and all I'd be doing was pushing things along a bit. Well, I needed the money. I said yes.'

The night porter fell silent now. I could see that he'd had little choice when faced with Lou Golding's indomitable nature, and I should probably have felt sorry for him. I said, 'You're scum, Graham, do you know that?' He did know that, and hung his head. 'I presume they haven't paid you?'

Now he looked up again. 'Never a brass farthing! Why should they? They've got what they wanted, and who could I complain to?' His eyes closed briefly as a painful thought came to him. 'Mrs Haig's going to hate me for this. I can't believe I did it.'

'Too late to whine about it now, Graham.'

'I suppose you're going to tell her?' The eyes pleaded.

'As a matter of fact, no.'

The relief was enormous. His whole face lightened. 'Oh, Mr Rickaby, thank you, thank you!'

'You're going to tell her yourself.'

He glared at me in disbelief. 'What?'

'First thing tomorrow, when Mrs Haig comes in. If I was in her shoes, I'd sack you and go straight to the police.'

There were real tears in Graham's eyes now. 'I've ruined everything, haven't I?'

'If you want to make amends, you could start by telling me what happened the night Giles Rawley was killed.'

'It's like I told that policeman, nothing happened. It was just a normal night.'

'But did you tell him that you were asleep most of the time?'

'Well – no, I – '

'Because that's a normal night for you, isn't it? You're at the betting shop all day, then you sleep the night away here at Mrs Haig's expense. So if anything did happen, you'd be none the wiser.'

Graham Leeds was silent again. He looked around the office, his gaze settling affectionately on one object after another. Then he said, 'Perhaps I should just go home.'

I shook my head. 'Work your shift out, Graham. And try to keep awake for a change.'

From beyond the door, a female voice called out, 'Hello?'

I said, 'That'll be your guests coming in.'

'They'll be wanting the room key.' Graham heaved himself up out of the low chair, and wiped his eyes. He said, 'Would it be all right if I – ?' I nodded, and he straightened his clothing and left the room.

Either Lena or Mickey must have called last orders just as I was strolling up from Wright Street, because when I stepped into the Grand Hotel Vaults a great crush of humanity was pressing forward against the bar, desperate to be served. There'd be no hope of a quiet chat with Mickey in such conditions, but just as I was about to make good my escape he saw me, stopped what he was doing, grabbed a bottle of stout, and waved it in my general direction while giving a tentative smile. Influenced more by the smile than the bottle, I nodded. He mouthed something which may have been 'Talk to you later,' began pouring the drink, then returned to his duties. I collected the glass and bottle from the bar and found a spot near the interior door to the hotel, suitable for hovering.

The Golding twins made an effective unit, gifted as they were with a prodigious knack for mental arithmetic, at least one more than the average complement of hands, and an intuitive ability to supply the other's need for crisps, glasses, or bags of nuts, without being asked. Watching them at work formed a helpful distraction from the inevitable craving for nicotine which had kicked in as soon as I entered the smoke-filled bar. As Mickey handed change to the final customer, Lena called time, and began draping beer towels over the pumps.

Mickey lifted the bar flap and came over to my vantage point. He said, 'It's very loud!' Which it was.

I said, 'Doing anything afterwards?'

But he hadn't properly heard me. He said, 'Can you stay a while? I won't be long.' So I nodded, and he went out into the room collecting glasses.

Despite being pretty well-oiled in advance, I'd finished my drink before the end of the statutory ten minutes' drinking-up time, and I gave the glass and bottle to Lena as she passed by. Soon she and her brother began the awkward task of persuading punters to exchange the bar's warm embrace for Marine Approach and the February night. There was no sign of First Ugly Bloke – or Cess, if that really was his name – but his ugly friend had been drinking heavily with other chums equally charmless and now had to be forced out of the building by threats of permanent exclusion. Gradually the clamour reduced, the last customer was thrust bodily out of the door, and Mickey bolted it top and bottom.

Lena called out to me, 'Kind of you to offer to help.'

Mickey said, 'Come on, Leen, he's a guest.'

Lena had begun wiping down the tables. She said, 'I'll finish up, if you like. As long as you're in around ten thirty tomorrow, for D-day.'

'What? Oh, yeah.' Mickey saw my puzzled expression, and said, 'We've got to switch the till to decimal and have a last rehearsal with Carlo, make sure we know what we're doing. It's sad, in a way. To think, I'll never have to work out shillings and pence again.'

'And you actually regret that?'

'It's a bit of history down the plughole, ain't it? Now – how about a quick one in the cocktail bar? It's still open for hotel guests, I can smuggle you in.'

'That would be good.'

'Just let me change first.'

I stayed to chat with Lena while Mickey disappeared in search of his civvies. She said, 'Any news about Giles?'

'Nothing definite. There's a new line of enquiry, I might know more tomorrow. Has Oscar been in at all?'

I thought she looked shifty. 'Oscar? No. Should he have been?'

Presumably he'd gone home after all. It hardly disappointed me to miss him yet again. I'd run out of ideas for getting the truth out of Oscar Hammond, and now I wondered whether there might be a case for setting Matt onto him the next day. Then I caught myself thinking about Matt and Eileen again, but at that point Mickey returned, wearing smart trousers and a crisply ironed floral shirt. It may have been the latest thing, but I preferred him in white really. We said goodbye to Lena and made our way through, up the few stairs into the hotel.

Trade in the rather over-decorated cocktail lounge was slack, but Herb Alpert was being piped in to help cover our conversation. Mickey treated me to a particularly fine Scotch on the house, and I asked myself what had become of the stern-faced M. Golding who'd given me such a hard time that morning. Then I stopped asking myself, and asked Mickey.

Mickey said, 'I may have been a bit hasty.' He smiled a half-smile which I took to be apologetic, then tucked into his lemonade as if it was worth drinking. He always said he could take or leave alcohol, and from what I'd seen to date he left it much more than he took it.

I said, 'But you were right. I need to get straight about Matt.'

'So there is something going on?'

'No.'

'But you fancy him?'

I wasn't sure whether this accurately summarised my feelings, but the important thing for the moment was to make things clear to Mickey even if they weren't clear to me. I said, 'I suppose I do, yes. And it's pointless, and I need to put it behind me. And I'm sorry if that messed up our morning.' It had messed up my afternoon as well, but I didn't say so.

Mickey's hand found mine, squeezed it, and withdrew. 'Don't worry about it. These things happen. I shouldn't have made such a big deal of it.' Then he said, 'Are we still friends? Please say yes, I've been fretting ever since I made that grand exit this morning.'

In part, I wanted simply to give Mickey the reassurance he was asking for. But the more I knew about the Golding family business, the less I liked it, so instead of answering directly I said, 'I met your mother today.'

I wasn't sure, but I thought he drew away from me a little. He said, 'Really?'

'A remarkable woman.'

'You think so?'

'I keep wondering what Southaven's done to deserve her.'

'She certainly knows how to stir things up.'

'So where exactly do *you* fit in?'

My question was abrupt, and it took Mickey a moment to gather himself before he could say, 'What do you mean, fit in?'

I said, 'Your mother clearly runs a large and profitable organization. I used to think it was your father who ran it, but of course that was just for appearances, wasn't it? By all accounts, your brothers manage the London end of things, yet your mother has you and Lena tending the bar in the Grand Hotel Vaults. Am I missing something, or is that strange?'

Mickey toyed with his glass. As if the situation didn't worry me enough already, Herb Alpert now sang *This guy's in love with you*. Mickey said, 'We've always been different from the others. We were a late addition – an accident, really. They'd had three already. You probably don't know about my big sister, she's the oldest, cleared out years ago, went to the States and married a hotshot lawyer. My folks didn't really want any more kids, and when it turned out we were twins that was like adding insult to injury. We've had to find a place in the family as best we could. We didn't mind, or anything, we've always had each other. It was obvious from the start that Artie and Benny were chips off the old block, but me and Lena were never business-minded.'

'Are you saying your parents were disappointed in you?'

Mickey thought about that. More familiar with his bar-room patter, I'd never seen him take such care over what he said. 'I suppose they were, yes. I think Lena resents it a bit. I mean, she'd like the chance to prove herself as a chef, but Mum won't even try her out in the hotel. I'm fine as I am, I've never been ambitious or anything and I've always got cash to spend. Besides, I like to stick near the old girl and keep an eye on her, she's not as tough as everyone makes out.'

Privately, I guessed this might be wishful thinking. And was it plausible that Mickey, as much a Golding as his brothers, could really be content to play so lowly a part in the family empire? I said, 'Does that mean you're going to be a barman for the rest of your life?'

I could see him taking exception to my tone. 'What's wrong with that? There's a lot worse things I could do. And if you must know, I was going to be involved in the casino side of things here. Carlo had me down for assistant manager, except thanks to the Malones we've got no casino to manage.' Suddenly Mickey's face lit up. He said, 'Would you like a look round? It's worth it, I'm telling you.'

So we knocked back our drinks, collected the keys from reception, and took the lift down to the basement, or the lower ground floor as it preferred to style itself. Along the corridor, Mickey drew back plush curtains to reveal a fine set of double doors. He unlocked them, and we entered the glamorous world of Goldings casino.

Mickey flicked switches. After the power cuts we'd suffered earlier in the winter, I no longer felt perfect confidence that such actions would produce results. This time, at least, all was well. Light flooded the room.

The lush décor of the cocktail bar upstairs had been repeated here with baroque knobs on. Chandeliers twinkled, red and gold dominated the colour scheme, and a deep pile carpet offered to cushion the punter's steps. Opposite, more curtains masked the main, canopied entrance from Marine Approach, while along the walls plush drapes were swagged on either side of a series of false windows with Mediterranean views. The mahogany tables hosted sets of plush upholstered chairs painted in gold. It was as if the sixties had never happened.

Not waiting to be invited, I took a stroll. One effect of the décor was to mute what might be termed the business aspect of the establishment. Among so much excess, the eye barely picked out the baize card tables, or the roulette table at the far end of the room. Even the bar, its grille currently lowered, seemed an understated presence in such assertive surroundings. I turned to look at Mickey, who wore a smile of obvious pride. I said, 'Who needs Monte Carlo?'

He said, 'Not bad, is it? I'd lay odds there's nothing else like it round here. It'd be a crying shame if we can't get the place up and running soon.'

Beyond the roulette table, a discreet door had been covered in the same regency striped wallpaper as the rest of the room. I tried the handle, but the door was locked. Mickey said, 'That's just the office.'

'So it's not where you run these illegal sessions we keep hearing about?'

Shaking his head impatiently, Mickey came towards me brandishing the keys. 'You can have a look if you want.'

'Why not? For the sake of completeness.'

Mickey swung open the door and walked in ahead of me. Harsh strip lighting announced immediately that we were no longer in the casino's fantasy world. A large, plain desk took pride of place, plain office fittings lined the walls, and a snug little safe squatted in one corner. Mickey leaned against floor-to-ceiling shelves crammed with box files. I said, 'You've got a lot of files for a business that hasn't even started yet.'

Mickey said, 'We're ready for anything. Satisfied now? You wouldn't like to look under the desk or rip up the floorboards?'

Of course, I wasn't satisfied at all. Somehow I felt increasingly certain that the Grand Hotel concealed some cosy hideaway where the stakes were high and the law of the land counted for nothing. I thought back to Thursday evening, and the strange concentration of posh cars I'd seen in Wright Street on my way to meet Giles in the Vaults. Could that have been the select few punters arriving – being dropped off in the side street, to make their secret way to the secret room which the police had somehow failed to find? But all I said was, 'I snoop for a living. You're going to have to get used to that.'

Mickey smiled without warmth. 'Fair play. But I'm a Golding. Maybe we've both got stuff to get used to.'

I liked the defiant set of Mickey's jaw as he said this. In fact, I liked it so much that I crossed the room to take a closer look. It was the second time that evening I'd had a man pressed up against office furniture, but this one needed more careful treatment. I slipped a hand behind Mickey's head and tried to read the expression in his eyes. My best guess was that they were trying to read the expression in mine, so I shut mine and kissed him. It went pretty well. It was still going pretty well ten seconds later when I heard something go clunk.

I said, 'What was that?'

I hoped Mickey wouldn't say, 'What was what?' but he did.

I said, 'Something went clunk. You must have heard it.'

'My mind was on other things.'

'What's on the far side of that wall?' I indicated the area behind the box files.

'Nothing. But we're under the pavement here, sometimes you can hear people walking. The whole place shakes when a truck goes past.'

I wasn't convinced that the sound had come from above, but now Mickey's hand came a-roving where it shouldn't, and soon we were kissing again. Mental arithmetic wasn't Mickey's only skill. I began to wonder how comfortable the desk-top might be. I broke away a little and said, 'Surely you're not going to ride that motor-bike in these trousers?'

He said, 'I'm not going home tonight.'

'No? What have you got planned?' Then, a little late, I caught up. 'Oh. You're coming back to my place.'

He said, 'Unless you've already got someone booked in. Now can we get out of here? These shelves are digging into my back.'

I don't know why, but I'd rather taken to this plain room with its fluorescent glare. In any case, when it comes to sex you have to seize the day. I crossed the room again and closed the door.

Mickey said, 'What are you doing?'

I said, 'You might like to hang that shirt up somewhere. You wouldn't want it getting creased.'


In due deference to Rosemary Pyle, I dreamed I was riding with someone in a tram. It could have been Matt, or it could have been Mickey, but whoever it was they said, 'We're going to crash,' and I said, 'Don't be silly, trams never crash,' and then we crashed and I woke up. This was what came of suppressing things. The other day I'd wanted to tell Miss Pyle that I knew far more about trams than she realized, but when interviewing people it's a mistake to start banging on about your own miserable past. So I suppressed the information, and this dream was the slightly disturbing consequence. No mystery there, then. Apart from the bit about Matt, or Mickey.

I lay on my back. It was still dark, but with time all messed up that no longer meant it must still be the middle of the night. The dial on my alarm clock was supposed to be luminous but it had lost the knack. I didn't feel like switching on the lamp.

Mickey said, 'Are you awake?'

I'd forgotten he was there. An irritating voice in my ear remarked gloatingly that if Mickey had been Matt I wouldn't have forgotten. I said, 'Yes. Are you?'

He turned on his side and slid a warm hand across my chest. 'I slept like a log. Everyone's on the move really early at my mum's, you feel you've got to be up and doing.'

I said, 'You won't find that problem here.'

He played with my nipple. After a while he said, 'Thanks for letting me come back.'

'You're very polite.'

'I might want to be asked again.' The hand moved to my belly. It had a nice touch. After another while, Mickey said, 'I knew a bloke did transcendental meditation for half an hour every day before breakfast.'

I curled an arm around his shoulder. 'Close pals, were you?'

'I was the one making breakfast. But it fizzled out. I prefer people who've got their feet on the ground.'

'Have I got my feet on the ground?'

'Not sure. You're an enigma. But at least you're not sat with your legs crossed going OM.'

'If you want to make the breakfast I won't stand in your way.'

The hand moved to my hip. 'We don't have to get up yet, do we? I'd got plans.'

'Like what?'

He gave some indication. And we didn't have to get up, so I tried to go with the flow. Last night Mickey had let me take my pleasure, now he seemed determined to give me pleasure every way he could. I liked the feel of him, the smell of him, he fitted just right where it mattered; but I couldn't relax, and daylight came before I did. I sensed Mickey's disappointment that I'd been such hard work. As I watched his neat, round backside heading out of the door en route for the bathroom, I was thinking that perhaps I'd learn to feel the buzz with him in time, that he'd been sent to me like a gift from the gods and what did it matter if I had trouble at first undoing all those knots and bows. But still the voice nagged on.

Though his sister might be the one who'd done the exams, Mickey had a handy way with an omelette. He made himself thoroughly at home in the kitchen, and I liked having him there, just as I'd appreciated his presence in the living room and the bedroom already. He gave not a murmur of complaint about my lax housekeeping, and when he discovered the potato on the stove he simply made use of it in the omelette. Matt would have scraped it noisily into the bin while lecturing me on my many shortcomings.

Afterwards we drank tea in the living room. That's when Mickey said, 'Are we still on for this evening?'

Though it was far too early for such things, my mind turned somersaults. I had, of course, invited Mickey Golding to eat with me at the Hen and Chickens. Convinced that the arrangement was doomed, I'd subsequently agreed to join Mark Howell at the same address, at the same time. What to do? Though there might be teething problems, Mickey was the best chance I'd had for a relationship in a long time, and a Valentine's dinner would be an ideal way to show him I meant business. It was unfortunate if I had to back out of seeing Mark, but perhaps we could just postpone for a while. I said, 'Yes, of course we are. Eight o'clock in Rustlers.' I hoped to goodness Matt wouldn't have sorted things out with Eileen and want the table for himself.

Braced for the rigours of D-day, Mickey left soon after ten. At the door he pulled the leather jacket around him and said, 'Can we do the same tonight? I always like to warn my mum if I'm not going to be home.'

I said, 'Are you sure you want to make a habit of this?'

He said, 'Why, aren't you?' And we stood there a moment

trying to read each other's eyes again.

I said, 'You're going to be late. Can't let Lena down in her hour of need.'

'What about tonight though?'

I pinched his cheek. 'Of course you're coming back here. I hate having to make my own omelettes.' Behind me the telephone rang.

He didn't smile. He said, 'You're a tricky one, Sam Rigby,' kissed me briefly, and made for the stairs. His smart leather shoes were thumping their way down as I turned back into the flat.

On the phone, an irate voice said, 'You cretin! You bungling fool!'

Though I'd often received similar compliments, it was the first time I'd heard them voiced by my landlord. I said, 'Good morning, Sidney.'

He ploughed on. 'You swear you've got everything under control, then we get this! You're incompetent, you're worse than useless! If there was any sort of register, I'd have you struck off!'

'What's the matter, Sidney?' He didn't reply. 'Sidney, tell me what's happened.'

He was making an odd, strangled sound at the other end of the line, but at first my brain refused to underwrite the simplest explanation. Only when the sound had continued for some time did I yield to the obvious. Sidney Flint was crying. It was a sound I'd have given a great deal of money never to hear. Eventually, in a weaker voice, he managed to say, 'They've taken him.'

'Who, Sidney? Who's taken who?'

He seemed to be forcing the words up from deep inside. 'Dennis. They've taken Dennis.' And with a cry – 'They've taken my boy!' He rallied a little now. 'You moron! You stupid, brainless... I'll have you shot for this!

# THE THIRD BOOK

## nineteen

Patience and empathy are admirable qualities. Their widespread practice has gone some way towards redeeming the human race's rather weak performance in moral affairs, and those particularly gifted in this regard stand as beacons in our midst.

But when, as in the case of Sidney Flint, someone has landed themselves in the dirt entirely as a result of their own obstinacy, to reward them with patience and empathy strikes me as a dereliction of duty. I could see no reason to protect my landlord from the consequences of his folly, so I said, 'I told you this would happen, didn't I? I asked you repeatedly if there was any weakness the Goldings could exploit, and all you did was lie to me.'

'How could they possibly know? I didn't think anyone knew, let alone some worthless mob of gangsters from London.'

'Especially since even Dennis himself doesn't realize he's your son. All the years he's been coming here, and it never occurred to me. No, that's wrong – perhaps the thought just drifted into my mind a couple of times, but I dismissed it as ridiculous.'

Sidney flared up. In this activity he didn't quite attain Bernie Foster's standard, but there was a good chance he'd have taken bronze. 'Why? What's so ridiculous about it?'

'Because I couldn't imagine that any father would treat their son as shabbily as you treat Dennis. You're a disgrace! I'm ashamed to be working for you.'

For a moment there was no response. Then, quiet again, Sidney said, 'I was afraid he wouldn't understand. He might have thought the worse of me if he knew I'd not stood by his mother. When the silly bitch got pregnant, I told her to go to hell. She was trying to force me into marrying her! She thought she was on to a good thing, but I wasn't going to be taken for a mug, was I? Besides, there was a war on, we'd all of us got better things to do.'

'Were you in the forces, then?'

'Er – not exactly. My health, you know. Anyway, one morning the girl turns up at my place, thrusts the baby in my arms and walks off, cool as you like. That's the last anyone round here saw of her. I had him taken into care.'

'Did the people at the home know you were the father?'

'Not in so many words, but I think it was understood. They always hoped I'd take an interest, and when Dennis got older, I did.'

'You had him come round to do odd jobs for you.'

Sidney's temper slipped again. 'Has he been talking? I've told him a thousand times not to talk to people!'

'It was my fault. He just thought he was doing what you wanted.'

I heard Sidney give a deep sigh. 'Yes, he's a good boy is Dennis. I couldn't have asked for a better.' Then suddenly he seemed to remember why he'd rung. 'And while we're stood here talking, they could be doing anything to him!'

'Tell me what happened.'

'I had a note pushed through the letter-box. It's typed, no address, no signature. They just say they've got my son, and they'll let him go as soon as I change my attitude. What if they tell him the truth? You've got to get him back!'

'There's no clue to where he might be?'

'Nothing.'

'Sidney, I really think you should go to the police with this.'

'No! It'll all come out then, won't it?'

'It's going to come out anyway.'

'He'll hate me. And he might – '

Sidney stopped himself. As I may have mentioned, I have a suspicious mind. 'He might what, Sidney? He might actually want what's been due to him all these years, is that it? He's been living in some godforsaken bedsit while you're sat on property worth thousands of pounds. And the worst of it is, he's actually grateful to you!'

Sidney whined. 'Oh! Why did these Golding people ever have to come here?'

'Because they're reality, Sidney, that's why. If you're living in cloud-cuckoo land, the Goldings always turn up sooner or later. So will you go to the police, or not?'

'The note said they'll hurt him if I do.'

I tried to calculate whether this might be an empty threat, and decided it wasn't. 'OK, Sidney, look – I'll see if I can find him.'

'But what if you can't? He could be anywhere!'

'You may have to call those solicitors of theirs in the morning and make positive noises.'

'They'll get nothing from me!'

'I think you've forgotten who's holding all the cards. But give me twenty-four hours to track Dennis down first.'

'You've got to find him, Sam. He's not strong, he can't protect himself.'

'On the bright side, they're not likely to perceive him as much of a threat. My guess is they'll leave him alone.'

'Well you'd better be right. I still blame you for this! If you'd not made me send that stupid letter to London – '

'They'd have taken Dennis just the same, it would have made no difference. Now – unless there's any other little secrets you want to share, perhaps you could get off the line and let me do some work.'

'There's no need to be sharp with me!'

'To be honest, Sidney, I've a good mind to come over there right now and break your neck.'

He hung up. I was glad to be rid of his wheedling voice in my ear. After ten long years I'd finally plumbed the depths of Sidney Flint's nature, to find them even muddier than I'd suspected. But even as I'd discovered the worst, it turned out that human feeling had some place in his crabbed little life after all. Inconveniently, I felt sorry for him.

Now something had to be done about Dennis, and that right speedily. Originally I'd thought of the Goldings as some large, formless organization currently weakened by the imprisonment of its chief executive. But now that I'd grasped that it was Lou Golding who called the shots, there couldn't be much doubt that she herself must have given the order for Dennis's abduction.

Where would he be kept? Surely it would be too risky to hide him somewhere at the Grand, with people coming and going all the time. From Mickey's report, Lou's house at Welldale not only afforded ample space for the concealment of asthmatic rent collectors, it also happened to back onto the Royal Welldale golf course, so that poor Dennis's shouts, if he was capable of any, were unlikely to be heard. A little light surveillance seemed called for.

In the pre-Matt days I would have dressed and left the flat at this point without much thought. Horrified by such lack of system, Matt had assembled two surveillance packs, one for each of us, containing notebooks, writing equipment, binoculars, a flask for hot drinks, a few snacks to snack on, and the all-important camera. The business still stretched to only one good camera, and if we both happened to be out doing similar work one of us had to settle for an unreliable second-hand Agfa with a shutter so noisy it could be heard several streets away. I now found that Matt had taken the good camera home with him after his adventures in Manchester, but I hoped this wouldn't matter. I didn't need pictures, I just needed to know where Dennis had been taken.

I dressed for the great outdoors and filled a flask with coffee. Then I opened the kitchen drawer, took out my abandoned cigarettes, pocketed them, unpocketed them, and shut them away in the drawer again. I was about to leave the flat when I decided that it would do no harm for someone to snoop around the Grand in any case, no matter how unlikely it seemed that Dennis would be there. That someone would have to be Matt, which meant that I would have to phone him and find out whether he was still giving me attitude about the previous day's unpleasantness. Standing in the hallway, I dithered, and while I was dithering the phone rang.

Matt said, 'How was your night?'

I hadn't expected this personal approach, nor the emollient tone. I said, 'Pretty fair, as a matter of fact. Mickey came back here.'

There was barely a pause before Matt said, 'Good. It was about time you made a move.'

I said, 'And how was yours?'

'Oh, OK, you know. Had better.'

'Did you ask Eileen about this evening?'

'No. She gave me enough grief the last time. But I've got a plan.'

I thought he was going to elaborate, but when he didn't I said, 'Anything you feel like sharing?'

'Not really. Need-to-know basis.'

I said, 'You're going to follow her and see where she goes.'

This astute insight into his mental processes seemed to annoy him. 'All right, yes, I am. But don't worry, I'm going to use Marie's moped. I'm sure I can get back in time for the Hen and Chickens.'

Up to that moment, the conversation had been going far better than I'd have dared to hope. The trouble, when it came, had arrived from a wholly unexpected direction. I took the less alarming aspect first. 'You haven't got a licence.'

Matt side-stepped this objection. 'I can probably borrow some L-plates. I've ridden the thing before, it's a doddle.'

Though the picture of Matt pursuing his girlfriend across country on his sister's moped held considerable pathos, I dropped it for now and went on to the main event. 'Matt – when you say, "The Hen and Chickens" – ' My voice refused to go on.

Matt said, 'Yeah, the Hen and Chickens. Our date in Rustlers at eight o'clock.' When I didn't speak, he added, 'Sam? Are you still there?'

I was, of course, but I wished I wasn't. I thought I could see what had probably happened, but to make sure I said, 'You know when you rang me from Manchester the other night and I told you not to cancel the booking – we were cut off, weren't we?'

'That's right, I tried to put more money in but the box was full up. Is there a problem? I didn't think it mattered because I knew what you were trying to say, you didn't want me moping, you were offering to go with me in place of Eileen.'

'Matt – '

'I don't need Miss Docherty around to have a good time. I'll show her! We could have a few beers afterwards too, if you're up for it.'

My back-room team, which had been roused from slumber at

Matt's first mention of the Hen and Chickens, had now knocked up a hasty contrivance suited to the purpose, and was trying to rush it to the front of my mind before I could say anything too disastrous. Under their guidance, I now said, 'Of course, I'd be happy to keep you company, you know I would. But I had second thoughts later.'

'Second thoughts? Why?'

'Isn't this another case of the Standish recklessness?'

'I don't follow.'

'What will people think if they see us eating together on Valentine's Night? What if it gets back to your mum?'

There was a fair-sized silence. I pressed on. 'I know you're angry with Eileen, but I don't want you to take a step you can't go back on. There's probably some perfectly simple explanation for what she's up to.'

More silence. 'I just want her to know that she isn't the be-all and end-all.'

'I thought she was.'

Silence again. 'Maybe you're right. Maybe it's not such a good idea. Damn, I'm confused now.'

I held the private view that Matt was confused most of the time, but this wasn't the moment to go public with it. 'Just let it go, Matt. And I'm not even sure you ought to risk following Eileen. Couldn't you try trusting her? It's the bedrock of relationships, isn't it? Besides, I've got a little job for you this evening.'

'Which is?'

'I'll tell you later. In the meantime, you could practise that Irish accent I've heard you doing. Listen, something's come up this morning.' I told Matt about Sidney and Dennis. 'I'm going out to Hepworth Road, but someone needs to stake out the Grand too. How do you fancy it?'

'Yeah, I can do that.'

'It might be smart to call in at the Marine Lodge on your way and check that Alice Haig's OK. Good customer relations.'

As I was about to ring off, Matt said, 'I'm sorry I've been moaning on so much about Eileen.'

'That's all right. Understandable.'

'I still think it would be a shame to let that booking at Rustlers go to waste. Why don't you ask Mickey if he'd like to go?'

Only the previous day, I'd been the last person on earth Matt wanted to talk to. Now he was showing consideration beyond the call of duty. I was baffled, but I was too busy being relieved to devote much thought to the question of why. My plan, if I'd had one at all, had simply been to turn up with Mickey anyway and hope that Matt hadn't bothered to cancel the booking, but now I could take Mickey out with Matt's blessing. 'That's really thoughtful of you. He's probably working, but I'll ask him.' And that's how we left it. I could hardly eat with Mickey and Mark Howell at the same time, but perhaps pressure of work would force Mark to drop out.

The morning wasn't particularly cold, and the Minx sparked into life without much difficulty. In a few minutes I was parking around the corner from Hepworth Road. The area boasted some of Southaven's most desirable real estate, the grandest properties built here since the war. Now that hardly anyone could afford to retain staff, the town's Victorian mansions were everywhere being converted into flats or demolished, but I suspected that few residents of Hepworth Road cooked their own food or scrubbed their own floors. I wondered whether they realized, these business tycoons and regional celebrities, that they had an East End gangster in their midst, and if so how they felt about it.

Since my face was known, I couldn't risk walking past the front of the house. The surveillance pack slung over my shoulder, I walked along the main road, slowly crossed Hepworth Road, and glanced to the right for evidence of life at the third house on the far side. The wrought iron gates stood open but there was no sign of Lou, her car, or its driver. If I'd half expected the place to be guarded by hoodlums in dark glasses, there was no sign of them either.

I continued past the houses and turned right onto the outer fringe of the golf course, a patch of hilly, scrubby land much favoured by dog walkers. In fact this was the highest ground in all of Southaven, rising to a giddy fifty feet or so above sea level. From here, the ground fell gradually away towards the dunes and the shore a quarter of a mile off, and behind me now the sun nudged weakly through the February cloud, picking out white tops on the distant sea.

A dense tangle of shrubs and bushes pressed up to the back walls of the Hepworth Road houses, giving good protection against burglars and private investigators. The walls themselves were low, but were supplemented by a variety of tall garden fences, many of which would have scotched all attempts at surveillance from this side. Luckily for me, Lou Golding's fence was topped by a decorative panel of cross-hatched slats, and a stunted hawthorn up against the wall would allow me to climb high enough to reach this handy viewpoint. I just hoped there'd be no obstruction on the other side.

Far away to the left, a group of golfers with their caddies trudged solemnly down the fairway. It was unclear to me whether golf was more a sport, a hobby, or an all-consuming way of life, but the main thing was that it got you out of the house on a slow Southaven Sunday while the wife toped sherry from the bottle and prepared the customary roast. None of these men was likely even to see what I was doing, much less take any interest. Some distance ahead of me, a young woman was walking a smooth-haired terrier, but she seemed intent on the shining sea ahead of her and I doubted if she'd look round.

I began to thread my way through the undergrowth, trying not to tear my trousers. Somehow I'd not found time to wash the trousers which had been drenched by God knew what in the toilets of the Grand Hotel a couple of days earlier, so I was wearing my good pair again. If the temperature outside the flat on Preston Road had seemed tolerable for mid-February, the north-westerly breeze currently making free with the Royal Welldale course corrected that impression. I was shivering already, even before my vigil had begun. Perhaps it was time I invested in something a little warmer than my leather jacket. Slowly I worked my way back towards the tree I'd spotted before, then stepped up onto the lower branches. A thorn forced its way through several layers of clothing into my upper arm. I detached myself and climbed higher, using the fence for additional support.

And now I could see between the diagonal slats into Lou Golding's garden. I settled myself as comfortably as I could, which wasn't very comfortably at all, and watched, with the binoculars ready to hand.

Here at the back of the house there were closed curtains or blinds at every window, with the exception of what I took to be the kitchen. This unsporting attitude to snoopers had not been replicated round at the front, where all had lain open to view. If Lou Golding wanted the place to stand as a metaphor for her business practices, then she was going the right way about it. I could only hope that there might be suggestive twitching at one of the curtains, or that someone might step to the kitchen window with a placard reading DENNIS IS UPSTAIRS. I raised the binoculars to my eyes and scanned every foot of the rear elevation. The wooden slats got in the way a little, but as stakeout views go it was far from being the worst. There was nothing whatsoever to be seen. I detached myself from another thorn, shivered again, and took a moment to curse Sidney Flint, who, as it seemed to me, was responsible for most of the suffering in the universe.

The blank aspect of Lou Golding's house was more than matched by its garden, or as much as I could see of it, which wore its winter drab with a kind of cussed pride. From a terrace running the width of the house, stone steps, flanked by barren rockeries, descended to a grey lawn. I guessed that the main action must take place in the bed out of sight below me, on the other side of the wall. Presumably in the spring this would host a blaze of colour, but no one was looking at it now. I couldn't imagine Lou Golding being much of a gardener, but then I'd not have guessed she was religious either. Perhaps she was still at church, and things would start to happen when she came home. Or she might go on to the Grand instead, and nothing would happen at all, and I'd be stuck up a tree all day freezing my arse off for no good reason.

After ten minutes, I drank some of the coffee from the flask. After another ten minutes I delved in the bag for a mint and popped it in my mouth, trying not to admit to myself that I'd have preferred a cigarette. But then my patience was rewarded at last, and something did happen, though not really the kind of something I'd hoped for. An Alsatian dog wandered into view, perhaps having just been let out of a side door. It paused on the terrace, sniffed the air, stretched, then sat down for a moment to scratch one shoulder with a back leg. Satisfied, it stood up again, trotted down the steps, and pissed freely on the lawn. She then (I could now be more sure of the gender) turned to look in my direction, pricked up her ears, and adopted a posture of intense stillness.

All of this I watched through the binoculars. Though she was a splendid animal, it seemed highly unlikely that she could have detected my silent presence at a distance of forty feet or more, with a fence between us and the wind blowing my scent away to the south-east. So when she now gave up her alert pose and started barking, I was as surprised as I was displeased. Fortunately, after just a few short barks she decided to change her approach, and she pelted back up the steps and out of sight around the corner of the house. I felt sure there must be someone there, and I trained the binoculars carefully, hoping they would show themselves. Instead it was the dog which now reappeared, barking as if her life depended on it. When she reached the middle of the lawn she came to a halt, continuing to bark savagely in my general direction.

I put down the binoculars to enable a wider view of the house. Perhaps the occupants, if any, had grown inured to this dog's habit of barking at shadows, and were ignoring her. Certainly no one drew back a curtain or peeked between the blinds. But this lack of reaction served only to provoke the dog to greater efforts. Her eyes were wolf eyes, wild and uncontrollable, and drool streamed from the corners of her mouth. When the performance had gone on for several minutes, I began to worry that she might be doing herself some kind of injury.

But then, unaccountably, the dog stopped barking, perhaps suddenly unsure whether to offer 'bow' or 'wow' as her next observation. As she fell silent she sat down, looking up at the fence with luminous intelligence.

I scanned the building with the binoculars again. The dog

must have heard someone in the house behind her, possibly Lou Golding coming home from church. But still there was no movement and nothing to see.

I dare say if this had gone on much longer I'd only have got bored, so I suppose I ought to be grateful that at this point something hooked me by the back of the collar and dragged me off my perch. My fall was broken by a generous quantity of thorns, all competing to puncture me in tender places. I struggled to get up, and just had time to glimpse a pair of fattish legs before their owner fetched me a nasty blow to the back of the head and the scene went dark.

## twenty

I'd been dreaming.

It had something to do with a dog and a wooden fence, but all that was slipping away now as consciousness returned. I could hear my mother talking with Reilly, the farmer, on the other side of the curtain which separated off the far end of the saloon, the part I thought of as my bedroom. My mother slept in the other, larger section, where we kept the table and the calor gas stove and most of our few belongings. Whenever I happened to wake up like this, it soothed me to hear my mother's voice. And besides, when Reilly came to call I liked it better if they were talking.

Now my mother seemed to say, 'Let's go through this again, shall we? What have I said about tying people to chairs?' When there was no response, she said, 'I've told you not to do it, haven't I? This isn't some old gangster film.'

'I'm sorry, Mrs Golding.'

'How long have you been working for me?'

'Two months. Maybe three.'

'And how many times have we had this conversation already? They said I'd find myself dealing with a bunch of apes if I moved up here, and they weren't kidding.'

The effects of temporary concussion were wearing off. I'd caught up now, and hadn't needed the explicit mention of the name Golding to confirm how things really stood. It wasn't the winter of 1947, and I wasn't sleeping in an old tram car at the edge of a field. It was 1971, and I was presumably somewhere in Lou Golding's house in Welldale, blindfolded and tied to a chair.

The act of withholding information from Miss Pyle concerning my familiarity with Southaven's trams had, it seemed, provoked another response from my unconscious mind. For the most part I tried not to think about that dusty corner of my childhood, nor any other corner of it for that matter. But still there was something compelling about the memory, which dragged me back there only half against my will.

I'd been ten years old when it started. As men returned from the war there were suddenly fewer jobs for women. After two years on the assembly line at Brockman's, making aircraft parts, my mother was laid off. She picked up bits of work here and there and tried to pretend we were all right, but we weren't all right. We'd been living in an attic flat above a shop in Merechurch. The landlord grew impatient. One Sunday morning in November 1946, we were out on the street.

My mother knew Reilly from the Coach and Horses. He farmed fifty acres in Marshfield, and back between the wars it had been his humour to buy up old tram bodies which the corporation were throwing out – the bogies went for scrap. Reilly then equipped these cars to house the migrant workers who descended on the region at harvest time, but before the war they'd usually stood empty for the rest of the year. They weren't empty now. The bombing had left thousands homeless in the wider county, and some of these people had found their way to Reilly's public transport graveyard. By then he'd acquired three single-decker tram cars, two double-deckers, and a bus.

We presented ourselves at Reilly's farmhouse. It looked reassuringly secure and permanent in the November drizzle. Reilly said we were in luck, a family of four had just moved on. As for the rent, it was only half what my mother had been paying before, and if even that was likely to be a problem then he felt sure they'd be able to come to some arrangement.

If you've never been ten years old and just about to move in to your first tram, you may struggle to grasp the full passion of my excitement. Our home was to be one of the double-deckers – Reilly, who took great pride in his fleet, referred to it as a 'Liverpool' – and though one platform had been completely enclosed and its staircase ripped out, at the other end the stairs still snaked up to the roof, where a washing line had been suspended from the trolley mast pole. The seats up there had been scrapped too, leaving the space open, and for the next few weeks it became the deck of the pirate ship the Death's Head, whose captain, Black Sam, was the scourge of the seven seas.

Above the windows, our new home sported advertisements for Hudson's soap on one side and the Botanical Gardens on the other. At one end, over the platform, the destination box still survived, as had the brass handle with which the motorman would change the information; but the mechanism was broken now, the destination stuck at CEMETERY. During the day, the enclosed saloon was always bright because of the three large windows on either side, now hung with ill-matched curtains for privacy. Still screwed to a bulkhead was a metal plate with the maker's name: Dick, Kerr and Company, Preston. I used to stare at this for long periods, debating internally whether there really had been both a Mr Dick and a Mr Kerr, or whether the comma was a mistake.

Even at first, life in the tram was no paradise. We had the stove for cooking, with its twin hot-plates, but the gas was expensive and we often ate cold food. Washing was another problem. There was a stand-pipe on the site, but I mostly washed at school, or at the public baths during the Christmas holidays. Reilly, who was a widower, let my mother use his own bathroom sometimes. There were public toilets in Marshfield near the local railway station on the Preston line, but you didn't always feel like hiking over there. An unofficial latrine had been set up in the field, well away from our once-mobile homes.

Despite all this, I was happier in the tram than anywhere we'd lived before, and I went round every day in an ecstasy of pride. I knew for a fact that none of my classmates lived in a tram, and I began to look down on them as a race of inferior beings. The only snag was that my mother had forbidden me from telling anyone about our change of address, saying there'd be consequences if word got out. In this she was eventually proved right, but in the meantime I found it hard to keep my counsel, especially since I had a school friend, Davey Horrocks, who I was desperate to impress.

But then, in January, it snowed. After it snowed, it froze, and stayed frozen for weeks on end. We all worked together on the site to dig our homes out of the snow. Coal stocks everywhere began to run low, and the whole country was almost brought to its knees. Only at school could I really get warm, but to save heating oil the school was reduced to opening three days a week. Now the big windows in the saloon were no longer a blessing; everything in the room froze solid. At night I slept in my clothes. My breath left a crust of ice on the bedding.

I could see that my mother had no plan to get us out of this. She said everyone was suffering the same, and the thaw would be bound to come soon. I knew Aunt Winnie and Uncle Fred would have helped us, but my mother and Winnie had fallen out back in the autumn, and she'd rather have died than go crawling to her sister now. Nor would she let me talk to Grandad Eli, who lived only a few streets away but had no clue of the mess we were in. Somehow I got the idea it was all my fault, that if I'd been a better son we'd at least have had a proper roof over our heads.

I wasn't getting enough to eat. At school I was lethargic and I couldn't concentrate. I didn't really know what I was doing or saying, and in that muddled state I finally let the cat out of the bag. I told Davey Horrocks where we were living, Davey told his mother, his mother told the school, the school told social services. My mother signed a form and I was taken into care.

I don't remember much about the home. I refused to believe that I'd be staying there. The other boys took against me, I had to prove myself with my fists, and for that the grown-ups thrashed me. My mother stayed away. I missed her so much I couldn't sleep, and if I'd ever learned how, I'd have cried.

Then, about ten days later, my mother turned up out of the blue and took me to our new home, another flat in Merechurch. It was quite ritzy by our standards. Though she still had no full-time job, my mother suddenly had money. Someone had bailed us out. I wondered if my father, my useless, faceless father, had come to the rescue at last.

In March, the thaw arrived. We went on as if nothing had happened.


Hoping that Lou Golding and the other voice, which I took to belong to First Ugly Bloke, might divulge information pointing to the whereabouts of Sidney Flint's son, I tried to give no sign that I was once more in residence with a light in the window. Lou Golding was saying, 'And why set about him with a snooker cue? I'll have to replace that now, or they'll want the money back off the deposit.'

'You never said anything about snooker cues, you just said I mustn't use the vases again. You said if we had intruders I was to use my imagination.'

'There are other ways to discourage people apart from smashing them over the skull with the first thing that comes to hand. Either you learn a bit of style, Cecil, or I'll have to let you go. Got that?'

'Yes, Mrs Golding.'

'I shouldn't have to waste my time on this sort of thing. Now – did we get a call from Carlo while I was out? Is our guest comfortable?'

In the circumstances these words were highly suggestive. And I might have found out more, but unfortunately for half a minute now the tip of my nose had been the playground of some unseen creature, possibly a house-fly which had chosen to over-winter in the balmy conditions of Hepworth Road. When this adventurer moved round onto my nostrils, the irritation became too great to bear, and I sneezed a sneeze so violent it would have lifted me clean off the chair if I hadn't been tied to it at the time.

First Ugly Bloke said, 'He's awake.'

'Take those ridiculous things off him.'

'But he might menace you.'

'What – Sam here? We're old friends. All the same, leave that door open a crack on your way out, and don't stray too far.'

The blindfold came off first. It turned out to have been a black silk scarf, the sort of thing Lou might have worn to the funeral of an unlucky business rival. While First Ugly Bloke squatted to untie the cords around my ankles, Lou Golding stood at a respectful distance, as if anxious not to embarrass a guest caught at a disadvantage. There was a window to my left, with Venetian blinds shut close. A couple of lamps cast moody shadows. We were in an office room, but not the kind of utilitarian space where I'd progressed my relationship with Mickey the previous night. Here, antique glass-fronted bookcases lined the walls, thick carpet covered the floor, and beside my chair a huge mahogany desk with a red leather top offered a seductive backdrop for the signing of those tedious cheques. I noticed a cigar box and guillotine and an onyx lighter on the desktop. A coal fire had recently been lit in the grate, but wasn't making much headway.

My wrists had been secured behind the chair, and the knots proved something of a challenge. But eventually these too were undone, and First Ugly Bloke took the ropes out of the room, along with his nasty, ugly self.

I said, 'I thought he worked for Joe Braithwaite.'

Lou said, 'Mr Braithwaite works for me now.' She made it sound so simple, and perhaps it was. Slasher Braithwaite was small beer beside the Goldings, and no doubt he'd been quick to recognize which side his bread was buttered. Lou turned towards me. 'I take it Cecil hasn't done any serious damage.'

Tentatively, I explored an area at the back of my head which throbbed unpleasantly. The bleeding seemed to have stopped. 'It's nothing. Just a scratch.'

'Cecil's very conscientious. He prefers visitors to use the front door.'

And I might just as well have done, for all I'd learned while skulking round the back. Apart from anything else, I felt a sharp pain whenever I shifted my buttocks, as if a thorn had broken off in the flesh. Whether Lou included mind-reading among her list of talents I don't know, but she now said, 'Perhaps you'd like to sit somewhere more comfortable,' and indicated a leather armchair on which my surveillance pack was currently reclining. I took up the offer, moving my bag to the floor. Lou crossed to a drinks trolley beneath the window. 'Drink? Scotch all right?' I took up that offer too. The crystal tumbler she brought over to me felt good in my hand. When she'd poured a glass for herself, she raised it to me and said, 'A fresh start – OK?'

I said, 'A fresh start,' and we both drank. It wasn't the kind of Scotch you get in cheap bars. Lou moved to a second armchair, settled into it and crossed her legs. She'd worn a dark trouser suit for church, but it would have looked no less appropriate in the boardroom.

To put Lou at her ease, I said, 'Good service this morning?'

'The Reverend Chadband certainly knows how to soothe his flock. Always the same message of mercy and forgiveness.'

No doubt if you were Lou Golding you stood in particular need of a merciful God. But she didn't say any more on the subject, and I was anxious to move on to other matters. I said, 'You've got a remarkable dog.'

Lou didn't quite smile, but she said, 'That's Lucille, I brought her with me. They'd told me the guard dogs up here were all amateurs.'

'You don't seem to have a very high opinion of this part of the world. I can't help asking myself why you came.'

Lou took another sip of the drink. 'It wouldn't have been my first choice, I don't mind admitting it. People here talk a different language, it's hard to make yourself understood. But that's just teething troubles. Because, when I hear of an opportunity – ' Instead of completing the sentence, Lou made a sudden grasping gesture with her free hand. You could almost see the opportunity having the life squeezed out of it. She sat further back in the chair and nodded complacently. 'Southaven's been dying on its feet for years, you're all just sleepwalking through your lives. That's going to change.'

'And I suppose you're the one who's going to change it.'

She regarded me keenly, or as keenly as was possible for a

woman with a turned-up nose. 'I get what I want. People resist at first, of course – you got to expect it. But they fall into line in the end.'

'Is that what you think?'

'I know it for a fact. They've got too much to lose.'

'Like your unfortunate husband for example. Didn't quite fall into line, did he?'

So far, my visit to Welldale had tended to disappoint, but I drew some consolation when this remark caused Lou Golding to frown. 'Frank's made of the right stuff. There was no one could touch him when he started out, and anyone that tried wished they hadn't. But the thing is, Sam, you got to keep up. That's what poor Frank never understood. Times change, you got to follow the money. He always said it don't pay to be greedy, that he'd been very lucky and you got to give something back. So much and no more, that's what he said. Bleed your customers dry and they can't pay, then you're all up shit creek together.' She sniffed now, an impressive effort which left her level of contempt in no doubt. 'Sentimental bollocks. I say, bleed 'em dry, then move on. What am I, a fucking charity?'

I said, 'You seem to be getting confused between business and organized crime.'

She dismissed this with a shake of the head. 'I can tell you the difference exactly. If you got friends in high places, it's business. If you ain't, it's organized crime.'

'And you've got friends here, is that it? That's what makes a dozy backwater like Southaven an "opportunity"?' I thought of the story in the Gazette which had first brought Alice Haig to my office. 'Is Morgan Williams on your payroll?'

Lou tried to laugh. She wasn't very good at it, but perhaps she didn't get much practice. 'You got quaint notions, ain't you? There's no payroll, Sam, just people looking out for each other, that's all.'

On reflection, I couldn't see Morgan Williams looking out for someone as alien to him as Lou Golding. Publishing that story without checking the facts could have been no more than a misjudgement. 'What about the cops? Who looks out for you there?' When Lou just shrugged, I said, 'I hear you've been rubbing shoulders with my old pal Chubby Fallon. Has he fixed protection for you? Who is it he's got the dirt on?'

'If you think I'll name names you're a damn fool. You got nothing on me, and you're going to leave this house empty-handed.'

Lou Golding was probably right. But after everything she'd said about business I'd have expected her to boot me out of the house and slam the door in my face, not give me the Scotch-and-armchair treatment. Perhaps there was something she wanted from me after all, in which case there was a chance I might get something in return. I said, 'Do we have to sit in Stygian gloom?'

'Eh?'

'Mind if I open those blinds?' Lou assented, and I went over to the window. It turned out we were at the north side of the house, where another high fence blocked the view of the property next door. Such light as now found its way into the room carried no warmth or cheer, but it was good to be reminded that there was a world outside. Returning to my seat, I said, 'Just renting, are you?'

'The owners are away for a year. But I'm starting to like it here, it's a good neighbourhood, you get a better class. When the owners come back they may have to find somewhere else.'

'You're staying, then?'

'Maybe, maybe not. I'm still not sure the climate agrees with me.'

'I thought everyone had to agree with you, whether they liked it or not. Take Sidney Flint, for example.'

Lou Golding rather let herself down now by saying, 'Who?'

'Come on, don't be coy. I'm talking about the man whose son is presently in Carlo's safe keeping.'

There was a brief pause while Lou sifted the implications. 'Oh. So you weren't out cold after all.'

'What exactly will you do with him if Sidney doesn't fall into line?'

'He will though, won't he. They all do.'

'And Alice Haig? She doesn't strike me as the type to buckle under pressure.'

'I've made Mrs Haig a very generous offer.'

'But I don't think for a moment she'll accept, and do you know why?' Lou Golding said nothing, but I had her attention. The tumbler rested forgotten on the arm of her chair. 'Because your offer's got blood on it. She asked Giles Rawley to nose into your affairs, next thing you know his brains are making patterns on the wall. I don't know yet who swung the hammer, unless it was that thug you keep for a pet, but it was you who gave the order, wasn't it?'

Lou Golding remained still for a moment. There was nothing flippant or facetious in her make-up, and she wasn't about to laugh off such a weighty accusation. I was trying to read her expression, the face day-lit on one side and lamp-lit on the other, but I probably wasn't the first person to have tried this and failed. At last she rose from her seat, crossed to the desk, and fetched the cigar box and guillotine. She opened the lid, and held it towards me without speaking. I put the tumbler down on the coffee table beside me, took out a cigar, snipped off the cap, and handed back the guillotine. While Lou replaced everything on the desk, I gave my nose a treat. I hadn't smoked a decent cigar in years, and this one threatened to be as decent as they come. As a bonus, it would put a nice dent in my nicotine craving, yet I could still claim that I'd been nowhere near a cigarette. Lou came back now with the onyx lighter. I rolled the cigar in the flame a few times, then lit it carefully. After a couple of puffs I took the smoke in my mouth, savoured it a while, then gently released it.

My normally inscrutable face must have betrayed some hint of pleasure, because Lou now said, 'Quite something, ain't they? I bought in a load for Frank, to help him pass the time. Trouble is, he never gets to smoke them himself. His new friends do show him respect for past glories, but I'm afraid he's nowhere near being cock of the walk. So I don't send them in no more. Want a top-up?'

I let Lou Golding refresh my glass, telling myself that if this kind of hospitality was her usual reaction when accused of vicious crimes, I should accuse her more often. Lou sat down again, and I puffed contentedly on the cigar. The fire in the grate had taken hold and was burning nicely, so I stretched my legs out towards its warming influence. The Scotch had had a warming influence too. Now that I more or less knew what had become of Dennis, I felt no great sense of urgency. The more Lou and I talked, the more I might discover.

Lou said, 'I take it Mickey was with you last night?' I didn't contradict her, and she gave a slight nod. 'I'm pleased. I know he likes you.' I felt grateful when she didn't add that there was no accounting for taste. 'Of course, it's not every mother who'd go overboard about having a ginger for a son. It was a while before Frank came round to it, if he ever really has, but it's like I said, times change, you got to keep up. Poof or no poof, Mickey's still my boy.' She sipped at the Scotch again. I was getting a lot more mileage out of it than she was. 'He thinks I take him for granted, Sam, but I don't. Him and Lena, they've always took care of each other, it's been hard to know what I could do for them.'

'Then why not give Lena a chance in the kitchen? She's a good barmaid, but I don't think it's what she wants.'

Again, Lou didn't quite smile. 'I like the way you're taking an interest. Perhaps you're right, perhaps I should let her loose at the Grand some time. I've already found something for Mickey, though.'

'If you mean helping out at the Casino, that rather depends on you and the Malones turning over a new leaf.'

'It's kind of a delicate situation. They got friends too, otherwise our licence application would have gone through first time. I'm working on it. Three or four weeks, Goldings Casino's going to be open for business.'

The label on my cigar was beginning to detach itself, so I finished off the job and tossed it into the fire. 'A little bird told me Goldings is open already, if you happen to be a favoured customer.'

Lou's eyes narrowed. 'What little bird? We got no licence, you know that as well as I do.'

'You're not the sort to let such a thing stand in your way, though, are you? The Grand's a big place, there must be somewhere you could hide a couple of tables.'

'In the middle of a police raid? They never found nothing. That little bird of yours is telling porkies.'

I allowed myself a small, frustrated sigh. Accusations were all very well, but without proof to back them up I was getting nowhere. It looked as if Lou was right, and I'd be leaving Hepworth Road empty-handed.

Then Lou said, 'I'm glad you called round,' which I thought was handsome of her considering that I'd just been caught up a tree spying on her home through binoculars. 'I'd been hoping we might have a little chat. If you and Mickey go on the way you're going, we might be seeing a lot more of each other. I may have discouraged one or two of his earlier associations, but he's ready to have someone special in his life, and I'm inclined to take a different attitude this time.' Perhaps spotting lint on the dark trousers, Lou brushed them down with one hand. Absorbed in this task, her eyes lowered, she said, 'I understand you ain't got much in the way of a family.'

Various images now arose unbidden. Of my Grandad Eli in the council care home at Marshfield, goosing the young girl who'd brought his tea. Of my aunt, savagely slicing carrots in the back kitchen at Crowburn House while Uncle Fred looked on in alarm. Of my mother asleep in a hospital bed. I said, 'We do all right.'

Looking up again now, Lou said, 'A man's nothing without a family. People he can turn to, people who understand. The world's a cold place if you ain't got family.'

I flicked ash into the hearth. 'I seem to have managed somehow.'

'That's right, and you should be proud of yourself. So you started on the wrong foot and went to work for Lily Law – what of it? You soon saw the error of your ways, you're in business now. Business. A chance to prove yourself, a chance to thrive. They tell me you played a fine hand over that murder case last summer. People will always need a good investigator, Sam. As a matter of fact, I need one myself; the Goldings need one. There's a place in the family for a man like you. I done some investigating of my own, and I reckon you'll be good for Mickey and good for the family too.'

Heat now disrupted the balance of the fire, and one wing of it collapsed. Leaning forward, Lou restored order with the poker, then she settled back again. 'But if you're going to thrive, you need investment. Think what your business could do with a little injection of cash – five grand, say, maybe ten.' A brief glance took in the rumpled surveillance pack beside my chair. 'You could upgrade your equipment. You could drive around in something smart for a change. You could employ a secretary, instead of bashing out your own letters on some beat-up old typewriter. But ten grand's a lot of money, no bank's going to lend it to you. That's where family comes in, Sam. You work with me, I'll see you right. I need a local man on the ground, someone bright who understands the ordinary Joe around these parts, someone who can winkle out the information my competitors don't want to give me. Why shouldn't that someone be you?'

Lou studied me closely as she awaited my response. Just to be moving I'd have liked to toke on the cigar, or slug down more of the deep, fiery Scotch, but something in her look held me paralysed. I knew exactly why the someone Lou was talking about should not be me. The Goldings were career criminals who followed the money no matter how dirty the road it took. Their true face was closer to that of First Ugly Bloke than the well-dressed woman sitting opposite me. But I also knew that Lou Golding meant what she said. This was a genuine invitation to join the family, and if I did I might never want for anything again. Firelight picked out the diamonds in Lou's earrings. The leather chair embraced me, as if I was already saying yes.

I drank the rest of the Scotch and set the tumbler aside. 'It's a tempting offer.'

'And you'd be a fool to turn it down.' Lou's eyes had never left my face. But now she read something new there, and her tone altered. 'Maybe you need a little time to get used to the idea. Offers like this don't come round every day.'

I said, 'No point in rushing things, is there?'

Lou tried to smile, then gave up when her face wouldn't cooperate. For all the glow of the firelight, her eyes were cold. They studied me closely now, as if I was some specimen on a slab.

There was a long silence.

Then Lou Golding said, 'What kind of person are you, Sam Rigby? I mean really, truly. When the chips are down, who are you?'

The fire flared up, a vein throbbed in my neck. Seconds ticked by, and still I had no answer to Lou Golding's question. She sat motionless, bravely making a show of patience against every instinct of her nature. She was taking a lot of trouble over me. I felt flattered.

But eventually Lou's patience reached its limit. Putting down her glass, she said, 'You know where to find me. Let me have your decision when you're ready.' And she rose to her feet. The interview was over.

I stubbed out what was left of the cigar, grabbed my bag from the floor, and stood up in my turn. I said, 'We've still got business outstanding. Sidney Flint.'

'Be reasonable, Sam. No one's going to shed a tear if that old Scrooge loses half his property. Why not try talking him round?'

'He's a hard nut to crack. I suggest you hang on to Dennis for another day or two and leave the rest to me. I take it Dennis is all right, by the way? You've not got him tied to a chair?'

'Carlo's worked in top hotels all his life, it pains him to see a guest treated badly. He's probably got this Dennis person living off the fat of the land, but Flint doesn't need to know that, does he?'

'So Dennis is at the hotel?'

It was a question too far, and the warm expression which Lou had been attempting quickly frosted over. She led me to the door. There she turned, and fixed me again with that uncompromising gaze. 'Be sure you take good care of my boy. I don't want you breaking his heart, understand?'

Something in Lou Golding's tone left little doubt what would happen to me if I did.

I couldn't park at the Marine Lodge, either front or back, so I drove round until I found a place on the street. I was impatient to talk to Matt and find out what he'd learned over at the Grand, but I thought I should see Alice Haig first. After all, if Lou Golding got her way then she and Alice and I would soon be part of one big, happy family.

The time was getting on towards two o'clock. To avoid the Valentine's Day diners, I slipped into the Marine Lodge by the back door, which stood wedged open. I expected to find Oscar Hammond and his team riding high on adrenaline.

And indeed, when I came to the kitchen door the scene was of purposeful activity, as waitresses bearing steaming plates and empty dishes passed in and out of the dining room. But the figure just piping cream onto what may have been Black Forest gateau didn't belong to Oscar Hammond. The hat appeared to be his, but it rested on the brow of Lena Golding.

Ever since I'd woken up this morning with one of them in my bed, there seemed to be Goldings everywhere. But the last place I'd have expected to find another one was here, at the nerve centre of Alice Haig's operation. In my surprise, I said, 'Lena!'

'Damn!' Lena stepped away from the gateau and glared at me. 'Now look what you've made me do!'

Alice herself marched in from the dining room. 'Is everything all right, Lena?'

'All under control, Mrs Haig. Apart from this clown creeping up on me.'

'You look a little stressed, if you don't mind my saying.'

'Take no notice. When it's over, I'm going to imagine I've really enjoyed this.' Then she resumed her work. She didn't quite seem her usual sunny self, but I'd never known her under this kind of pressure before.

Alice crossed to where I hovered in the doorway, and shepherded me out into the corridor. 'Mr Rigby – it's the most extraordinary thing! Oscar never turned up for work this morning. He'd been going to do the breakfasts because we have so many people staying. I coped all right myself, but when I sent Evan down the road to Oscar's house he wasn't there! I had all these lunch bookings and no chef.'

'Did you call the police?'

'Yes, they're looking for him now. He's always been so reliable, I can't think why he'd suddenly go off like this without telling me.

When it got to half past ten and he still hadn't appeared, I got desperate, I didn't know where to turn. But then I thought of Mrs Golding. She'd been so keen yesterday to impress on me that we had interests in common. She said if my business needed help, I only had to ask.'

The line sounded all too familiar. 'She likes to put people in her debt. It's a way of neutralising them.'

'But what choice did I have? I rang the number she'd given me, but I was told she was at church, so I went next door and asked to see the manager. I told him what had happened and begged him to spare me someone from the Grand kitchens to help out, but he said they were far too busy, which of course is what I'd feared. Then Lena – oh, isn't she wonderful, Mr Rigby? Mrs Golding is *so* lucky. I can't see Bobby turning out anywhere near as useful.'

'And Carlo let her go? Isn't she supposed to be working behind the bar?'

'He grumbled, of course, but Lena said he could easily find someone to cover, and she came straight back here with me. Oscar had prepared the menus last night, the ingredients were ready to hand. So she cooked exactly what Oscar had been going to cook himself. It's been rather slow and to be honest I have had complaints about that, but it could have been a *disaster* and thanks to Lena it was nothing of the kind.'

Over Alice's shoulder I could see Lena ladling gravy onto a plate. I said, 'By the way, did Graham Leeds speak to you this morning?'

Alice's expression darkened. 'He did. Thank you for clearing that up for me, I should never have doubted you. Perhaps if I'd brought you in earlier instead of asking Giles Rawley – ' She left the thought unfinished.

'What did you decide to do?'

'My instinct was to let him go straight away. Such a betrayal! I could hardly bear to look at him. But where was I going to find a night porter for this evening? I tried to give him a week's notice, but I kept thinking what Ian would have said about it.'

I wondered if it might have been Graham Leeds who'd suffered a vase to the head while visiting Hepworth Road. I said, 'Surely you've not kept him on – after everything he's done?'

But before she could answer, Alice's eye was caught by a movement behind me, and a voice I recognized said, 'Mrs Haig.'

'Ah! Detective Constable. Any news of my chef?'

We'd been joined by Mark Howell. He gave me a brief smile, then to Alice Haig he said, 'Not yet, I'm afraid. But I need to see Cordelia Lane. We've arrested her husband.'

'Arrested, why? I'd no idea he was even in Southaven.'

'Surrey police went to question him yesterday evening, but he'd flown the nest. They circulated his registration number. We thought he might turn up here, and one of our men stopped him out on the coast road at Otterdale a couple of hours ago. Howard Lane assaulted him and tried to get away.'

It seemed that Southaven had been possessed by a rare frenzy of activity while I'd warmed my toes at Lou Golding's hearth. I said, 'Has he admitted anything?'

'Not yet. But DI Hargreaves is with him now.'

This announcement didn't inspire the confidence it might once have done. Hargreaves had never been quick, but few villains could resist the steady pressure of his scepticism. Recently, something must have changed. Whether he'd been put off his stroke by the reorganization of the local force, or perhaps the looming prospect of retirement, I couldn't say, but whatever the reason I'd been astonished that he seemed to accept Oscar Hammond's story at face value. Oscar claimed to have gone straight home after dinner on the night Giles Rawley died, but I felt convinced he was lying, and I'd fully expected Hargreaves to grind the truth out of him. That hadn't happened, and now Oscar Hammond was missing.

Once again, Alice Haig was distracted by some development behind me. I turned to see a uniformed officer hurrying towards us from Wright Street. Mark went out to talk to him.

Alice said, 'Cordelia's going to be in shreds. First her father, and now this. Do you know why the police wanted to talk to Howard Lane?'

'He has no alibi for the night of the murder.'

'But why would he need an alibi? Surely no one could possibly be suggesting – '

Alice stopped talking. Mark had rejoined us, and she could see that he brought news. Mark said, 'We've found him.'

'Oscar? Oh, thank goodness! I've been so worried.'

For a couple of seconds Mark let Alice enjoy this flush of hope. Then he said, 'I'm sorry, Mrs Haig. Oscar Hammond is dead.'

Alice Haig's face registered mere blank disbelief. But the news had a far different effect on someone else, someone who'd been listening through the open doorway. From the kitchen, Lena Golding howled one great, primal howl of pain.


## twenty-one


Oscar Hammond's body had been discovered in a bus shelter facing the sea, on the coast road between Welldale and Otterdale. I'd noticed the shelter often enough as I drove by, the sort of place a person might go to sit and think and watch the light slowly changing over the distant waves. A brandy bottle with most of its contents spilled lay open on the bench beside the corpse. The signs were that Oscar had been poisoned.

Lena Golding said, 'If I just hadn't been so vain! I didn't want people knowing. I mean – he was a lot older than me, and he wasn't exactly Robert Redford, was he? And then, if my mum found out I knew she'd put a stop to it. Oscar wasn't the sort she wanted in the family. But he was the sweetest, kindest – ' She gave herself up to tears.

When Lena had said she wanted to talk, I'd followed her and Mark Howell into Alice Haig's office, leaving Alice herself to substitute for Lena in the kitchen as best she could. My attendance at this interview didn't exactly chime with official procedure, and at every moment I expected Mark to throw me out.

The discovery that Oscar and Lena had been having a relationship answered several questions. As her tears subsided,

Lena dried her eyes with the handkerchief which Mark had given her. Personally I'd have had nothing to do with this dubious square of cloth, but Lena seemed not to notice its deficiencies. I risked saying, 'I take it Oscar was with you on Thursday night – the night Giles Rawley was killed?' I glanced apprehensively at Mark, but he seemed content to let me do some of the leg-work.

Lena nodded. For Mark's benefit, she said, 'I've got one of the staff rooms at the Grand, next door. Oscar used to stay over. He was always pestering me to go to his place, but I was afraid someone might come looking for me in my room and there'd be questions if I wasn't there.'

Mark said, 'Did anyone else know about this?'

'My brother Mickey knew, but that's all. I'd made Oscar swear he wouldn't tell anyone.'

I said, 'I can't imagine that went down very well.' I was thinking of Oscar's mood whenever I'd bumped into him during the past forty-eight hours, of his stubborn refusal to tell me where he'd been on the night of the murder.

'You're right, it didn't. He said if I really cared about him I'd want to tell the world, not hide him away like I was ashamed of him. When I tried to explain, he used to get angry.' Almost to herself she added, 'We couldn't have gone on the way we were.'

Lena, hatless now, had adopted the armchair, while I leaned back against the filing cabinet and Mark stood near the desk, taking notes. He said, 'And when was the last time you saw him?'

The tears rose to her eyes again. 'Oh God – this is awful!' But this time she bit her lip and pressed on. 'It was the middle of the night, last night.'

'When exactly?'

Irritably, she said, 'I don't know, do I? I never looked at the clock. Maybe two, maybe three. He was upset about something, he'd been drinking, and when he drank a lot he snored and tossed around in the bed. It's only a single bed and he's a big man, he kept waking me up. I told him to bugger off home. If I'd just been a bit more patient with him – '

I said, 'Lena, it's not your fault.'

Mark said, 'Upset? Do you know what Mr Hammond was upset

about?'

Lena shook her head, dabbing at her eyes with the handkerchief. 'He wouldn't tell me. But I think it had something to do with the army, he was talking a lot about Kenya. He was out there during that bad time.'

'The Mau Mau rebellion?'

'That's the one. Only he said it wasn't a rebellion, it was a – what did he call it? – a war of liberation, that's right. He said we was treating the blacks like filth, and they had no choice.'

I remembered something Oscar had said, about the things he'd seen and done. 'I got the impression Oscar wasn't very proud of his service record.'

Lena said, 'He loved the army. Your average soldier was like a hero to him, he was dead proud to have been part of it. It was the top brass he couldn't swallow. And then, he was ashamed how he ended up.'

Lena stopped there, as if we knew the rest of the story and wouldn't want to hear it again. Mark said, 'We need to know all the background, Miss Golding. It might be relevant to what's happened.'

I felt the same myself. Laurence Glass had pointed out that what linked himself and Giles Rawley was that they were both old soldiers, and now another old soldier was dead. If there'd been anything unusual about Oscar's military career, it could offer a vital clue. Vital clues had been in short supply lately.

Lena Golding tried to collect her thoughts. 'I may not get all this right. He told me in bits, you know? I've sort of pieced it together.' Distractedly, she was winding and unwinding the handkerchief around her wrist. 'It started up in the hills.'

'This was in Kenya?'

She nodded again. 'There was fighting, he saw some terrible things. That's when he began to go off the rails. They pulled him back to base camp, thinking he'd sort himself out. He was cooking for the prisoners – there was loads of them, hundreds maybe. And they was being – I don't know, beaten, stuff like that. The way Oscar told it, the C.O. was this monster, got a kick out of hurting people. Then one day, Oscar saw him – ' Lena winced at some internal picture. Then she took a breath, and went on. 'Oscar saw the C.O. squeezing a prisoner's eyes out. Several people saw it, but it was all hushed up. Only Oscar couldn't get it out of his mind, it sort of tipped him over the edge. He wasn't a well man by then, he didn't know what he was doing.'

Again Lena paused. Mark, never the most patient of police officers, was about to give her a verbal nudge, but I held up my hand. Lena's delivery may have been on the slow side, but as witnesses go she was one of the best. After a while, she said, 'Sometimes he cooked for the officers' mess. There was half a dozen high-ups, he said they all acted like they was at Claridge's or something. Anyway, there was these dogs in the camp, dozens of them, they had to shoot them sometimes to stop them raiding the supplies. Oscar started giving the officers dog-meat. But they didn't seem to notice, and he got more and more angry. That's when he did it. He served them dog-shit stew.'

I thought back to the cake I'd eaten at Giles's birthday party, hoping Oscar hadn't been too creative with it.

Mark said, 'Presumably this time they did notice.'

'Oscar was questioned, and he said some wild things, and there was talk of him being court-martialled. But in the end he was dishonourably discharged. Thrown out, nowhere to go. He fetched up in a mental hospital in London somewhere, he was there three years. When he come out, no one would give him a job. So he moved up north, where no one knew anything about him, and finally Mr Haig took him on here. Oscar was too honest for his own good sometimes, he told Mr Haig the whole story. But Haig just said it was all in the past, as long as Oscar knew his way round a kitchen and didn't serve dog poo for breakfast they'd get along fine.'

There was a knock at the door, and the uniformed officer we'd seen before came in, an evidence bag in his hand. To Mark, he said, 'This was found in the victim's pocket. Hargreaves wants the handwriting identified.'

Mark examined the contents of the bag, then crossed to show it to Lena. She said, 'Sorry, no idea.'

Then it was my turn. The plastic bag held a white envelope,

from the Marine Lodge's own stationery, with the address printed on the back flap. The words *Oscar Hammond* had been written on the front in a vigorous script, then underlined. I'd seen something like it recently, but I wasn't sure where. To the constable I said, 'Anything found inside the envelope?'

But apparently he could see no reason why he should answer my questions. Whether this was because I was a stranger, or because he knew exactly who I was and didn't like it, I couldn't tell. Only when Mark seconded the query did he grudgingly say, 'No, it was empty. There's a search team going over Hammond's place now – number thirteen, down the road.' Then he left the bag with Mark and quit the room, giving me an unpleasant reverse glower.

Lena said, 'I need to be doing something. Is it all right if I get back to the kitchen?'

Mark said, 'Just one more thing. Did Mr Hammond have the brandy bottle with him when you last saw him?'

'I didn't let him bring drink into the room, he'd have had to go home and fetch it. He drank brandy all the time – Sam'll tell you.'

Mark seemed to check the back of his mind for points he might have forgotten, then said, 'You've been very helpful, Miss Golding. If you think of anything else – '

'I'll let you know. Or I'll tell Sam.'

Mark frowned. 'Actually, you need to tell us. The police.'

'But I thought you two was friends? I saw you chatting at the Grand when we got raided.' While Mark and I exchanged a look, Lena got out of the chair. She said, 'I keep thinking I'll wake up and it's just been a nightmare.' She let a couple of seconds go by, but when she still didn't wake up she nodded to us and silently left the room. Her eyes were red and her face was streaked with tears, but there was no mistaking her determination. I was berating myself for having taken too little notice of Lena Golding in the past, perhaps dazzled by her brother's attractions. I made a mental note never to underestimate a Golding again.

To Mark I said, 'Thanks for letting me sit in on all that.'

'So what do you think happened?'

'It's obvious, someone's slipped poison into the brandy bottle.'

'No chance of it being suicide?'

'Why are you asking me?'

'Because you knew him.'

I thought about this. 'No, no chance at all. He was disturbed by Giles Rawley's death, but if he'd survived the army and Kenya then I don't see why he couldn't survive this too.'

'What if it was him that killed Rawley? Perhaps he was overcome by remorse.'

'But he had no motive, and in any case it sounds like he was with Lena Golding at the time. Besides, if you want to kill yourself you're not going to slip poison in your own brandy, are you? It's murder, I'm sure of it. What I don't understand is, how they got at the brandy. He often brought a bottle here with him, to the hotel, but if someone had spiked it here yesterday evening then why was it so long before Oscar actually drank any?'

Mark said, 'And where does all this leave Howard Lane? We picked him up on the coast road, only about a mile from where Hammond was found. Presumably he'd visited the Marine Lodge in the past?'

'I don't know.'

Mark looked unhappy. 'I thought we were getting somewhere, now I'm not so sure. Perhaps the search of Hammond's home will turn something up – maybe even the contents of this envelope.' He waved the evidence bag in his hand. 'I'd better go round the hotel and see if anyone recognizes the writing.' Mark picked the remains of his handkerchief off the chair where Lena had left it, and stuffed it in his pocket. Moving towards the door, he said, 'You still OK for the Hen and Chickens this evening?'

I hesitated. 'Er – of course I am.'

Mark said, 'You hesitated.'

'No I didn't.'

'There's a problem, isn't there.'

'Of course there isn't.'

'Why would you hesitate and say "er" if there isn't a problem?'

The man had a point. My backroom team were running round in a panic, spilling tea and falling over each other, but if there was a plausible answer to Mark's question they seemed to have mislaid it. Then I managed to say, 'Are you sure you'll be able to get away? You've got two murders to solve.' When this seemed to give him pause, I pressed my case. 'You need to get on to Aldershot and find out more about Oscar Hammond's service record. And it would be good to know the name of that sadistic officer.'

'Yes – thank you, Sam, I do know how to investigate crime. But I'm only going to slip away for an hour or two. It doesn't take long to make a gesture.'

I followed Mark out into the corridor, intending to escape to the Grand as fast as possible and find out what Matt had been doing. But in the hallway we found Alice Haig, relieved of her kitchen duties by Lena's return. Evan Bickerstaff was in charge of the reception desk, his absurd bell-boy outfit looking tighter on him by the day. A party of diners was just leaving, and Alice said to them, 'Thank you so much, I do hope you've enjoyed your lunch,' before turning back to address Mark. 'I'm not needed here, am I? I promised I'd visit the Major this afternoon and it's already after three.'

Mark said, 'Do you know this handwriting, Mrs Haig?' and showed her the envelope.

Alice took the bag in her hand and screwed up her eyes. She said, 'I'd be more confident if I had my reading glasses, but surely it's Giles Rawley's?'

Yes – of course. The script resembled the marginal notes I'd seen in Giles's copy of *King Lear*, but on a larger scale.

Mark said, 'I'm going to talk to Mrs Lane anyway, so I'll ask her to confirm that. You're free to go to the Infirmary, but I'd be glad if you could come straight back here afterwards. We might be due another visit from DI Hargreaves.'

Alice looked appalled. 'That man, *again*?' Then she checked herself. 'I'm so sorry, Detective Constable. Please forget I said that.' There was even a little colour in her cheeks.

As I've probably mentioned, Mark's sense of humour has never been his defining characteristic. Nevertheless, I think he was trying not to smile as he said, 'Do you know if Mrs Lane is in her room?'

Alice said, 'Why not get the boy to put a call through?'

While Mark crossed to the desk, I said to Alice, 'Shall we go together? My mother's on the ward in the cardiac unit.'

'Oh – I didn't realize. Well, yes, if you like.'

'I'm afraid my car's quite a trek away along the Promenade.'

'Then we'll go in mine. It's in the yard as usual.' Having said our farewells to Mark, we went out by the back corridor. I noticed Matt walking up from Wright Street. He looked exceptionally pleased with himself, as if he'd just come back with Apollo 14. Alice Haig said, 'Could you give me a moment to run up to the flat and fetch my coat?'

The eddy left by Alice's retreating form had barely subsided when Matt's arrival provoked a new one. He said, 'Mickey Golding changed the Red Barrel twice.' He seemed to be expecting applause for this shattering observation.

I took a close look at my assistant. 'Have you been drinking?'

'No! Well – yes, but that doesn't alter the facts. I was having a beer in the Vaults and keeping an eye on your little friend, and he changed the Red Barrel twice. It's not right.'

'Matthew – ' I only called Matt Matthew when I wanted to remind him that, unlike the pope, he was a fallible human being with a long history of stupid mistakes. 'It's been a very busy day. Sidney Flint's son is missing, I've been beaten about the head with a snooker cue, and now Oscar Hammond has turned up dead. Why would I be interested in what Mickey does or doesn't do with that revolting keg bitter?'

Wide-eyed, Matt said, 'Dead? As in, murdered?'

Expecting Alice to reappear any second, I told the story as briefly as possible, though slowed by Matt asking questions which I couldn't answer. Then Matt said, 'Damn! I wanted to go to band practice. I suppose we'll have to make enquiries now.'

I chewed on this. Though in general I considered the coming together of talentless young people to form pop groups a pressing social evil calling for immediate legislation, I had to admit that Matt's weekly session with the Sand Lizards had a steadying effect on his psyche. I said, 'Not necessarily. For once, I think the police have got things covered. I'll find out what they know when I see Mark this evening.'

'But I thought you were seeing Mickey Golding this evening.'

Unwisely, I hesitated again. 'Er – yes, I am.'

Matt said, 'You hesitated.'

I hadn't enjoyed this routine the first time, and I certainly wasn't about to go through it all again. I said, 'Never mind about that. You've not told me whether you saw anything unusual at the Grand.'

Matt protested. 'I did tell you! Mickey changed the Red Barrel twice.'

I began to wonder whether the pint Matt claimed to have drunk had been more like three or four. 'I mean, about Dennis. It seems he's in the tender care of Carlo, the manager, but I'd like to know exactly where in case we need to spring him.'

Matt shrugged. 'I saw Carlo talking to Mickey, but there was nothing odd going on at the hotel, apart from a few people complaining because they didn't understand the prices in decimal. I don't see the problem. Sixpence is two and a half new pence, a five-year-old could work it out. Anyway, the place was heaving. Do we know if Carlo lives in?'

I didn't know, but if he did then it would enable him to drop in on Dennis from time to time without having to leave the premises. I said, 'I'll find out. In the meantime, I think Dennis is safe enough, and he's probably eating a lot better than he does at home. I'd like to leave him where he is overnight.'

'Why?'

'Because the longer Sidney thinks his son's in danger, the more chance there is that he'll treat him decently when he shows up safe and sound. Now – you know what you've got to do this evening?'

Matt sulked. 'It's horribly illegal.'

'What's the matter with you? I thought you'd leap at the chance to break the law in a good cause. Call me around bedtime, I'll be able to tell you how it worked out at my end. You'd better get moving, or you'll be late for your practice.'

'I'm on Marie's moped. It's brilliant, I nearly got forty out of it this morning.'

'For God's sake, be careful.'

Matt pulled a face and said, "*'For God's sake, be careful.'*" I hoped I didn't really sound like that, but I probably did. Then he ambled off towards Wright Street. It's amazing how even the back of people can annoy you sometimes.

I'd been standing alone in the yard for another couple of minutes, wondering if we'd ever make it to the hospital before the allotted hour came to an end and visitors were chased from the building at gunpoint, when Alice Haig emerged from the doorway to her flat, wearing the green coat and putting on a good turn of speed. She set off towards the two-tone Wolseley which I'd previously decided must belong to her, and as she went she said, 'Sorry I was so long. Bobby and Nigel were arguing and I had to intervene.'

Trying to keep up, I said, 'Is Nigel better?' I wondered if she'd told the children about her engagement yet.

'Not a hundred per cent, but I'm sure he'll be fine for his exam tomorrow.'

I chose not to speak while Alice manoeuvred the vehicle out of its space and onto Wright Street. She wasn't what you might call a natural driver, and I feared that if I distracted her there might be consequences. Even so, Alice appeared so wrapped up in her own thoughts that I doubted whether she was sparing much attention for the road. There was a rattle somewhere, as if the exhaust was working itself loose. The car was seven or eight years old and neither clean nor tidy. From the start I'd found it difficult to warm to Alice Haig, but here at last was evidence that we did share common ground. After a while, I stopped worrying about Alice's driving and wrapped myself in some thoughts of my own, which is where I was when a voice said, 'I never did get there yesterday afternoon.'

Deducing that the voice must belong to Alice Haig, I said, 'What? Oh – to the Infirmary, you mean.'

'Poor Laurence will have been all on his own. I expect he's fed up with that place by now.'

'It's only been a couple of days.'

'This time, yes, but he's been in there before. In October, I think it was, soon after he came to Marine Lodge. A grumbling appendix.'

'Did they operate?'

'No, they kept him under observation for a few days and when it all calmed down they decided to leave well alone. And he got terrifically bored, because he wasn't really very ill. He spent his days wandering around the hospital talking to people. He's told me all this since, of course. I'm afraid none of us from the hotel knew him well enough at the time to visit him.'

Alice swerved to avoid a pedestrian who'd been careless enough to cross the road at a zebra crossing. Then she said, 'What is it about men?'

Strangely enough I'd sometimes asked myself the same question, but Alice pressed ahead without waiting to hear my views. I didn't know the answer anyway.

Alice said, 'Why do you all seem to think we women need protecting? What we actually want above all else is to know where we stand. We need you to tell us the truth.'

I maintained a guilty silence. If I can possibly help it, I never tell anyone anything.

Alice said, 'I'd be so much easier in my mind if I didn't think Laurence was keeping things from me.'

So this was about Laurence Glass, of course, not me. I said, 'Such as?'

'Well – his hand, for example. He's always said losing those fingers was an accident, but it wasn't, was it? I'm sure he lost them in action somehow and doesn't want to tell me the details. I'm going to be his wife! If something dreadful happened to him, I want to know. I want to know everything about him.'

I said, 'He seems to be a rather private person.'

'That won't do! Ian used to keep things from me too, and it nearly ruined us. Laurence will have to change his ways.'

We pulled onto the forecourt of the Infirmary, and Alice parked the Wolseley in an awkward corner space, leaving me very little room to get out. Two things were puzzling me. Firstly, Alice Haig hadn't even mentioned Oscar Hammond's death. And secondly, despite everything she'd said about keeping our relationship professional, Alice had just opened her heart to me as if I were her most intimate confidant. But I thought the explanation might be the same in both cases. Alice was in love. Her thoughts revolved around a single topic, and she was quite happy to break her own rules if it allowed her to talk about the object of her affections. Love makes fools of us all, even the Alice Haigs of this world. We parted in the reception hall, and I watched as she trotted off towards the stairs, every fibre of her being intent on Major Laurence Glass.

There was no sign of Bernie on the women's ward in the cardiac unit. I tended to switch off whenever she started talking about the staff rota, so I couldn't remember whether she was supposed to be on duty today or not. I carried on down the ward, looking to left and right.

My mother was sitting up in bed, casting a dyspeptic eye over the goings-on around her. She wore a coral pink bed-jacket which I hadn't seen before, and if she didn't exactly look well she looked a lot less ill than she had done the previous day. When I was still some distance away, she loudly said, 'What have you brought me?'

Now under close scrutiny from various patients, visitors and members of the nursing profession, I delayed my reply until I was seated at the bedside and could deliver it quietly. I said, 'Nothing, I'm afraid. Just me.' Though the patients, visitors and members of the nursing profession probably hadn't heard this, it was all too obvious that I'd come empty-handed, and they now turned their backs on me as one, tut-tutting their disapproval. 'I thought Aunt Winnie would be bombarding you with stuff.'

'She brought this jacket.' My mother fingered the pink wool.

'You look nice in it.' The colour stood out strongly against the hospital green of the walls.

'I don't appreciate wearing Winnie's cast-offs. It's like when we were girls.'

'Has she been this afternoon?'

'No. She said you'd be coming.'

'And here I am.'

'It's quarter to four.'

'I've been busy. I'm working on a murder case.'

My mother considered this for a second or two before saying,

'If you ask me, you make these things up.'

'Are they looking after you all right?'

Suddenly my mother seized my wrist. 'Get me out of here, Sammy love!'

The surprise had got the better of me, and I could feel my heart racing. 'Why? What's the matter?'

'It's horrible! Everybody's ill!'

'It's a hospital.'

'But why do they have to rub our noses in it? I can't drink, I can't smoke – '

'Surely you can smoke in the day room?'

'I've not got any ciggies. In any case, they won't let me out of bed. Until the consultant sees me tomorrow I'm supposed to sit here like a stale bun and mind my own business. On top of that, it's all women. They resent me. I've learned to expect it, but that doesn't mean I like it.' Then she added more quietly, as if I wasn't supposed to hear, 'How I came to have such a plain son, I'll never know.'

I said, 'You seem more yourself today.' I was thinking how much I'd preferred it when she wasn't.

'There's nothing the matter with me. I'm being kept here under false pretences. I've a good mind to leave them to it and go home.'

'Then why don't you?'

My mother didn't answer immediately. A young man on his way out of the ward happened to catch her eye, and she gave him one of her more extravagant smiles. When he'd gone, she retrieved her default expression from store and said, 'As a matter of fact, Sammy, I've not been feeling too good lately.'

'In what way?'

'Oh, it's probably nothing. I expect I need to get out more.'

If my mother got out any more, she'd be able to leave off paying rent and hand back the keys. I said, 'I hear you stopped going into work at the toffee factory. Didn't you like it?'

'Yes and no.' Her face brightened a little. 'Enid Gregson was working there. You remember Enid? We used to push you out in your pram together when she was still Enid Cook. Then she married, only Albert got shot in the war so after that she was stuck looking after him. You'd see them in the Co-op all the time with him in his wheelchair. Then last year he died, I remember seeing it in the Gazette, only I never went to the funeral because I had a dose of the runs. I hate funerals, all that standing around in the cold and the rain. And black's not my colour, never has been. Anyway, with Albert gone Enid's a different woman. She says she's back on the market now and folk had better watch out.'

I smiled. 'Sounds like you were having a pretty good time.'

The brightness dimmed. 'I was only there a few days, but I tell you this much: I'd sooner eat my own shoes than ever wrap another toffee.'

'So you left because you were bored?'

'No! You're getting the thin end of the stick, as usual. I told you, I've been ill.'

'How ill?'

'Quite bad, if you must know. I was in bed with the doctor for a week, not that it did any good.'

I thought I knew what my mother meant by this, but I didn't check with her in case I was wrong. 'Why didn't you call me?'

'What for? Are you a doctor now? Anyway, I tried to get up after that, I thought I might feel better if I was up and doing. And this is where it's got me.'

At least it was clear enough now that my mother's attack hadn't come out of the blue. I said, 'What have they told you in here?'

'Not much. You know what they're like, the patient's always the last to know.'

'But you do realize you've probably had a heart attack?'

My mother looked away from me. 'Is that what it was?' She was trying to sound unconcerned.

'The ward sister said it might be something to do with your liver.'

In a sudden burst of energy, my mother smacked the bed with a bony hand. 'I knew it! They're trying to blame it on drink. I've had this all my life, the minute anyone sees me enjoying myself, out comes the book of rules. Your grandad started it, and Winnie keeps it going. There's nothing wrong with having a little drinkies now and then. Look at Mavis Tweddle – eighty-two if she's a day, and never misses a Saturday night at the Coach.'

'Is that where you'd been when they found you?'

My mother thought about this. 'I'm not sure, to tell you the truth. I just remember feeling cold, I've never felt so cold in my life. Next thing I knew, I was here.'

I tried to pat the back of my mother's hand, but she drew away. I said, 'Well you're in the best place now. You've got to let them do their job and find out what's wrong.' She didn't respond. She began looking around the ward again, as if I wasn't there. After half a minute of this, I said, 'Talking of being cold, I was remembering that terrible winter after the war.'

'What winter?'

'You know, when we lived in the tram.' I smiled. 'Crazy! But we got through it, didn't we?'

My mother now looked directly at me and said, 'Tram? What do you mean, tram?'

I had the old familiar feeling of the ground turning to jelly under my feet. I said, 'On Reilly's farm. We were there four months.' Then, when this failed to spark recognition, I added, 'In a tram.'

My mother closed her eyes, shook her head pointedly, and gave other signs of saintly forbearance. 'There's something a bit Billy Liar about you, isn't there? First you pretend to be Sherlock Holmes, and now there's all this tram nonsense. It's one fantasy after another, I really don't know where you get it from.'

Not feeling particularly charitable at this point, I said, 'Perhaps it's come down on my father's side.'

The response was swift and sharp. 'Don't bring your father into this.'

A vein was throbbing in my temple. The ward seemed very hot. 'You said he was here. Yesterday. Was that true?'

My mother looked away from me again and shifted in the bed. 'Of course he wasn't here. Why would your father come here?'

'To see you.'

'They had me sedated yesterday, I didn't know my backside

from a tin of fruit.'

Now it was my turn to do some wrist-grabbing. 'You're lying! You always do this, I can never get an honest word out of you. He was here, wasn't he? Tell me!'

The bell rang for the end of visiting time.

My mother said, 'You'd better go.'

'I'm not going anywhere till you tell me the truth.'

'You will come and see me tomorrow, won't you?'

I tightened my grip. 'I mean it! I'm sick and tired of this, I want to know!'

She turned back to me. The face was grey, the eyes dull, and the skin of her forehead was flaking. Quietly, she said, 'Sammy, love – my wrist.'

I looked down. My knuckles were white. When I let her go, my mother took the freed wrist in her other hand and rubbed it. I tucked my own hand into the opposite armpit, where it could do no more damage.

Unaware of the drama playing out around my mother's bed, visitors were moving towards the door. Some looked over their shoulders to wave at their loved ones. Others, eyes lowered, were getting out as fast as they could.

Eventually, when the ward was nearly empty, my mother said, 'When you come tomorrow, Sammy love, do you think you could bring me a teensy bottle of lemonade?' I didn't answer, and I didn't look at her. I hated it when she used this little-girl voice. 'And if you like, you could just pop the top off first, and *slip something in*. You know. Just to pep it up a bit. You will do it, won't you, Sammy? I'll go mad if I don't get a drink soon.'

## twenty-two

When I got downstairs, Alice Haig was standing near the reception desk, looking out for me. She said, 'Laurence wants to see you. It's about Oscar.' We went back up the stairs together. When I asked why she didn't use the lift, she said, 'I don't like waiting, Mr Rigby. I never have done.' We were working against the current of departing visitors, but soon enough we reached Laurence Glass's ward, where I had to negotiate with Sister Wolfe again before being permitted to see the man. Cilla Donnelly's former place outside the door was taken by a different officer now, who acknowledged us briefly as we went in.

As on the previous day, the Major was sitting up in bed and looking healthier than anyone else in the building, provided you ignored the bandage around his torso. Somehow he'd once more contrived to have the window left open, but the February air made little impression on the stifling conditions in the room. Glass seemed in a better mood than before. Apparently Sister Wolfe had assured him there was every chance he'd be sent home in the morning, as soon as the doctor had taken another look at him. He said, 'You know, despite everything that's happened I can't wait to get back to the good old Marine Lodge. It's home more than ever now. Did Alice tell you what we've been planning?'

Alice said, 'There wasn't time, Laurence.' Then she turned to me. 'I think we might not wait before we marry. I agree with Laurence, at our age it would be absurd to have a long engagement. All we need is a week or two to make the arrangements.' She squeezed Laurence's hand.

The Major said, 'It won't be a big do, obviously. Registry Office, a bite to eat at the hotel afterwards. Alice doesn't have much family and I doubt my sister in Broadstairs will be fit to travel. Do come if you want, by the way, we'd be glad to have you.'

Though I usually avoided weddings if possible, I thanked the Major and said, 'You had something to tell me about Oscar.'

'That's right, yes. Here we are, blabbing on about our nuptials, when I'm sure you must have a thousand things to do. Well, I won't keep you five minutes. Oscar came to see me yesterday.'

'At visiting time?'

'Yes. That policewoman might have a record of the time.'

'WPC Donnelly.'

'Seemed like a fine, well-adjusted young person. Bit broad in the beam for my taste, but still.'

Alice Haig said, 'Laurence!'

'Oh, you mustn't mind me, Alice dear, I don't mean anything by it. Eyes for none but you these days.' He squeezed her hand in return, then to me he said, 'Oscar wanted my advice. He'd received a letter from Giles Rawley. By hand, of course – well it had to be didn't it? No post at present. But the thing was, it didn't arrive until yesterday morning, a whole day after poor Giles was killed. It seems someone had dropped it in at number fifteen by mistake, and Oscar's neighbour, not being the sharpest tool in the box, sat on it for twenty-four hours before she brought it round.'

Alice said, 'I'm surprised at Giles, making a slip like that. He was normally so careful.'

I said, 'Perhaps someone less careful delivered it for him. Did Oscar say what was in the letter?'

'He had it with him, but he didn't show it to me, he just kept revolving the envelope in his hand. Giles had found out that Oscar was involved with this girl Lena Golding at the Grand, and he wanted to warn him off. He said the Goldings were up to no good, he'd done some digging and he was now in a position to expose them. He advised Oscar to disentangle himself from the family while he could. You see what this means, don't you?'

I did. It was the first piece of hard evidence linking the Goldings with Giles's murder. I said, 'But why would Giles put all that in a letter? Why not take Oscar on one side and have a quiet word?'

Alice said to me, 'Have you ever tried having a quiet word with someone at Marine Lodge? There's always half a dozen people listening.'

The Major nodded. 'Perhaps the old fellow thought a letter would be more secure. Then he goes and shoves it through the wrong letter box. Obviously wasn't as smart as he thought.' It was clear enough that Laurence Glass's animus against Giles Rawley had survived Giles's death.

I said, 'But I don't see why Oscar needed to bring this to you.'

'Wanted to know if he should take the letter to the police. Respected my opinion, old soldier and so forth. He was afraid that he might get this wretched girlfriend of his into hot water.'

'And what did you say?'

'Told him to square up and do the decent thing. If these Goldings are a bad lot, they need dealing with. They've certainly done Alice no favours. But it sounds as if he chose to ignore my advice, doesn't it? Oscar must have held onto the letter, and then been killed for it, poor chap.'

Alice said, 'I'm worried that Laurence might be in danger. He's been attacked once already, and if the Goldings realize that he knows what was in the letter – '

Glass said, 'They'll not get me a second time, my dear. Just let them try, that's what I say.'

I said, 'I don't think very much is likely to happen while the Major's under guard.'

Alice said, 'They ought to put a window in these partition walls, so that patients can be kept under observation.' There was in fact a glass panel in the door, but the usefulness of this was negated by a blind on the inside.

Rather patronisingly, the Major said, 'But then you see, it wouldn't be a private room any more, would it?' And he smiled at what he took to be his own joke.

I said, 'Major Glass, have you talked to the police about this?'

'How could I? Alice has only just told me that the Corporal's dead.' His expression changed. 'Oh, God. They won't send in that Hargreaves person again, will they?'

'But I thought you were interviewed yesterday by DC Howell?'

'That came later. Hargreaves was first on the scene. "Are you *sure* there was someone in the room? Are you *sure* you were stabbed? Are you *sure* you're Major Laurence Glass?" Twenty minutes of that, and I was damned if I knew.'

I found this reassuring. Perhaps Hargreaves wasn't losing his touch after all.

The Major had nothing to add. Leaving word with the officer on duty to summon a member of the investigating team, Alice Haig and I headed back to the hotel. In the Wolseley, something had changed. It seemed that Alice had been revitalised by half an hour in her fiancé's company, and she was taking up twice as much space and air as she had done before. My mind revolved the Major's testimony. It directly implicated the Goldings just when a case appeared to be developing against Howard Lane. I said to Alice, 'I was meaning to ask you – has Mr Lane ever stayed at the Marine Lodge?'

'Certainly. The entire family came up for Christmas three years ago.'

'So he would know his way around the hotel?'

'Of course. My husband was alive then, he and Howard got on rather well.'

I left it at that. There was no need to spell out that with a little inside knowledge Howard Lane could easily have collected the murder weapon from the workshop, broken into the building, and slipped quietly up the back stairs to the room which his father-in-law returned to every year.

The business of the letter was more puzzling. According to both Miss Pyle and Laurence Glass, after coming upstairs on the night he died Giles Rawley went out again, and was gone no more than five or ten minutes. This didn't seem long enough for Giles to have walked all the way to Oscar's house at the far end of Wright Street and back again. There were two possibilities: either Giles had delivered the note earlier, before joining me in the Vaults, or he'd given the letter to someone else, who'd then taken it to the wrong address. Alice had been correct, to confuse house numbers was not quite Giles Rawley's style. Which left only the second possibility. Someone had delivered the letter on Giles's behalf, and I had a good idea who that someone might be.

Alice said, 'I've been thinking about Mrs Golding's offer. She wants my answer by this evening.'

This surprised me. 'I'd got the impression she was giving you plenty of time to come round to the idea.' Not that I knew exactly what the offer was, of course. I could only speculate that it ran along the same lines as Lou Golding's offer to myself.

'Perhaps our Southaven idea of plenty of time is different from hers. But you see my problem? If Giles really did discover something compromising about the Goldings, it's hardly a good moment for me to be – how can I put it? – joining the firm.'

I said, 'You need to slow things down. Call her and ask for more time.'

'I'm not sure she'd respond at all well. She doesn't strike me as very accommodating.' Alice sighed. 'I wish I'd asked Laurence what to do.'

'You can ask him tomorrow. He'll probably be back at the hotel.'

'But by then it might be too late.'

I didn't like the sound of this. 'Why? Did Lou Golding threaten you in some way?'

'Not in so many words. She said that if I didn't come on board she would have to consider alternatives.'

'That could mean anything.'

'Exactly. And I've already seen the kind of thing Mrs Golding is capable of.'

I'd been reflecting on the change in Alice's position since Giles Rawley's death. I said, 'Surely, with the cash that's coming your way from Giles's estate you can afford to go it alone now.'

'It's not as simple as that. If I have a larger competitor on my doorstep who is determined to drive me into the ground, I can't hold out indefinitely, no matter how secure my business may seem. I'm a minnow in a lake full of pike.'

Alice was probably right about this. I didn't know what she should do, and I didn't pretend that I did. I sat quietly as we covered the remaining half mile of the journey, feeling more than usually helpless in the face of forces I couldn't control.

And I kept thinking about Lou Golding. What she'd said was true, I could be a useful addition to the family business. Why shouldn't I say yes? I wasn't getting any younger, and whenever I consulted the crystal ball year after desperate year of insecurity loomed up out of the mist. Perhaps some of Lou's dealings were unconventional, but God knows I'd bent the rules myself often enough. And it wasn't as if the Goldings were a bunch of murderers.

Unless, of course, they were.

Climbing out of the Wolseley in the back yard at the Marine Lodge, Alice said, 'Will you be going straight home? If DI

Hargreaves puts in another appearance I'd rather appreciate your moral support.'

I pointed out to Alice that she had in fact parked right next to the great man's car, an old brown Rover 90 which looked as tweedy as Hargreaves himself. She said, 'Oh, dear. You know, I think I'll just run up to the flat and check on the children before I come in.' I admired this approach. I've always believed that any chance to postpone an interview with Harry Hargreaves should be seized with both hands. Promising to catch up with Alice later, I carried on into the hotel.

As I passed the open kitchen door, I could see two girls juggling cakes and pots of tea. They looked up, and I nodded to them. There was no sign of Lena, who according to Alice had undertaken to repeat at dinner her celebrated lunchtime performance. Presumably Lena was talking to Hargreaves somewhere in the building. He wasn't much of a man for lending handkerchiefs to distraught young women, and I hoped Lena would be all right.

Though I could hear the distant chatter of guests from the lounge, where afternoon tea must be in progress, the entrance hallway was occupied only by the long case clock and Evan Bickerstaff, who'd remained at his post on the reception desk. As usual, his face registered complete indifference as I came into view from the back corridor. But all that changed when I strode round behind the counter and bore down on him. Indifference quickly turned to alarm, and he backed up against the telephone switchboard. This wasn't going to do him any good. I grabbed his ear and pulled. He said, 'Ow.' Then I dragged the ear through into Alice's office, with Evan following at a discreet distance.

I pushed Evan further into the room, closed the door, and remained standing in front of it in case he should try to mimic the perfidy of Graham Leeds. Some young men would have complained about such rough handling, but Evan's protestations had been limited to that initial 'Ow'. Perhaps if you were as obtuse as Evan Bickerstaff you came to expect this sort of thing.

I said, 'You asked Nigel Haig whether it was right to keep secrets for people. The answer comes in two parts. In general, for people you trust and respect, yes. But if they've been murdered, and revealing the secret might help to catch their killer – '

Evan said, 'I promised him.'

'I refer you again to my second point.'

'But he said I mustn't tell anyone! He said he'd have delivered it himself only he was tired. And he looked it, too, he looked more like a hundred than seventy-six.'

At least, now that the secret was out, Evan seemed happy to talk freely. I said, 'Tell me what happened.'

Evan plunged straight in. He wasn't the type to collect his thoughts first, not that it would have taken him long. 'It was about midnight. I'd been out for a walk, along the Prom. I was just turning into the yard when Mr Rawley comes out of the hotel with his hat and coat on. I thought it was odd, with it being so late and that, but I was just going to say hello and then keep walking. Only he stopped me, and took this envelope out of his coat pocket. He said he was on his way to Oscar's with it, but perhaps I wouldn't mind doing it instead. He gave me a couple of bob and said I was a good lad and I shouldn't take any notice of what people said.'

'What do you think he meant by that?'

Evan shrugged. The tight jacket threatened to burst open, propelling brass buttons in all directions. 'Search me. Anyway, I took the envelope from him and set off, but I'd not gone two steps when he called me back and made me swear not to tell anyone. I left him there, in the yard. Next thing I heard, he was dead.'

I now wondered how to proceed. On the whole I thought it better that Evan should hear the facts from me rather than the police. 'Evan – what number on Wright Street is Oscar Hammond's house?'

'Thirteen. He rented it, it's one of those pint-sized terrace jobs up the other end. There's a great row of them, all the same.'

'The thing is, Evan – you delivered the letter to the wrong house.'

'What? No! I'm sure I put it through at number thirteen.' Then his thoughts turned inward, and I could see his certainty dissolving. 'At least – '

'At least what, Evan?'

He spoke more reluctantly now. 'Well – I'd been out, like I said. I'd been thinking about stuff.'

'What kind of stuff?'

He tried to meet my eye and couldn't. He began to study the carpet instead. 'You know. Stuff.' He shuffled from foot to foot. Mark Howell would have urged him on, but I waited until he was ready to say more. Still addressing the carpet, he said, 'I've not got much of a life, have I? It's no wonder if I get a bit – ' He dried up.

'Bored?'

There was a long silence before he brought himself to say, 'Lonely. I get lonely.' Briefly, he looked up again, into my eyes. 'You're the same as me, aren't you? You and me and Mickey. There's not much goes on here. Southaven, I mean. There's places to go if you just want – you know. But I'd like something more than that.' The admission came shyly, and he made most of it to the floor.

Who could have guessed that inside Evan Bickerstaff's sturdy frame there beat the heart of a true romantic? I said, 'Anyone particular you've got in mind?'

He said, 'Might be.'

My opinion of the Bickerstaff youth continued to fluctuate wildly. There was something touching in this reticent display, something of a piece with the warm-hearted young man who'd obliged us all to sing at Giles's birthday party. I was going to have to disappoint him all the same. While I searched for a good way to do this, I said, 'Have you got family, Evan?'

He scowled. 'Slung me out, didn't they.'

'Why would they do that?'

'My mam found these pictures under my bed. Dad says it's not natural.'

I'd heard this story often enough before. 'And I suppose he thinks turning his own son out of doors is natural?'

'He's all right, is my dad. But he never learned how to think for himself.'

This was another, familiar part of the saga – rejected offspring defends indefensible behaviour of parent. 'Do they know where you are now?'

'Yeah. But they don't get in touch.'

This new information did little to help me break the unwelcome news. I decided to be blunt and get it over with. 'Evan – if it's Mickey Golding you've got your sights on, then I'm afraid he's got other ideas.'

Evan looked up sharply. 'What do you mean? What's he said?'

'You'd better forget it, it's just not going to happen.'

'Why? Because of you, is that it? Mickey would never be interested in you, you're too old!'

'It may surprise you to learn this, Evan, but I'm actually thirty-four.'

'There, see? Mickey could have anyone he likes. If he's making up to you just now, it's only because he wants something.' The bell rang on the reception desk. Evan glanced towards it, then turned back to me. 'It's you that's wasting your time! I know he likes me, he hardly takes his eyes off me when we go swimming. He's not going to throw himself away on some fat old bloke when he could have me!'

The bell rang a second time. I now found that my opinion of Evan Bickerstaff had taken a fresh turn, and I decided it might be a good thing if he left the presence as soon as possible. Without speaking, I opened the office door and stood to one side. I rather suspect Evan may have given me a meaningful glare as he passed by, but if so I didn't see it, because I was too busy studying the ceiling at the time. There was a long crack in the plaster, and the whole thing needed a few good coats of paint.

When Evan had gone, I pushed the door gently shut, breathed deeply, and counted to ten. Apparently, being written off as some fat old bloke was too much even for me. Only when I felt confident of presenting the unruffled Rigby my public knew and loved did I open the door and step out into the world. Several afternoon tea customers were making their exit through the front door, while Evan struggled to make sense of an elderly couple who, from what I overheard, had got the idea that Marine Lodge was a residential care home and wanted to be shown around. The grandfather clock struck five. I slipped out round the counter and made my way towards the lounge, where I hoped I might be able to tie up another loose end. Unusually, the door to the dining room was closed. Perhaps Harry Hargreaves was in there, just tightening the rack on Lena, or some other unlucky witness. I pressed on to the lounge.

Here, I found only two groups of guests. To my left as I came in sat Cordelia Lane with two very similar women, who differed from Cordelia mainly in that large sums had been lavished on their appearance. I could guess who they were. We'd now moved on from *King Lear* to *Three Sisters*. I was pleased to note that, despite putting up at the Grand, Cordelia's siblings were nevertheless prepared to risk afternoon tea at the Grand's humble neighbour. From the debris of plates, crumbs and discarded paper napkins on the low table in front of them, it seemed that grief had failed to dull their appetites. I nodded to Cordelia, then crossed to join Rosemary Pyle and Sarkis Aznavorian, who were sitting near the window in the opposite corner of the room, next to a small writing desk. Their own more modest leavings consisted only of a tea-pot and two empty cups. Compared with Giles's robust daughters, they looked as if they couldn't have managed a fairy cake between them.

Miss Pyle got straight down to it. 'Mr Rigby! What on earth is happening to us? First Giles, now Oscar – are we all going to be murdered in our beds?' She wore the mulberry suit still but she'd changed to a darker blouse, and the effect was to age her and point up her slightness of build.

Aznavorian said, 'Now, now, Rosemary love, give the man a chance to get settled.' To me he added, 'Sit down, won't you. We're just waiting our turn with the Spanish Inquisition.'

Miss Pyle said, 'I hoped I would never see that rude man again. Do you have any facts for us, Mr Rigby? No one will tell us anything.'

It was likely that I knew a good deal more about Oscar's death than they did, but I hadn't come here to be helpful. I said, 'Why did you both lie to me?' It wasn't a friendly thing to say, and they looked at one another for support. When they turned to face me again, they wore identical masks of indignation.

Miss Pyle said, 'I find that extremely offensive.'

Aznavorian said, 'I'll not have you talk to Rosemary like that!'

'You can bluster all you like. There've been two deaths in forty-eight hours, the gloves are off. You lied to me, and I want it all cleared up now.'

Miss Pyle said, 'But Mr Rigby – '

'You left the hotel on Friday morning with a large brown bag, but you came back from your trip without it. I want to know what was in it.'

Aznavorian said, 'I told you before, you're mistaken. There was never any bag. A great deal happened on Friday, you just got confused, that's all.'

'If someone here in the hotel attacked Giles Rawley, their clothes will have been marked with blood. The police searched the place from top to bottom and found nothing. But you two had left the hotel earlier, before the body was even discovered, and some time during the day you disposed of a bag.'

'I'm telling you, you're wrong.'

'Do you want me to mention this to DI Hargreaves? Would you rather leave it to him to beat the story out of you? Because that missing bag is going to mean one thing to him and one thing only.'

A brief silence followed. My speech seemed to have had some influence on Miss Pyle. She touched her friend's sleeve and said, 'Sarkis – '

But he hadn't been similarly affected. 'I won't be cowed by threats! Just because you've dreamed up this imaginary bag – '

'But Sarkis, dear – '

He turned on her. 'Shut up, Rosemary! Don't meddle in what doesn't concern you.'

'But it does concern me.' Apparently Miss Pyle couldn't be cowed by threats either. 'After all, we're as good as engaged, aren't we?'

Aznavorian lowered his eyes. 'I don't know about that, my love.'

This was not what Miss Pyle had hoped to hear, and it went over badly. I wouldn't have cared to be Aznavorian the next time those two were alone together. A heavy frost descended on Miss

Pyle's manner. 'The fact is, Mr Rigby, Sarkis hasn't quite retired yet.'

'Rosemary – ' He placed a restraining hand on her arm, but she pulled away.

'He still has a small collection of rare books, and contacts all over the world. Naturally, from time to time one of these people will get in touch with him, and if Sarkis is able to oblige them – '

'Then I make a sale. It's as simple as that.'

I was pleased that Aznavorian had decided to cooperate now, not that he looked pleased himself.

He said, 'A dealer from Manchester had contacted me by phone, interested in some of those Michael Arlen books I told you about. The buyer's Armenian. It was too good a chance to miss.'

'I'd have thought you'd want to hang onto them. Sentimental reasons, your childhood friend and so on.'

'I'm running a business, Mr Rigby.' Then he seemed to want to qualify this bold statement. 'In a small way, I mean. Like I told you, Arlen's out of fashion, but suddenly I had a buyer who was prepared to offer good money. Sentiment doesn't come into it.' He sat back in his chair. 'So there you are, mystery solved. You did see a bag, but it was full of books, not bloody clothes.'

I could see Miss Pyle preparing to chide Aznavorian for his language, but a second later she caught up and stood herself down. I said, 'I don't understand – why all the cloak and dagger nonsense?' Then I caught up myself and said, 'Oh.'

Aznavorian said, 'I hardly make any money at all now.'

Miss Pyle said, 'It's more of a hobby, isn't it, Sarkis?'

'That's right, my love, yes. I'm not quite a vegetable yet, I like to be doing something.'

I said, 'You don't pay any tax, do you?'

Aznavorian coloured. 'It wouldn't amount to a row of beans. Honestly, it would cost them money to collect it!' He studied my expression. 'I suppose you're going to shop me to the Inland Revenue now, and I'll be banged up in chokey for the rest of my life.'

'Just a minute – these books. Presumably you don't keep them in your room?'

'What, and have Mrs Clark douse them in detergent every five minutes? No, they're all packed away in a lock-up.'

Miss Pyle said, 'It's one of those in the yard. Sarkis always parks in front of it.'

Aznavorian looked briefly annoyed with Miss Pyle, then tried to disguise his irritation. 'Very cheap, of course. Cool and dry, too – perfect conditions for books.'

'And naturally you told the police about this lock-up?'

'Well, no. Do you think I should have?' The affectation of innocence was almost convincing.

I said, 'I promise you, DI Hargreaves won't be remotely interested in your tax affairs. Tell him about the lock-up now, then he can have someone take a look at it. If he finds out about it later, your life won't be worth living.'

'Yes – of course, Mr Rigby, I'm sure that's the right thing to do. Very wise. I'm sorry if I was less than truthful with you before. And you mustn't blame Rosemary, I'd specifically asked her to say nothing. My fault. My fault entirely.' With this he beamed at Miss Pyle, who could only manage a thin, purse-lipped smile in return, devoid of her usual sugary excess. Clearly, Aznavorian was still in the dog-house.

I asked the two friends if they could think of anything which might shed light on Oscar Hammond's death. They'd seen nothing, heard nothing, and claimed to be shocked and baffled by the whole affair. After the fiasco of the brown bag I could hardly take their word as gospel, but with no evidence linking them to the murder I saw no point in pressing them too hard. I thanked them, and took my leave. While we'd been talking, the three sisters had moved on too.

Alice Haig was now at the reception desk, Lena's place on the rack having been taken by Evan Bickerstaff. I hoped it might occur to Evan to call Hargreaves some fat old bloke, and see what good it did him. Alice and I chatted for a couple of minutes, but there wasn't much I could say. Giles was dead, Oscar was dead, Lou Golding still had the upper hand, and I was fresh out of ideas. Alice must have been wondering why she'd ever bothered to employ me. When at one point she paused and said, 'Mr Rigby – ' I thought I was within seconds of getting the old heave-ho. But she simply said that she could manage Hargreaves well enough by herself, and asked me to be sure to ring in the morning. I agreed and left her, before she could reconsider and sack me after all.

In the kitchen, Lena and the sous-chefs were hard at work. I called out to Lena, 'Are you all right?'

She looked up and said, 'No. But thanks for asking.'

'I hope DI Hargreaves didn't give you too much grief.'

Lena said, 'That man is an arsehole,' and went back to her work.

Apart from the Cradock woman, no one likes to be watched when they're cooking, so I gave up loitering in the doorway and set off in pursuit of the Minx.

## twenty-three

As a general rule, Southaven Sundays are an uneventful, even tedious affair, distinguished only by a spike in the local suicide statistics. Back in the flat again, I was wishing that this particular Sunday had conformed a little more to type. My body ached, my head wound throbbed unpleasantly, and there was a kind of white noise in my mind generated by shrill voices demanding that something must be done immediately. I threw myself down on the settee and tried to sprawl, but it wasn't big enough. There would now be a lull of almost two hours before my double date at the Hen and Chickens, and I hoped this would be time enough to restore the various bruised and disaffected aspects of myself now screaming for attention.

I say double date because it had been slowly dawning on me that, rather than letting either Mark or Mickey down, there was no reason why I shouldn't turn up for both engagements at the same time. Roosters, after all, was on the first floor, and Rustlers on the ground floor. Surely it shouldn't be beyond my powers to dine in both restaurants at once. True, Mark did happen to be a notorious late-comer, and I'd have to be careful that he didn't spot me and Mickey as he came in. But the stairs to Roosters were very close to the street door, and Mark would probably run straight up without looking around. What, I told myself, could possibly go wrong?

To silence one of the more persistent of the shrill voices, I made a dive for the telephone and rang Sidney Flint. Though I might regret it later, I'd weakened since the afternoon and decided to tell him at least that Dennis was safe. I couldn't risk mentioning the Grand in case Sidney took it into his head to turn up in the lobby and make a nuisance of himself, so I invented underworld contacts who'd divulged only limited information. Sidney then gave me an earful, insisting that I leave no stone unturned until I'd freed Dennis from his captors. Assuring him that I'd shelved all other activity and would work on through the night if necessary, I rang off and went into the kitchen to make toast.

Among the other shrill voices, one took the view that I should currently be at Crowburn House, typing up my notes. There were two main reasons why I was trying to ignore this voice. Firstly, the place was so quiet on Sundays that I'd never be able to sneak in without attracting the attention of Aunt Winnie, who would complain about me working on the Sabbath and force me to talk at length about my mother. And secondly, I couldn't type up my notes because I couldn't think. My capacity for thought had been slowly dwindling all day, until I was now the dull boy at the back of the class who stares vacantly out of the window. It was lucky that the evening ahead held nothing more intellectually challenging than being in two places at once.

I brought the toast back to the settee. I hadn't eaten since breakfast and could hold out no longer, even with the promise of two evening meals on the horizon. While I ate, I leafed through Bradley looking at the pictures, and paused on a fine old shot of upper Marine Approach in the pre-Cattermole days. Visitors making for the beach thronged the narrow track between the cafés and oyster sellers. I wondered whether it was true that the ghosts of these buildings still existed beneath the road outside the Grand Hotel. Such stories were usually fables, serving to ease the pain of perpetual change, but short of taking a drill to the tarmac there was no way of finding out. I left the book open on the coffee table, returned to the kitchen, and removed the cigarettes from the drawer. For a few seconds I stood paralysed, cigarette and lighter poised in mid-air. This was no way to kick the habit; what had become of my celebrated self-control? On the other hand, if I did give up I might put on weight and provide the boy Bickerstaff with further ammunition. But then, on the other other hand, what did I care if a charmless juvenile who couldn't even post a letter through the right door started calling me names? My reaction had been a temporary weakness of character, nothing more, and to demonstrate that I'd now risen above it I lit the cigarette and smoked defiantly.

This done, I tried tidying up my wound with the aid of hot water and cotton wool. It started bleeding again. I ran a bath, and found when undressing that the thorn which had been nagging at my left buttock since the morning was actually stuck in my trousers. I took a cautious look at my body profile in the mirror. Though my ambition to model swimwear might need a rethink, I felt that Evan had wildly overstated the problem. As Mickey had said, I needed more exercise, that's all.

I'd bathed and dressed and was pulling on my shoes when I felt a sudden flutter of anxiety about the evening ahead. Mark could be tricky to handle if he thought you weren't taking him seriously, and it was possible that my dining simultaneously with someone else lay open to such interpretation. Mickey would hardly be overjoyed if he discovered that I was dividing my attentions between himself and an ex-lover who also happened to be a local plod. I remembered the ominous atmosphere as those two had first come face to face during the raid on the Grand Hotel. Any further confrontation must be avoided at all costs.

Thankfully, I then spotted the flaw in my thinking. There was nothing written in the universal plan to the effect that Sam Rigby's projects must always be doomed. It was true that in the past some of them had failed. Indeed, many had failed disastrously. But past performance was no guide, and dismissing my fears as alarmist I laced up the shoes, took the cigarettes from the kitchen drawer, put them back again (was I giving up or wasn't I? – I'd lost track), and let myself out of the flat.

It was a mild enough evening for February, but a silent drizzle fell, making haloes around the street lights. I checked my watch. Though I'd seen off those irrational worries, it could do no harm to brace myself with a quick one in the Velvet Bar. There wasn't much time, so I upped the pace a bit as I came onto the Prom and arrived in Leslie Lush's presence with heart-rate noticeably quickened. Somewhere between my brain and my mouth, the Scotch I'd intended to order became a double. On the juke box, a chanteuse in the role of Nancy was belting out *As Long As Hay Nayds May*, her vowels perhaps distorted by the awareness that no matter how often she sang this, nor how well, Bill Sikes invariably beat her to death soon afterwards. I looked around. The drizzle had perhaps deterred some regulars, and the bar was quiet, but Leslie had his hands full with a burly man in a rather heterosexual car coat who was complaining that all the prices had been rounded up on conversion to decimal, a fact – and it was a fact – which Leslie adamantly denied.

If I'd stood in need of reassurance when I strode in, the Scotch and the familiar scenes around me were providing it. The Velvet Bar was a life-saver, and it was possible I took it too much for granted. I could recall various tense occasions down the years when owners of the George, the parent hotel, had tried to boot out the Velvet Bar's particular clientele, no doubt weary of the hilarious innuendo they must have endured at meetings of the Licensed Victuallers' Association. For weeks or months we would move on like orphans from one drinking hole to another, only to drift back gradually to the Velvet Bar, dislodge its new customers by fair means or foul, and take up from where we'd left off.

My watch read seven fifty, the clock behind the bar seven fifty-five. Either way, it was time to go.

The drizzle drizzled on. Heedless, Victoria kept her vigil at the top of Marine Approach, the narrow shoulders and voluminous skirt suggesting one of those crocheted toilet roll covers favoured by people in headlong flight from their bodily functions. I peeked out from the corner of the swimming baths, but there being no sign of Mark or Mickey I hurried on down the slope to the Hen and Chickens and pushed my way inside.

My first task was to run up to Roosters, in case by some miracle Mark had arrived early. He hadn't. The place was busy, and I had to wait a couple of minutes for my friend Alf the waiter to take a complicated order before I could draw him on one side.

'Good evening, sir. I'd not have expected to see you again so soon.'

The man looked genuinely pleased. As I think I've mentioned, few people rend the air with whoops of joy on my appearance, so I put this down to the fat tip I'd given him on Friday. I said, 'I was afraid you might have the night off.'

'No chance of that, sir, all leave's been cancelled. We're fully booked upstairs and down.'

'So am I.'

Alf said, 'I'm sorry, sir, you'll have to explain.'

There was no point in trying to dress this up. 'I'm eating here in Roosters with a bloke called Mark, and I'm eating downstairs in Rustlers with a bloke called Mickey. At the same time. Now, in fact.'

He raised one eyebrow. Personally I thought the situation deserved both, but Alf's strict formal code may have precluded such displays. He said, 'I can't recall ever seeing that done, sir.'

'Well you're going to see it done tonight. If either of them finds out what's going on, it could start a third world war. Can I count on your help?'

'I'd consider it an honour, sir.'

I gave Alf his instructions and headed back down the stairs to Rustlers. On the half landing, a payphone, invisible from either restaurant, hung on the wall near the toilets. Everything I needed was in place.

In Rustlers, Mickey Golding stood beside the till, watching an efficient-looking young woman with a pony tail as she ran her finger up and down a list of the evening bookings. He said to her, 'It must be there somewhere. Rigby, Sam Rigby.'

'We have nothing under that name, I'm afraid.'

Over Mickey's shoulder, I said, 'Try Standish.'

Mickey said, 'Hi, Sam! Why Standish?'

The woman said, 'Yes, there's a table reserved at eight for Mr Standish.'

I said, 'That's me.'

'I thought your name was Rigby?'

'Mr Standish is my assistant. I asked him to book me a table, and he must have stupidly given his own name.' I tut-tutted. 'You can't get the staff these days, can you?'

The woman with the pony tail came out from her lair, led us to a table in the window, and left us. Mickey then inconsiderately lowered himself into the chair facing the door, from which he'd have a perfect view of Mark's arrival. I said, 'Actually, Mickey, would you mind if I sat there?'

He said, 'Why?'

It was a reasonable enough question, but I still found it obstructive. When you're at work on your masterpiece, as I was, you don't want people quibbling over your chiaroscuro. 'Er – it's a thing.'

'A thing?'

'A thing. I've got a thing about being able to see the exit. I get nervous otherwise.'

Mickey seemed amused. 'Who'd have thought it? Funny what you learn about people, ain't it?' And he very decently got up to let me take his place. He was looking good, as always, but I think he might have been over-liberal with the Brut because a bloke at the next table now took out his lighter to check it wasn't leaking.

Mickey said, 'I heard about Oscar, Lena dropped in. I couldn't believe it. I mean, who would want to do away with poor old Oscar? I was all for cancelling our date tonight so I could keep an eye on Lena, but she said she wanted to work, keep her mind busy. I'm glad I didn't have to let you down.' He smiled a smile which under other circumstances would have been the highlight of my day.

I said, 'I'd have understood.' It would have saved me a lot of bother, too, but I didn't mention that. I kept wondering when Mark was going to show up.

Mickey said, 'Do you know if the cops have got any leads?'

'They've got someone in custody over Giles's death, but I'm not sure they can link him to Oscar.' Since the Major's new statement, the police could certainly link Mickey's family to Oscar, but it was too early in the evening to advance such a delicate topic.

Mickey had hung his jacket round the back of the chair. He said, 'Aren't you hot in that coat?'

I said, 'Bit chilly in here.' I still needed the coat for my second arrival upstairs.

The restaurant, or joint as Aznavorian might have called it, was closely packed with warm bodies and hot food, and Mickey appeared on the point of questioning my inner thermostat. But just then a sullen waitress appeared, took our order for drinks, and went away again. Mickey ran his eye over the menu. He said, 'Not bad, if you like steak and chips.'

'I should have checked with you first, I'm sorry.'

'No, it's fine, honest. I used to be a vegetarian until a couple of years back, but I fell off the wagon.'

I said, 'Anyway, it's all on me, have whatever you like. To be honest, I'm not massively hungry myself.'

'Been at the snacks, have you?'

I shook my head. 'Dodgy stomach. Don't take it personally if I suddenly have to get up and leave you for a few minutes.' I thought I'd placed that quite nicely.

'Does that rule out a starter?'

'You have one if you want. I'll just sit and admire the view.'

'Yeah, I expect you can see the Grand from there.' And he looked over his shoulder to test the hypothesis.

'I don't mean that, you berk, I mean you.' Mickey smiled becomingly. I said, 'How's D-Day been going?'

'Not bad. There's been a few moans, but people love it, don't they? Forget football, moaning's our national sport.' He leaned closer and took my hand. 'I've been thinking about you all day. I told the old girl I'd not be back tonight. I've got this whole exercise programme worked out for you.'

The waitress's return might have caused Mickey to release my hand, but it didn't. Either not noticing, or not caring what customers got up to with their hands, she rather carelessly set down my pint of beer and a half of cider for Mickey, then took out her pad and pen. She said, 'What can I get you boys?' and looked away down the restaurant, as if almost anything would be of more interest to her than our order.

I said, 'You're busy tonight, aren't you? Still, I expect it makes the evening go faster for you.' I must have taken her manner as a challenge.

She said, 'What do you want? I've got people waiting.'

Mickey chose the garlic mushrooms and a rump steak well done, while I thought the fish and chips might be my least worst option. If memory served, it also provided the fish relief on the menu upstairs, so I wouldn't need to confuse the palate with ill-matched dishes.

Then, as the waitress moved away, the back of Mark's head came in sight and passed across the window. My adrenal glands went into production on a large scale. Mickey hadn't seen Mark, and Mark hadn't glanced in, so that was the first hurdle safely jumped already. Mickey said, 'This place is all right really, isn't it? Don't know about the décor though. Trouble with Southaven, it's five years out of date.'

'Only five?'

'OK, ten. I didn't want to upset you.' The design seemed quite modern to me, with a lot of brown and beige and what I took to be hessian wallpaper, but I was prepared to defer to the expert.

Now I could see Mark through the doorway, just at the foot of the stairs. I swept my paper serviette onto the floor and bent down out of sight in search of it. By the time I straightened up again, Mark had gone. I would be needed upstairs now.

'Actually, Mickey, talking of being upset – '

He looked sympathetic. 'The old tum, is it?'

'I'd better just dash out for a minute before the food arrives. You don't mind, do you?' He didn't, or he said he didn't, which was good enough, so I got up from the table and made for the stairs. On the half landing I paused for breath. I hoped to goodness Mark wasn't feeling pernickety. He had a nasty habit of taking a microscope to my deficiencies, and this really wouldn't be a good time. But the longer I delayed, the longer I was keeping

Mickey waiting, so I pulled myself together, ran up the remaining stairs, and burst onto the scene in Roosters with every show of haste. With Alf in attendance, Mark was settling at a corner table away from the window, so I waved and crossed to join him.

'Sorry I'm late.' Alf drew my chair out a little and pushed it in again when I'd sat down. Previous establishments had trained him well; you didn't get service like that in Rustlers. Then he took our drink order and drifted away. One of my instructions had been that under no circumstances should Alf reveal that we'd met before. He'd passed this first test well.

Mark said, 'I thought you might be going to stand me up.'

'I'd only have been sat here fifteen minutes twiddling my thumbs. Why are you always, always late?'

'I'm on a murder inquiry.'

'Today, yes, but it's never been any different. I've wasted hours of my life waiting for you.'

Mark said, 'Are you in a bad mood again?'

'Me? No.'

'You look a bit strained.'

'If you want me to look relaxed and casual, you should try turning up on time. Anyway, we're here now. Let's just try to enjoy it, shall we?' Any remark better calculated to spoil a social occasion would be hard to imagine, but it was too late to take it back.

Mark frowned. 'You are, you're in a really bad mood. Is it your mother? Did you see her today?'

'Yes, and she's looking better. Do you know what you want to eat?' Feeling that I had to divert Mark's attention away from me somehow, I pushed a menu across the table. 'I can recommend the chicken.'

'I thought you said you'd never been here?'

'It was meant to be a joke.'

Temporarily silenced, Mark studied the menu, while I pretended to do the same. After a while, without even looking at me, Mark said, 'Aren't you hot in that coat?'

I said, 'Bit chilly in here.' If I reappeared in Rustlers without a coat, Mickey would be sure to notice.

'Do you want a starter? To be honest, I haven't got much time. I'm supposed to be meeting the rest of the team back at the nick before we call it a day.'

Alf returned, with my beer and Mark's glass of wine. Mark rarely drank, and I guessed that this deviation from normal practice could be put down to anxiety. After all, by means of this intimate dinner he intended to inform Southaven, and especially its constabulary, that he was indeed the raging poofter they'd all been trying to pretend he wasn't. This was quite some bridge to cross; a lot of people would have needed the whole bottle. He ordered the chicken cacciatore which I'd eaten myself the other day, while I stuck to my plan and asked for the fish. When Alf had gone, Mark looked around glumly and said, 'I don't think this is going to work.'

'What isn't?'

'Well – just look. I thought it would be more, you know, Valentiney. It's mostly families. And see this.' He fingered the solitary red carnation in its slim vase. 'They didn't even fork out for roses. I'm trying to make a gesture here, but everyone probably thinks we're just two blokes having a meal.' Then something caught Mark's eye. 'Wait a minute, though – '

He directed my gaze towards a young couple who were being extremely Valentiney on the opposite side of the room. 'I think that's the Super's daughter, Penny Sturges. We chatted for hours at this charity do last year, she's bound to remember me. What a stroke of luck! I need to get her attention.' He grabbed the lapels of my jacket, pulled me towards him, and kissed me.

It wasn't much of a kiss, but I'd rather have settled for none at all. When Mark let go, I said, 'Was that absolutely necessary?'

He was looking across the room again. 'It's no use, they're too wrapped up in each other.' Which was true. The Sturges girl was gazing deep into the eyes of a bland, whey-faced bloke resembling a young Cliff Michelmore but without the rugged sex appeal. I thought she could have done better.

However, the unwelcome smacker Mark had planted on me hadn't gone unnoticed by a middle-aged couple at a nearby table, who were now watching us with suspicion. I gave them a friendly smile, which went for nothing, then drank off a fair proportion of the beer, hoping to get the most out of it before any resumption of Mark's antics could send it flying. Then I said to Mark, 'I suppose there's no sign of that missing letter yet?'

Still preoccupied with the possible failure of his famous gesture, Mark said, 'What letter?' But he was first and foremost a policeman, and needed no further prompting. 'Oh, you mean the note from Giles Rawley to Oscar Hammond. An interesting development. Puts the Goldings right in the frame. We didn't find it at the house on Wright Street, but there was evidence of a break-in, a back window had been forced. Tidy job, though – Hammond could easily have come back to the house for the brandy and gone out again without noticing.'

I said, 'Which is presumably how the poison got into the bottle.'

Mark nodded. 'They're saying it could be strychnine. The body was contorted, he'd had convulsions before he died. The tests should confirm it.'

'How easy is it to get hold of strychnine?'

'Too easy, if you ask me.'

'Excuse me, sir.' With impeccable timing, Alf had materialised at my elbow. 'Would your name be Rigby, by any chance?'

I admitted as much.

'There's a telephone call for you, sir. A Mr – there now, I've forgotten the name. Leyland, was it? Chorley, perhaps?'

'Standish?'

'Oh, yes, that's right. I knew there was an L in it. He says it's important.' And Alf winked at me.

If he'd meant this wink to be sly or surreptitious, then Alf's efforts were in vain. It came across instead as the wink of a lifetime. Why he couldn't have winked a confused, minimal, Giles Rawley sort of wink at such a crucial juncture, I really didn't know. There was no hope whatever that Mark would have missed it. I said, 'Have you got something in your eye?'

Skulduggery doesn't come naturally to everyone. Alf looked perplexed and said, 'I don't think so, sir.'

Deciding it might be better if I dropped the optical theme

altogether, I said, 'Could you tell me where the phone is?'

'You'll find it on the half landing, sir. If you'll excuse me.' Alf pootled off.

Mark said, 'He winked at you.'

'Who did?'

'That waiter.'

'No he didn't.'

'Yes he did. A great, fat, juicy wink.'

'I think he just had something in his eye.' I pushed back my chair. 'Sorry, Mark, I'd better go and see what Matt wants. I told him I'd be here with you. I've got the poor lad working, while I'm living the life of Riley. Won't be long!' And I left Mark looking sceptical. A sceptical Mark was not the variety I needed just at the moment, but I couldn't do anything about that now. Instead I legged it down the stairs and resumed my seat opposite Mickey Golding.

Mickey, who was just finishing off the garlic mushrooms, looked up and said, 'Are you all right? I was beginning to think you'd flushed yourself away.'

'I'm sure I'll be fine. How were the mushrooms?'

'People never put enough garlic in garlic butter, do they? If you tried passing that off as garlic mushrooms in London, you'd get done under the Trade Descriptions Act.'

I said, 'This is what happens when you reside among oafish provincials.'

'All right, all right, point taken.' The waitress removed Mickey's plate. In terms of service she was Alf's polar opposite, giving the impression that once she'd had her novel published the Hen and Chickens wouldn't be seeing her for dust. When she'd left us, Mickey said, 'I hear you called on my mum.'

It seemed that members of the Golding family were all well versed in the art of euphemism. I said, 'I'd certainly give her full marks for hospitality. And I got a fantastic welcome from the servants too.' I turned to show the back of my head.

Mickey winced. 'How did that happen?'

'Your friend Cess.'

'He's not my friend. The old girl has to keep muscle round the place, she's got no choice. When you're in business, you make enemies.'

Of all the euphemisms they employed, 'business' seemed to be the Goldings' favourite. I said, 'She invited me to join the family.'

Mickey looked down at the table for a moment, then picked up his cider and sipped at it. 'And?'

'And what?'

'What did you say to her?'

'I said I'd think about it.'

There was another brief silence. Suddenly Mickey put the glass down and took my hand again. 'Say yes, Sam, say yes! I can't tell you what it would mean to me.'

I liked the feel of Mickey's hand in mine. I liked the keen, warm, welcoming expression on his face, an open door leading to an easier life. I liked Mickey Golding. But I could hear Evan Bickerstaff saying, if he's making up to you he wants something. I wished I could believe that the only thing Mickey wanted was me.

The waitress brought our meals. When Mickey asked for French mustard, the waitress said, 'We've only got English,' and went to fetch it.

Mickey said, 'Don't you want ketchup?'

'There's tartare sauce with it already.'

'That stuff is shit. They just invented it to try to give scampi a bit of class.'

The waitress thumped a small dish of mustard on the table without comment. When Mickey had helped himself she took it away again immediately, as if he couldn't be trusted with it.

I said, 'The thing is, Mickey, you Goldings aren't quite the kind of family I'm used to.'

'I don't get you.'

'For instance, your mother's currently holding a man against his will. Somewhere in that hotel of yours, as a matter of fact. I'll admit my own family's not much to write home about, but at least we don't go in for kidnapping with menaces. Know anything about it, by the way?'

Mickey hesitated, then cut into his steak. When I scattered salt over the fish and chips, he said, 'You shouldn't have so much salt, it's not good for you.'

I said, 'And now there's evidence linking your family to the death of Oscar Hammond. You go on like you're the Waltons, but the Goldings have got more baggage than Speke Airport.'

Stung from silence, Mickey jabbed in my direction with the steak knife. 'That's not fair! Give a dog a bad name, that's what this is about. We're Londoners, but to you lot we might as well have come from Timbuktu, and you think we've brought all the bad things in the world with us. Why won't you give us a chance? Why won't you trust me?' He paused, puzzled. 'What is it? What are you looking at?'

Although Mickey's speech had in its way been compelling, so too was the sight of customers and staff filing out of the Grand Hotel and congregating in the drizzle. Two police cars stood outside the main entrance, their lights flashing. Mickey screwed his head round to follow my gaze, but his chair was badly placed for looking back up the road. He said, 'What do you think's going on?'

'I couldn't tell you.' To be strictly truthful, I'd have had to say 'won't'.

'Sam – is it all right if I just run outside and ask someone what's happening?'

I said, 'Be my guest,' and as soon as he'd disappeared through the door I told the waitress to keep an eye on our food and ran hell for leather up the stairs.

Back in Roosters, Mark said, 'How was Matt?'

'Who? Oh, yes, Matt. Making a huge fuss over nothing, as usual. Fab, the food's arrived.' And I got stuck in. I may have been dining in two restaurants, but the fact is I was starving. There hadn't been much opportunity to make inroads on my downstairs meal, and I was hoping the upstairs one would go better. I flagged Alf down to ask for ketchup. Generously, he left it with me. I said to Mark, 'How's the chicken?'

'All right. Actually, I've had better in the staff canteen.'

Unless standards had risen since my time on the force, this review was pretty damning. There'd been a summer day in 1960 when so many of us were off with food poisoning that the criminal fraternity had Southaven all to themselves. I said, 'Did Hargreaves get much out of Howard Lane?'

'Yes and no. He claims he was with someone the night Giles Rawley was killed, but he won't say who so we can't check it. An affair, presumably, and he's trying to protect the woman. But he admits Rawley had phoned him recently and threatened to go to the police if Lane didn't leave his wife and kids.'

'What did Howard Lane do?'

'Refused, obviously. He said the housekeeper's note was all lies, she'd taken a dislike to him for some reason and just wanted to make his life difficult.'

'So Howard Lane still has a motive for the murder and no alibi. What about Oscar?'

'Lane says he left his house in Reigate at four in the morning and drove straight here, but again we can't confirm that yet. If it's true, he couldn't possibly have broken into Hammond's place last night in time to poison the brandy. Besides, there's no link between him and Hammond. He says he doesn't even remember meeting the chef when he stayed at the Marine Lodge.'

While Mark had been giving this cogent summary, I'd spotted the Superintendent's daughter navigating a path towards us between the tables. She now moored alongside and said, 'DC Howell, isn't it? We met at that fundraiser last year – Penny Sturges.' She smiled an engaging smile, freely exuding goodwill.

Mark stood up in his place and shook her hand. 'I remember it well, we had a good chat. Enjoying your evening?'

'I'm here with Hector.' She looked across at this human dumpling and glowed with misplaced pride. 'We're getting married in a few weeks.'

'Congratulations.'

'All a bit daunting really, but we're just so right for each other. How about you?'

From time to time Penny Sturges had let her eye wander in my direction, regarding me in the light of an exhibit without a label. Mark said, 'Me? I'm here with Sam.' And he looked at me as if the sun was at that moment shining gaily from my every orifice. He'd not looked at me that way in earnest for seven or eight years. He was faking now, of course, but he did it well.

Penny appeared mystified for a moment, and I wondered whether she might have led such a sheltered life that Mark's meaning would be lost on her. But after a while you could see the bulb light up. She said, 'Oh. Oh. Yes.' She glanced at me again, and I distinctly caught her thinking that Mark could have done better. 'Well – they put on a good spread here, don't they?'

Mark said, 'We like it. Don't we, Sam?'

Eight years earlier, before the law was changed, when we'd been trying to keep our relationship secret, the notion that we'd one day play out a romantic scene such as this in a public place would have seemed an impossible dream. It was a shame I couldn't throw myself into the role with more conviction. In fact, when I opened my mouth to speak nothing happened, so I shut it again. To Mark, Penny Sturges said, 'I expect you're working on this dreadful murder case.'

'That's right. I'm just taking a quick break. With Sam.' The scary smile again. Penny Sturges wasn't going to forget this in a hurry.

Sensing an opportunity, I said, 'Would you two – ? I'm just going to – ' I couldn't seem to manage anything more coherent at the time, but it would have to do, and leaving Mark in the care of the Superintendent's daughter I put my serviette on the table and slipped quietly away.

When I reached the bottom of the stairs, Mickey was just coming inside, his hair and shirt damp from the drizzle. 'Guess what – there's a bomb!' He probably thought he knew where I'd just been, so I said nothing about it.

'Really?'

'You don't look very surprised.'

'Let's go and sit down.'

Mickey followed me back to the table in the window, saying, 'An actual bomb! Though the cops think it's most likely a hoax. Carlo's doing his nut, it's really bad for business. Apparently there was a call from a phone box, some bloke with a Scottish accent.'

Although I'd made a fair start on my upstairs meal I was still really hungry, so it was with a mouth full of chips that I now said,

'Scottish?'

'Yeah, Scottish.'

'Not Irish?'

'No. Which probably rules out the IRA.'

I took a swig of the beer and said, 'If it's a hoax, it's going to be the Malones again, isn't it? They already had a go at you with that raid the other night.'

Mickey said, 'No, it's definitely not the Malones.'

Alarm bells rang. This happened to me so often I should have had them playing on a loop. 'How can you be sure?'

'Because the Malones are stood outside now, with my mum. They'd been having a celebration drink in the cocktail bar. Apparently we've ironed out our differences, from now on the Goldings and the Malones work together.'

With these innocent words, my whole plan to take the heat off Alice Haig by ramping up the turf war between Southaven's two shadiest families sank ingloriously beneath the waves. Momentary guilt nibbled at my conscience. I'd involved Matt in something horribly illegal, as he'd said, and to no useful purpose. Lou would now have all her considerable energies free to put pressure on Alice.

And then, like some spectre in a dream, Matt himself appeared. I briefly supposed that my guilt might have caused me to hallucinate, because this was a strange, phantasmagoric version of Matt, caked with mud down one side, his hair standing on end, his moustache a-quiver, and wearing an expression of mingled rage and despair which I'd never seen on his face before and hoped never to see again. Striding past both the till and pony-tail woman, who seemed perturbed by this apparition, he made a bee-line for our table, and on arrival said, 'I'll never forgive you for this, never!' I mightn't have minded so much if he'd been talking to Mickey, but he wasn't.

The line was rather hackneyed, but Matt had delivered it with such sincerity and force that several diners now looked round and tuned in to the unfolding drama. I said, 'For what?'

'Oh, as if you didn't know.'

'But I don't. What's happened?' I was becoming aware of a

strong smell of ditch.

'How long's it been going on? Weeks, is it, or months? And all this time you've let me carry on making a complete fool of myself. You knew what I was going to find this evening! You could have spared me, you could have saved me the humiliation, but I suppose in your sick, twisted way you thought it would be funny and you wanted your little laugh. You've all been laughing at me, haven't you, all three of you!'

Pony-tail woman had arrived at the table during this tirade, and now said to Matt, 'If you wouldn't mind, sir – '

I said, 'Was Eileen with someone else, is that it?'

Matt said, 'Still pretending, are you?' Steam was rising off him. Not metaphorical steam, steam. 'Thanks to you I've had the worst evening of my whole life. Driving miles round the sodding countryside on that useless machine, soaked to the skin, trying to keep up with Eileen in the cab, and then when I get there – '

Pony-tail woman said, 'Please, sir – ' and went so far as to put a hand on Matt's less muddy arm, but he threw it off.

I said, 'Where was she going?'

'You *know* where. The Lord Derby. Out in the middle of nowhere, big Valentine's party in the function room, but not just any Valentine's party, something a bit special, a bit *different*.'

'Did she meet someone?'

'I don't believe this! Of course she did, you know very well she did, and you know who it was too.'

'Excuse me, sir, I really think you ought to – ' Pony-tail woman again.

I said, 'Who? Who was it?'

'You've got some nerve. You know, you've always known!'

'Matt, I swear to you I don't know what you're talking about.'

'I don't believe you. After all, she tells you everything, doesn't she?'

'What – Eileen?'

'Not Eileen, you idiot. Bernie Foster. Your old pal Bernie Foster!'

The apparition shimmered a little now as some subterranean force took Rustlers restaurant and shook it from side to side. For a second I thought the bomb must have gone off, but then I remembered that the bomb was fiction and I'd invented it myself. Weakly, I said, 'Eileen was with Bernie Foster?'

'They were all over each other! Talk about electricity, you could have run Blackpool illuminations off them.'

To give pony-tail woman her due, she wasn't one to give up easily. 'I'm afraid I'm going to have to ask you to leave, sir.'

Matt said, 'I didn't try to talk to her. What was the point? If I'd gone charging in they'd have got a kick out of it, wouldn't they? So I just left, then I did that bit of business for you. No, not for you, I did it for the client.'

I considered butting in and complaining about the quality of Matt's Irish accent, then thought better of it.

Matt said, 'But that's me finished. You can stick your job! I'm finished with you, understand? I never want to see you again!' Then he sighed and added more quietly, 'It should have been me and Eileen at this table tonight, not you and this Cockney cretin. I hope you've enjoyed yourselves.' He turned, and with a dignity surprising in one so muddy he walked out of the room.

Mark Howell, who'd joined our little group during the later moments of Matt's performance, now looked coldly from me to Mickey and back to me again. He said, 'Sam, what the bloody hell is going on?'

I said, 'I can explain,' and hoped he didn't ask me to.

Pony-tail woman said, 'If you're going to make a scene could you please do it out in the street.'

Mickey had been wearing a puzzled frown for some time. 'What did he mean, this table should have been his?'

Alf said to Mark, 'I'm very sorry, sir, but you've inadvertently left without settling your bill.' I hadn't noticed Alf bowling up, but then there was a lot going on. He looked ill at ease down here in Rustlers and I felt anxious for him.

I said, 'Alf, this isn't a good moment.'

Mark said to me, '*Alf?* I thought you'd never been here before?'

Mickey said, 'Wait a minute – there's nothing wrong with your stomach at all, is there? You've been eating upstairs with *him!*'

Mark hurled Mickey an evil look and said, 'I've got your

number, Mickey Golding!'

'Oh, yeah? I'm not scared of you, copper! You want trouble, I'm ready for you!'

I said, 'Mickey – '

Our waitress now stuck her nose in and said, without enthusiasm, 'Are you two boys done, or are you just having a breather?'

Mickey threw down his serviette. The principle was sound, but for a gesture like that to work you need something heavier than paper. He rose to his feet and said, 'I'm sorry, Sam Rigby, you're too much for me. I've tried to keep up, but I can't.' He picked his jacket off the back of the chair. 'Whatever my mum may have said, the offer's closed.' But then he hesitated, and our eyes locked. Mickey seemed to be searching for something, something that would make him change his mind. When he couldn't find it, he said, 'Goodbye, Sam.' And keeping to the trail pioneered by Matt, he left the premises.

Mark said, 'What is it with you? I ask you to do a simple thing for me, and you turn it into a three-ring circus! You'd think I'd have learned my lesson by now.' He turned to leave, but came back to deliver the postscript. 'And if you don't want to screw up this investigation, I suggest you stay away from Mickey Golding!' He then followed Matt and Mickey out into the night. Pony-tail woman kept pace with him as far as the till, addressing requests for payment to the back of his neck, but he ignored her and swept on.

Our audience, realizing that the show was now over, began to seek alternative entertainment. The waitress had long since mooned away, and apart from a faint whiff of rotting vegetation no trace of the recent mayhem remained.

I said to Alf, 'I think that went pretty well on the whole, don't you?'

He looked miserable. 'Are you sure, sir? Your friends didn't seem very happy.'

There was no reason why both of us should have a lousy night, so I slipped him another fat tip and said, 'I couldn't have wished for a better partner in crime.'

Alf's gloom lifted immediately. 'Very kind of you to say so, sir.' He pocketed the cash, wished me good evening, and with a light step withdrew to the safety of the upper floors.

The food had gone cold by now, but I ate it anyway. Then I paid both bills and went home.

## twenty-four

When the phone rang around half past seven next morning, I almost spilled the tea I was carrying through from the kitchen. Phones always seem louder before daybreak, and the grey of dawn had only just begun its contest with the yellow of the street lamps. I'd been awake half the night waiting for the other shoe to drop and was confidently expecting bad news, so it surprised me when a cheerful voice said, 'Sam? Sam Rigby?'

'Who is this?'

'It's me, Nigel Haig. I've cracked the case!'

Given that some of the sharpest minds in the north west had just spent several days failing in the attempt, a degree of scepticism could be forgiven. 'Who was it then – Professor Plum?'

'If you're going to be like that, I'm not telling you.'

The rebuke was fair. 'Come on, Nigel. It's too early in the morning for games.'

'You started it.'

'Yes, all right, I'm sorry. What have you come up with?'

His tone softened. 'To be honest, I don't actually know who did it.'

'But you said you'd cracked the case.'

'I have! Well, possibly. I may not know who did it, but I think I know what it's about. Anyway, I can tell you when you get here.'

'What – am I coming over?'

'Yes. Now. My mum asked me to call you, she's busy doing breakfast with Lena Golding. God, that girl is sexy! Those tits! All wasted on you, I suppose.' He lapsed into a preoccupied silence.

'Nigel, why does your mother want to see me?'

'She doesn't, she just thinks you'll come when you hear the latest. Aznavorian's done a runner. In the night, bag and baggage. The police are here now, searching his room again.'

'Did he take Miss Pyle?' I don't know why, but that was my first thought. Perhaps I had a fantasy of them going on the run together, like a senior citizens' *Bonnie and Clyde.*

'No, he's left the old bat here. She'll be livid. *"Oh, Sarkis, how could you? You know I'd follow you to the ends of the earth!"'*

It was a remarkably accurate impression, and triggered a half-reminiscence which I couldn't quite place at the time. I wondered whether Nigel could do the smile as well. I said, 'I'll be there as soon as I can.'

'Well hurry up. It's my exam this morning, I've got to be on the train to school at eight and I'm not dressed yet.'

'How about giving me a clue what you've worked out?'

'All right then: I just keep thinking, why only three?'

'Only three what? Nigel? Nigel?' But the wretched youth had rung off.

Apparently, what little sleep I'd had was insufficient for solving riddles. I couldn't imagine what Nigel Haig meant, nor why Sarkis Aznavorian should have fled the Marine Lodge so suddenly. The fact was, I'd put too much effort into rational thought overnight when I should have been sleeping. Whatever my mother might have said, I've never fancied myself as Sherlock Holmes, and on the rare occasions when I do have a useful idea it's generally the back of my mind which supplies it and not the front. The bedroom floor was littered with the scraps of paper I'd scribbled on during the small hours – names, lists, diagrams, and questions questions questions. Every avenue I went down seemed blocked.

For a while then I'd given up and tried to read instead. At last the Pequod left harbour to pursue its destiny, Captain Ahab still an unseen presence brooding in his cabin on the Great White Whale. But though in imagination I may have been cutting through the icy waters of the north Atlantic, images of the past evening, of Matt's forlorn figure as he spun his tale, kept on breaking through. I discovered now that I was furious with Bernie. Given what Matt had seen out at the Lord Derby, there seemed no possibility of a mistake. Bernie had taken my request to keep watch on Eileen Docherty a little too much to heart. She'd been playing a dark game, she should have told me the truth, and she should have persuaded Eileen to tell Matt. At half past two in the morning I felt all this so strongly that I rang the woman and gave her both barrels.

People don't take kindly to finger-wagging at the best of times, so it's no surprise if at half past two in the morning they tell the finger-wagger where he can stick it. Bernie went on to say that Matt had been culpably naïve and deserved everything that was coming to him. Provoked, I said some offensive things. Offended, Bernie repaid them with interest. When the call ended five minutes later, I didn't know whether Bernie Foster and I were still friends.

Low-spirited now, I went back to Ishmael and the Pequod, hoping that the pace might pick up a bit. It had taken Melville a hundred pages just to get the ship out of the harbour, and there were still five hundred to go. Perhaps I should have started my new Melville habit with *Redburn*, which wasn't especially long, or *Billy Budd*, which was short. I was still waiting for the library to notify me about *The Confidence-Man*. Then, belatedly, I realized that they could hardly send me a card while there was no postal service. I would have to go in and check.

But Melville once more failed to grip. A thought had been pestering me ever since I'd spoken to Alice Haig the previous morning, just before Mark told us that Oscar was dead. I got up and rang Graham Leeds at the Marine Lodge. He seemed startled to receive a phone call in the middle of the night, thought not half as startled as he was by the time I'd finished with him. The information he unwillingly gave me was suggestive, but of what? More confused than ever, I trailed back to bed and switched out the light.

At last I slept. Before long, I found myself on stage at the old Pier Pavilion, now magically restored from ruin, where my act involved performing impressions of all the suspects in the present murder case. (Hence, I suppose, the odd sensation I experienced later when Nigel Haig gave me his Miss Pyle.) All went well until I came to the last suspect. I tried everything, and failed and failed again. There was nothing I could get a grip on – no mannerisms, no quirks of language – no character – no soul. This one had to be the murderer! If I could just find a way into the role, the killer would be unmasked, and I turned to Giles Rawley for help. But he said, 'Who are you, Sam Rigby? Really, truly? Who the devil are you?' And then he winked.

I woke up remembering that those had more or less been Lou Golding's words. They implied that if I wanted to become a Golding I needed to free myself of illusion, to understand what really drove me. Though Mickey had told me the offer was closed now, I suspected such decisions weren't his to make.

There was probably a lot I didn't know about myself, but two things I did know. First, I had no intention of joining Lou's precious family. Yes, I'd been tempted. The cigar, the Scotch, the armchair. The chance to be part of something. But the costs were high, the rewards were doubtful, and I didn't much fancy the idea of becoming related to Chubby Fallon. I would have to turn Lou Golding's offer down.

And second, though I might have been blown off course lately, for months now there was only one person I'd really wanted here in the bed beside me. And it wasn't Mickey Golding.

The light strengthened to reveal a clear, cold morning. As I drove over to the Marine Lodge, my mind kept drifting back to the strange remark Giles Rawley had made at the close of his birthday tea party. After quoting the Bard on the subject of playing many parts, he'd said, 'But you'd know all about that, wouldn't you?' and winked one of his ill-defined winks. At the time I'd believed he was talking to me, but what if his lazy eye had deceived me? Was there someone else among the group Giles identified as a fellow-actor? It seemed such a trivial point, but the back of my mind wouldn't let it drop.

I parked in the yard alongside the police car whose former occupants must now be searching Sarkis Aznavorian's room. I wondered whether the bag and baggage he'd absconded with in the Armstrong Siddeley included the contents of his lock-up. Something must have spooked him, something more serious than the threat of paying tax on modest earnings. Had he grown tired of Miss Pyle, recognizing that he'd either have to marry her or escape while he could? What if his occasional trading was less innocent than he'd made out – involving obscene books, perhaps, or books stolen to order for rich clients? Or had it in fact been Aznavorian's hand which swung the fatal hammer? Rosemary Pyle might not know all the answers, but she seemed like a good place to start.

I got out and locked the car, and at the same moment my assistant, if he still was my assistant after the previous evening's performance, emerged from the staircase next to Alice Haig's, the one leading up to Evan Bickerstaff's accommodation. Though his face and hair were clean now, Matt wore the same muddy clothes which had so impressed pony-tail woman the evening before. There was something different about him this morning, but I couldn't think what. He took a couple of steps towards me, then came to an uncertain halt and bowed his head, the asphalt surface of the yard having suddenly acquired a strange fascination. I crossed to join him, but a few feet away I too faltered, and my eyes fell. There could be no doubt about it, this was the most spellbinding asphalt I'd ever seen, rich with stony charm. I felt particularly drawn to the area around Matt's shoes. It became clear to me that all our previous notions of the picturesque would need to be revised to take account of this extraordinary composition.

Then I heard myself say, 'I'm sorry.' This was a mistake. If Matt now took full advantage, I'd only have myself to blame.

He said, 'Why? It's me that should be sorry.' I risked looking up, and saw that he'd looked up too. He said, 'You really didn't know about Eileen, did you? I could see it in your face. But I was angry, I wanted to make someone pay.'

I glanced over his shoulder towards the stairs he'd just come down. He saw me do it, and probably saw me leaping to conclusions. I said, 'You and Eileen have been falling apart for ages.'

'Yeah, I know.'

'You'd even slept with someone else.' He looked as if he was about to deny it, so I added, 'In Manchester, on Friday night. Let me guess – the bloke with the motor-bike who helped you go after Gordon Asprey.'

Matt sulked. 'It's none of your business.'

'What about Eileen – did you tell her about it?'

He shook his head. 'When I saw her on Saturday she made me angry, I knew she was lying to me about doing that training course the next day.' He was wrestling with some particularly unwelcome recollection. 'There was a moment when I wanted – I wanted to hurt her.'

'What, make her jealous or something?'

'Not that.' He clenched and unclenched his fists. 'When you think you care about someone it can make you crazy.'

I noted the choice of words. 'Matt, you didn't actually – '

'Of course not. It was like you and me the other day. I stopped myself.' He'd returned to studying the asphalt.

I moved a step closer. I was going to touch him, put a hand on his arm. Then he looked up again, and it didn't seem like such a good idea. I said, 'I'd never hurt you.'

'You can't know that.'

'But I wouldn't!'

'You're a powder keg. It only needs one spark – ' He didn't complete the idea. 'But apparently I'm not as different from you as I thought. We'd better not risk – ' He didn't finish that one either. 'Anyway, you're with Mickey now.'

'Matt – '

'Let's just leave it, shall we? You haven't told me what you're doing here. You realize it's not even eight o'clock yet?'

There was a kind of violence in the sudden change of subject. I said, 'Do you want to know what these murders are all about?'

'Course I do.'

'Then come with me. Nigel Haig's about to tell us.'

I led Matt up the stairs to Alice Haig's flat. Though I'd never yet found the door locked, I was surprised to see it standing open. In the cramped hallway I called out, 'Nigel?' There was no reply.

We turned into the kitchen, where two eggs were dancing gaily in a pan on the stove. It seemed that Nigel had taken the advice of the Egg Marketing Board and was about to go to school on them, though perhaps one was intended for Bobbie. Back in the hallway I tried again. 'Nigel? Bobby?'

Matt said, 'Perhaps he's upstairs.'

Again I led the way. The door to Nigel's room stood open too, and we went inside. The bed had been neatly made, and Nigel's school clothes lay ready to hand on the chair, but on the floor beneath the shelves books lay scattered randomly where they'd fallen. It looked as if there'd been some kind of struggle. Then I heard footsteps on the stairs. A voice shouted 'Nigel! Nigel!'

I said, 'Up here!'

Alice Haig half ran into the room. Not finding what she'd hoped to find, she clutched her head in her hands and said, 'No!'

'What is it? What's happened?'

'That woman!'

'Who? Lou Golding?'

Alice turned to look at me now. 'She rang, a minute ago. She was cold, heartless. She said I'd given her the wrong answer!'

'What answer? I don't understand.'

'But that's the point, I hadn't contacted her at all. She said she'd teach me to be more cooperative in future. She said – oh God! She said children have a way of disappearing.'

'She's insane.'

Really I'd been talking to myself more than to Alice Haig, but Alice said, 'I don't think she is, it's worse than that.' She sighed. 'At least Bobbie's safe.'

'Was she not here?'

'I've sent her to stay with her friend until all this is over. Oscar's death was the final straw.'

'You need to ring and make sure she's OK. And the police – '

'The police have been worse than useless. I'm going to sort this out myself!' She removed the apron she'd been wearing and threw it down on the bed.

'How? What can you do that the police can't?'

'I'm going to do what I should have done before. I'm going

straight over to see Mrs Golding and talk it through, woman to woman.'

I put a hand on her shoulder. 'Don't! Please don't. Think about Nigel. You could make things worse, you don't understand what you're walking into.'

Alice turned on me and snarled into my face. Up to that moment, I'd have said that snarling lay outside her range, but apparently not. 'And you do understand, is that it? I'm not a fool, Mr Rigby. You told me you had a plan to disrupt Valentine's Day at the Grand. That idiotic bomb hoax was you, wasn't it? Obviously Mrs Golding thinks that was my reply to her proposal, and now my boy's been taken and it's your fault!' She moved to the door, pausing there to deliver the parting shot. 'Consider your contract terminated. Good morning.' And she left us.

I sat down on the bed. In the light of these new developments, Miss Pyle would have to wait. Matt said, 'Why are you sitting down? We should be out there doing something!'

I said, 'Sit.' He sat. I then found it necessary to take one of his hands in mine and play with it, purely as an aid to concentration. The last time I'd sat on a bed with him and taken his hand, things had ended badly, but I refused to be bound by the miscalculations of the past. 'I've done nothing but run around ever since Giles Rawley was murdered, and it's been a total waste of energy. You know what I should have been doing instead?'

'Do you have to fiddle with my hand like that?'

'I should have been talking to you. My assistant Matthew Standish, finest of all the Marshfield Standishes. Wait a minute – your moustache!'

'What about it?'

'It's not there. I mean – you've shaved it off!'

'What if I have?'

'Nothing. Forget I mentioned it.' I could fresh hope surging through me. This marked the beginning of a new era, free of unsightly facial hair. 'The point is, for days now I've hardly seen you. How can we be expected to work this out if we don't put our heads together?'

'We've been making enquiries. It's what we do.'

'Well it's not enough. We need to get back to the flat and *think*. Only, not the sort of thinking I do when I'm on my own. The sort you do. The sort that gets us somewhere.'

'You want me to solve the case for you?'

I patted the hand. 'I knew you'd understand. If Nigel can do it, I'm sure you can do it too.' I outlined the salient points of the recent telephone conversation. '*Why only three*, that's what he said. But only three what? I don't know what the bloody hell he was talking about. I'll meet you back at the flat in an hour – we've both got things to take care of first.'

'Such as?'

'Have you seen yourself? You're going home to change. Are you still on the moped?'

'It's parked on Marine Approach. I don't think Marie's going to be very happy with me when she sees it.'

'You can easily get home and back within the hour. If you arrive first, brew large quantities of tea and start without me.' I let go of the hand and stood up.

'Where are you going yourself?'

'I intend to take a leaf out of the Standish Book of Recklessness.'

'Yes, but where?'

'The cop shop. Wish me luck. If I don't come back, I want to be cremated.'

On the way out, Matt remembered to switch off the gas under the eggs. It was that sort of attention to detail which sometimes made me toy briefly with the idea of increasing his wages. Out in the yard, I climbed back into the Minx and watched him run off towards Marine Approach. I didn't know whether Evan Bickerstaff was still in his flat, or hard at work in the hotel. But wherever he was, I suspected he might not be feeling quite so lonely any more.

Detective Inspector Henry Hargreaves generally delayed his first pipe of the day until mid-morning, after which he kept it almost continuously smouldering. At present it lay dormant on the table between us. Not a great tea drinker himself, Hargreaves had nevertheless requested a mug of the stuff to help me pass the time while I waited for him to deal with more pressing matters. Protestations that my visit was of vital importance had probably done nothing but add several minutes to my wait in the interview room. When Hargreaves eventually returned it was with the air of a man hoping for little and expecting less.

He began by sniffing. I'd heard him sniff before, and I wasn't going to let it scare me. 'So, Samuel, what is this important contribution you claim you wish to make? And before you answer, I should warn you that if it's on a par with some of your past contributions I will personally lock you up and throw away the key.' His hair looked more than usually wayward this morning, like a bad wig put on in a hurry. I doubted whether he'd had much sleep.

I said, 'It's getting out of hand.' Considering that I'd had ten minutes to prepare my remarks, this was a disappointing opener. I'd worked out several better ones, but they all ran and hid when Hargreaves came into the room.

'Out of hand, you say?'

I nodded.

Hargreaves nodded back, sagely. 'Out of hand. Well, that's very interesting.' Picking up the pipe, he pushed back his chair. 'Now, if there was nothing else you wanted to share with me, I have duties to attend to.'

'You see, this is what you do!' The words came out all of a rush.

Hargreaves said, 'What I do? I wasn't aware of doing anything.'

The DI's failure to do anything was the exact nub of my complaint, but instead of seizing on this helpful admission I said, 'You – you *play* with me, when you ought to be trying to get to the bottom of things!'

'Oh. I see.' Hargreaves put down the pipe. 'I play with you, do I? And what else would you expect me to do with a child?'

There was no mirror handy, so I can't say for certain that the colour now rose into my face. 'Why will you never show me any respect?'

The answer was a smug half-smile. 'When you earn respect, Samuel, I'll be the first to give it.'

'How? How do I earn it?'

He picked up the pipe again to underline his point. 'It's very simple.' Now the pipe came into play, jabbing towards me for emphasis. '*Bring me something I can use.*' He laid the pipe aside. 'But you won't, will you? All I ever get from you is airy-fairy rubbish. You were the same on the force, fanciful, full of ideas. Your ideas are worthless to me. In fact, you're worthless to me. If I had any sense I'd see you barred from these premises.'

'Then why don't you? Do you think I want to come here, nagging at you to do your job properly?'

This caught his attention. 'Is that why you're here? You think after more than forty years in this God-forsaken place I need you to tell me how to do my job?'

'These Goldings – you're giving them the run of the place! They seem to think they can get away with anything. Maybe even murder.'

'I'm keeping a very close eye on Mrs Golding.'

'You think she cares? While you've been watching, she's had two people kidnapped.'

Suddenly more serious now, Hargreaves made to get up from the chair.

I said, 'It's all right, I saw DC Howell on the way in, I've given him the details.' In return, Mark had told me the interesting news that the chemist's shop on Marine Approach had been broken into over the weekend. Some strychnine was missing. I said, 'You know Joe Braithwaite works for Mrs Golding these days?'

'I'd heard rumours.'

'Rumours! Airy-fairy rubbish. You need to get out there and get stuck in. I went to see Lou Golding, she told me herself. So now she's got all the muscle she needs, she's added Braithwaite's dodgy business to her own, she's got a property scam going, she's leaning on the local betting shops, she's in cahoots with the Malones – '

Hargreaves was shaking his head with a condescending pucker of the lips. 'The Goldings and the Malones are at daggers drawn.'

'Not since yesterday they aren't. What's more, she's running an illegal gambling club at the Grand.'

'We went there, it was clean.'

'You just didn't find anything, that's all. Then to put the icing on the cake she's gone in for kidnapping with menaces, and you lot are sat here on your arses. I'm telling you, it's getting out of hand!' The expression seemed much pithier with the aid of a little context.

Hargreaves had been chewing the stem of the pipe. He said, 'I admit we may have underestimated Mrs Golding's ambitions. We're not used to her type in Southaven.'

I sniffed. I didn't see why Hargreaves should have all the fun. 'That's not what's really going on, though, is it? There's plenty of people on the force would be only too happy to go after her, but someone here keeps slamming on the brakes.'

Hargreaves didn't like that. 'If you're saying what I think you're saying – '

'You remember DS Fallon? Works for the Goldings now, when he's not too busy skiing in some fancy resort. Fallon's got the screws on someone here, someone right at the top.'

Hargreaves turned this over. Then his expression hardened and he looked at me with even less warmth than usual. 'If you're suggesting that you think I could be corrupted by a nasty, vicious piece of work like DS Fallon – '

'That's not what I meant.'

He loosened his collar. I wasn't sure I'd ever seen him loosen anything before.

I said, 'The fact is, you know something dodgy's going on, but you've been turning a blind eye.' I tutted a couple of disappointed tuts. 'You've always been down on me, but I could put up with that as long as I thought you were straight and decent and prepared to do the right thing.'

'I'm not taking lectures from you! I don't know why I wasted my time letting you in here this morning.'

'Did you realize that Sarkis Aznavorian has a lock-up in the yard at the Marine Lodge?' When Hargreaves once again made to leave his seat, I said, 'Don't worry, I told DC Howell about that as well. Airy-fairy rubbish, is it, or something you can use? Aznavorian promised me he was going to tell you himself, but instead he's flown the nest and taken God knows what evidence with him. What's the matter with you? You interviewed him twice, in your prime you'd have cracked him open in five minutes!'

Hargreaves didn't respond. He took his tobacco tin from a pocket and began to load the pipe. This prop of his had been annoying me for years, and I'd half a mind to grab it now and hurl it across the room. Eventually he said, 'You may have heard I'm thinking of retiring.'

'Someone did mention it.'

He picked apart the threads of tobacco and gently tamped it down in the bowl. 'Whatever you might say, I believe I've got a few more useful years left in me – retirement age is a grey area in the force, as you know. Then suddenly we get this reorganization foisted on us. There'll be no dedicated Southaven team, and I'll have a DCI from Preston breathing down my neck every move I make. It's not the same police force I joined.'

'Everything changes, Henry.'

He transferred his attention to my face. 'I must remember to write that in my commonplace book.'

'The force still needs you. Southaven needs you. You can't always have things on your own terms.'

He looked away again and fussed with the pipe. 'I'd have imagined you'd be only too pleased to see me go.'

For the first time I had a sudden vision of my life with no Henry Hargreaves in it. The sense of freedom made me giddy. Perhaps this was how agoraphobics felt when stranded on the open plain. I said, 'You're not going though, are you? This is all a bit of drama because you don't feel appreciated.'

'Edna's been wanting me to retire for some time now.'

'Then Mrs Hargreaves'll have to be patient. Come on, Harry, buck your ideas up!' He was about to object to this familiarity, but I steamed ahead. 'You've got Lou Golding to deal with, and two murders. I want results! I want to see the bad guys quaking in their shoes!'

'You don't want much, do you?'

'And another thing I want to see is DC Howell promoted, like he should have been six months ago. He's done the exams, he just needs you to recommend him.'

Hargreaves lit the pipe. This enforced a ten-second pause in the conversation, exactly when I'd hoped I might be making ground. Now partly obscured by the smoke he'd created, Hargreaves said, 'On the surface, DC Howell is an effective and conscientious officer. But it's my personal opinion that he's a liability.'

Hargreaves had all too often used this word against me, but against Mark it seemed even more unfair. Nor did it take much decoding. 'If you mean that in your personal opinion homosexuals have no place in the constabulary, why not say so? We wouldn't be a liability if you supported us instead of leaving us to be blackmailed by the likes of DS Fallon.'

Hargreaves sneered one of his least appealing sneers. 'He's admitting it at last, is he? This is no job for pansies.' He pounced gleefully on the plosive. 'DC Howell has been deliberately misleading us for a number of years. I understand he was engaged to WPC Donnelly.'

'Not exactly.'

'How can we trust a man who wilfully deceives us?'

'You've as good as forced him to lie or be drummed out!'

'He should have been frank with us.'

'You mean, like I was? Look where it got me!'

Hargreaves leaned back and took consolation in the pipe. He said, 'I find this whole subject extremely distasteful.'

'That's the best you can manage, is it? Henry Hargreaves finds the subject *distasteful*, so DC Howell can forget any chance of a career?' It was my turn to push back the chair. 'I can see I've been wasting my time. You've got to have everything on your own terms or you start throwing your toys around like a great big baby in a tweed suit. If you think you can refuse to play just because Lou Golding's the wrong kind of villain, or Mark Howell's face doesn't fit in this cosy boys' club of yours, then it's you that's got your head in the clouds, not me. Why not come down and join the rest of us? Because if you don't, you'll find yourself waking up on the scrapheap one morning, with the mangles and the wind-up gramophones.' I was on my feet. For some reason, my knees felt a little insecure. 'Now if you'll excuse me, I've got duties to attend to.'

Hargreaves didn't budge as I made for the door. There was enough smoke in the room to cure kippers.

Then I heard him say, 'How's your mother?'

I said, 'Ill,' and left him to his habit and his thoughts.

Matt was sitting, as usual, on the window seat, supporting a mug of tea on his leg. Though it was pleasing to have the old, mud-free Matt restored to us, I doubted whether a change of clothes by itself could obliterate all memory of his recent adventures. Bitter reflection has a way of furring the deductive arteries, so it was little wonder that Matt had still made no sense of Nigel Haig's last utterance. Privately I kept thinking he'd do better if he came and sat next to me on the settee. How could we put our heads together with Matt's over there and mine over here? Besides, if he sat closer I might feel able to turn down the gas fire, which was burning decimal currency at the frantic rate familiar from the dear dead duodecimal days beyond recall.

But it wasn't only bitter reflection which could sap deductive power. For the last five minutes I'd thought of little but the intriguing nakedness of my deputy's upper lip, with occasional breaks to admire the mud-free trousers proudly displaying themselves a few feet away. When I tried to return to the problem in hand – easily summarised as, *Why only three?* – but only three what? – I found the entrance locked shut against me. If in spirit Matt was indeed lost somewhere on the Lancashire lanes in hot pursuit of Eileen, then neither of us was doing anything useful at all.

I went to the bedroom to fetch *Moby Dick*, then sat down again and tried to read.

Matt said, 'What on earth are you doing?'

I said, 'I'm trying to read.'

'I can see that. Why?'

'I thought if I stopped trying to solve the riddle I might be able to solve the riddle.'

Matt said, 'That's all right then. For a minute I thought you weren't doing any work.'

'How's it going where you are?'

'Not well. I keep thinking I should have said something to Eileen last night and not just stalked off. I wish I'd given her a piece of my mind, she's got away scot free!'

'But think of it from her side. She's probably been going through hell, and you haven't even noticed.'

'Oh, great, thanks for the sympathy.'

'I mean, her brother's a priest. They're not going to want a dyke in the family, are they?' Then when Matt threw me a distinctly chilly look, I added, 'I'm only trying to help.'

'Then don't. Let me concentrate, this is driving me nuts. *Why only three?* Only three what?'

'Is that as far as you've got?'

He didn't answer. Either he'd finally focused his mind on the job, or he was back in the Lord Derby again having the scales ripped from his reluctant eyes. From time to time he sipped the tea, but it was hard to tell whether these were the sips of a man bright with intellectual fire or a similar-looking man reliving a year-long romance and consumed with regret.

I returned to the book. Unfortunately, I'd arrived at Melville's, or Ishmael's, lengthy defence of the practice of whaling, which subsequent events had rather undermined. I was soon thinking about something else entirely, and after a while the thought formed itself in speech. 'So how did it happen? Did you just bump into Evan Bickerstaff in the street?'

'Ssh! I'm trying to think.'

I shrugged my shoulders, and skipped to the next chapter. But I hadn't read more than a few lines before Matt said, 'When I left the Hen and Chickens, I walked around for ages, up and down the Prom. I thought about going in the Velvet Bar.'

'But you hate it.'

'Yeah. Sort of. Anyway, I couldn't because of the mud. Then I found Evan hanging around by the pier. He was staring at the rubble where the Pavilion used to be. He didn't look very happy.'

'So you thought you'd put a smile on his face.'

Matt didn't respond at first. Then he said, 'I don't think I want to talk about this with you.'

'Why not?'

'We should be working.'

He was right, of course, so once more I tried to read in order to try not to try to solve the Nigel Haig conundrum. But now, perversely, instead of the book distracting me from the riddle, the riddle kept distracting me from the book. *Why only three?* Only three what? I couldn't work it out, and I couldn't read either. I threw the book aside and said, 'Oh, for Pete's sake.'

Matt said, 'I thought Melville was supposed to be your favourite writer.'

'He is. Or he will be, if I can finish this flaming book.'

'*Moby Dick*'s the only one I've heard of.'

'He wrote quite a lot. I got three out of the library.'

Matt said, 'Why only three?'

'I'm saving my last ticket for one called *The Confidence-Man*, they've ordered it for me. Great title, isn't it?'

I paused. While it would be wrong to claim that my assistant always hung on my every word, or even on alternate ones, at present he wasn't hanging on any of them. Instead, his gaze rested in mid-air somewhere beyond my shoulder, gripped by a vision which he alone could see. I said, 'Hello? Is there anybody there?'

Partly back amongst us, Matt said, 'Giles Rawley was a big reader, yes?'

'That's right. There isn't much to do at the Marine Lodge, he got through books like sweets.'

'So if he had four library tickets like everyone else, why were there only three books by his bed?'

I got up and attempted to pace. I said, 'Those books on the floor of Nigel's bedroom – '

'We thought there must have been a struggle when Nigel was taken, but he was leaving you a message. There wasn't time to write a note, he just pulled them off the shelves. *Books.* Only three books!'

I saw a possible snag. 'There was blood all over Edith Evans.'

'What?'

'The top book in the pile.'

'That doesn't mean anything. The killer could easily have

removed a book from lower down, or it may have been somewhere else in the room altogether when Rawley was killed.'

I gave up pacing, or shuffling, and went to turn off the fire.

Matt said, 'Are we going somewhere?'

'Of course we are. This may not be significant, but we've got to find out.'

Matt slipped down from the seat. 'What book could be so dangerous that Giles Rawley had to be murdered just for reading it?'

Though Rawley might not be the first person to die because of a book, I remained sceptical. Things like that didn't happen in Southaven, unless perhaps the world was changing and Southaven wasn't Southaven any more.

But at least I knew now what we had to do. I dug out my one remaining library ticket, stuffed it in a pocket, and shooed Matt ahead of me out of the door.

It was time to track down the fourth book.

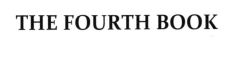

# THE FOURTH BOOK

## twenty-five

Curiosity propelled us at speed along the Boulevard. Queues had formed outside some of the banks, which had been closed for several days to facilitate the currency switchover. The newspapers had predicted trouble, and extra police were in evidence, patrolling on foot instead of hurtling past in panda cars like they usually did.

Our visit to Southaven Central Library, which stood on the Boulevard a few doors south of the Town Hall, was short and productive. Confronted with one of the less approachable members of the library staff, I chose to deal with *The Confidence-Man* first – it turned out that the book had been waiting for me for almost a week – and then set Matt on her.

There was nothing smarmy about my second-in-command. Nor would I have described him as oily, greasy, or ingratiating. It was true that the teeth flashed, and upon some of us the eyes cast a certain spell, but none of this explained why Matt could charm the birds out of the trees and I couldn't. His secret lay in the great void in his personality where guile should have been. Even when required to fib, something occasionally forced on him by his line of work, he fibbed with absolute sincerity.

But in tackling the librarian, a woman of years and experience, Matt saw no need for such subterfuge, falling back instead on his favourite tactic: a ruthless deployment of the unvarnished truth. When I saw that he meant to risk all on this flimsy device, I shook my head internally. The woman would be sure to see right through it, and pitch us empty-handed out of doors.

Though naturally I was anxious to know whether the fourth book existed, and if so what it was, it still annoyed me when the librarian acceded immediately to Matt's request and produced Giles Rawley's four tickets, with the book slips tucked neatly inside them. I could have tried a dozen cunning ruses and still got nowhere. Worst of all, so familiar was this smooth path to him that Matt wasn't even looking pleased with himself.

She read out the titles one by one. We had no interest in Dame Edith, nor in Olivia de Havilland, nor in McKechnie's *Popular Entertainments Through The Ages*. But when she read the fourth title a thrill of triumph shook me. Without looking at me, Matt touched my hand to show that he'd understood.

I said, 'Do you have another copy in the library?'

'I'm afraid not. We had to order this one from Liverpool.' The woman seemed keen to help. I began to wonder whether the frostiness I'd originally detected had all been in my head.

Then something I'd heard recently came back to me. 'Where can I find the contact details for local clubs and societies? You do keep them here, don't you?'

They did, and we came away with a telephone number. I wanted to drop in at the office and try it straight away, but Matt insisted we went back to Leigh Terrace. On the way to the library he'd glanced up Marine Approach, and an idea had occurred to him which he wanted to pursue in my copy of Bradley.

In the flat, I saw no point in making tea, or taking off my coat, or lighting the hungry fire again. If things went well, we'd not be staying long. I was too excited to sit properly, so while Matt slumped on the settee studying Bradley I perched on the arm beside him with the phone on my knee, and put the call through.

A woman answered. No, her husband wasn't in, he'd not be back until tea-time. What was it about, perhaps she could help? I didn't quite tell her the unvarnished truth, but I told her enough to make her say, with an appealing laugh, 'Oh, you don't want Alan! He's the best in town if you need your brickwork pointing, but Alan's never read a book in his life! You should talk to the archivist.' And after a pause while she looked it up, she gave me the number.

The archivist had the dusty voice of a man waist-deep in works of reference, but he sprang to life immediately on learning that my enquiry touched his specialist subject. Yes, he had the book there, he'd read it himself when it came out a couple of years before.

Would I like to come round and take a look? I asked him to put it aside for me, but in the meantime I needed to know only one thing. I told him a story.

He said, 'Yes! It's all in the book. There's a few details different, perhaps, but – '

'Sam – ' Matt was tugging at the back of my coat.

To the archivist I said, 'Thanks, you've been really helpful.'

He said, 'Not at all, it's what we're here for.'

'Sam!' More tugging.

Wishing the archivist every success with the group, I rang off and put the phone down on the floor.

Matt said, 'Have you seen this?'

I swivelled round onto one buttock, and found that Matt was waving Bradley at me. I said, 'It's Bradley's *History of Southaven*. I've seen it thousands of times. Come to that, so have you.'

'I don't mean that, I mean *this*.' And he stuck a particular page under my nose.

I took the book from him. He'd picked out the photograph of the track at the top of Marine Approach, the one I'd been looking at myself the evening before. 'What about it?'

'Look at the café on the left. What does it say above the windows?'

'It says, -EL DINING ROOMS.' From the photographer's vantage point, that was as much of the establishment's name as you could see.

'And what do you think the complete name is?'

'I don't know – Mabel? Hazel? Strudel?'

Matt made that annoying face, the one where he thinks he knows something. 'What if it's GRAND HOTEL?'

That thrill again, for the second time within an hour. Much more along the same lines and I'd be joining my mother in the cardiac unit. 'Grand Hotel Dining Rooms!' Thoughts spun off in all directions. 'They'd have needed access from somewhere in the hotel, under the pavement.'

Matt said, 'Mickey Golding changed the Red Barrel twice.'

I remembered now that on the night of the raid, when the constable had stepped into the Vaults and boomed out his instructions, Mickey had supposedly been down in the cellar changing the Red Barrel. But what if he'd really gone below to warn the staff and punters in the old dining rooms concealed beneath the road?

Matt said, 'What do you think they've got down there?'

'There's only one way to find out.' I stood up, but when Matt stood up too I said, 'You're not coming.'

'What! You can't leave me out of this!'

'It could be dangerous. If they're holding Nigel and Dennis there'll be security, I don't want you running up against Joe Braithwaite's Neanderthals.'

'You'd be mad to go there on your own!'

I harrumphed. 'And this from a Standish! But I won't be on my own, I'll have Mickey with me.'

'I know he's your boyfriend, but you seem to have forgotten he'll be fighting on the wrong side.'

Matt had a point. I was taking a chance, relying on my instincts, and they'd let me down often enough before. I said, 'He's not my boyfriend, I dumped him last night.' Well, some of that was true. 'Anyway, I'm not arguing with you. See if you can find Mark Howell and tell him what's going on.'

Still sulking about being excluded from the serious action, Matt set off for the police station. There was no one I'd sooner have had alongside me in a scrap, but I daren't risk a repeat of the previous summer's farrago. I still bore the scars where Matt's mother had set about me at the hospital while he lay fighting off an early date with death.

I took the Minx, parked behind the Marine Lodge, then walked round onto Marine Approach and in through the main entrance of the Grand Hotel. Carlo, the manager, stood chatting with the receptionist. I wasn't sure whether he knew who I was, but I gave him a friendly smile in any case. There was a fair possibility he'd be out of a job by lunchtime and I wanted him to enjoy his last minutes. I trotted down the steps towards the toilets, then cut along the corridor to the interior entrance to the Vaults. I tried the handle but the door was locked. Familiar music seeped out from within, and I wondered what the source might be. There was no juke box in the Vaults, and the piped music polluting the hotel's public spaces was also wisely excluded from this more humble environment.

Pressing my nose against the glass panel, I could see Mickey behind the bar, setting up for the late morning session. I tapped on the glass, and when he failed to respond I tapped again, with feeling. He looked round then, and I was sorry to discover that Mickey had now joined the great mass of humanity who greet my appearance with open disappointment. Nevertheless, he came over and unbolted the door to let me in.

I've never quite grasped the point of classical music. In fact I've sometimes wondered whether the whole thing might be one gigantic spoof, with the players sniggering behind their music stands when they see the audience falling for it yet again. But I can still recognize a tune when I hear one, and I now identified the music-while-you-work which Mickey had chosen as the *1812 Overture*, currently labouring its way through the preliminary stages before Tchaikovsky really gets stuck in. A tape recorder stood on the work surface beneath the spirit optics, its reels gently rotating. The volume level was set too high for the machine's internal speakers, and I dreaded to think how they'd cope with what lay ahead.

Mickey and I stood near the door, each waiting for the other to speak first. Eventually, Mickey said, 'Did you see *The Music Lovers* yet? A bit over the top. I used to quite fancy that Richard Chamberlain in *Doctor Kildare*, but he makes a rubbish Tchaikovsky.'

I said, 'Mickey – I'm sorry about last night.' He looked unimpressed. 'In fact, I'm sorry about everything. You deserve someone who's really – ' I hit an obstacle there. I wasn't sure yet what Mickey did or didn't deserve.

He said, 'As it happens, Sam, I'm busy.'

I was meant to feel the chill of that, and I did. I said, 'But I deserved better from you, too.'

'How do you work that out?'

'You kept asking me to trust you, but you don't even know who you are. It's decision time, Mickey. Are you just another cog in the

Golding machine, or are you a man in your own right? We can still be friends if you want. It's your choice.'

He looked up at the wall clock. 'I ain't got time for this.'

Hoping that wouldn't be Mickey's last word on the subject, I said, 'I've come to collect your guests.'

'Guests, what guests? What are you talking about?'

'Somewhere out there under the road you're holding two people in that private club you claim to know nothing about. It's over, Mickey. You're busted.'

There was a brief delay while Mickey took this in. 'Have you come on your own? You're pushing your luck a bit.'

'Like I said, Mickey, it's decision time. I've seen a new side to Lena this past twenty-four hours, and you two are more alike than I'd realized. I reckon you're going to help me.'

Another anxious pause followed. I could see Mickey wasn't happy about this latest turn of events, but I still had no idea whether I was dealing with friend or foe.

Then, without speaking, Mickey went back behind the bar and lifted the trapdoor. He stood above the empty space and looked at me evenly. The horn calls had started. Any minute now, cannon would be blasting out across Marine Approach. Mickey said, 'After you.'

A steep wooden stairway took me down into the half-darkness, the reek of damp and history growing stronger with each step. My eyes had barely begun to adapt to the gloom when Mickey joined me on the flag-stoned floor, and with a low hum modern strip-lighting flickered into life. Metal kegs stood piled against the wall, while those currently in use were ranged in a line beneath the bar, linked by tubes to the upper world. It only needed Peter Cushing in a blood-stained coat to suggest some cheap remake of *Frankenstein*. Fresh white paint covered the cellar walls, but a door at the far side had been left its original varnished brown. Above the lintel, a sign in faded gold script read *To The Dining Rooms*. Mickey opened it, went through, and flicked on another switch.

I followed, shutting the door behind me. Tchaikovsky's mad cannonade was barely audible now. I whispered, 'Where are we?'

Mickey said, 'It's all right, no one can hear you. We're under the pavement. Come on.'

The walls here were wood-panelled to dado height, with a white vaulted ceiling, low but not oppressive. Fittings on the wall held ancient and redundant oil lamps, one or two of them missing now. In a few yards we came to a broader passageway, running across us. I said, 'Where does that come from? I presume there's an entrance from that office in the casino, where you and I – '

'The casino was all kitchens in the old days. There's a door behind the office shelves, you heard someone going past in the corridor that night. But the one we use most is from Carlo's flat, out in the yard. Used to be part of the stable block.'

'So punters coming down here need never go into the hotel at all.'

'That's right. Ain't no one going to notice if Carlo has a few personal visitors. It's this way.'

We turned towards the sea, at least if my sense of direction wasn't playing me false. At the end, the corridor angled to the right. We must be under the road now. Ahead of us stood another varnished door topped by another sign, modern this time. It read, THE OYSTER BAR. I was about to comment when Mickey put a finger to his lips. I mouthed, 'Who's in there?'

Mickey mouthed something back, but when after several attempts he'd failed to make me understand what he meant, he resorted to mime, giving a very creditable impression of First Ugly Bloke's lumbering waddle. I said, or whispered, 'We can take him,' but Mickey gave no response. If he intended to fight for team Rigby once we were inside, he was certainly being coy about it. Then Mickey opened the door for me, and I stepped in.

There was only just time for me to observe that there were three people in the room before ordnance of a smaller but more alarming nature than mere Russian cannon came into play, and a bullet ripped apart the door jamb to the left of me. I turned and fled, treading on at least three of Mickey's feet in the process, then slammed the door shut and threw the heavy bolt which someone had thoughtfully installed above the handle. Mickey and I came to a halt side by side, pressed back against the corridor wall and breathing hard. We glanced occasionally towards the door, as if one of First Ugly Bloke's most celebrated skills was the ability to walk through solid matter.

Mickey said, 'She's only gone and given him a fucking shooter! She's off her fucking trolley!' From this, it was easy to judge the strength of Mickey's feelings, since he was normally as much a stranger to effing as he was to blinding.

I said, 'Haven't you seen it before?'

'No I fucking haven't! He must have brought it in this morning. Jesus!' After a moment's thought he added, 'We ought to go.'

'We can't leave those two in there with that maniac waving a gun around. All right, here's the plan. First, we get in, all submissive. Then we split up and try to confuse him – shouldn't be too difficult. When I say *now*, we rush him and get the gun. How about it?'

If I'd hoped for enthusiastic agreement, I was disappointed once again. But then Mickey moved a little closer to the door. He called out, 'Cecil?'

'Go away.'

'It's me, Mickey. Look, Cess, it's all right, yeah? I told Sam he could just pop in for a minute and make sure our guests are OK. Then he'll leave, and he won't tell no one.'

There was a short break for reasoning, but First Ugly Bloke can't have used it very productively because he then said, 'Go away,' again.

Mickey said, 'Cess? He's coming in now, with his hands up, OK? There's two of us and there's only one of him, so don't go making a big drama out of it.'

That last line didn't reassure me, but I told myself it was only what Mickey needed to say if I was to gain access to the room in some other character than Duck on Fairground Stall. There was no answer from the man Cecil, but Mickey still withdrew the bolt and slowly opened the door. With hands raised somewhat half-heartedly, I inched my way over the threshold.

The survival instinct is strong, and although I was keen to confirm who else was present and in what condition, my attention inevitably focused first on the pistol which Cess was pointing at me. In my day, hardly anyone on the Southaven force was put through the firearms training, and as a result I knew nothing at all about the weapon I was looking at beyond the fact that it was apparently loaded and could do nasty things to wood at ten paces. To respect its potential seemed the wisest course, especially since I felt no such respect for the hand which held it. I gathered from Cess's awkward stance that he'd not done the training either, and hadn't expected to find himself using the pistol in anger on its first day at work. But it would be wrong to pretend that having this new power at his disposal made him nervous. Some people enjoy having a gun in their hand, and Cess was clearly one of them.

Having learned what little it could about the gun, my eye moved on to the other occupants of the room. Dennis sat perforce in a chair to my right. I say perforce because he was tied to it. He looked morose, but then he always looked morose, and if he was afraid it certainly didn't show. Off to my left, seated in pyjamas and dressing gown beside an elegant roulette table, Nigel Haig appeared to be making calculations on a notepad. Without looking at me, he said, 'Did you get my message?'

'I did, thanks. You were right, you'd cracked the case.'

'Who was it, then?'

First Ugly Bloke, perhaps annoyed by the half-heartedness I mentioned before, now said to me, 'Stick 'em up. Properly.'

I stuck 'em up properly. Then I said to Nigel, 'What are you doing?'

'Trying to work out a system. It's got to be possible to beat this thing. Only I'm having to do all the sums the long way, it's really irritating.'

'Has Mickey been looking after you?'

'This is the first I've seen of him. Someone called Carlo's been playing host. Stocky chap with a Welsh accent.'

Mickey had moved towards Nigel, passing beyond the line of fire of First Ugly Bloke, who seemed unconcerned by this action on the part of an ally. I said to Mickey, 'Now I understand why your mother brought her own contractors up from London to do the work.'

'Local builders would have gossiped. What do you think of it?'

The note of pride was unmistakable.

'I'm impressed.' And I was. The room was larger than I'd expected, and much better appointed, more or less in the style of its counterpart in the hotel. In addition to the roulette table, there were card tables, a couple of dining tables, plush settees, and a small bar in the far corner. Against the wall nearest the main building, two huge classical vases full of dried flowers reposed on classical plinths. But the chief glory and surprise of the décor lay not within the room but beyond it. The old windows had been restored, and the idle punter looked out on an uncanny vision of the past, as half a dozen poor but honest Victorian holiday-makers and a donkey cart made their way beneath electric sunlight towards the beach and the retreating sea. On the opposite side, a shop front had been meticulously recreated under the sign, *T. Cropper, Oyster Merchant*. Although mid-morning traffic must be running above our heads on Marine Approach, sound-proofing ensured that the room remained eerily silent.

I said, 'Whose idea was all this? It's amazing.'

'You'd have to ask the old girl.'

But then the back of my mind lobbed something forward. Chubby Fallon had told me that his grandfather sold oysters up by the Prom. Only a local would have known about this vanished world, and it wasn't much of a stretch to imagine that Fallon's mother might have been a Cropper before she married.

'And where on earth did you find the stuffed donkey?'

Mickey grinned. 'That's my favourite. She's called Clementine.'

Cecil said, 'If you've just come down here to gawp, you can go.'

I said to him, 'Why have you tied up poor Dennis here? You know Mrs Golding doesn't like that kind of thing.' At least poor Dennis wasn't gagged like I had been.

'He tried to escape.'

'He was only showing the proper spirit. But he won't do it again, will he? Not now you've got the gun. What is it, anyway?' I moved a little closer to take a look.

'Get back!' He raised the weapon higher.

I got back, and said to Dennis, 'How are you keeping?'

'Not too bad thanks, Mr Rigby. But there's rents to collect

today, Mr Flint'll be wondering where I've got to.'

Whatever Dennis may have said, it was clear from his oddly nasal delivery that all was not as it should be. It also seemed to me that he had more spots than usual. I said, 'You've got that thing that's going round, haven't you? I warned you on Friday you shouldn't be out without a scarf.'

'I'm fine, honest.' He sneezed. 'When can I leave?'

'Dennis – can I ask you a question?'

'We had enough of that the other day.'

'Suppose – purely hypothetically – suppose your father suddenly turned up out of the blue. How do you think you'd feel about it?'

The reply was immediate. 'I don't need a father. I've always had Mr Flint.' Then while I considered where to go from there, he said, 'I want to blow my nose.'

I appealed to Cecil's better nature. 'Come on, now – why not untie him? You'll not try to get away, will you, Dennis?'

Mickey said, 'He's right, Cess. Untie the man.' Here at last was some slender evidence of Mickey's cooperation.

First Ugly Bloke said to him, 'Do it yourself.'

As Mickey passed behind me, I wandered towards the roulette table, so that Cecil couldn't pose a threat to both me and Mickey at the same time. I said to Nigel Haig, 'You don't seem very concerned by all this.'

Still immersed in his calculations, he said, 'These things happen. How's mum?'

'Disturbed. As a matter of fact, she sacked me.'

'She's always been a hopeless judge of character. You know she's got engaged to the Major?'

'She did happen to mention it.'

'I may have to run away from home. Anyway, I'll be at Uni in the autumn, it's Bobby I feel sorry for.'

Behind me, First Ugly Bloke said, 'That's enough. It's time you cleared off.'

I turned. Dennis, newly released from captivity, was just digging in his pocket for a handkerchief. The plan, if you remember, had been to rush Cecil and get the gun, but it was proving difficult to identify a moment when the damned thing wasn't pointed straight at me. We'd already been made aware of Cecil's advanced trigger-happiness, and I feared that any sudden move would result in my being perforated with extreme prejudice. I caught Mickey's eye over Cecil's shoulder, but couldn't read what, if anything, it was trying to say.

Unexpectedly, Dennis provided the solution. He blew his nose. I'd never heard him perform this act before, so hadn't realized that he was one of those world-class nose-blowers who model their tone on the trombone section of the Grimethorpe Colliery Band. Startled, Cecil wheeled round towards him, and in that moment I shouted, *'Now!'*

No specific training in rushing people had been provided by the Southaven police, but nevertheless I was pretty good at it, and I rushed First Ugly Bloke now as if my life depended on it, which it probably did. Unfortunately, I was the only rusher present. Mickey stood stock still while I hurled myself without restraint against the bloated monolith who'd subjected me to so many indignities in recent days. The impact caused Cecil to rock on his feet, but not to drop the gun. When he noticed Dennis seizing this opportunity and abandoning his chair like the favourite bursting out of the gate at Aintree, Cecil quickly levelled the gun and fired. I smacked the weapon out of his hand, but it was too late. Dennis had gone down.

Cess now went to retrieve his pride and joy, which had landed some distance away, beyond the still stationary form of Mickey. I grabbed the back of Cess's collar with my hand, there being no snooker cue available, and hauled him towards me. He spun round, and, deciding to deal with this irritant once and for all, fetched me a vicious rabbit punch which lifted me off my feet. In the next second I was flat on my back, with First Ugly Bloke coming down on top of me.

I suppose I ought to have been glad that in pursuing his personal vendetta Cecil had prioritised this gun-free approach to violence, but to be honest I'd rather have been shot than forced into the kind of repellent intimacy I was experiencing now. Cecil was astride me, and before I could do anything to defend myself he'd lifted my head with both hands and smashed it back into the floor. This hurt, and dark blobs occluded my vision. When he lifted my head again, it went through my mind that a second blow like that would probably finish me off. I wondered what had become of Matt. It was a shame he'd had to miss the action, he'd have loved every moment. And I wondered if he'd be upset when I was dead or just get another job and carry on as if nothing had happened. His face rose before me, bright in the summer sun. The scent of lime flowers drifted down.

Then the second blow fell.

But this time it had been First Ugly Bloke's head on the receiving end, not mine. Insensible, he slumped sideways, surrounded by shards of classical pottery. I could only imagine what Lou Golding would have to say about this renewed outbreak of vase abuse.

Mickey threw aside the base and said, 'Are you all right?'

I slid out from beneath Cecil's legs. Nigel Haig was crouched beside Dennis, his fingers on Dennis's neck. A pool of blood was spreading on the carpet. Nigel said, 'He's alive. I'll call an ambulance.' He let himself out of the room, and I took his place beside the wounded man.

Mickey said, 'Where's he hit?'

'The right shoulder.' Then I couldn't help adding, 'You took your time.'

'Better late than never.' The line was unoriginal, but also true.

I said, 'Dennis, can you hear me? Just twitch a finger or something.' But nothing twitched and there was no reply. I hoped Nigel Haig wouldn't get lost on his way to the phone. I said to Mickey, 'You've probably got time to disappear if you want.'

He shook his head. 'Wouldn't look good, would it? But thanks for the suggestion.' He glanced over at First Ugly Bloke, then turned back to me again. Lowering his eyes, he said, 'I didn't want to lose you.'

In truth Mickey had lost me before we'd even started, but while I was failing to tell him so the door swung wider open and Nigel Haig came back into the room. He said, 'I met them coming down.' Mark Howell appeared behind him, leading a uniformed officer.

Matt must have been responsible for raising this posse, but that still didn't explain where he was now. I stood up, and had to battle with dizziness for a few moments. I said, 'We need an ambulance.'

Mark said, 'Cilla was with us, I've sent her back to sort it out.' Then he saw the blood and said to me, 'Is this bloke badly hurt?'

'There was only one shot fired, it got him in the shoulder.'

'Who is he, anyway?'

'His name's Dennis. He's a pawn in a property scam Lou Golding's trying to pull.'

Mark transferred his attention to the dormant mass which was Cecil. 'How about that one? Any serious injuries?'

'Don't know. Don't care. He tried to kill me.'

Nigel said, 'Mickey saved Sam's life.'

Mark said, 'How touching.'

'He did, though.' Then to Mickey Nigel said, 'I've heard about you, you're Lena's brother. You've both got the nose.'

Mark had been examining First Ugly Bloke. 'He's breathing, anyway.'

I said, 'What else is happening? Has anyone spoken to Carlo?'

'It was him that gave us directions down here. He could see the game was up.'

'What about Howard Lane? Has he been released yet?'

'They were doing the paperwork when I left the station.'

This was good news. No doubt Howard Lane's first move would be to visit Cordelia at the Marine Lodge. 'Did you find anything in Aznavorian's lock-up?'

'Books. Lots of them, in crates. Nothing special, as far as we could tell, but we're trying to get hold of an expert.'

Mickey said to Mark, 'I'd like to make a statement. Down the nick.'

'Seen the error of your ways, have you?'

'There's no need to get sarcy. I want to talk, that's all.'

To the constable Mark said, 'Harper, escort Mr Golding back to the hotel. He can go to the station with the manager.'

As Mickey passed me he tried to smile, but it didn't work out too well. I felt a stab of regret. I had no idea when I'd see Mickey Golding again, or on what terms. Watching his back disappear round the door, for a moment I seemed to be watching the story of my life. Mark must have seen something in my face, because he said, 'Come on, Sam – he's low-life! He's a Golding, for God's sake.'

I said, 'I'd like to take Nigel back to the Marine Lodge, if that's OK.'

Nigel said, 'I can take myself.'

'I know you can, Nigel, but humour me. I'm trying to crawl back into your mother's good books.'

Mark said, 'We'll need statements from both of you later. But go, if you want.'

'By the way, I know who killed Giles Rawley and Oscar Hammond.'

'What do you mean, *by the way?*'

I couldn't understand why Mark had suddenly become so animated. I said, 'You'd better send a couple of plods over to the Marine Lodge. Oh, and tell Hargreaves that Nigel Haig cracked the case. It's no use saying I had anything to do with it, or he'll take no notice. In fact, he might like to wander over to the Lodge himself, if he's not too busy.'

'Are you all right, Sam? You're talking a bit different.'

'Me? I'm tip-top. Can you lend me an evidence bag?' Puzzled, Mark obliged, and Nigel and I left the room. First Ugly Bloke was just beginning to stir as we made our exit.

We left the same way I'd come in, through the cellar of the Vaults. I didn't want to get tangled up with the rest of the police operation, and besides, this enabled me to switch off Mickey's tape recorder, which was revolving silently now with one spool empty. I unbolted the street door and let us out onto Marine Approach. I said, 'A shame you had to miss your exam.'

'But what a fantastic excuse. Beats "the dog ate my homework," doesn't it?' As we came round onto Wright Street, Nigel said, 'Bobby's going to be livid when she finds out what's happened. "Why couldn't *I* have been kidnapped? It's *so* unfair!"' Apparently his repertoire as an impressionist wasn't limited to Miss Pyle. Then he said, 'You're going to unmask the killer now, aren't you?'

'Do me a favour, Nigel, and stick close to your mother, OK?'

'All right, but why?'

We'd come to the back yard, where an ambulance was just disgorging a very healthy-looking Laurence Glass, complete with bag. I called out, 'Major! Good to see you!'

Nigel whispered, 'Don't say that, he's a prat.'

'Ah! Mr Rigby. Still haunting the premises, are you?'

'Not for much longer. Here, let me take that bag– we don't want you tearing your stitches.'

'Very decent of you.' He turned to Nigel. 'Young man – why are you wandering around in your night clothes at half past eleven?'

Nigel seemed reluctant to respond, so I answered for him. 'He's had an interesting morning. Shall we go in?'

The Wolseley was parked in the yard again, so I knew Alice Haig must have returned from her threatened visit to Lou Golding. We found her in the hallway, having a heated discussion with my assistant while Evan Bickerstaff looked on from behind the counter. As I might have expected, there was a definite smile on Evan's face. When Alice saw me flanked by Nigel and the Major, it was clear that she couldn't decide who to greet first. Wisely, she threw herself at Nigel, who submitted to a fierce embrace. On release, he said, 'Sam saved my life.' Apparently he'd got hold of this life-saving motif somewhere during the course of the morning, and decided to run with it.

Alice Haig said, 'I'm very grateful, Mr Rigby. Forgive me if I spoke hastily before.'

Nigel said, 'The Goldings have got this whole secret casino under the road. It's brilliant!'

The Major said, 'Don't I get a hug too?'

Alice said, 'Your chest, Laurence - or had you forgotten? Welcome home!' She smiled awkwardly, he smiled awkwardly, and they sort of kissed.

Nigel suppressed a grimace and said, 'I want to go and change. Don't start without me!' He ran back down the corridor.

I said, 'Did you have any luck with Lou Golding?'

'Blast the woman! I was told she was in a business meeting. I've been calling her all morning, but no joy.'

The telephone rang. Evan answered it, then handed the receiver to Alice. He said, 'It's Mrs Golding.'

She took it, and the rest of us moved a little way off to give her space. The Major said, 'Perhaps I should go up and unpack.'

Matt said, 'Why not do that later? I expect you'll want to join the others.'

'The others? I don't understand.'

Matt said, 'I'm gathering all the suspects in the lounge.'

I suppose I shouldn't have been surprised, but I said, 'You're doing *what?*'

'I thought you'd want me to! You can't pass up a chance like this! Mrs Haig was furious, she was about to throw me out.'

The Major said, 'I strongly resent being described as a suspect.'

I said, 'I'm sorry, Major, he didn't mean it. Did you, Matt?'

Laurence Glass reconsidered. 'Still, if there's going to be a show I wouldn't care to miss it. I take it there've been developments?'

To the telephone, Alice said, 'The infernal cheek of it! If you want my cooperation, Mrs Golding, then I suggest you come round to the Marine Lodge and ask me in person. Good morning.' And she handed the phone back to Evan.

The Major said, 'What was all that about?'

'It's the most extraordinary thing! She was calling from the Grand – apparently the manager has been arrested on suspicion of false imprisonment. Mrs Golding asked me – can you *believe* that woman? – if I wouldn't mind stepping in and covering for him!'

I drew Matt away while Alice Haig and the Major chewed over this latest slice of Golding chutzpah. I said, 'You're right, of course. Get everyone you possibly can into the lounge. And there might be latecomers. Stay near the door and show them in.'

Matt said, 'You don't look well.'

'Why's everyone so bothered about my health all of a sudden? I've just got to run upstairs for a minute, then I'll be ready to start.' Behind Alice Haig's back, I borrowed a pencil and the master key from Evan. From time to time he threw Matt appreciative glances in which memory and anticipation mingled. I called out to the Major, 'I'll leave the bag outside your door!' He thanked me, and I set off for the back stairs.

When I returned some minutes later, Alice was showing the small, proud figure of Lou Golding into the lounge. Clearly she'd responded to Alice's invitation by turning up for a face-to-face parley. Lou's morning hadn't been going well, and I hoped it would get worse. Matt had taken the usher's position by the door. I explained what I meant to do. Then, since there was still no sign of Howard Lane, I took a minute to call Sidney Flint from the front desk. I hadn't expected his attitude to be friendly, and it wasn't. To hear him go on, you'd have thought I'd shot Dennis myself. When I pointed out that if Dennis hadn't been so desperate to get out collecting rents he'd have come through unscathed, Sidney put the phone down on me.

In the hallway outside the lounge, Matt was talking to Cordelia Lane. I said to her, 'Are your sisters not with you today?'

She pulled a face, devoid of sisterly affection. 'They're where they always are. Shopping.' Then she spotted something behind me, and at once everything else seemed to become invisible to her. I looked round, keen to learn what had wrought this transformation.

Evan Bickerstaff was guiding towards us a tall, silver-haired man in a rumpled suit. WPC Cilla Donnelly followed behind them at a respectful distance. The man had been smiling amiably, but when he saw Cordelia the smile showed signs of faltering and his steps ceased altogether. Husband and wife then appeared to conduct some kind of telepathic tennis match, during which the twin issues of Howard's unfaithfulness and his having spent the last twenty-four hours in police custody were whacked silently back and forth across the net between them. Then Howard Lane said, 'Cordy – I've been an ass.'

Apparently this admission decided the game, because I could sense Cordelia softening beside me. She extended her hand. 'I'm glad you're here, Howard. Let's face this together, shall we?' Howard took the hand, and they walked through into the lounge. On the settee, Miss Pyle had to shift up so that they could sit side by side.

Cilla Donnelly said, 'Are you all right, Sam? You don't quite seem yourself.'

Evidently there was a conspiracy afoot to persuade me that I was ill. As it happened, I wasn't feeling my best, but I put that down to the fact that the suspects were all gathered in the lounge and my public awaited. I wondered if Giles had felt this way in the moments before quitting the safety of the wings to become Vanya or Polonius. I said to Cilla, 'Is Mark coming?'

'He went back to the station.'

I hoped my disappointment didn't show. 'Anyone else?'

She raised an eyebrow at me. 'Like Hargreaves, for example? I couldn't tell you.'

I sighed. There was blood rushing in my head and my heart had chosen this inconvenient moment to take up clog-dancing. Matt said, 'You'd better get on with it or they might turn ugly.' He shepherded Cilla and Evan into the room then smiled at me uncertainly. I wanted to run my finger along his recently denuded upper lip.

I said, 'Are you doing anything this evening? We could go out somewhere if you like, try and make up for last night.'

Matt said, 'I'm seeing Evan.' Then he said, 'Sorry.'

'Of course, of course. Doesn't matter. Some other time. Are we ready, do you think?'

He said, 'As we'll ever be.'

But I wasn't ready at all. My mouth was dry and my legs had got bored with me and gone off to work for someone else. Not that there was much point in having legs when the floor was pitching like the deck of the Isle of Man ferry. 'What if I make a tit of myself?' This was almost certainly what people like Cilla, or Evan, or Lou Golding, were confidently expecting of me, though it wasn't really them I was bothered about.

Matt said, 'Don't worry.' He touched my wrist. 'I won't care. It's not important.' He was looking hard at me, but I couldn't read him. Then he said, 'Look – I don't have to see Evan tonight if you don't want.'

'No – no, if you've got plans that's OK.' I took a deep breath. I could have done with a cigarette but I'd left them in the kitchen drawer. I said, 'No use prolonging the agony, is it?' Then I turned from Matt abruptly and stepped into the room.

The show was about to begin.


## twenty-six


For a Monday, it was a pretty good house.

Seated in the armchair near the window, the one in which Giles had enjoyed his birthday tea, was the Major, with Evan standing beside him in his usual self-effacing manner. Also in armchairs were Lou Golding and Alice Haig, while Nigel Haig kept watch on his mother from an upright chair beside the buffet table. Opposite, with one elbow on the writing table, Lena Golding waited impatiently to learn why her kitchen duties had been interrupted. Cilla Donnelly stood next to her. As I said, the settee held Howard and Cordelia Lane, together with Miss Pyle, who was looking down, perhaps with envy, at the couple's entwined hands. We were missing only Sarkis Aznavorian (whereabouts unknown) and Bobby Haig, about to commence the last lesson of the morning at Shoreside High School.

Strictly speaking, of course, we were also missing Giles Rawley and Oscar Hammond, but that was why we were all here.

Leaving Matt to take care of the door, I advanced a few feet into the room, coming to a halt in the magic spot where I could see and be seen by everyone. The hum of conversation died away. Laurence Glass said, 'Will this take long? I need to phone my sister in Broadstairs.'

Though she still wore the mulberry suit, Miss Pyle seemed to have shrunk since the last time I'd seen her. She said to the Major, 'I do believe Mr Rigby has solved the case.'

Cordelia said, 'Is that right? Do you know who did it?'

Reflecting that Giles Rawley had never had to take questions from the audience before beginning his performance, I said, 'Yes and no.'

Irritated, Cordelia said, 'You realize you're keeping us all from lunch?'

Miss Pyle said, 'I thought you'd got to the bottom of it!'

I said, 'I know who the killer is, but I don't know who they are.' This prompted a general murmur of exasperation. If I didn't get a grip soon, people might start walking out.

Lou Golding looked at her watch and said, 'I've got a business to run.'

'I wouldn't be too sure, if I were you. We're old-fashioned in Southaven, we don't take kindly to threats and blackmail.'

Lou was smiling, as far as she was able. 'I told you before, this town's going to have to change. We're doing things my way now.'

'The law's not going to turn a blind eye to abduction and attempted murder.'

'I'm as shocked as anyone to learn that such things could happen in my own hotel. But I think you'll find there's nothing to link me personally to these – ' She hunted for the word. 'These – regrettable crimes.'

Cordelia Lane said, 'I don't see what this has to do with my father.'

'Or with Oscar.' This had come from Lena Golding. I saw now that her eyes were red-rimmed from weeping, or lack of sleep, or both. It was possible that she cared more than anyone present what might result from this assembly.

I said to Lena, 'Let's clear something up first. Was it you who asked Oscar to defect to the Grand?'

She shook her head. 'That was Carlo. But Oscar would never have abandoned Mrs Haig, she'd been good to him, her husband had been good to him.'

'Was Carlo acting on his own initiative?'

Lou Golding said, 'If you're trying to say that I put him up to it, why shouldn't I? I've been trying to put the screws on the Marine Lodge for weeks, everyone knows it. And I ain't got nowhere. Now I'm thinking there might be another way forward for me and Alice.'

Coolly, Alice Haig said, 'I'll thank you to call me Mrs Haig, if you don't mind.'

'Suit yourself. But we've still got lots to talk over, you and me.'

'I'm afraid that came to an end when you kidnapped my son.'

'Kidnapped? We just borrowed him for a few hours, that's all.'

Nigel now piped up. 'Mrs Golding, is there any chance you'd let me have access to the roulette table again?'

Alice said, 'Nigel!'

'But mum, I'm working on this system.'

Lou Golding said, 'I'll get you together with my croupier, if you like. He's hanging around on half pay until I can fix the licence.'

'Nigel, I forbid you to go anywhere near that hotel!'

Such enthusiastic audience participation might be all very well in panto, but it was forcing me off-script. I said, 'Could you all concentrate, please, and cast your minds back to last Thursday. Mrs Lane – '

'Yes?' She seemed startled at being picked out like this.

'I believe you and your father were having a difficult time.'

'Not exactly. It was a misunderstanding, that's all.'

'He'd just cut you out of his will, he was demanding that you leave your husband. That's some misunderstanding. You fought with him.'

'He wouldn't tell me what it was all about!'

'Then I will. Giles had had a letter from his former housekeeper, written on her deathbed, claiming that it was your husband who'd arranged the theft of his coin collection.'

Cordelia was thunderstruck. Her jaw hung open, and the plump hand withdrew itself from Howard Lane's. When she'd recovered the power of speech, she said, 'Howard? Is this true?'

Smoothly, he said, 'What – about the coins, or the letter?' Then noticing that such fine distinctions appeared to be lost on his wife, he continued. 'That awful woman did send him a letter, yes. Making allegations which I have to say are totally groundless. Your father rang me and cut up rough about it, wanted me to leave you and have nothing more to do with the family. All on the word of a servant! I told him to go to hell.'

I said, 'He didn't mention that he intended to cut you both out of his will?'

Howard Lane said, 'The first I knew about that was when Cordy rang me from here, the day she arrived.'

'Which would have given you plenty of time to make a plan.'

'Plan? What plan?'

'You'd already trained the au pair to cover for your absences, because of the affair you've been having. All you needed to do was drive up from Reigate, remove a hammer from Ian Haig's workshop, climb the back stairs, and end the life of a man who'd been nothing but a thorn in your side for years, and whose only benefit to you was the prospect of an inheritance.'

Cordelia had backed away, into the arm of the settee. 'Howard?'

Howard Lane flushed. 'You can't think – I mean, you *know* I'm not capable of such a thing!' He tried to take his wife's hand, but she pulled violently away. 'I'm no saint, Cordy, I've never pretended I was. But to do something like that – '

Miss Pyle said, 'But Mr Rigby, Giles had changed his will already. What use would it be for Mr Lane to kill him?'

I'd put considerable thought into all this, and found it gratifying that at least one person was following the plot.

Lena said, 'And my Oscar – Mr Lane didn't even know him, it don't make no sense.'

Evan Bickerstaff said, 'What about the note?' He clearly subscribed to the universal opinion that our own part in any affair is bound to be the most significant.

I said, 'Yes, you're right, all of you. But we need to go back to the will. Miss Pyle – '

It was Rosemary Pyle's turn to be startled by this direct address. 'Oh – yes, Mr Rigby?'

'Mr Aznavorian and yourself both told me that you knew nothing of the contents. That's not true, though, is it?'

Miss Pyle wrestled visibly with her sense of loyalty to absent friends. She said, 'Really, I didn't see anything.'

'But Mr Aznavorian?'

She hesitated for a moment, then said, 'I'm afraid – oh, dear – I'm afraid he may just have caught a glimpse.'

'Tell us how it happened.'

'We were up in Giles's room. I'd already witnessed Giles's signature on the will, and Sarkis was about to do the same when a call came through from reception. It was the courier from Giles's solicitor's. He'd taken himself off somewhere for a cup of tea, and come back earlier than Giles was expecting. Well, Giles had his back to us, and I was looking at him, wondering what the call was about. But then I did just happen to glance round, and Sarkis was – well, he was tidying the documents, as if he'd somehow disarranged them. I think he must have taken a quick peek. But he understood things like that, he could have picked out the main points in a few moments.'

'Did you ask him about it later?'

'Heavens, no! It would have been far too embarrassing.'

'So we have to assume that Mr Aznavorian knew something of the contents of Giles Rawley's will.'

Still hot on the scent, Miss Pyle said, 'But Sarkis wasn't a beneficiary either.'

'That's right. So it seems that no one knew the details of the will except for Mr and Mrs Lane and Sarkis Aznavorian, but none of them stood to gain by Giles Rawley's death. The only person who did gain, financially, was Mrs Haig.'

Alice Haig, who'd been observing the proceedings in a rather detached way, as if she was merely a guest in her own hotel, now roused herself and said to the room at large, 'But I had no idea all that money was coming to me.' Then she appealed to me personally. 'You know how shocked I was, I told you at the time.'

'And I believed you. It was a very convincing performance, but a performance is all it was. Because you did know, didn't you, Mrs Haig?'

This created something of a sensation, especially when Alice Haig didn't immediately leap to dispute my claim. There was a good deal of shifting in seats, and Lou Golding gave her business rival a look marked by fresh admiration. Only Evan seemed to have failed to grasp the implications, perhaps because this new information had nothing to do with the note. Nigel Haig, his face stricken with anxiety, said, 'Mum?'

Alice chose to bluster. 'This is all nonsense! How could I possibly have known? Giles would never have told me, it would have seemed as if he was trying to buy my affection. He was far too much of a gentleman.'

Standing in one spot for so long had begun to disagree with me, so now I walked a few paces this way and that to loosen my joints and my thinking. I said, 'You know, I couldn't understand why you were so lenient with your night porter, Graham Leeds. Quite apart from the fact that he was rubbish at his job, he'd handed over the Marine Lodge's financial secrets to Mrs Golding. By rights, you should have thrown him out on his ear.'

'I told you the reason. My late husband would not have wanted me to be harsh.'

'So it had nothing to do with the fact that Graham Leeds had overheard Mr Aznavorian telling you about the will?'

Another sensation. Miss Pyle said, 'But why would Sarkis do that? He was normally so discreet about money.'

'It was an accident. He wrongly assumed that Mrs Haig was already aware of it. You all knew that the Marine Lodge was in financial difficulties, and Mr Aznavorian's history made him particularly anxious about the threat of the hotel suddenly closing, leaving him homeless. Late one evening, about ten days ago, he found himself alone with Mrs Haig in the hallway. He asked her outright how serious the problems were, and she was honest with him. She painted a pretty bleak picture.'

Alice Haig objected. 'The Marine Lodge is a perfectly sound business.' And she gave a quick squint sideways towards Lou Golding.

'But perhaps you'd had a bad day, and in any case this was before your bank loan had been agreed. Aznavorian could see how low you were, and he tried to make helpful suggestions, all of which you dismissed. So finally, in desperation, he pointed out the light at the end of the tunnel. He said Giles Rawley couldn't last for ever. Then it all came out.'

On several occasions during our brief acquaintance, Alice had looked at me as if I'd just made a nasty scratch on her favourite Frankie Vaughan LP. Her expression now went far beyond that. The mask she'd been raised to wear fell aside, treating me to my first glimpse of another Alice Haig, one whose behaviour would be harder to predict. She said, 'I don't recall your having been present on that occasion, Mr Rigby. You seem to be letting your imagination run away with you.'

'I'm only reporting what I was told by Graham Leeds. He was in the office at the time, setting up for the night's shift. He'd arrived a little early, you'd no idea he was there, and he said nothing about it until you tried to sack him yesterday morning. Then he pointed out that it wouldn't look good for you if the police discovered you'd known about the will all along.' To squeeze these juicy facts from the night porter over the phone, I'd had to threaten a personal visit which he would never forget. But this wasn't the moment to publicize my methods.

Bluster having failed, Alice now blew up. 'All right! So I knew about the will. Is that a crime? If I'd told the Detective Inspector about it, I'd have been thrown in the cells before I knew what had hit me.'

Howard Lane said, 'I don't recommend it. The food's shocking.'

'I couldn't take the risk, I'm needed here, running the hotel! But if you think that I could possibly have *killed* Giles – ' She came to a halt, struggling to express herself with the force the occasion demanded. 'I am not a murderer! Laurence – you know me better than anyone. Tell them!'

But the Major didn't tell them. Instead, Evan said, 'What about the note?'

Sensing activity behind me, I turned to find Mark Howell entering the room. He said, 'Could I have a word?' and led me out into the corridor, where I saw that he'd brought another uniformed officer with him. If I'd expected the assembled crowd to break out in a babble of discussion, they now confounded me by maintaining a tense silence. I said to Mark, 'What is it? I'm just getting to the important bit!'

'Sorry to break your flow, but I thought you'd want to know what's happened. Superintendent Sturges has resigned, with immediate effect.'

I could hardly believe what I was hearing. 'Resigned?'

'Resigned. Stepped down, quit, thrown in the towel – '

'Yes, all right, I get the idea. Have you seen Hargreaves?'

'He's pacing around the station, smoking enigmatically. Why, do you think he had something to do with this?'

I did, but I didn't say so. 'Are you staying for the last act?' Leaving the constable outside, Mark and Matt both came back into the room with me, and Matt closed the doors. The others sat down, and I resumed my former position.

I said, 'This won't mean anything to most of you, but an era in the history of the Southaven police has just come to an end. Superintendent James Sturges has resigned his post.'

I'd directed this information at Lou Golding. She said nothing, but I could see her mind working frantically. If it was Sturges who'd been protecting her interests, she'd need to come up with a new strategy, and fast.

I said, 'To return to Evan's question.' Evan looked astonished by this move. Up to that point, he'd probably lumped me in with that overwhelming majority of people who took no notice at all of anything he did or said. 'Evan, of course, has a point. What about the note? We need to go back to last Thursday afternoon again. Giles Rawley had discovered something which he wanted to share with Oscar Hammond in private. As we've just seen in the matter of the will, the hotel's a bad place for confidences, and otherwise Giles and Oscar only used to meet in the Grand Hotel Vaults, which is probably worse. Rawley's discovery was of such importance that he decided to write Oscar a note and take it along to Oscar's home late that night. But he bumped into Evan in the yard and delegated the task to him, after which Evan accidentally posted the note through the wrong door.'

Careful of his reputation, Evan said, 'I'd got stuff on my mind.' No one took any notice.

'By the time Oscar received the letter, more than a day late, Giles was already dead. The envelope was in Oscar's pocket when he himself died, but the actual note's never turned up. Luckily, though, he'd taken it to the Infirmary on Saturday afternoon and told the Major about it. So we know what it said, don't we, Major?'

Laurence Glass nodded. 'In outline, yes. Somehow Giles had found out that Oscar was seeing Lena Golding.'

Lou Golding stepped in. 'I couldn't believe it when Mickey told me last night.' She turned towards her daughter. 'Oscar

Hammond! A cook at the Marine Lodge, of all places!'

'Not a cook, Mum, a chef. He was a chef.'

'And the state of the man – four stone overweight, and a face like a raspberry mousse! With your looks you could have anyone you want.'

I said, 'Major, you were telling us about the note.'

'That's right. Alice had asked Giles to do some sleuthing over at the Grand.'

Alice Haig said, 'It was foolish of me. I hadn't realized it could be dangerous.'

Laurence Glass continued. 'At any rate, he must have been successful, because in the note he warned Oscar to distance himself from the Goldings. I presume he'd unearthed something pretty significant.'

I said, 'In which case it's easy to see why the Goldings might want Giles out of the way.' Lou Golding seemed about to interrupt, but I went on. 'Lena – did you ever notice Giles snooping, asking awkward questions about the business?'

She frowned. 'Not exactly. Once or twice he tried to lead me on to say something. We'd be chatting, you know, mucking about, and then he'd suddenly pretend to be horrified that he was hob-nobbing with this – what did he call me? – this *underworld moll*, that's what he said. He was quaint, the things he came out with. Then he said he'd bet good money I had dark secrets. You know, like he wanted me to spill the beans. I never said nothing, though.'

'Mrs Golding – did you ever hear of Giles Rawley poking around in the hotel's affairs?'

'I can't say as I did. My staff report back to me personally. If there'd been anything like that going on, I'd have been told.'

I said, 'Puzzling, isn't it? It seems that Giles had done barely any sleuthing at all, yet it seems he'd managed to discover something so incriminating that he felt he must warn Oscar about it. But wouldn't he be worried that Oscar might tip the Goldings off? And even if we assume that someone acting for the Goldings killed Giles and Oscar – '

Lou Golding said, 'I've had enough of this! We never had nothing to do with it.'

'But even if that did happen, why would they also attempt to kill the Major at the Infirmary on Friday night, *before* he knew anything about Giles's investigations?'

Laurence Glass said, 'Perhaps they supposed he would confide in me.'

'Really? When everyone knew that Giles couldn't stand the sight of you?'

'I say – that's a little strong.'

Alice Haig said, 'It was banter between them, that's all.'

To my surprise, Evan Bickerstaff now spoke up again, and on a subject other than the note too. 'You're wrong! Mr Rawley hated the Major. I heard them arguing, the afternoon he died. He seemed to think the Major would be leaving soon, he said it would be good riddance.'

Mark Howell said, 'Why on earth haven't you mentioned this before? Didn't you realize it might be important?'

Evan looked wounded. 'I never thought you'd be interested. They were always arguing, ask anyone.'

I said, 'Major – do you happen to remember what that particular disagreement was about?'

'To be frank, he'd seen that Alice and I were getting on well and he didn't like it. Sheer childish jealousy.'

'Weren't you afraid he might try to drive a wedge between you?'

'But how? What could he possibly have done?' He smiled complacently at Alice, and she returned a smile of perfect understanding. 'We're in love, Mr Rigby. Giles could grumble all he liked, it wouldn't have made the least difference.'

All this time, the evidence bag I'd borrowed from Mark, together with its contents, had been burning a hole in my pocket. I should probably have brought it out earlier, but I'd hoped it wouldn't be necessary. Now I removed it and held it up for everyone to see.

Alice Haig said, 'Is that our writing paper?'

Mark Howell said, 'Have you found the note?'

The bag contained a single sheet of Marine Lodge notepaper, shaded in pencil on one side. I said, 'Giles Rawley wrote the note to Oscar in biro, in his usual firm hand. The rack of paper in his room is exactly like the one over there.' I indicated the writing table where Lena Golding was sitting. 'When he wrote the note, he took all the paper out of the rack, so that he'd have something to lean on. Afterwards, he put the unused sheets back. This is the one from the top.'

Miss Pyle said, 'You've rubbed over it in pencil, so you can see the impression! You clever thing!'

Mark Howell said, 'What does it say?'

I turned to the Major. 'Well, Major. What does it say?'

Laurence Glass chose not to speak. Alice's expression had clouded, and I was pleased to see that Nigel was keeping a close eye on his mother as I'd requested.

I said, 'One thing it certainly doesn't talk about is the Goldings. That's right, isn't it, Major? That whole saga of yours was an invention, like everything else you've told us. You needed to divert suspicion onto someone plausible: why not the Goldings, who already had a bad name? You thought you'd be safe, because you asked Oscar to let you keep the note and think about it for a while. I dare say we'll never find the original, but we do have this.' And I dangled the bag by way of illustration.

Laurence Glass smiled thinly and shook his head. 'You should be careful what you're saying. I believe it's you who's making up stories, Mr Rigby.'

I said, 'Giles Rawley had probably realized that there was something wrong about you from the start. He was an actor, he knew the tricks, he could see what you are – a confidence man. If you'd not had your sights on Mrs Haig he might have let it go, but he couldn't risk her getting hurt. He suspected your whole spiel was phoney, that you'd probably not been in the army, that you'd certainly never been in Burma during the war. All he needed was proof. He decided to read up on the subject, to try and catch you out. He borrowed a book from the library – '

Matt said, '*A Decent War – living and dying on the Burma railway*, by Fred Michie.' He'd been sitting very quietly, and if I knew anything about him he was probably a bit bored.

I said, 'You used the expression yourself the first time we saw you at the Infirmary – you said you'd gone out East expecting a decent war. But that wasn't the only thing you'd borrowed from the book when you researched your role.'

Matt said, 'On a trip down-river, Michie's friend was thrown overboard by one of the guards. When Michie protested, the guard cut off his ear.'

'You decided this would make a perfect explanation for your missing fingers, the sort of thing that would convince anyone that you'd genuinely been there. Anyone, that is, apart from Burma veterans, which is why you had to keep away from the local Burma Star group.'

A silence followed. People needed time to absorb this new information. One person needed it more than most. In a weak voice Alice Haig said, 'Laurence?'

He said, 'So perhaps I elaborated my service record a little. That doesn't make me a killer.'

I said, 'No, it doesn't. What makes you a killer is the bloody clothes.'

Matt said, 'You planned everything. You faked an attack when the body was discovered so that you'd be taken to the Infirmary, together with your bag and the clothes. You'd been there before with your appendix, on the same ward, and you'd had loads of time to scout the place out.'

I said, 'You knew that private room would enable you to come and go as you pleased in the middle of the night. You knew where the waste bins were. You were taking a gamble; you disposed of the clothes and the book on the Friday night, and they sat in the hospital waste all weekend. Which is where they turned up an hour ago.'

Laurence Glass said, 'That's impossible! They empty the bins first thing every Monday morning.'

Matt said, 'They would have done today, too, but for the strike.'

Though nothing he'd heard so far had made any visible impact on Glass's smooth demeanour, this last detail seemed to hit its mark. He said, 'Strike? Is there a strike?'

I've often thought that Cilla Donnelly should in fact be

running the Southaven police force rather than making her present lowly contribution. Some days I go further and picture her running the country, not that we'd ever stomach a woman as prime minister. She now nodded with every appearance of sympathy and said, 'I'm afraid so, Major. A little local squabble, that's all.' Where she'd learned to lie like that, I'd no idea. I hadn't even primed her beforehand.

Laurence Glass now sighed, and settled further back in the chair, smoothing the upholstery on the arm with an impatient hand. 'A strike. Does no one in this country do any bloody work?'

Clutching at straws, Alice Haig said, 'But Laurence couldn't have intended to smuggle the clothes out in his bag. It was my idea that he should take it to the hospital, not his.'

Glass said, 'Oh, I knew you'd suggest it.' A sneer crept into his voice. 'Efficient, predictable – '

'Laurence!'

'If you'd slipped up, I'd have asked for the bag myself at the last minute. Like that boy says, it was all very carefully planned.'

I said, 'The phone message you received from Broadstairs on the Thursday afternoon – that was you, wasn't it? You'd gone for a walk – Mrs Haig and I saw you go – then you rang the hotel pretending to be your sister's neighbour, so that you'd have a reason to pack a bag that night.'

Rosemary Pyle, who seemed to have forgotten her own personal woes and was following events like a bloodhound, now said to the Major, 'But I don't understand. Why didn't you just leave in the morning and disappear while you had the chance?'

'Oh, I couldn't have done that. Go away empty-handed? Alice here was about to become a rich woman. I needed more time.'

He looked at Alice then, and smiled a greedy smile. It was sickening, and we all saw it. But for Alice Haig, who'd been on the receiving end, it was too much. The colour drained from her face. Fighting back tears, she said, 'Excuse me,' and left the room. Nigel followed her, and Cilla Donnelly followed them both.

Miss Pyle said, 'We all trusted you! Poor Oscar was so dreadfully sorry for you, he was convinced the army had let you down after the war.'

Lena said, 'Why did you have to kill him? He never done you no harm!'

'Oh, the man doted on me. He told me everything – about his past, about his new girlfriend, it all poured out. But of course Giles couldn't bear it, someone else was getting the attention, you see. So he had to tell Oscar my little secret.'

'You're a maniac! You ought to be hanged!'

'No great loss, was it? A man who'd driven himself off the rails, and all because he was upset about the fate of a few darkies.'

Mark Howell said, 'How did you do it, Mr Glass?'

Glass said, 'It's *Major* Glass, actually.'

'You can cut the act now. I doubt whether your name's even Laurence Glass, is it?'

Momentary confusion troubled the face of the man we'd been calling the Major. It was all very well asking him to cut the act; what if he didn't know how?

Mark said, 'I don't understand how you managed to poison Hammond's brandy when you were stuck in the Infirmary.'

I said, 'He wasn't stuck, though, was he?'

Matt said, 'My girlfriend – ' He stopped, and started again. 'Some of the nurses cycle in to work, most of them don't bother to lock their bikes. All he had to do was borrow one.'

To Laurence Glass I said, 'You seem particularly adept at breaking and entering – first the back door here, then the chemist's on Marine Approach and Oscar Hammond's place. And you must have known that strychnine would act quickly and be undetectable in alcohol.'

Mark Howell said, 'Where did you pick up skills like that?'

Again, Laurence Glass chose not to speak.

Howard Lane said, 'Perhaps he went to boarding school.'

Miss Pyle said, 'Whatever can you mean, Mr Lane?'

'Amazing what you learn. I could pick the padlock on the tuck-shop door in fifteen seconds. Not so sure about the poison, mind.'

Evan Bickerstaff said, 'But it can't be the Major, can it? Someone stabbed him on Friday night!'

This display of slowness caused a look of disappointment to scud across Matt's face. He said, 'Glass had taken the knife in with him. He probably bought it somewhere on the Thursday afternoon when he was out. He stabbed himself.'

Evan made an appreciative face, conceding credit where it was due. To Glass I said, 'You did it partly to throw us off the scent, but you wanted the attention too, didn't you? Not just from Mrs Haig, though it did give you the chance you'd been waiting for to pop the question. When we saw you on Saturday morning, you were lapping it up from every side.'

Mark Howell said, 'What exactly happened between you and Giles Rawley on Thursday?'

Laurence Glass seemed to be recalling the events with a certain fondness. 'Giles had been reading his stupid book. He cornered me that morning and told me he'd found the story of the guard and the river trip – it was only a few weeks since I'd given him my own version, to shut him up one day when he'd been making light of my flashbacks. He said he knew what I was, and if I didn't clear off within three days he'd tell Alice.'

Miss Pyle said, 'Why didn't he just tell her straight away?'

'Alice isn't the sort to laugh it off when she's been made to look foolish. If Giles exposed me, Alice would be almost as angry with him as with me. So I was meant to trump up some excuse and slink away before Alice got in too deep. But I couldn't allow that, could I? – I was about to reel her in. She'd confided in me about the will, and with Giles dead I'd be marrying a small fortune. I decided to act fast, before he could tell anyone else. And I thought I'd got away with it, too, until Oscar came to visit me in the Infirmary.'

Lena Golding said, 'Oscar should have shopped you to the rozzers straight off!'

'But why? He trusted me – you know, old soldier, all pals together. He thought Giles must have made a mistake. The note said nothing about Giles having confronted me already, so I pretended it was the first I'd heard about it. I told Oscar to make allowances for Giles, since the poor chap was knocking on a bit and everyone knew how jealous he'd been of Alice and myself. I kept the note, and he went off reassured. But I couldn't have him walking round like an unexploded bomb, it was too dangerous.'

He smiled again. 'I had no choice, did I?'

Mark Howell said, 'The net was closing in. We'd begun to make enquiries into everyone's background, we'd have rumbled you eventually.'

'But these things take time, don't they? I knew the risks were piling up, in a few weeks I'd have had to move on. Meanwhile, the longer I waited, the more I could hope to get out of Alice. But it doesn't do to milk them, you know – bad for business. I'm always content with a few thousand, and besides, one mustn't make too big a splash in the newspapers. I'd decided that my wonderful sister was going to need expensive treatment in the United States, for which Alice would lend me the money. Then I'd be gone. No use hanging around too long, is it? Pastures new, that's the thrill of it. Always pastures new.' Even now, when there was little hope of him moving on to anything but a prison cell, he seemed to relish the prospect.

Mark Howell stood up and said, 'If you'd come with me now, sir.'

But Cordelia Lane was on her feet too, standing squarely opposite Laurence Glass. She said, 'I've got something to say to this man. I don't know who you are, but I agree with Miss Golding, they ought to hang you. I loved my father, my sisters loved him, my children loved him, and you've taken him away from us for no reason at all. He'd always known how to enjoy life, even when the work stopped coming and people didn't recognize him like they used to. He was slowly winding down, making a good end of things, and you robbed him of that. Hearing you talk I think you must be sick, but I don't care. If there's a hell, I hope you burn in it.' Calmly, she turned and walked out. After a few moments of indecision, Howard Lane went after her.

I said to Mark, 'You'll be wanting this,' and held out the evidence bag. 'No – just a moment.' I opened the bag and removed the sheet of notepaper, and Mark put the bag in his pocket. Then I tore the paper into small pieces and dropped them on the floor.

Evan Bickerstaff protested. 'You can't do that – that's evidence!'

Despairing, Matt rolled his eyes.

I said, 'Smoke and mirrors, Evan, just smoke and mirrors. I don't know what Giles leaned on when he wrote the note, but it certainly wasn't this.'

Understanding that he in his turn had been conned, the Major, or whoever he was, allowed his head to droop briefly onto his chest. Then, his military bearing restored, he stood up and walked towards the door, with Mark coming in beside him.

At the door, he turned. 'You know, Giles Rawley was a perfectly terrible actor. Have you seen those films? Not a moment of truth in them, it's all surface, all laid on from the outside. He knew nothing of how to get under a character's skin, so that if necessary you could play the part all day long. That's what I call acting – real acting. In the end, the reason Giles hated me is that I'm an actor, and he was not.'

Laurence Glass scanned the faces of his audience. Then, apparently satisfied with the effect of his exit speech, he swept through the double doors and on to his next engagement.

With Laurence Glass gone, a strange emptiness settled on the room. Miss Pyle was playing with her hands, Evan Bickerstaff had withdrawn into his old passivity, and I was suddenly conscious of being surplus to everyone's requirements.

Then Lou Golding said, 'Are we done? I got a man coming at two to fix the downstairs lav.'

In the Minx on the way back to Leigh Terrace, Matt said, 'Smoke and mirrors! I've never seen anything so hammy in all my life.'

'Not even Jason King in *Department S*?'

'Fair enough, but apart from that. What were you playing at?'

'It was your idea to get everyone together in the lounge. What did you expect me to do, read out the phone book?'

'Well, I suppose it did work, that's the main thing.'

'And we finally know the answer to the question that's been nagging us for days.'

Matt nodded. 'Who killed Giles Rawley.'

'No, not that. I meant, Exactly how stupid is Evan Bickerstaff?'

Matt frosted over. 'He may not be Bronowski, but he's a very nice person.'

We were just coming round onto the Boulevard. 'You realize this very nice person you're talking about called me a fat old bloke?'

Matt laughed. Such was my reward for nurturing ability in the young. 'A fat old bloke! Priceless!'

'His day will come, you mark my words. People with that sort of square build always fill out in their twenties.'

'Oh, so you've been studying Evan's body, have you? Didn't take you long to get over Mickey Golding.'

'No? Well it hasn't taken *you* long to get over – '

I stopped myself, but it was too late. We were held up in traffic, while a lorry tried to make a right turn up to the building site which until recently had been the Empire cinema. Suddenly I felt reckless. I was probably still on an adrenaline high from my performance at the Marine Lodge. If I was going to say things I shouldn't say, I could at least say things that mattered. Again I had the sensation of the sea pitching beneath me. I said, 'If you really had to sleep with someone on the rebound, why couldn't it be me?'

The block eased, and we were moving again. I was aware of the car in front of me, a black Jaguar, and I was aware of Matt chewing his lip in the passenger seat. After all, what could he say? It had been a stupid remark, the latest in a long line of stupid remarks which Matt had inspired during the past six months. In his shoes, I'd have chewed my lip too.

Then I was aware of the clear day darkening, of black blobs blotting out the sun, and of Matt saying, 'Sam? Sam, what is it?' After that, I put my foot down and drove hell for leather up the kerb and into the nearest tree. Or so I've been told. But I knew nothing about it, because by then I was unconscious.

Wild scenes followed, playing out on the screen of my restless mind – lurid, extravagant, impossible. I'd had gas as a child to put me under while two teeth were extracted, and it had been the same then, an experience as glorious as it was intense and terrifying. I'd happily share the details, but the images belonged so exclusively to a world elsewhere that they burned up on re-entry. Half relieved, half sorrowful, I slowly let them go.

The first thing my consciousness knew was a smell, a familiar, sickly smell with overtones of urine. The smell of hospital. My eyes still closed, I allowed reality to flesh itself out one piece at a time, and with it arrived the knowledge of who I was and how I must have got there. The splitting headache provided a leading clue: the word 'concussion' came to mind. With all that straightened out, and the last of the nightmare visions banished, I opened my eyes.

Someone must have been hovering nearby, because within seconds a face interposed itself between my eyes and the ceiling. Nurse Eileen Docherty said, 'I hope you know Bernie's furious with you.' Left to myself, I'd probably have chosen some other reintroduction to waking life, but at least this one had the merit of accurately reflecting the world I'd left behind.

As it happened, I didn't give a stuff whether Bernie Foster was pissed off with me or not. I said, 'How's Matt?'

## twenty-seven

Laurence Glass went up before magistrates and was remanded in custody in that name, for want of any other. It turned out, though, that his acting career wasn't over yet. But I'll leave him on one side for the time being, while I tidy up the mess left by the rest of us.

My spell of unconsciousness lasted only an hour or so, but this was enough to worry the professionals, who muttered that the effects of concussion could be serious and I would need to be kept under observation. When I tried sitting up in bed I felt distinctly green about the gills. Still sporting this hue prominently, I was visited towards four o'clock by Matt, fresh from A & E, the broken little finger of his left hand neatly strapped to its neighbour. He was able to calm my anxieties about the Minx, which had been towed away by my pet mechanic Paul Sidebottom with the promise that he'd see what could be done with it.

Matt, a true-blooded Standish capable of emerging from the

business end of a combine harvester without a scratch, was otherwise unharmed. But I could see that something was troubling him, and finally he came out with it. If I'd genuinely been unconscious, why had my foot not relaxed instead of jabbing down hard on the accelerator pedal? It was a good question, but I didn't have the answer. He gave me funny looks. Even now, I think he half believes I crashed the car on purpose.

Though his injury was slight, it wasn't without consequence. When his mother noticed it, in the middle of a fraught discussion about his failure to come home the night before, she swore that Sam Rigby would one day be the death of her darling boy, and demanded that Matt seek other employment. He declined. She made it a condition of his remaining beneath the Standish roof. He threw some things in a bag, and walked out.

Matt spent the first night of his independence on the settee at Leigh Terrace, a feat unlikely to spawn imitators. I was still in hospital, so I don't know why he couldn't have taken advantage of my empty bed. The following night he spent with Evan Bickerstaff. Then Sidney Flint found him a bedsit in a house near Crowburn Park, and he's still there now. The building's a dump, like all Sidney's properties, but Matt has transformed his own corner of it into a shining outpost of civilisation. It's just a pity he can't do much about the shared bathroom.

Dennis Flint – he's taken his father's name – made a full if rather slow recovery, and lives with Sidney these days. In a rash moment, Sidney bought him a new coat. Other than that, I don't think anything's changed.

A flurry of court cases followed over the next few months. Howard Lane – bound over to keep the peace. Carlo – eighteen months for false imprisonment (both his guests having praised him warmly as a model host). And finally, First Ugly Bloke – ten years for being unpleasant while in possession of a firearm. Sidney Flint said Cecil should be horse-whipped and offered to administer the punishment himself, but the killjoy State said no. When I'm in the mood to wind Sidney up, I tell him he shouldn't be so hard on poor Cecil, who probably had a terribly unhappy childhood. Then I sit back and watch the show. This doesn't get the roof fixed, but as a spectacle you can't beat it.

After a couple of days, the police ran Sarkis Aznavorian to earth at a hotel in Eastbourne. He had nothing with him except his personal belongings. I still believed he must have removed something of interest from the lock-up in the yard and relocated it, though what it was I couldn't be sure. He'd paid up at the Marine Lodge until the end of the month, and since it's not yet a crime to leave Southaven without saying goodbye, the police took no further interest in him.

Whether Rosemary Pyle forgot about him so quickly, I don't know. She stayed on at the Marine Lodge, a somewhat reduced figure stirred to life only when someone happened to mention the crowded state of Southaven's roads. Then out would come the history of the local tram system, enlivened by anecdotes from her father's days as the man in charge. Although other eligible men soon replaced the missing long-term residents, from Miss Pyle they drew no more than a prim good morning. If she really was the Jezebel Giles Rawley had claimed, she hid it well.

My mother and I were both discharged from the Infirmary on the Thursday morning. She'd been given dark warnings of the doom that awaited if she didn't mend her ways, and until the Sunday lunchtime she appeared to treat these with the utmost seriousness. But then she just happened to feel that it might do her good to pop along to the Coach and Horses for one little drink, and after that normal service was resumed. I try to drop in at the Duck Lane cottage at least once a week now, if only to check that she's got food in the house and isn't living in a tip of empty bottles.

As Lou Golding had predicted, despite the fact that serious mayhem had been perpetrated on property she owned by men she employed, none of the mud stuck to Lou herself. Further to the reorganization of the local force, DS Sturges was replaced by a Detective Chief Superintendent dividing his time between Southaven and Preston. Perhaps this was what Lou Golding meant when she began to tell people that the climate in Southaven no longer agreed with her. By mid-March, she and Mickey were back in London for good. Mickey's initiative in making a voluntary statement to the police had allowed him to distance himself from the derring-do in the Oyster Bar. No charges were brought against either him or his sister. Lena remained in town as permanent chef at the Marine Lodge.

Every couple of weeks or so, Mickey writes me long, poorly-spelled letters about his exploits up the Smoke. He says he's joined something called the Gay Liberation Front, though apparently you don't so much join as turn up looking fabulous. His mother has a new problem. Having acquired a taste for greater control during her absence, Mickey's brothers are now trying to sideline her, as she herself once sidelined Frank. With Lou's attention fully occupied by this infighting, I suppose it's not surprising that no further communications have arrived from Messrs Tipton, Buxton and Lamb. It looked as if Lou Golding might write Southaven off completely, and withdraw from all her interests here. And perhaps she would have done, but for Alice Haig.

In my hospital bed I'd worried that the blow Alice had taken from Laurence Glass might be enough to finish her. I could hardly believe it when I saw her again, a week or so later. Alice had come out fighting. On Lou's invitation, she'd taken Carlo's place at the Grand, and within days she was offering to buy a controlling share in the business as soon as probate came through on Giles's estate. Lou Golding, baulking at the thought of becoming a mere junior partner, negotiated, and now she and Alice are to hold an equal stake.

Alice has big plans for the Grand. One of these is to re-jig the Oyster Bar as a function room with a novelty theme. Unfortunately, she must first wade through a legal quagmire, while it's decided whether the site of the former café beneath Marine Approach still belongs to the hotel. All the relevant papers have gone missing. Recently, Alice drafted me in to help with the search, and I've done a couple of other jobs for her too – vetting new suppliers, and keeping an eye on a light-fingered guest. It all helps to pay the bills.

Goldings casino opened with great fanfare in April, the Malones having withdrawn their objections. Sometimes, out of hours, Nigel Haig can be found there working on his system at the roulette table. He once tried to talk me through the probability theory which lay behind it, after which I had to take two aspirin and lie down. I don't much like the look of the croupier, and I suspect that the apparently smooth functioning of the wheel may in fact be open to influence. This would be a shame, as it could invalidate all Nigel's work. Unless, of course, he knows about it and has factored it in.

The suspect wheel isn't my only worry. Alice now employs a couple of Slasher Braithwaite's men, and she became uncharacteristically vague when I asked her why. Recently, too, there's been a fresh spat with the Malones, who've lost business share after an unexplained fire at the Roxy. There's nothing conclusive in all this, but when I deal with Alice Haig these days I find myself troubled by questions. What kind of business does Alice think she's buying into? Which is the real Alice, the honest, small-town hotelier who sought my help in a crisis, or the Alice who so easily persuaded me she knew nothing about Giles Rawley's will?

And last but not least – what if I've actually ended up working for Lou Golding after all?

I saw Lena Golding this morning. It was one of those mild, soft mornings in early May that remind you why you bothered to survive the winter. I'd been taking a mid-morning constitutional along the Prom, and I spotted Lena sitting on a bench in the gardens opposite the Marine Lodge, enjoying a quiet cigarette. I'd long since given up giving up, so I took the opportunity to cadge one. Then I sat down and said, 'How's it going?'

Lena blew out smoke. 'Just taking one day at a time, really. He'd have loved this.' With a gesture she took in the gardens, the lake, the pulse of spring. 'I keep thinking, why should I get to enjoy it and he can't?'

There was no need to ask who 'he' might be. I said, 'Anything new at the Marine Lodge?'

'No, worse luck. I mean, I love the cooking, best work I've ever had. Alice gives me free rein, the guests don't know what's hit 'em some days. But she's that taken up with the Grand and all her big notions, she's letting the old place slide. It may not be much, but it's got something, know what I mean? If Alice don't invest, people won't come.'

'Have you tried telling her?'

'Sort of, but she only changes the subject. It's like she's had her head turned. Between you and me, I wouldn't be surprised if she sells up.'

I wondered if the ghost of Ian Haig had heard that. If so, it would surely have broken his spectral heart, but perhaps in truth the Marine Lodge had had its day. Ian's widow was a serious businesswoman now. She couldn't afford to end up crushed under the wheels of progress.

For a while, we puffed away in silence. Far out beyond the lake and the coast road, the banished sea waited, biding its time. Then Lena said, 'You know, you and Mickey would have been good together.'

A young woman went by, pushing a big, old-fashioned pram with all the trimmings. I said, 'It's not like we didn't try.'

'Mickey said he never stood a chance, because of that boy who works for you. Do you mind if I give you a piece of advice?'

I didn't answer. I was probably in for it whether I minded or not.

Lena said, 'Forget him. He's still sowing his wild oats, at your age you need to think about settling down. You know he's seeing Evan?'

I did know, of course, though exactly how often or on what terms I wasn't sure. Both of them had had birthdays in the past couple of months, but Evan was still below the legal age of consent, and this gave Matt the excuse he needed to keep the relationship behind closed doors and his family in the dark. It was only a couple of weeks since his mother had found out he wasn't seeing Eileen any more.

When I got home later, a picture postcard of the Tower of London had arrived with the second delivery. The message read: *'Languishing. Visit soon! M x'* Despite my views on the capital city, I might take Mickey up on that.

\* \* \*

In February 1857, Nathaniel Hawthorne – celebrated writer, friend of Herman Melville, and American consul in Liverpool – became a victim of crime. The rooms his family had taken on Southaven Promenade were burgled, and the police swung into action. The culprits were soon found to be two young lads from Liverpool, who'd arrived and departed by train. In his diary, Hawthorne wrote: 'A rogue has a very poor chance in England, the police being so numerous, and their system so well-organized.'

Either Laurence Glass had somehow missed this passage, or else he'd decided to ignore its warning, because en route for the remand centre at Hindley he escaped.

The escorting officers could hardly be blamed if no one had thought to warn them their prisoner had form for drama. He faked another attack, and in the resulting confusion made a discreet exit. Convinced he wouldn't elude them for long in open country in the middle of winter, the police launched a manhunt.

The case against Laurence Glass no longer relied solely on his confession. The truck which had collected waste from the Infirmary was stopped on its way to the depot, and the book and clothes – a dressing gown and a pyjama jacket – were discovered wrapped in a bag from Butterworths store.

Now the police faced the task of establishing Glass's true identity. A local bank released the security box in which he'd held fake ID documents in a variety of names – Leslie Grainger, Leonard Gray, Captain Lester Graham. His photograph was circulated, and women began to come forward with their stories. Glass's MO had varied, but most frequently he'd targeted vulnerable women, often older than himself, via the personal columns in local newspapers. Finally, a woman from Sidmouth told police that back in 1955 a certain Leopold Goodman had conned her out of sixteen hundred pounds. Beyond that, the trail went cold.

Ten days after he'd escaped, Laurence Glass's partly eaten body turned up in a barn at the edge of the moors. He'd died of septicaemia following a ruptured appendix.

I've dreamed about that barn. I lie on my bed of straw, the rats expectant in a circle all around me, and I know my days are done.

Strangely enough, it's a good dream; when I wake to find death postponed, life seems doubly sweet.

I never liked Laurence Glass, and it annoys me that I still think of him. In my mind I quarrel with him about Giles Rawley – Giles may not have been Olivier, but I enjoyed his performances just the same. I puzzle over the truth of the missing fingers. I imagine how it must have been to rise each morning to a new day of deception, a new role, a counterfeit self, year after rootless year.

But most of all I wonder about the end, and whether in the final hours, when Laurence Glass had only rats for an audience, he lay with the tide of death creeping over him and tried one last time to remember who he really was.

Printed in Great Britain
by Amazon